A
BURTON & SWINBURNE
ADVENTURE

THE RETURN OF THE DISCONTINUED MAN

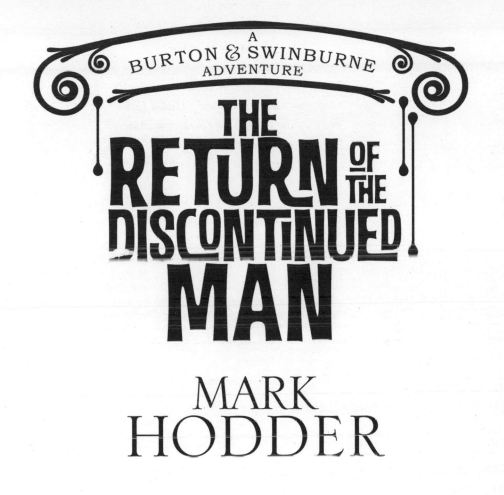

A BURTON & SWINBURNE ADVENTURE

THE RETURN OF THE DISCONTINUED MAN

MARK HODDER

DEL REY

1 3 5 7 9 10 8 6 4 2

First published in the United States in 2014 by Pyr®, an imprint of Prometheus Books

First published in the UK in 2014 by Del Rey, an imprint of Ebury Publishing
A Random House Group Company

The Random House Group Limited Reg. No. 954009

Addresses for companies within the Random House Group can be found at
www.randomhouse.co.uk

A CIP catalogue record for this book is available from the British Library

The Random House Group Limited supports The Forest Stewardship
Council® (FSC®), the leading international forest-certification organisation.
Our books carrying the FSC label are printed on FSC® -certified paper.
FSC is the only forest-certification scheme supported by the
leading environmental organisations, including Greenpeace.
Our paper procurement policy can be found at:
www.randomhouse.co.uk/environment

MIX
Paper from
responsible sources
FSC® C016897

Printed and bound by CPI Group (UK) Ltd, Croydon, CR0 4YY

ISBN 9780091950651

This one is for

MICK FARREN

(1943–2013)

THE FIRST PART

THE VISIONS

You can never plan the future by the past.
—Edmund Burke

CHAPTER 1

AN APPARITION IN LEICESTER SQUARE

He fragmented. Decisions taken were unmade and became
choices. Successes and failures reverted to opportunities
and challenges. Characteristics disengaged and withdrew
to become influences. He lost cohesion until nothing of him
remained except potential. Yet, set apart from this strange
process, something observed and wailed and grieved as it
watched itself disintegrate into ever smaller components. Who
was he? Where was he? Why was he here? What must he do?

There was a name: Edward Oxford.

And an enemy: Burton.

— *The Strange Affair of Spring Heeled Jack*

"Y ou're a drooling, bulge-eyed drug addict!"

The accusation, which Algernon Charles Swinburne screeched in his characteristically high-pitched and excitable tones, caused the entire saloon bar to fall momentarily silent.

Sir Richard Francis Burton glowered at his diminutive friend. "A little less volume, if you please."

"You're hooked! An addle head! What next for you, hey? The gutters, perhaps? Bedlam lunatic asylum? A Limehouse opium den?"

"Limehouse doesn't exist. It burned to the ground last year, as you well know."

"Pah! And I'll say it again! Pah! In fact, once more for good measure! Pah to you, sir!"

Burton sighed, raised his glass, and took a gulp of ale.

Around them, the Black Toad's other customers—a slovenly crowd of thieves, dollymops, and chancers—returned their attention to their beers, gins, whiskies, and absinthes.

Burton and Swinburne had occupied a table in a dark corner of the disreputable drinking den, there to wet their whistles for a couple of hours prior to a gathering of the Cannibal Club, during which their whistles would no doubt become thoroughly sodden, as they usually did when the pair joined with their friends ostensibly to discuss issues of anthropological and atheistic interest but, more often than not, to instead carouse a night away.

Of these Cannibals, there was no more dedicated a roisterer than Swinburne. His tiny, slope-shouldered body—with its oversized head made all the bigger by the mop of long carroty-red hair curling almost horizontally from it—could hold astonishing quantities of alcohol. The excess of electric vitality that coursed through the young poet's system, making him constantly twitch and jerk, endowing him with such a skittish nature that many thought him either possessed or crazed, appeared to burn off the effects of his overindulgences at a prodigious rate, so that one moment he might be a slurring, staggering mess, and the next so perfectly clear-eyed and *compos mentis* that he could, on the spot, compose a sonnet of astonishing beauty and technical grace.

Swinburne was an eccentric, a drunkard, and an absolute genius.

He was also, at this particular moment, thoroughly peeved.

He slapped a hand down onto the table and squealed, "Three months! For three whole months you've been off with the fairies. Have you achieved anything in that time? No! Have you worked on your books? No! Have you planned any new expeditions? No! And look at you. Your eyes are hollow. Your cheeks are sunken. You've become a shadow of the man I met last year. It has to stop. No more Saltzmann's, Richard! No more!"

Burton drew his lips back tightly over his teeth, a snarling expression that exposed his long canines and made him appear so barbaric that most men would have fled from him at once. Not so Swinburne, who was by now accustomed to the famous explorer's savage countenance and fully cognisant that Burton often took advantage of it to intimidate when challenged.

"It's not the bloody Saltzmann's Tincture," Burton countered. "The stuff is perfectly harmless."

"Sadhvi Raghavendra doesn't share your opinion. She says it contains cocaine."

"She theorises that it does. She doesn't know it. I think otherwise."

"Based on what?"

"Based on the fact that I'm thoroughly familiar with the effects of cocaine and Saltzmann's doesn't share them."

"That doesn't mean it's not addictive."

"I repeat: it's not the Saltzmann's, Algy."

Swinburne curled the fingers of his right hand into a fist and considered it, as if deciding whether to swing it into his friend's nose. He clicked his tongue, picked up his glass, and swallowed the contents in a single gulp. "Then explain your bedraggled mien."

Burton looked down at the stained tabletop. His mouth moved, trying to frame words that wouldn't come. His eyes flicked evasively from side to side.

Swinburne watched him. Softly, he said, "Isabel?"

Dumbly, Burton nodded. He rubbed a hand across his forehead, wiping away perspiration that wasn't there. "I can't eat, Algy. I can't sleep. I feel like one of Babbage's clockwork men, going through the motions, hardly alive. I was never meant to exist without her."

"I sympathise, Richard. Really, I do. But you'll not escape your loss by obliterating your senses. Put the Saltzmann's aside. Get out and confront the world. Allow it to distract you."

"I'm here, aren't I?"

"Ha!" Swinburne said. "I'm thankful that you are, too, though getting thoroughly sozzled isn't quite what I meant." He grinned mischievously. "Though one must start somewhere, what!" He slapped the table again and yelled, "Pot boy! Another couple of ales over here, lad!"

The beer was duly served, and the poet made a solemn toast:

And grief shall endure not forever, I know.
As things that are not shall these things be;
We shall live through seasons of sun and of snow,
And none be grievous as this to me.
We shall hear, as one in a trance that hears,
The sound of time, the rhyme of the years;
Wrecked hope and passionate pain will grow
As tender things of a spring-tide sea.

The moment of crisis passed. Burton knew his friend wouldn't challenge him again. In some matters—just some—Swinburne knew where to draw the line. Instead, the poet would put his advice into practice by providing diversions, entertainments, and intellectual stimulation. No doubt, after they'd got sloshed with the Cannibals, he'd suggest a visit to Verbena Lodge, his favourite brothel. At that point, Burton would go home. He didn't share the poet's taste for the lash, as distracting as it might be.

They drank and, around them, men and women flirted coarsely and squabbled loudly and cackled obscenely and shouted incoherently. The air was thick with tobacco smoke and heavy with the vinegary odour of cheap wine, souring beer, and unwashed bodies. A startling contrast, then, that amid this unrefined pandemonium, Swinburne talked of his affinity with the Pre-Raphaelite artists and his hopes for the forthcoming publication of his poem, *Rosamond*; of his summer holidays at his grandfather's house, Capheaton Hall, in Northumberland; and of his love for that wild and romantic northern county.

Despite his odd sense of detachment, Burton couldn't help but be fascinated. Swinburne's ability to hold an audience was astonishing. When performing—and Burton had no doubt that his friend was purposely putting on a performance for him—the tempo and cadence of his voice was spellbinding, his choice of words ingenious, and his gestures extravagantly expressive.

Automatically, Burton found himself responding. He described his childhood, during which he'd been dragged around Europe by his restless father and long-suffering mother; spoke of his subsequent inability to fit in at Oxford University, where he was scorned as a thoroughly un-English ruffian; described his explorations of Arabia; and confessed his ambivalent feelings about his current commission as the king's agent.

While he spoke, a separate part of him observed Swinburne watching and judging.

He thinks my manner is all wrong. I'm making an unconvincing show of it.

After a while, the poet consulted his pocket watch and declared it to be a minute past nine. "Shall we be off? The Cannibals await, hurrah, hurrah!"

He's eager to consult with Monckton Milnes. He thinks my oldest friend will know how to bring me out of this confounded funk.

They stood, donned their coats and hats, and took up their walking canes, the contrast between them attracting the amused attention of the saloon's clientele, for where Swinburne barely scraped five feet, Burton was just an inch below six and looked considerably taller by virtue of his broad shoulders, deep chest, and imposing presence. Were it not for the famous explorer's infernal physiognomy and challenging gaze, the pair might have invited catcalls as they crossed the room. None were forthcoming. There occurred, instead, a slight hush accompanied by sly grins and exchanged winks. One muscle-bound lout spat into the floor's sawdust as if to show that were Burton to challenge him there'd be no contest, but he averted his eyes when the king's agent glanced at him and thus revealed it to be nothing but empty *braggadocio*.

Perhaps I should pick a fight with him. Perhaps the violence would snap me back into myself.

Swinburne pushed open the door, and they stepped out onto Baker Street.

Frigid air hit them.

They stopped dead.

"My hat!" Swinburne cried out. "The sky is bleeding."

The atmosphere was thick with falling snow, and it was bright red, a near opaque cloak of vermilion, falling vertically, the variations in its density making the illumination from the street's gas lamps pulsate, causing the length of the thoroughfare to resemble the interior of a throbbing artery.

Burton scraped his heel across the pavement. "Thin," he observed. "I'll wager it just started, but if it keeps going at this rate London will soon be half buried." Curiously, he held out his right hand then withdrew it and examined his powdered palm. "Remarkable. Can you see? It has seeds mixed in with it, like those from dandelions, but red."

Swinburne exclaimed, "It's winter! Quite apart from them falling out of the sky in such profusion and being a startling colour, how can there be seeds floating about at this time of year?"

"Blown across the globe at a high altitude, I suppose," Burton mused. "I don't know what species of plant, though. The effect is rather uncanny, don't you think?"

The poet shivered and turned up his collar. "And rather penetrating, too. I shall require a brandy to warm my cockles."

They trudged southward for a few yards, the scarlet snow crunching beneath their feet, until they heard the chugging engine of a steam cabriolet. Swinburne put fingers to his lips and emitted a piercing whistle. The vehicle emerged from the cascading curtain and drew to a halt beside them, its furnace hissing like a box of angry serpents.

"Bloomin' well bonkers, ain't it?" the driver said, his voice filled with wonder. "I've not seen nuffink like it in all me born days. Red snow! Cor blimey! Whatever next? Where to, gents?"

"Leicester Square, please," Burton directed as they climbed in. They brushed cigar butts from the seat, settled, and the cab jerked into motion.

The king's agent said, "As it happens, I've experienced stranger weather phenomena than this."

"Last year's aurora borealis, you mean?" Swinburne said.

"I'm referring to my time in Sindh, when it one day rained fish during the monsoon."

"Flying fish?"

"Falling fish. They're lifted from the sea by tornadoes, thrown into the upper atmosphere, and carried over the land, onto which they descend."

Their carriage rocked and bumped southward, and by the time it reached Leicester Square, the red snow had given way to the normal white which, still falling thickly, was rapidly turning the ground from blood-red to a sickly bright pink.

"Hallo! What's all that kerfuffle about?" the driver commented as they disembarked and Burton paid him. They followed the man's gaze and saw, half obscured, a commotion on the western side of the square. A crowd was milling about outside Bartolini's Dining Rooms, where Burton and Swinburne were due to meet their friends.

"Is that Trounce?" Swinburne asked, pointing.

Burton spotted the burly detective inspector, gave a grunt of confirmation, and set off with his companion in tow. As they traipsed closer to the throng, he saw members of the Cannibal Club among it—Richard Monckton Milnes, Thomas Bendyshe, Henry Murray, Doctor James Hunt, Sir Edward Brabrooke, and Charles Bradlaugh.

The restaurateur, Signor Bartolini, was shouting at William Trounce and gesticulating wildly.

Trounce saw them approaching and bellowed, "By Jove! Thank the almighty you're here! I can't get any sense out of this fellow. He's utterly unhinged."

"He's utterly Italian," Swinburne corrected.

"The same bloody difference, if you ask me."

"Has something occurred?" Burton asked.

Trounce, thickset and blunt in features, with a wide snow-speckled brown moustache and bright-blue eyes, threw out his hands. "I've not been here ten minutes. My mind is still befuddled by this freakish red stuff. Now it appears I have to deal with a costumed intruder playing silly beggars, too."

Bartolini shook a fist at Burton and cried out, "*Hanno esagerato*, Signor Burton! I can have no more of this! Your trick, it scare my customers! Your Club Cannibal, it not welcome here no more. *Non più! Non più!*"

Burton glanced beyond Bartolini and waved for Monckton Milnes to come over. He then held up his palms at the dark and slightly built Italian and said, "*Per favore, signore, fidati di me*—trust me—whatever has happened, I had nothing to do with it. Tell me. An intruder?"

"*Un fantasma!* It crash into my *ristorante*. It call for you! Smash! Smash! Throwing the tables and the chairs, and it shouting all the time, Where is Burton? Where is Burton? Through the *sala da pranzo* it run, and up the stairs to your friends. Where is Burton? Where is Burton? Then back down again and—*meno male!*—out and away!"

"Fantasma?"

Monckton Milnes arrived, took Burton by the arm, and said to the others, "Pardon me, gentlemen." He pulled the king's agent aside and murmured, "It was Spring Heeled Jack, Richard. No doubt about it. The hellish thing burst in on us and demanded to know where you were, then bounced away on its stilts. It frightened us all witless."

For a moment, Burton's mind froze. It wasn't possible! He coughed to clear his throat. "Just now?"

"About forty minutes ago. We called a constable, and he gathered some of his fellows. They're scouring the area in search of the monster."

Burton frowned, took off his top hat, banged snow from its brim, and put it back on. "Spring Heeled Jack? Are you certain? Describe it."

"It resembled a naked man, tall and rangy in build, but it was entirely white and featureless. No hair, eyes, nose, ears, or mouth. No fingernails. No genitals."

"Helmet and cloak?"

"Not at all."

"A disk on its chest?"

"No adornments or clothes to speak of."

"But it was raised on spring-loaded stilts? So it was wearing boots?"

"No. The stilts appeared to grow straight out its heels, an extension of them."

Burton raised his fingers to his chin, feeling the tuft of hair that grew in its cleft. "Yet, despite the lack of a mouth, it spoke?"

"Shouted like a madman. Bradlaugh practically fainted with the shock of it."

"Why did Bartolini think it was me?"

"Tom Bendyshe's fault. You know how he enjoys a good jape. His first assumption was that you'd decided to put the wind up us, and Bartolini cottoned onto it. He can't decide whether it was you dressed up or a ghost."

Burton gazed into the gradually thinning snow, his thoughts turning over, searching for a workable theory to explain the bizarre visitation. He couldn't find one.

He briefly gripped Monckton Milnes by the elbow before striding back to Bartolini. "Signor, please accept that this was none of my doing nor, I am sure, that of anyone with whom I'm acquainted."

The Italian gave a wide, exaggerated shrug. "If you say it, I believe it. But what was it? Why have the *neve rossa* bring it here?"

"The red snow?"

"*Sì!* It start to fall and, *immediatamente, il fantasma* come crash crash crash into my *ristorante*!"

"Wait. What? The snow and the intruder arrived simultaneously?"

"*Sì! Sì!*"

"I'm at a loss, but I shall endeavour to get to the bottom of it." Burton touched two fingers to his hat and returned to where Monckton Milnes had joined Swinburne and Trounce. "Both at nine o'clock! Scarlet snow and Spring Heeled Jack."

The detective inspector cupped his hands and blew into them to warm his fingers. "Lord help me, are we faced with another of your damnable affairs?"

"My affairs, Trounce?"

"More king's agent ballyhoo."

"Ah, I see. I don't know, but if Bartolini's was really invaded by Spring Heeled Jack, then I fear we might be."

They joined the other Cannibals.

"The devil himself was among us!" Bendyshe trumpeted. His voice was never less than stentorian. "Gad, what a horror!"

"You should have seen it, Richard," Henry Murray said. "A ghost? A mechanism? I'm utterly flummoxed."

"I thought it was a man in a costume," Sir Charles Bradlaugh added. He put a finger to his right cheek, which was darkly bruised. "But when the thing shoved me aside—the feel of it!"

"What do you mean?" Burton asked.

"Like fish skin but solid and waxy." Bradlaugh shuddered. "Hard. Not clothing at all."

And calling for me. Why?

As if reading his thoughts, Bendyshe cried out, "I say, old horse, we all know you've been up to your devilish eyebrows in some bizarre business recently, but this takes the biscuit! Care to explain?"

"I can't, Tom," Burton responded. "I have no notion what the apparition was or why it was searching for me. Would you excuse me for a moment?" He addressed Trounce. "I need to know where it went."

Trounce pointed to a constable who was moving among the gathered crowd. "There's Honesty. He was with the men who chased after it."

Burton, Swinburne, and Trounce strode over to P. C. Thomas Honesty, a wiry and dapper man with immaculately trimmed eyebrows and an extravagantly curled moustache. Only a few months previously, he'd been the groundsman at New Wardour Castle, the seat of Isabel Arundell's family. After the events that led to her death, he'd joined the Police Force and, on government orders, had been rushed through training.

Burton hailed him. "Hallo, Tom!"

Honesty saluted. "Sir! Strange night. Snow. Stilt man."

"Strange is the word. It's been a while since I saw you, old fellow. Has your wife joined you in London? Are you settled?"

"We are. Nice little place in Hammersmith. Baby on the way."

"My good man! Congratulations!"

Honesty accepted a handshake then pointed to the side of the square opposite Bartolini's. "Consensus is, the phantom jumped down from the rooftops over there."

"Phantom?" Swinburne queried.

"Or whatever it was."

Burton said, "Judging by the mark on Bradlaugh's cheek, it was rather too substantial to qualify as a spook."

As if it had been adjusted via a control, the snowfall suddenly slowed and thinned until only a few stray flakes were left drifting down.

The men surveyed the square.

"Looks like an iced cake," Trounce murmured.

Honesty nodded his helmeted head in the direction of Charing Cross Road. "Made off in that direction. We chased. Too fast. Lost it." His eyes widened. He gave out a strangled yelp and pointed. "There! It's back!"

Burton whirled in time to see a figure apparently falling from the sky. Its stilts hit the ground and slipped from beneath it. The apparition crashed down onto its side, scrabbling wildly in the snow, limbs flailing. It howled—its voice filled with despair.

Someone shouted, "Bloody hell! What is it?"

The creature gained its feet, shrieked wordlessly, then cried out, "Prime Minister, where are you? Please! Where are you? Guide me! Guide me!"

The crowd outside Bartolini's screamed and scattered.

Shaking its head as if to clear it, the stilted man raised its featureless face to the sky and yelled, "Burton! Burton!"

"Here!" the king's agent called, striding forward. He drew the rapier from his silver-handled swordstick.

Spring Heeled Jack—Burton couldn't think of it as anything else—crouched and turned toward him. "Sir Richard Francis bloody Burton."

"You've inserted one name too many, my friend, but I shall overlook that. Now be so kind as to introduce yourself and explain what you want with me."

"I don't know."

Burton stopped in front of the creature and examined it. The description given by Monckton Milnes was accurate; it was totally lacking in any human detail.

"You don't know?"

"Perhaps—"

"Perhaps what?"

"Perhaps I have to—"

Without warning, it pounced.

"Kill you!"

A swinging fist knocked the point of Burton's blade aside. He felt himself grabbed by the upper arms, solid fingers gouging into his biceps, and was lifted high into the air as if he weighed nothing at all. With tremendous strength, Spring Heeled Jack dashed him viciously to the ground. Even through the padding of snow, Burton's head cracked with such force against the paving that his senses reeled.

"Got you!" his assailant shouted. "Stop interfering! Leave me alone! Tell me why I'm here!"

A shrill scream of outrage echoed through the square, and Swinburne came racing to his fallen friend's assistance. The poet swiped at Spring Heeled Jack with his cane. It impacted against a broad shoulder and snapped in half, its lower end spinning away. "Get off him, you brute! Scat! Scat!"

The stilted figure turned and swatted the poet. Swinburne cartwheeled and landed in a tangled heap.

Tom Honesty put his whistle to his mouth and blew.

Jack squatted over Burton. "What am I supposed to do? Where is the prime minister? What is your significance? What happened at nine o'clock?"

Flat on his back, the king's agent looked up at the blank countenance. "I have no idea what you're talking about."

His attacker reached down, clasped the front of his coat, yanked him upright, and threw him. Burton saw the black night sky and the pink ground of Leicester Square alternating around him as—with shock slowing everything to a crawl and causing him to feel like a dispassionate observer—he pirouetted through the air. He passed over Trounce and the members of the Cannibal Club and glimpsed them looking up at him with expressions of sheer horror. Then he impacted against a plate glass window. Fragments exploded around him. They glinted and flashed. They rained like a thousand jewels.

This surely hurts, yet I don't feel a thing.

He crashed down onto a table. It collapsed beneath him. Cutlery and broken crockery danced up, colliding with the showering glass. A symphony of clatters and smashes and bangs and clangs sounded from afar. Distant voices ululated. Everything was dreamlike.

Of its own accord, his right hand rose into his line of sight, and he was fascinated to find that it still held his rapier. He watched as the weapon's point lowered toward his feet until it was directed at the jagged rectangular hole where the window had been.

Poor Bartolini. He's having a bad evening. His restaurant is wrecked.

Spring Heeled Jack bounded in and dived forward. Burton's sword adjusted itself and struck the apparition in the middle of its chest. The blade bent, scraped across to the left, gouged a scratch in the hard white skin, but didn't penetrate it.

Jack snatched the weapon, wrenched it from Burton's hand, and cast it aside. Planting a stilt to either side of the fallen man, it looked down and gave vent to an agonised whine.

Burton whispered, "What the hell is wrong with you?"

"I must serve Queen Victoria," it responded. "But I've forgotten how."

Trounce came pounding into the restaurant. Bellowing, he thudded into the creature, wrapped his arms around it, and declared, "You're bloody well nicked, old son!"

Jack staggered. Burton quickly pushed himself out from between its legs and dragged himself backward through splintered wood and glass.

Trounce's grip broke as his captive flung out its arms. A solid elbow smacked into the detective's face, sending him tottering backward with blood spurting from his nose. His legs hit the ledge of the window, and he toppled out into the snow.

Burton heaved himself to his feet. He lunged at his opponent. They locked arms and grappled, twisting this way and that, thudding into tables, knocking them flying.

The king's agent was no match for the other. Sent reeling, he plummeted out through the doorway and went slipping and sliding outside, somehow maintaining his footing, though he possessed hardly any sense of what he was doing.

Spring Heeled Jack followed and laid into him with its fists. It wailed, "Where am I? What must I do, Prime Minister? I'm alone! I'm alone!"

Blood spattered the snow. Burton fell and was hauled up again. He became vaguely aware that constables were running toward him.

"Please!" his opponent screamed. "Help me!"

Swinburne suddenly came cannoning from one side and dived at its ankles, locking his arms around them. Caught off balance, Spring Heeled Jack pitched face-first into the snow. Immediately, Burton delivered a vicious kick to the side of its head before he, too, lost his footing and fell.

Trounce blundered back into the melee. He stepped over the king's agent and thudded down knees first onto Jack's back. Honesty and three other constables swooped in and grabbed at the creature's arms. The detective inspector had a pistol in his hand. He raised it and cracked it down onto Jack's head. The white cranium split, and a bolt of blue electrical energy sizzled across its surface. A transparent skin detached itself from the prone figure and began to expand outward.

Burton knew what would happen next. "Get away from it!" he roared, as the world snapped back to normal speed. "Move! Move!"

He scrambled across the ground on all fours, grabbed Trounce by the back of his coat and heaved him aside, then gripped Swinburne's ankle and, dragging the poet with him, slithered backward. The constables rolled aside just as the transparency swelled into a bubble and popped with a thunderously echoing retort.

Spring Heeled Jack vanished, taking with it a bowl-shaped section of Leicester Square's paving.

Trounce sat up, fished a handkerchief from his pocket, and applied it to his bleeding nose. "By Jobe! Whad a monstrosidy!"

Flat on his back, with cold moisture soaking into his clothes, Burton lay panting, his mind awhirl, his body finally starting to register the pain.

Beside him, Swinburne said, "Is it as bad as it looks?"

Burton moved his tongue around, feeling his teeth to check they were all present. They were. After a few moments' preparation, he managed to croak, "What?"

"Your condition."

As reality continued to reestablish itself, the king's agent struggled to his feet and stood swaying. His clothes were hanging in tatters. Blood dribbled inside his ragged sleeves and slowly dripped from his fingertips.

After a little exploration, he discovered that the left side of his chin bore the most serious of his many lacerations—it was small but through to the bone—and there was another, longer and more painful cut at the side of his left elbow. None were incapacitating.

"I'm an atheist, Algy," he murmured, "but I must confess, the fact that I went through a window and can still stand strikes me as somewhat miraculous."

"You must have hit it head first. Broke it with solid bone before the rest of you passed through."

The poet rose from the ground and helped Trounce up. The detective inspector drew a second handkerchief—clean—from his pocket and passed it to Burton, who uttered a grunt of thanks, wiped his hands on it, then pressed it to his chin.

The king's agent said, "For certain, that was not a man in a suit."

"A clockwork device, then?" Trounce asked.

"More sophisticated."

Thomas Honesty and his fellow constables had risen and brushed themselves down. Honesty looked at Burton, who, seeing that Monckton Milnes and the Cannibals were poised to rush over, said to him, "Would you hold everyone back for a minute, Tom? Just while I gather my wits."

Honesty nodded and got to work.

Burton put his left hand to the back of his head. His scalp was ridged with scars—gained last year when he'd narrowly missed being killed by an explosion—and had now acquired an egg-sized bump.

Pain was beginning to overtake him. His legs were shaking.

The snow all around was gouged with broad furrows, cutting through to the bright red beneath. Leicester Square—flesh-coloured and mutilated—appeared to reflect his own injuries, as if he and the world he perceived were a single, wounded being.

He shivered, fumbled for—and failed to locate—a cigar, and said, "I want to find my topper and swordstick, Algy. We should then make our way to Battersea Power Station. We need to consult with Brunel and Babbage. They know all there is to know about mechanical men."

Swinburne gave a small and reluctant grunt of agreement.

Burton's fingers, still absently in search of a cheroot, encountered a solid object and withdrew it from his coat pocket. It was a small, ornately labelled bottle. Saltzmann's Tincture. Incredulous, he whispered, "Good Lord! It didn't break."

"I wish it had," Swinburne grumbled. "Put it away."

"My head is thumping. It'll help."

"So will Sadhvi Raghavendra. We'll send a lad to summon her to the station. She'll treat your wounds better than that stuff can."

Burton hesitated, nodded, and slipped the bottle back into his pocket.

"Humph!" Trounce muttered. "I'd better get to work. There's a crowd that requires dispersing. I'll post a guard outside the restaurant. See you later. Keep me informed, will you?"

He stamped away.

Limping slightly, Burton started off toward the Cannibals. They hurried forward to meet him.

"God in Heaven!" Monckton Milnes exclaimed. "Are you all right? I've never seen such a scrap! How can you even walk?"

"I hurt all over," Burton said. "But I'll survive."

"He wants to gulp down a bottle of Saltzmann's," Swinburne revealed. "So obviously his brain has been bruised, despite its small size and the thick layers that surround it."

For an instant, Monckton Milnes locked eyes with the king's agent. Both men knew that Swinburne operated in a very peculiar manner, often experiencing and expressing the opposite of what would be expected from any normal individual. When the poet felt pain, he considered it pleasure. When he was deeply concerned, he most often articulated it as humour or sarcasm.

"Lay off the confounded mixture, Richard," Monckton Milnes advised. "I've told you before."

"Enough! Enough!" Burton protested. "Will you both please give it a rest? I shan't touch the stuff, I give you my word."

Monckton Milnes responded with a brusque nod. He stepped aside as the other Cannibals crowded forward to voice their consternation and amazement. Burton endured their attentions. He was aware that Monckton Milnes and Swinburne were both watching and assessing him, and it irritated him that they considered themselves better judges of his condition than he. At the same time, he was touched, and cursed himself for a fool that he harboured such an idiotic spark of resentment.

Too much self-sufficiency. Why be so contained? Few men have such loyal friends. Swinburne, Monckton Milnes, Bendyshe, Bradlaugh—all of them. They are not attached to you. They are integral.

He felt the void that marked Isabel's absence.

Bendyshe was hollering, "Bartolini will never forgive you, old thing! You went straight through his bloomin' window! The restaurant is wrecked! Why aren't you dead?"

Burton thought, *I might as well be.*

CHAPTER 2

AN EXPERIMENT GONE AWRY

THE POWER OF TAROT

Your Future Foretold
Every combination of cards is unique
Each describes your journey into the future
The Opportunities. The Challenges. The Lessons.

MADAM TABITHA KNOWS

Apply within

Swinburne grabbed at a hand strap as the landau in which he and Burton were riding bounced over the kerb while rounding a corner. He coughed and muttered, "Drat the thing!" He was referring to the carriage's side window, which was jammed half open, allowing smoke from the vehicle's steam engine to coil in to assault their eyes and noses.

"Spring Heeled Jack!" he exclaimed. "How is it possible? I thought Edward Oxford was dead."

Burton, grimacing with the pain caused by the jolt, had finally located a Manila cheroot in his waistcoat pocket, and now shakily held a lucifer to it. He set about adding to the abrasive atmosphere. Blood was congealing on his chin and neck, and his tattered left sleeve was wet with it.

He gathered his thoughts for a moment then said, "Let's consider what we already know. Oxford was from the future. In the year 2202—"

"Inconceivably distant!"

"—he created a wearable machine, comprised of a one-piece skintight suit with a flat disk on its chest, a black helmet that encased his head fully but for the face, a cloak, and boots to which powerfully sprung stilts were attached. These latter were necessary to propel him into the air, so that nothing touched him, there to be thrown backward or forward through history by the microscopic components of his device."

"I can see why you've delayed your translating of *A Thousand Nights and a Night*," Swinburne said. "You must find its tales positively pedestrian." He produced a flask from inside his coat and unscrewed its top.

Burton grunted his agreement. "Oxford leaped back to the year 1840 to observe his ancestor's failed attempt to assassinate Queen Victoria. He intervened, inadvertently caused the assassination to succeed, and accidentally killed his forebear. His suit, badly damaged, then threw him farther back through time to 1837."

Swinburne took a swig, smacked his lips, and passed the flask to Burton. "He changed history and wiped himself out of the future. What an idiot."

"Indeed," Burton agreed. He took a drink and returned the vessel to the poet, wincing as brandy burned the cuts where the insides of his cheeks had been mashed against his teeth. He sucked at his cigar. His ribs creaked. They were badly bruised. Through billowing smoke, he went on, "Oxford had caused time to bifurcate. There was now the original history and, running parallel to it, a new one in which he was trapped. His prolonged exposure to the past caused him to rapidly lose his mind. He embarked upon a desperate hunt for the woman his ancestor would have married."

"Meaning to impregnate her in order to reestablish the chain of descent that would eventually lead to his own birth," Swinburne said. He giggled and hiccupped. "Only a lunatic could *conceive* of such a scheme! Please forgive the rotten pun."

Burton waited for the landau to pass a loudly clanking pantechnicon. When he could again be heard, he said, "He was repeatedly spotted by the public, who regarded him as something of a bogeyman and named him Spring Heeled Jack. Meanwhile, the man who gave him shelter relayed to Isambard Kingdom Brunel some of Oxford's hints about the machineries of 2202. Employing the materials and knowledge of our age, the great engineer acted upon this information, and, over the course of two decades, the British Empire quickly filled with his diverse and ever more eccentric inventions."

Swinburne gestured at the interior of the landau. "Behold! A horseless carriage! The great age of steam!"

The vehicle's motor produced a horrible grinding noise followed by a thunderous belch. They heard their driver swearing at it.

"Yes, but our history is not the one we're discussing. For us, now, it is 1860. Where Oxford was trapped, the next significant event takes place a year hence, when a version of me—who, to avoid confusion, we shall refer to by the name he'll later adopt, Abdu El Yezdi—will learn the truth about Oxford. He'll also discover that a cabal of scientists intends to seize the time suit, repair it, and use it to create multiple histories in which to experiment with evolution and eugenic manipulation. To prevent this, and hoping to forestall any further interference with the flow of time, he'll break Oxford's neck and will take possession of the suit."

"What a brute!" Swinburne muttered.

"He is—or was—or will be—me."

"As I said."

"Oaf."

"I hope they have some brandy at the power station. My supply is dwindling fast. Are we nearly there?"

Burton peered out of the window. "We're on Piccadilly. Just passing Green Park."

"How very germane. That's where Victoria was gunned down."

"It's snowing again."

"Red?"

"White." Burton considered his cigar and calculated how many more puffs he could drag out of it. It was, he concluded, good for another four or five. He moved his wounded arm and winced, tried and failed to position it in a manner that hurt less. The pain of his wounds was intensifying. It caused him to lose track of his thoughts. He furrowed his brow, gritted his teeth, and tried to battle through the discomfort.

"1862," Swinburne prompted.

"Ah yes, a year after Oxford's death. El Yezdi will discover that parts of the suit contain tiny shards taken from one of the three mythical "Eyes of Nāga," rare black diamonds, each a fragment of a fallen aerolite. Remarkably, they're able to store and maintain subtle electrical fields, such as those generated by the human brain. My *doppelgänger*, setting out to find all three stones, will learn that in every existing variation of history, a devastating world war is coming. During that conflict, the diamonds will be used to psychically enhance three great dictators: Britain's Aleister Crowley, Prussia's Friedrich Nietzsche, and Russia's Grigori Rasputin. One of those men, Rasputin, will send his mind back through time from the year 1914 in order to alter the course of the war."

"My head hurts," Swinburne complained.

"My everything hurts," Burton responded. His hand drifted to a pocket. He felt the outline of the Saltzmann's bottle.

Don't. You gave your word.

Swinburne said, "Your counterpart will defeat the Russian and cause him to die in 1914, two years earlier than he would otherwise have done."

"Resulting in yet another split in history. El Yezdi will become aware that such bifurcations can't be controlled and are occurring in profusion."

A flurry of snow blew in through the jammed window. Swinburne lifted his top hat from his knees, upended it, and tapped it with his knuckles. Snowflakes rained onto his boots. "Really," he muttered. "We might just as well sit on the roof."

"So," Burton said, "having gained through his battle with Rasputin two of the Eyes of Nāga, El Yezdi will organise an expedition to recover the third, which is located in the Mountains of the Moon close to the source of the Nile. He'll be challenged by a rival group financed by Prussia, and the two safaris will fight their way across Africa, unaware that they're both being manipulated by the Nāga, a prehistoric race of intelligent reptiles whose consciousness has been trapped in the stones for millennia."

"As if all the rest wasn't sufficiently fantastic," Swinburne said, "now we have lizard men. Shall we get drunk and forget all this nonsense,

Richard? We could live out our remaining days in a pleasant haze, oblivious to all absurdities bar our own."

Burton dropped his cigar stub and crushed it beneath his heel. "Pass that flask."

"Hurrah! He toasts the motion!"

The king's agent imbibed and returned the near-empty container. "I might be tempted, but I fear the absurd has a tendency to seek us out wherever we might be, as the events of this evening have demonstrated."

The landau lurched to a halt, there came a knock on the roof, a hatch lifted, and the driver looked down at them. "'Scuse us, gents. Won't be two shakes of a lamb's tail. Got to shovel more coal into the furnace. Just a tick. Half a minute. Quick as a flash, like. I shan't keep you. It won't take long."

The hatch slammed shut.

"He certainly took his time telling us how fast he's going to be," Swinburne observed. "Where were we? Ah, yes, Abdu El Yezdi is going to realise that the Nāga arranged his experiences from the start. That's when his trials will really begin."

"Quite so. The reptiles will tattoo black diamond dust into his scalp, it being required for a technique they'll then employ to send him forward through time to 1914, where for five years he'll endure the terrible global conflict and witness its devastating effect on Africa. Traumatised, with his memory in pieces, he'll evade the British psychic Aleister Crowley and make his way back to the Mountains of the Moon, there to return to 1863. The Nāga will inform him that the experience was a parting gift, intended to give him a better understanding of the nature of time. They'll then be liberated from the diamond, which El Yezdi will take back with him to England."

"As gifts go, that one was lousy."

"I can't disagree. It certainly influences his subsequent determination to restore history to its original single stream. Emulating the Nāga's method, and taking the diamonds and damaged time suit with him, he'll travel back to Green Park in 1840."

"Hooray! We can return to the past tense. It feels so much more *normal*."

"I quite agree."

The carriage rocked as the driver climbed back up to his seat. The engine gave a roar, settled into a more subdued chugging, and the vehicle jerked back into motion. Burton hissed and clutched at his arm.

"All right?" Swinburne murmured.

"Yes. So my counterpart waited for history to repeat itself, which it did: Edward Oxford arrived in 1840, having jumped from 2202. My other self immediately killed him and took possession of his undamaged suit. Thus Oxford couldn't be thrown to 1837, history wouldn't be altered, and everything would be back as it should be."

"Except it wasn't. Somehow, he failed to prevent Victoria's assassination." Swinburne shook the now empty flask and heaved a forlorn sigh.

"Correct. El Yezdi had created yet another strand of history, *this* one that you and I inhabit, and he was trapped in it, knowing that a younger version of himself, the nineteen-year-old *me*, was already here."

"Two Burtons," Swinburne mused. "How perfectly dreadful."

The one at his side gave a wry smile. "I'm glad I was oblivious to the fact until last year."

The poet held up the empty brandy flask. "I wish I was a little more oblivious. All this is giving me a terrible thirst. I also feel obliged to remind you that our current conversation was begun with the intention of perhaps shedding light on what or who it was that wrecked Bartolini's and beat you black and blue. We appear to be no closer to any insight."

"I want to outline events in their proper order that we may think clearly."

"Where hopping through time is concerned, I'm not sure there's any such thing as a proper order. And do you really think clarity of thought is possible after going through a window headfirst? You're ambitious, I'll give you that. Well, carry on. You have my undivided attention."

"Now that the brandy is gone."

"Precisely. What happened next, oh Scheherazade?"

"With the Eyes of Nāga and the two time suits—one damaged, one not—in his possession, Abdu El Yezdi—he now took that name—went into hiding, aided by Isambard Kingdom Brunel and Charles Babbage, and over the next two decades influenced them, along with our key thinkers and politicians, to shape our world into one that, he hoped, would avoid the terrible war he'd witnessed."

"The scene: 1859. Enter Richard Francis Burton, stage left, El Yezdi's younger self, native to the history he'd created. You."

"And, unfortunately, enter Aleister Crowley, who sent his spirit not only backward through time but also sideways, crossing from the future where El Yezdi had encountered him into this, our history. He hunted me and—and—"

Killed the only woman I have ever loved.

"And kidnapped scientists and surgeons," Swinburne interjected, "forcing them to construct a body for his disembodied spirit to inhabit."

"I defeated him," Burton said flatly.

"You met Abdu El Yezdi."

"My other self succumbed to old age."

"His allies—Brunel, Babbage, and the Department of Guided Science—are now *your* allies, and his reports, in which all the aforementioned is explained, and which are filled with the wealth of his experience, are at your disposal."

Burton was silent for a moment. The stench of the River Thames wafted in through the window. They were close to their destination.

Three steam spheres passed the landau, their drive bands humming.

"What's your opinion of them, Algy—of the reports, I mean? Specifically, the manner in which the material is presented."

Swinburne chuckled. "I think his propensity for inflicting them with penny dreadful titles proves conclusively that he was you. *The Strange Affair of Spring Heeled Jack. The Curious Case of the Clockwork Man. Expedition to the Mountains of the Moon.* They sound like the tales that young valet of yours reads in his—what's the name of the story paper little Bram's so addicted to?"

"*The Baker Street Detective*, featuring Mr. Macallister Fogg."

"Sheer hokum, and I'd say the same of the reports had I not met El Yezdi in person. I must say, though, for all their outlandishness, I'm just as fascinated by what he omitted from them than by what he included, especially where the third is concerned. Was he protecting himself, do you think?"

Burton shook his head. "I've been in many positions where concealing information would have been the wisest course. The report I made, at Sir Charles Napier's behest, into male brothels in Karachi ruined my military career and my reputation because it was, quite simply, too complete. That was in 1845, when I was twenty-four years old. El Yezdi had been with us for five years by then. We know from the first of his accounts that, in his native history, he'd presented the very same report when *he* was twenty-four and suffered the identical consequences, yet he made no move to prevent me from repeating the mistake. It appears that he and I, being one and the same, have shared an utter lack of caution where personal reputation is concerned."

"So maybe the omissions were to protect others."

"That's my suspicion. Perhaps there are some matters his associates are simply better off not knowing."

"Myself among them."

"Most assuredly," Burton agreed. "He never revealed the fate of the Swinburne who, in his own variant of time, accompanied him to Africa. Exactly what happened to you amid the Mountains of the Moon?"

"And why didn't I return from them?"

With a jerk and a loud detonation from its engine, the landau came to a stop. The driver shouted, "Battersea Power Station, gents!" He saluted down to his passengers as they disembarked. Burton stepped out of the cabin stiffly and with a groan.

Snow fell around them. The cabbie waved a hand at it. "At least it's turned the right bloomin' colour, hey? White, just as snow aught to bloomin' well be!"

"A shilling, I take it?" Swinburne asked.

"Beg pardon?"

"The fare."

Burton pushed his friend aside and handed up the correct coinage and a little extra. "My companion is convinced that every cab ride, no matter the destination, costs a shilling," he explained.

"They do!" Swinburne protested. His left leg twitched, causing him to hop up and down.

"Funny in the head, is he?" the man asked.

"Extremely. He's a poet."

"Oh dear!"

"An unmitigated loony," Burton clarified.

"I say!" Swinburne screeched.

The driver clicked his tongue sympathetically. "Got you into a scrap, did he? Caused a rumpus? You look proper done over, you do, if yer don't mind me a-sayin' so."

"He did, I am, and I don't. Good evening."

"Night, sir."

The landau departed.

Battersea Power Station stood tall before them, its four copper rods rising high, like chimneys, scraping the underside of the blanketing cloud. Both men knew the rods extended even farther below the edifice, penetrating deep into the Earth's crust. Brunel had designed the station to render geothermal energy into electricity. It was one of his few failures, and generated only sufficient power to light itself.

They started across the broad patch of wasteland that separated the station from Queenstown Road. Burton limped, pain stabbing through him with every step. Their feet sank into the snow, which was already lying a foot deep, startlingly pink beneath the illuminations of Brunel's creation.

"Red snow," Swinburne muttered. "Spring Heeled Jack. Men from the future. Multiple Burtons. And he calls *me* a loony!"

Off to their right, a gargantuan rotorship rose from the nearby Royal Navy Air Service Station. Light glowed from the many portholes along its sides, and its spinning wings sent a deep throbbing through the atmosphere. It powered into the sky on an expanding cone of starkly white steam until it was swallowed by the cloud. A lozenge of fuzzy luminescence marked its position as it slid southward.

"The *Sagittarius*," Burton noted. "According to the *Daily Bugle*, it's off to China today."

"To bomb the Qing Dynasty into submission at the behest of Lord Elgin," Swinburne added. "That man is the consummate politician. He possesses not one jot of conscience. Can we return to the matter at hand? Edward Oxford? Did we encounter him tonight?"

"The problem is that the apparition resembled Oxford's time suit only in that it was mounted on stilts," Burton responded. "It was a mechanism, not a man."

"So if not him, what?"

"In design it appeared more advanced than Oxford's invention. I wonder, then, whether its origins lie even farther into the future than 2202. Conversely, it said it served Queen Victoria, meaning it must have come from some point during her reign, between 1837 and 1840."

"Which makes no sense at all."

"As you say. And why was it hunting for me? And why didn't it know what to do with me when it found me? And why did it—did it—wait. Stop." Burton gasped, stumbled to a halt, and leaned heavily on his cane. "I just need a moment."

"Not far to go," Swinburne said. "Then warmth, brandy, and a chair to sit in. Sadhvi shouldn't take too long to get here, either. She'll soon have you as right as rain."

"I share your—your faith in her abilities," Burton mumbled. "Nevertheless—"

He fished the bottle of Saltzmann's Tincture from his pocket.

"Please," Swinburne pleaded. "You promised."

"I have to break my word, Algy. I'm sorry, but my legs are folding beneath me. I can barely function."

"Just hold on a little longer."

"I can't." Burton sucked in a juddering breath, uncorked the bottled, raised it to his lips, and downed the contents.

"All of it?" Swinburne shrieked. "You're only meant to take a teaspoonful!"

"Nonsense."

"You're out of your bloody mind!"

Burton felt honey-like warmth oozing through arteries and spreading into capillaries. His aches immediately shifted to one side, as if vacating his wounds. He felt the odd sensation that countless possibilities stretched away from him into an infinitude of futures.

The tincture had never acted with such rapidity.

He was thankful for it.

"Better," he said after a minute had passed. "Let's get out of this snow."

They trudged onward, Swinburne glaring angrily at the explorer, and came to the power station's big double gate, in which was set a smaller door. Burton rapped his stick against it and, within a minute, it swung inward and one of Brunel's engineers greeted them. "You got here quickly!"

"What do you mean?" Burton asked, stepping through into the courtyard.

"Weren't you called for?"

"No. Why? Has something happened?"

"I'll say! You'd better go straight through to the central work area. Mr. Babbage will explain. Or more likely Mr. Gooch. Babbage—*Mr. Babbage*—is rather—um—upset."

Puzzled, Burton and Swinburne crossed to the tall inner doors, which were standing slightly open, and entered the station's vast cathedral-like interior. It was filled with machines whose function could only be guessed at. They pumped and hammered and sizzled and buzzed while, overhead, in glass spheres suspended from the distant ceiling, lightning flashed without surcease, casting a harsh light over the scene.

The two men followed a passage through the various contraptions until they came to an area that was filled with workbenches. Normally, this part of the station was crowded with engineers and scientists, all labouring night and day over their creations, but now it was empty but for a small group of men and women among whom Burton spotted Babbage, Gooch, and Brunel. The latter was so utterly motionless that he resembled a statue.

Isambard Kingdom Brunel was a remarkable figure. No longer human, he stood there, a hulking man-shaped contraption, comprised of armour-like brass plating, rods, springs, pistons, and cogwheels, and etched all over with intricate decorative designs. He had six arms—one with a big Gatling gun bolted to it—and a mask-like face fashioned into a likeness of the human features he'd possessed until his death last year. The electrical fields of his conscious mind were stored in fragments of a Nāga diamond and were articulated through one of Babbage's famous probability calculators housed in his metal skull.

As they came closer, Burton saw that one of the great engineer's hands had been cleanly shorn off at the wrist. He also saw a workbench upon which the pristine time suit—the one Abdu El Yezdi had taken from Edward Oxford in 1840—had been laid out. Beside it, an oblong box-like contraption was hanging by long chains from the ceiling. Constructed from dark wood and polished brass, it somewhat resembled a curve-topped sea chest. Its upper surface was inset with dials, switches, and gauges. On the other side of this box, in an area that looked as if it should have been occupied by another workbench, there was a circular smooth-sided bowl-shaped depression in the floor. Though considerably smaller, it exactly resembled the one left in the paving at Leicester Square after Spring Heeled Jack had vanished.

Burton felt his skin prickling with a disconcerting presentiment.

"By God, what happened to you?" Daniel Gooch exclaimed upon spotting the king's agent. "You look like you lost an argument with an omnibus."

"Something like that," Burton said. He looked at Brunel. "Isambard?"

Gooch, a short, plumpish, sandy-haired man who, as usual, was wearing a harness to which was attached a pair of mechanical arms supplementing his own, extended all four limbs in a wide shrug. "You'll not get anything out of him, I'm afraid. I think his babbage calculator has been knocked out of whack. He's completely paralysed. We've had an—er—*incident*." He turned and called to Charles Babbage. The aged scientist, though stooped and liver spotted, had about him an air of zealous energy that belied his years. That energy was currently being expended in frenetic pacing. He was also tapping the fingers of both hands against his forehead, as if pressing imaginary buttons.

"Charles! Charles!" Gooch repeated. "Sir Richard and Mr. Swinburne are here."

"Irrelevant!" Babbage snapped.

"I hardly think so, sir. The suit belonged to Sir Richard, after all."

"Belonged?" Burton queried.

"The damaged one," Swinburne said. "Where is it?"

"Ah," Gooch answered. "That's the question."

"Not one we should be required to ask," Babbage shouted in a querulous tone. "It shouldn't be possible. Even if it had become functional, there was no one inside the blasted thing to command it. What could have instigated it to jump?"

Burton struggled to clarify his thoughts. The Saltzmann's was sending wave after wave of heat through him, flushing out the pain of his wounds, but also causing his mind to apprehend a plethora of variations, so that when Babbage turned to face him, he was also dimly aware of the old man *not* turning to face him, and when Babbage raised his right hand with his forefinger pointing upward, Burton imagined or vaguely perceived—he wasn't certain which—the scientist raising the left instead.

"Nine o'clock on the fifteenth of February, 1860," Babbage announced. "Does that moment mean anything to you?"

"I'm aware that it is today's date," Burton responded. "And the hour of nine has made itself significant."

"Ah! So you recognise the anniversary?"

Burton removed his top hat, shook snow from it, and placed it on a worktop. He put his cane beside it and started to unbutton his coat. "I don't, Charles. Enlighten me."

Babbage slapped his right fist into his left palm. "Edward Oxford! It is at nine o'clock on the fifteenth of February in the year 2202—his fortieth birthday—that he'll make his first foray into the past; departing his native time period at that precise moment, exactly three hundred and forty-two years from now."

Stepping to a wooden stool, Burton lowered himself onto it, feeling his injured arm complaining but experiencing the pain as a somehow disassociated flare of light that didn't properly belong to him.

Swinburne, who'd also divested himself of his outer garments, said, "What of it, Charles?"

"Have you not read the reports Abdu El Yezdi left for us? Did he not always insist that coincidences are of crucial importance? He referred to time as having echoes and rhythms, ripples and interconnected moments. In truth, what he was clumsily expressing are matters of algorithmic probability. They cannot be ignored."

"An anniversary strikes me as more a matter of sentiment than of mathematics," Swinburne said.

"You are a *poet*, sir!" Babbage spat the word as if it were the worst insult in the world.

Burton addressed Gooch. "Have you a cigar, old fellow? I appear to have smoked my last."

Gooch dug mechanical fingers into his pocket and passed a *Flor de Dindigul* to the king's agent.

"Thank you." After putting a flame to his smoke, Burton returned his attention to Babbage. "I take it you marked the occasion in some manner." He gestured toward the indentation in the floor. "And perhaps that is the result?"

"It doesn't make any sense."

"What doesn't?"

Babbage started tapping his head again. "Nothing to provide the impulse, you see," he muttered. "No one in it."

"I don't see." Burton turned to Gooch. "In plain English and to the point, please, Daniel."

The engineer grunted and said, "I'll try." He folded his four arms. "It concerns the multitude of histories. They must all contain Edward Oxford's burned and malfunctioning time suit because they all originated either from the moment he caused the first division in time or from events that occurred subsequent to it. However, our iteration of history is absolutely unique in that Abdu El Yezdi brought to it a second version of the outfit." He nodded toward the nearby bench. "The undamaged one. That's what made Charles's experiment possible."

"Two suits. Where is the other?"

"We don't know. Charles was attempting to repair it." Gooch strode over to the bench. "The suit is comprised of four principal components." He put a metal hand against the white fabric. "Its material absorbs light and converts it to power." He touched the flat disk on the suit's chest. "The Nimtz generator stores that power and converts it to what we might refer to as chronostatic energy." He moved to the end of the work-table. "Immediately prior to the suit's transference from one moment in history to another, the generator extends around it a pocket of the aforesaid energy. Were this to intersect with anything possessing more density than air, the object would be sliced through and part of it carried with the traveller through time. The boots, with their spring-loaded stilts, were therefore designed to thrust Oxford high above the ground so only the atmosphere surrounded him." He waved a fleshy hand toward the other end of the bench. "Finally, the helmet contains microscopic semi-biological machinery that calculates, initiates, and directs all aspects of the journey. The crucial constituent of this machinery is called a BioProc. One word, capital B, capital P. There are thousands of BioProcs in the helmet, and every one of them contains a granule of powdered black diamond. Larger shards of the stone are also present in the generator. We are all aware of the peculiar qualities of the gem, yes?"

He received sounds of confirmation from Burton and Swinburne.

"The immense calculating power of the helmets," Gooch went on, "is made possible by an inconceivably complex electromagnetic pattern existing within the diamond dust; a pattern that employed Edward Oxford's mind as its template. When he was killed by El Yezdi in 1840, his terminal emanation—a powerful burst of energy from the brain—instantly overwrote it, but since this matched what was already there, there was no untoward effect." He stood back. "The damaged suit didn't fare so well. Its electrical composition was already badly impaired by prolonged exposure to the madness of the Oxford who'd become known as Spring Heeled Jack, and when he died, whatever vestiges of sanity that remained in it were erased by his last mental gasp."

Passing back along the side of the bench, Gooch reached out and picked up the helmet. "This is a truly remarkable machine. It can enter a state called 'self-repair mode,' which allows its internal components to alter their function in order to carry out whatever maintenance is necessary. Had we, like the other histories, only the one ruined suit, we would have rerouted what power remained in its Nimtz generator to the headpiece, hoping that somehow, in its insanity, there was retained sufficient an instinct for self-preservation to instigate repairs. Perhaps it would have somehow reordered its synthetic intelligence." He turned the helmet in his hands. "But we were lucky. We had this pristine version, which is why Mr. Babbage created that—" He jerked his chin toward the box-like affair. "A Field Amplifier."

Burton swayed slightly, in the grip of a synaesthesia that suddenly made the sound of Gooch's voice a floral scent, turned the scene before him into a symphony of visceral sensations, and transformed the oily odour of the workshop into a melodious purring. He glanced at the glowing tip of his cigar. It was a miniature sun.

"With it," Gooch went on, "we intended to record the electrical pattern present in this helmet and copy it across to the defective one, replacing the insanity therein."

"Marvellous!" Swinburne exclaimed. "What went wrong?"

"Charles has a curious sense of occasion. To him, every event is a mathematical formula and its every possible outcome an elaboration of the calculation. Applying this hypothesis to the suits, he proposes that they manipulate a single great equation—a stupendous envisioning of time's structures and processes—and that by observing coincidences and sequences, he might one day comprehend it. This is why today's anniversary was significant, and why he initiated the experiment at exactly nine o'clock."

Charles Babbage suddenly came out of his self-absorption, stepped forward, and slapped a hand down onto the worktop. "The synthetic intelligence is responsive, not active. I could not have issued the command independently."

A particularly violent bolt of lightning whipped through one of the overhanging globes. The crackling detonations echoed around the massive hall, and the white light momentarily illuminated the normally shadowed sockets of the scientist's eyes, revealing a fanatical glint within.

Burton felt the inexplicable suspicion that, rather than being present in Battersea Power Station, he was somewhere entirely different.

From afar, he heard Swinburne cry out, "Command? What command? My hat! In all the many histories, is there a single Charles Babbage who can get to the confounded point?"

As the king's agent splintered into innumerable renditions of himself, Gooch said, "At the exact moment the Field Amplifier accessed the ruined headpiece, a bubble of chronostatic energy formed around the damaged time suit. It sliced through Isambard's wrist, popped, and the suit, along with our friend's hand, vanished."

"It travelled into time," Babbage snarled. "Of its own accord."

CHAPTER 3

AN EVENING WITH ORPHEUS

The world is divided into two classes, those who believe the incredible, and those who do the improbable.
—Oscar Wilde

From amid the complex of jointed metal limbs that hung from the centre of the ceiling like angular jungle lianas, one emerged with a sword clutched in its mechanical digits. Gently, it tapped the blade first against Captain Richard Francis Burton's right shoulder, then against his left.

The king's agent stood, now a Knight of the Most Distinguished Order of Saint Michael and Saint George.

Due to the damage done to the monarch's vocal apparatus during the attack on Buckingham Palace, a white-stockinged royal equerry had spoken the words of the ceremony. Burton felt relieved by this. King Ernest Augustus I was demented at the best of times, and the past three months had been far from the best. Had he been able to express himself, he'd no doubt have ranted endlessly about the violence done to him—for the palace was, in effect, his own body; his limbs were built into every part of it, all controlled from the Crown Room, where his brain floated in a tank of vital fluids. The destruction of the western wing had been the equivalent of having an arm blown off. His Majesty was nettled, to say the least.

Burton took three steps back, bowed, and returned to his seat.

"Did your leg fall asleep?" whispered Monckton Milnes, who was sitting to his left.

"No. Why do you ask?"

"You were limping."

Burton made a sound of puzzlement. "Was I? By Allah's beard, I do feel a little strange. My mind was wandering all over the place. I imagined myself to be at Battersea Power Station."

"Maybe it wasn't just the leg, then," his friend suggested, *sotto voce*. "Perhaps all of you fell asleep. I wouldn't be at all surprised, despite the occasion. Not after what you've been through."

"I was daydreaming, that's all. You know I have no patience for these official functions. When can we get out of this asylum?"

"Shhh! The walls have ears."

Burton mentally kicked himself. "I mean no disrespect to the king, but I was probably thinking of Battersea Power Station because I have to be there by nine o'clock. Babbage is activating Oxford's suit."

An abstruse thought intruded. *What? Again?*

"These ceremonies don't usually occur so late in the day," Monckton Milnes observed, "but His Majesty spent all morning with his architects, and the meeting went past its allotted hours. It's rumoured that he wants the palace rebuilt and made the tallest edifice in the city. I expect he's eager to get back to his plans and sketches, which is why, believe it or not, formalities are proceeding at such a rapid pace."

"This is rapid?"

"By comparison to the norm. Be patient, there are only three more to be knighted, then we'll depart."

One of the palace footmen gave them an uncompromising glare. They stopped their whispering.

Burton ran his forefinger around his collar. It was too tight. He'd forgotten how uncomfortable a freshly laundered army uniform could be.

Wearily, he endured the pomp and protocols.

Forty minutes later, in the reception hall, the foppishly attired Lord Palmerston approached him and drawled, "My dear Sir Richard, may I be the first to congratulate you."

"On what, sir?"

"Your title, man! Your title!"

"Ah. Thank you, Prime Minister."

"I've read your report. *The Mystery of the Malevolent Mediums.* Do you intend to give all your accounts such lurid titles?"

"I felt it appropriate. It was a dramatic affair."

"I can't disagree with that. Is it really over?"

"Nietzsche is dead, sir—in our time, in his own, and across all the other versions of history."

Burton couldn't shake a curious sensation of unfamiliarity. The environment felt unutterably askew. Even the words that came out of his mouth felt wrong.

"And the future war?" Palmerston asked.

"That rests with you. Now we know it's coming, you have the opportunity to develop policies that will steer us along another course. There's no need for the conflict to erupt in 1914. We have fifty-four years in which to prevent it."

Palmerston rubbed his chin thoughtfully. "Hmm. Or fifty-four years in which to prepare. Perhaps it would be better to spend that time undermining Prussia and the Germanic states rather than indulging them."

"That might send us into battle earlier."

"Nietzsche told you the conflict is inevitable. If that's the case, better we strike hard and when least expected than not at all."

Burton shrugged and murmured, "As the premier, it's your choice to make. I don't envy you."

Palmerston hemmed and hawed.

"I have to go," Burton said. "There's business to take care of at the Department of Guided Science."

"The what?"

"The—the—I'm sorry, I meant to say, at the Federation of Mechanics."

"A rather unusual slip of the tongue."

"It's this uniform. It's too tight. I'm hot and uncomfortable. Can't think straight."

"Hmm. So what are the Empire's boffins up to? Anything I should be aware of?"

"No, sir, I don't think so."

The prime minister nodded distractedly and waved him away.

Burton returned to Monckton Milnes, who was flirting—fruitlessly, as usual—with Nurse Florence Nightingale.

"I'll see you at Bartolini's at eleven."

"The Cannibal Club convenes," Monckton Milnes confirmed. "I'll be there."

Burton made for the exit but was intercepted by Detective Inspector Krishnamurthy, a handsome young Scotland Yard man of Indian extraction who was sporting a shiny new medal on his jacket.

"It's done, sir."

"All of them?" Burton asked.

"Yes. Countess Sabina and Isabella Mayson killed the last at two o'clock this morning. It was hunting Sergeant Honesty through the British Museum."

"Bismillah! Is he all right?"

"Unharmed. The countess has confirmed that not a single berserker remains."

"Good show. What of Trounce?"

"His eye can't be saved, but he'll pull through."

"Thank you, Maneesh. I'm sorry about Shyamji. Your cousin was a good man."

"Yes, sir, he was. A brave one, too."

Burton left the chamber and stepped out of the palace into thick London fog. He stopped, frowned, and tried to identify whatever it was he appeared to have forgotten. Nothing occurred to him, but the sense that something vital had been misplaced didn't go away. He snapped his fingers irritably and walked on, passing along the edge of the parade ground to the Royal Mews.

He came to the stables. His mechanical horse raised its head as he approached. It whirred, "You need to wind me up. My spring is slack."

"Hello, Orpheus. Slack? Have you been gallivanting? I told you to stay still."

"I know, but I felt restless. You've been in there for ages. I needed to stretch my legs."

Pulling the key from its housing in the horse's side, Burton inserted it into the hole beneath the steed's decorative tail and began to rotate it. Speaking over the loud ratcheting, he said, "Your legs are metal. They can't be stretched."

"I was speaking metaphorically."

"I shall have words with Babbage. I'm not sure a mechanical horse should know how to employ metaphors."

"While you're at it, you could ask Isambard Kingdom Brunel to completely redesign me."

"You say that every single time I wind you up."

"Because it's humiliating."

"You don't possess emotions."

"Having a key shoved up my arse on a regular basis appears to have instilled them in me."

"And you become ever more bothersome each time your spring is tightened."

"If you want a dumb steed, buy a fleshy one. You'll find its maintenance a far less convenient affair. Hay must be shoved into one end, and it emerges rather messily from the other. I assure you, in our relationship, I'm the one that suffers."

"You never stop reminding me."

Having fully rewound the horse, Burton clicked the key back into its bracket and hoisted himself up onto the saddle. "Take me to Battersea Power Station."

"Walk, trot, or gallop?"

"A brisk walk, please."

Orpheus headed toward the palace gates. "I didn't include a brisk walk among the options. In my book, it qualifies as a trot."

"Just be quiet and try not to get lost."

"I can't get lost. The route is engraved into my memory. I could navigate it blindfolded."

"How about gagged?"

"Well! Really!"

They left the palace and proceeded along Buckingham Palace Road in the direction of Chelsea Bridge. The fog was so thick that when Burton extended an arm his fingertips disappeared into it. Sounds were muffled and darkness hung over the city, penetrated here and there by nebulous balls of orange light that may have been street lamps, windows, or distant suns; it was impossible to tell.

There were very few people out and about. The weather wasn't solely to blame; the recent invasion of berserkers had terrified the entire city. People weren't yet convinced the danger had passed.

The stench of the Thames assaulted his nostrils. Bazalgette's new sewer system promised to solve the problem, but the tunnels had only been in operation for a few days, and it would take many months before the river's water ran clear. The fog always made the stink worse, too.

Five minutes later, Orpheus clip-clopped over the bridge, passed a patch of wasteland, turned onto a path that skirted the edge of the Royal Battle Fleet Airfield, and arrived at the gates of the power station. The many windows of the Mechanics' headquarters lit up the vapour, making of the illumination a physical mass that swirled around Burton as he dismounted.

"Wait here," he ordered.

"In the cold?" Orpheus complained. "It's bloody freezing."

"You can't feel cold."

"I'll get bored again."

"You'll wind down before that happens."

"Ugh. I hate entering the void. Even worse, I hate waking from it with that bloomin' key stuck up my whatsit. You're very mean to me."

"I might swap you for a velocipede."

Burton knocked on the door set into the massive station gates.

"Wheels!" Orpheus exclaimed. "Unstable. You'll fall off and crack your head. Deservedly so."

The door opened, and an oil-stained engineer ushered Burton in. "Hello, sir," she said. "They're waiting for you in the workshop. Follow me, please."

The woman led the king's agent across the courtyard to the tall inner gates, which, after manipulating a complex combination lock, she pushed open. They entered and crossed the vast floor space to the central area of workbenches.

Sir Charles Babbage looked up as the king's agent arrived. "About time!"

"Good evening," Burton responded. He acknowledged Daniel Gooch, at the scientist's side. "I apologise if I'm a little late. I was being knighted at the palace. You know from personal experience how such things drag on."

Babbage grunted disdainfully. "Well, if you must involve yourself with trivialities."

"I wasn't given any more choice in the matter than you were. Incidentally, the probability calculator you put in my mount—it's one of the new models, yes?"

"A Mark Three. My best design yet. It has personality enhancements."

"So I've noticed. Is there any way to diminish them? The confounded thing keeps answering back."

"Tut-tut!" Babbage barked. "Tut-tut! Always complaints. You're nothing but a Luddite, sir!"

From behind a nearby apparatus, a badly dented silver ball, twelve feet in diameter, appeared and rolled unsteadily to join them. It stopped and wobbled in front of Burton. A panel on its surface slid aside. A multi-jointed arm unfolded from inside, and the pincer-like hand at its end reached to a second panel, which opened with a click. Reaching in, the pincer extracted a long, thick cigar—already lit and glowing at one end—and inserted it into a small hole at the top of the globe. The tip of the cigar burned brightly, and smoke plumed from another orifice.

The king's agent said, "Hello, Isambard."

Isambard Kingdom Brunel clanged, "Sir Richard. Congratulations. Are you recovered?" His voice sounded like handbells being spilled onto a church organ.

"From the ceremony or from my injuries?"

"Heh! Your injuries, of course."

"My bruises pain me, but for the most part, yes, I'm fine, thank you."

He put his right hand to his left elbow and felt for a wound that wasn't there.

Why did I do that? My arm received no injury.

He turned his attention back to Brunel and, as he always did, wondered how much of the famous engineer still existed inside his life-maintaining machine. Brunel had suffered a serious stroke last year and would have died had Gooch not quickly designed and constructed the globe in which he was now preserved.

"You summoned me, Isambard?"

"I did. Sir Charles is about to perform an experiment that, as the guardian of the time suit, you should witness."

Burton looked at the workbench around which they were gathered. Edward Oxford's burned and blistered outfit had been laid out on it.

A powerful sense of *déjà vu* blossomed from the pit of his stomach. Its heat filled him, made his senses reel, and caused him to lean unsteadily on his walking cane.

Why am I here again?

It was a thought that made no sense.

Burton suddenly had no control over himself. Everything appeared unfamiliar. The inside of the station was crammed with contraptions, but they weren't the ones he knew. Babbage and Gooch were dressed in oddly tailored clothes. And Brunel—

A battered sphere? Shouldn't he be a man of brass?

He struggled to piece together recent events and glanced at the next workbench along, wondering why it was there and puzzled by the expectation that there should be a dent in the floor instead.

Memories welled up. Red snow. Leicester Square. Spring Heeled Jack.

"What experiment?" he asked, his voice hoarse.

It went wrong. The suit vanished of its own accord. Yet here it is.

Babbage pointed at the dented and blistered helmet. "As you are aware, this contains a synthetic intelligence, though its thought processes have been crippled by Edward Oxford's lunacy. During the course of the past three months, I have asked it questions, and it has replied to them with—"

"You've been wearing it?" Burton interrupted. "I thought Abdu El Yezdi left strict instructions that you should never—" He stopped.

Babbage and Gooch peered at him curiously.

Brunel chimed, "Who is Abdu El Yezdi?"

"No one. Nothing. My apologies. I'm—I'm tired. My mind is wandering."

"Rein it in!" Babbage snapped. "Pay attention! This is important! As I was saying, the headpiece has never responded to my queries with anything other than garbled nonsense. I've had to sort through all manner of irrelevancies to locate the merest crumbs of pertinent information. It has not been sufficient. I've gained little understanding of how the machinery of the suit functions, and now the power held in the helmet is almost drained." He leaned over the workbench and tapped a finger on the device attached to the suit's chest. "However, all is not lost. This is called a Nimtz generator. It holds a reserve of energy. Considerably more, in fact, than was ever in the headpiece. I've learned how to connect them together. It is done. I'm ready to issue the command that will cause the helmet to be reenergised. I believe it will then be able to repair itself." Babbage wriggled his fingers, said—"Hmm!"—and pulled a chronometer from his waistcoat pocket. "So, let us record that the procedure commences at nine o'clock on the evening of Wednesday the fifteenth of February, 1860. You understand the significance of the time?"

"I do," Burton murmured.

Nine o'clock! How can it be nine o'clock again?

The scientist reached down and traced a shape on the side of the Nimtz generator. The disk began to glow. It crackled. Suddenly, a shower of sparks erupted from it. Babbage flinched and cried out in alarm.

"What happened?" Gooch asked.

"I'm not sure. Perhaps the power has been routed to the wrong—"

The scientist stopped as a transparent bubble materialised around the helmet, suit, and boots. It rapidly expanded. The men quickly backed away from it, but Brunel didn't roll fast enough; the edge of the bubble touched him just before, with a deafening bang, it popped. The suit, the workbench, and a small section of the famous engineer vanished into thin air.

Gooch placed a hand on the sphere. "Are you all right, Isambard?"

The silver globe didn't respond. It was silent and still.

"What's wrong with him?" Burton asked. He looked down at the floor and saw a familiar smooth round indentation where the floor had been scooped out by the edge of the chronostatic energy field.

"It's hard to say," Gooch replied. "Maybe his probability calculator has been damaged."

"Pah!" Babbage put in. "A trifling matter. The suit has gone. Gone!"

"Into time, Sir Charles?" Gooch asked.

"Obviously! Hell and damnation! What have we lost? The knowledge! The knowledge!" The scientist lowered his face into his hands and moaned. "Go away, all of you. I have to think. You're distracting me. Leave me alone."

Burton cocked an eyebrow at the eccentric old man, glanced at Gooch, then looked down and was surprised to see that his hands, apparently of their own volition, were buttoning his coat over Army reds. Puzzled by the uniform, he retrieved its cap from a table, took up his silver-handled swordstick, and heard himself say, "I'll leave you to it. There are matters I need to attend to."

"Is the Nietzsche affair not done with?" Gooch asked.

"It's over," Burton answered, not really knowing what the Nietzsche affair was. He bid Gooch farewell, eyed Babbage and Brunel for a moment, then turned and left the station. As he stepped into the courtyard, he expected to see snow falling. It wasn't. There was just a solid wall of bitterly cold fog.

Crossing to the main gates, he exited through them and was greeted by a whirring voice. "That was quick."

Startled, Burton took a pace backward. A large horse-shaped contraption of brass loomed in the murk, regarding him with big, round, glowing eyes.

"What—what are you?" the king's agent stammered.

What is wrong with me? Have I amnesia?

"Orpheus, your trusty steed, of course. Have you come to test my knowledge of things you already know or are we going somewhere? I need to get moving. I haven't much enjoyed standing here with this damp air seeping into my joints."

"Orpheus," Burton mumbled. It was the name of the airship—captained by Nathaniel Lawless—that had flown him into central Africa last year, enabling his discovery of the source of the River Nile.

The contraption said, "Are you going to climb aboard or stand there with your jaw dangling?"

Hesitantly, Burton moved to the horse's side and mounted it.

"Where do you want to go?" it asked.

"Um. Home."

"Walk, trot, or gallop?"

"Can you trot in this fog?"

"Of course. I can't guarantee I won't collide with anything, though."

"That's not very encouraging. Proceed at the safest pace."

Orpheus set off, heading for Nine Elms Lane. The vehicle's eyes projected twin beams of light into the darkness. It picked up speed and traversed the thoroughfare to Vauxhall Bridge. Burton paid the toll. They crossed the river then travelled on up to Victoria, past Green Park and Hyde Park, and along Baker Street. For the duration, Burton's mind was practically frozen with bewilderment.

The city was quieter than he'd ever heard it. There were no steam horse-drawn cabs, no pantechnicons, no steam spheres, no velocipedes, and no rotorchairs—just a few riders on mechanical horses. Disconcertingly, the steeds greeted one another as they passed:

"Evening, Orpheus."

"How're you doing, Flash?"

"Hallo, Orpheus."

"What ho, Blackie."

"All right, Orpheus?"

"Fine, thank you, Heracles."

"Will you please stop that," Burton complained.

"Can't," his horse replied. "You know full well the exchanges are necessary."

"Necessary for what?"

"For passing route and traffic information."

"All I'm hearing are variations of *hello*."

"That's because those pathetic biological ears of yours have limited sensitivity. You're not hearing the coded tones beneath the words."

Burton ground his teeth. He was frustrated that the dense pall blocked his view of the city. His explorer's instinct was stimulated by what was—as his mind cleared he was becoming convinced of it—a variant London. He had no idea how he'd got here and wasn't entirely certain where he'd come from, but he desperately wanted to observe the metropolis. Unfortunate, then, that all he could see were vague smudges of light!

How was it possible that the weather was different? It had been snowing where he came from, he was sure. Wasn't history a matter of human affairs, rather than natural? Then he noticed soot and ash suspended in the fog, and he realised that this capital must be even more industrialised than his own, and the snow was perhaps held in abeyance by the blanket of fumes. The work of man affecting the climate! What an extraordinary thought!

At the corner of Gloucester Place and Montagu Place, a familiar voice hailed him through the gloom.

"What ho, Cap'n!"

"Is that you, Mr. Grub?" Burton called, for the greeting had come from the corner where Grub the street vendor always had his brazier or barrow.

"Aye, an' no one else," came the answer. "Fair solid, ain't it?"

"The fog? It is. I can't see you. How did you know it was me?"

"Recognised yer nag's footsteps."

"They *are* distinctive," Orpheus murmured.

"One o' the back feet drags a little. Needs—what's the word?"

"Recalibrating?" Burton offered automatically.

How did I know that?

"Rather an impertinent suggestion," Orpheus complained.

"Aye! Recalcifyin'!"

"What on earth are you doing out in this weather?" Burton asked.

"Toastin' corn on the cob fer 'em what wants it."

"Well, you're a braver man than I. I'd rather be toasting my toes by the fire."

"Aye, there ain't nuffink like the comforts of 'ome."

"Do you actually have one, Mr. Grub? I don't think I've ever passed this corner without seeing you on it."

Not that you can see him now. And be careful. What is true of your world may not be true of this. Watch what you say.

"We all 'ave our place, don't we, Cap'n? This 'ere is my patch."

"I suppose we do. Good afternoon to you, sir."

Though his words and thoughts had come without volition, Burton's mind was clearing. "My world" was starting to mean something to him—and it was most certainly something different to "this world."

A few minutes later, he stabled Orpheus in the mews behind his house—"I'll wait here and wind down," the horse said grumpily—and entered Number 14 by the back door. He strode to the foot of the stairs where he found his young valet, Bram Stoker, polishing shoes and boots.

"Hello, Bram. You're up late. Off to bed with you."

The boy looked up. It wasn't Stoker at all, but Oscar Wilde, who'd been Captain Lawless's cabin boy during the African adventure and who'd recently been accepted by the flight officer's training school.

"Bram, guv'nor?" the youngster asked.

"Sorry, I was thinking out loud."

"How were the toffs?"

"Toffs?"

"At the palace."

Burton struggled with confused memories. Had he been to Buckingham Palace?

He gave a safe answer, "Tedious, as usual."

The Irish boy grinned. "Ye should never speak disrespectfully of Society, sir. Only people who can't get into it do that."

"Then I feel at liberty. The high and the mighty don't make me welcome at their clubs and dinner tables."

"It's 'cos ye have a brain in your head, so it is. What a danger for 'em! Ignorance is like a delicate exotic fruit; touch it and the bloom is gone."

Burton chuckled. He placed his cap on the stand, hung up his coat, and put his cane into its elephant foot holder. He glanced around the hallway. It was as it should be, except the pictures on the wall were arranged a little differently, and the grandfather clock at the far end was a different model.

He said to Wilde, "When you've finished those boots, and before you go to bed, come up to my room and put this uniform away, would you?"

"Right you are, sir. Shan't be long."

Burton went up to his bedroom on the third floor. There, he divested himself of the scratchy and constricting regimentals, threw them onto the bed, and donned shirt and trousers.

He checked his pocket watch. It was a quarter to eleven.

His reflection watched him from the wall mirror. He gave a start, crossed to the glass, and discovered that his hair was a little shorter, a devilishly forked beard adorned his jaw, and the scar on his left cheek had become longer and was angled a little more toward the horizontal. There were marks on his skin—cuts and bruises—but they were healing, not the fresh and painful wounds he knew he'd suffered a couple of hours ago. Or was it three hours? Four? A day?

Squaring his shoulders, he addressed his opposite. "I trust you have a good supply of brandy and cigars, Captain Burton. This is a three-Manila problem."

The king's agent went down to his study. Upon entering it, he was insulted by a colourful parakeet.

"Stench pool! Lard belly! Dribblesome jelly head!"

He looked in surprise at the perched bird, shook his head in wonder, and began to slowly move around the room, examining every detail of it. At a glance, it looked unchanged, but on closer inspection he found his paperwork had been reorganised and items moved, including his collection of swords, which though still affixed to the chimneybreast were displayed in a different arrangement.

He investigated his principal work desk and found that he was apparently authoring a book entitled *A Complete System of Bayonet Exercise*. After reading the first few paragraphs, he muttered, "A truly excellent idea. I shall write it myself."

He went to the bureau, poured a drink, and crossed to the old saddlebag armchair by the fireplace. When he sat, he found it as familiar and as comfortable as his own.

"It *is* your own," he said and, reaching down to a box on the hearth, took a cheroot from it, poked its end into the fire, and started to smoke.

"Let me see now. I met Algy for a drink. Where? The Hog in the Pound? No. The Black Toad. After which we went to meet with the Cannibals at Bartolini's. Ah! Spring Heeled Jack. That explains this wound to my arm." He flexed his left elbow. "Except it's not there. But anyway, one hell of a scrap, I'm certain of that. Then young Swinburne and I headed off to consult with Babbage. Am I still at Battersea?"

"Nose-picking, mould muggling arse pot!" the parakeet cackled.

"You may be right, my brightly feathered friend," he agreed. "But that doesn't explain how I've somehow slipped into the body of a different Burton. Have you any insight into that?"

"Buttocks!" the bird responded.

There came a tap at the door.

"Enter!"

Mrs. Iris Angell, his housekeeper, stepped in. A basset hound padded beside her.

"Will you require any supper before I go to bed?" She hesitated then gave an awkward bob. "Should I address you as Sir Richard, now?"

"No, Mother Angell, no formalities and no supper. I haven't any appetite."

He looked down at the dog as it walked across to the hearthrug, sat, and gazed back at him with an eager thump of its tail on the floor.

"Fidget wants a walk," Mrs. Angell observed. "The greedy little mite. He doesn't care about the hour, nor that he's already been exercised twice today by Quips."

"Quips?"

"Master Wilde. Are you all right? You look a little flustered, if you'll forgive me a-sayin' so."

"It's been an odd sort of day. The dog will have to wait. I have to go out again in a moment."

"So late? I do wish you'd take a rest for once in your life."

Burton watched his housekeeper depart. He smiled. There was a peculiar sort of satisfaction in knowing his other self enjoyed the same comforts of home.

He took a gulp of brandy and noticed a puckered scar across the back of his left hand. He recognised it at once. It was common in men who favoured the blade as a weapon—a mark of their earliest days of training when in attempting to sheathe their weapon they missed the scabbard and sliced the flesh, cutting it to the bone. A painful mistake, but one that Burton had never made. This was not his scar.

"And this is not my place," he said decisively.

He stood, put his drink aside, lifted a jacket from the back of a chair, and slipped it on.

"Crapulous ninny!" the parakeet squawked.

"And up your pipe," he replied.

He left the study and descended the stairs.

"I'm all done here," Oscar Wilde said. "I'll go and fold your uniform, guv'nor."

"Thank you, lad."

After shrugging into his coat and taking up his top hat and cane, Burton passed through the house, went out into the yard, and crossed to the mews. He entered them with the instinctive expectation that he'd see his two rotorchairs, two velocipedes, and single steam sphere, even though he knew they weren't there.

"Again?" Orpheus said. "Can't I enjoy a moment's peace?"

"Earlier you complained you'd wind down," Burton noted.

"Where do you want to go?" the contraption asked.

"To visit my brother."

"I didn't know you had one. You never tell me anything. Where does he live?"

"At the Royal Venetia Hotel on the Strand. He's the minister of chronological affairs."

"I've never heard of such a thing."

"You're a horse."

The contraption jerked its head toward the street-facing doors. "Stop dithering and open up."

Burton crossed to the portal and slid it open. He waited while Orpheus walked out, then secured the stable, mounted the vehicle, and said, "Trot, please."

They set off.

Again, Burton was surprised by how subdued the city felt. There was none of the hustle and bustle he was accustomed to. Vague memories— not his own—nudged at the periphery of his conscious mind. Nietzsche. Berserkers. Death. Destruction.

Please, no! I lost Isabel in this life, too! Isabel! Isabel!

Forty minutes later, Orpheus stopped outside the hotel.

Burton jumped to the pavement and crossed it. People moved past him like wraiths, quickly and silently, as if in the grip of some nameless dread.

He tipped his hat to the doorman, entered, walked across the opulent black-and-white chequer-floored reception area toward the staircase, then suddenly hesitated and changed course. He approached the front desk.

"I'm here to see Mr. Edward Burton," he said. "The minister. Suite five, fifth floor."

The night clerk pursed his lips, causing the ends of his waxed moustache to stick out like little horns, checked the guest register, and shook his head. "We don't have anyone by that name, sir."

"He's a permanent resident."

"I'm afraid not. Suite five, you say? Those rooms have been empty for the past three days. The last occupant was the Spanish ambassador, Signor Delgado. He was killed during the troubles. Perhaps you have the wrong hotel."

Burton said thank you and departed. He remounted his steed. "Take me to Cheyne Walk."

"Mr. Swinburne's?"

"Yes."

"Are you going to get drunk?"

"Mind your own damned business."

Orpheus trotted westward following the Thames upstream back toward Chelsea Bridge. Foghorns sent their mournful blasts into the pall. Big Ben chimed midnight.

"By God! Where am I?" Burton cried out, for St. Stephen's Tower had been blown to smithereens last November, and, even before that, its bell had cracked and stopped working. Suddenly, he felt horribly lost, terribly alone.

A sense of urgency—near panic—overtook him. Why was he in this familiar yet alien London? What had thrown him here? How could he return to his own world?

"Go as fast as you can," he commanded.

"Hold on tight," the clockwork horse advised. "I might have to stop abruptly."

With metal hooves clacking, the steed set off at a gallop.

A breeze had got up, and the blanket of fog was shredding. It parted just ahead, revealing the back of a slow-moving hansom cab. Burton had to quickly jerk the reins to steer his armadillidium around it.

He looked down.

Armadillidium?

CHAPTER 4

RECURRENCES

BREATHE EASY WITH THE
POTTLEWORTH AIR MASK

**Prevents Dust, Smoke, Ash,
Coal Dust and Chemical Fumes
from Entering the Lungs. Promotes Good Health.
Instant Relief from Asthma, Bronchitis,
Croup and Whooping Cough.**

*Send £2 to Pottleworth & Heck, Ltd.,
10–11 Stonecutter Street, London, E.C.*

"From what yer might call a filler-soffickle standpoint," Herbert Spencer declared, "I ain't averse to the idea what that time can divide into separate 'istories. An' I must admit, I quite likes the possibility that there's more 'n one o' me, an' that some o' the others might 'ave 'ad better hopportunities than what I've 'ad. It's a rum do—hey?—to fink there might be an 'Erbert Spencer somewhere what's a bloomin' toff with an heducation n' all!"

Spencer was sitting behind Lieutenant Richard Francis Burton on a saddle-like seat mounted on the back of a massive woodlouse—of the genus *armadillidium giganticus*. Burton was steering the crustacean along Nine Elms Lane toward Battersea Castle. There were many more of the creatures on the road, some with as many as five passengers upon their plated backs.

"In your case, Herbert," the explorer responded, "I suspect the profundity of your intelligence is probably the same in every version of the world. If, in a parallel existence, you are better educated, then perhaps it allows you to express yourself in a rather more erudite manner, with the consequence of greater attention and respect from the intelligentsia, but you've never struck me as a man who particularly desires to be feted."

"Nah," Spencer agreed. "All that attention? It ain't fer the likes o' me. The appeal of bein' a toff is a full stomach, that's all."

Burton was suddenly hit by a vertiginous sense of falling. He tugged at the armadillidium's reins, as if trying to avoid something that wasn't there, and gave a cry of alarm. From behind him a voice said, "Cor blimey! Steady on! You nearly 'ad us off the bloomin' road!"

Twisting around, he saw a bearded vagabond sitting behind him.

"Watch out!" the man said, pointing ahead.

Burton returned his attention to the woodlouse and steered it back onto the left side of the thoroughfare.

He gasped. Though low snow-bearing clouds obscured the night sky, the cold air was so incredibly crisp and clear that every street lamp blazed like a star, and, to his right, the River Thames glittered as if filled with phosphorescence. He looked down again at the thing beneath him.

"Um."

"Somethin' wrong, Boss?"

"No," Burton lied.

He struggled to recall the man's name. Wells? No. Speke? Spencer. Yes. Herbert Spencer. How did he know that?

The accounts left by Abdu El Yezdi. Herbert Spencer was a vagrant philosopher. He was killed while holding shards of one of the Nāga diamonds. Due to his proximity to them, the dying emanation of his brain was imprinted into the gems. They were later transferred into a clockwork man's babbage device, giving Spencer's still-conscious mind a means through which to express itself and, after a fashion, live again.

This memory suddenly felt profoundly significant to Burton, though he couldn't fathom why.

A huge dragonfly hummed by overhead, with a man saddled upon its thorax and glowing paper lanterns trailing on ribbons behind it.

Burton watched it pass and was startled when a lock of hair fell over his eyes. He reached up and found himself possessed of a shoulder-length mane. For some strange reason, he imagined he'd always worn it short. He pushed his fingertips into its roots and along his scalp. No scars.

What is wrong with me?

He must have been daydreaming. He'd imagined something about a mechanical horse. His thoughts were jumbled and erratic. Fantasies were intruding into them. Berserkers. Spring Heeled Jack. Lord Palmerston.

He muttered, "I must be going barmy."

The four copper towers of Battersea Castle were just ahead. He felt it to be his destination, so guided the woodlouse off the road and into the edifice's decorative gardens. Frost had whitened the grass, hedgerows, and skeletal trees. The flowerbeds to either side of the path were barren.

"Pull yourself together," he whispered as he drew his steed to a halt outside the castle's gates.

"Beg pardon?" Spencer asked.

"Sorry. Nothing."

As they climbed to the ground, Burton reeled to one side and would have fallen had Spencer not caught him by the wrist.

"Flamin' heck, Boss! What's got into yer?"

"Too many late nights." Burton steadied himself. He put a hand to his ribs, to his left arm, to his chin. Ghostly pain inhabited them but didn't hurt him.

Spencer said to the armadillidium, "Wait."

It rolled itself into a ball. The king's agent marvelled at the way the creature made of itself such a perfect sphere, completely protected by its armour, with the saddle balanced on top. It was astonishing. The achievements of the geneticists never ceased to amaze him. Sir Francis Galton certainly deserved all the honours he'd received.

Geneticists? Galton? Galton the lunatic? The father of that illegal science?

"Why are we riskin' this visit?" Spencer asked. "The Master Guild of

Engineers is defeated, an' if Gladstone finds out we're consortin' wiv the enemy, 'e'll likely 'ave us 'ung, drawn an' quartered."

"Gladstone is an ass," Burton replied involuntarily. He looked up at the building, noting that, in contrast to its well-tended gardens, it appeared shabby and neglected. Many of its windowpanes were cracked. It didn't feel right. Not at all.

He knocked on the door. A motor-driven mechanical guard opened it and ushered them through. Like so many of the devices created by the Master Guild, it was a rickety thing that wobbled on its wheels and coughed black smoke from a clanking oil-powered engine. It led the king's agent and his companion to the tall inner gates and opened them. Burton and Spencer entered.

Wending their way past the machinery, they arrived at the central work area, where they found Algernon Swinburne waiting with Charlie Babbage.

"Hey ho, fellow rabble-rousers!" the diminutive poet cried out. "Welcome to the dark heart of the insurgency. My hat, it's like the jolly old Gunpowder Plot. What! What! What!"

Babbage said, "We've been waiting. Why are you late?"

"I don't know," Burton replied truthfully.

"We was at the Penfold Private Sanatorium," Spencer put in. "Sister Raghavendra says they can't save Monty Penniforth's arm an' will 'ave to remove it an' grow 'im a new 'un."

Babbage waved a hand dismissively. "Immaterial. Immaterial."

"Not to Monty," Swinburne observed. "That's his drinking arm." He quivered and spasmed in his usual over-excitable manner.

Isambard Kingdom Brunel trundled into view. One of his wheels squeaked annoyingly. His brain was plainly visible, floating in a dome-shaped glass container, and his many thin metal tentacles were in constant motion, writhing and curling restlessly.

"Hello, Lieutenant Burton," he said. His voice sounded like bubbling liquid. "Mr. Spencer."

Burton nodded a greeting then looked at the ruined attire spread out on one of the workbenches.

"Edward Oxford's time suit," he observed.

A recurrent dream. Or nightmare.

"Yes," Brunel replied. "Charlie will explain. He feels he might have a solution to our problem."

Babbage hissed impatiently. "Feels? Feels? Don't impose the imprecision of emotions upon me, Brunel. My theories, premises, hypotheses—call them what you will—originate in logical thought. There is no room for doubt in science. Either something is, or it isn't, or it's unknown. If I say I have a solution, it's because I do. My feelings don't enter into it."

"The terminology I employ has no influence upon the facts," Brunel countered.

Babbage rasped, "Just the attitude that has weakened the Master Guild of Engineers to the point of extinction. Accuracy! Accuracy! I'll have exactitude, if you please!"

"Must I stand here listening to you two squabbling?" Burton asked. "What is your proposition, Charlie?"

"That we give up the fight."

Before Burton could respond, Swinburne screeched, "That's it? That's your idea? Gladstone's dictatorship continues unabated, he's taken Isabella Mayson as his unwilling mistress, Prince Albert is incarcerated in the Tower of London and due to be executed next week, the Libertines are employing their mediumistic powers to incite a war with Prussia, most of our allies are dead, and your great plan is to give up? By my Aunt Carlotta's cruelly constraining corsets! Why would you propose such a thing? It's perfectly monstrous!"

"I suggest it," Babbage said, "so that we might start the rebellion from scratch."

Burton looked from Babbage to Swinburne to Brunel and back at Babbage. "I have no idea what you're talking about."

The scientist placed his right hand on the time suit's headpiece. "This," he said, "contains what amounts to a synthetic intelligence, though one virtually incapacitated by the ravings of a madman. Nevertheless, by putting carefully considered questions to it, I have managed to ascertain that the suit transcends the natural flow of time by employing an extraordinarily sophisticated mathematical equation. What fragments of it I've had access to leave me convinced that, were I to extract it in full, I'd be able to construct a machine to emulate the function of the garment."

Herbert Spencer said, "Yer mean t' say, you could build another of the bloomin' things?"

"If that is what I meant to say, I'd have said it," Babbage responded. "No. The techniques available in the year 2202 are beyond even my understanding. Without them, we cannot create microscopic systems. I might, however, be capable of constructing a macroscopic equivalent. It would perhaps, be the size of a room or, more significantly, of a large vehicle." He looked meaningfully at Burton. "One that might carry the core of our rebel group three years back through history."

Swinburne squawked, swiped a fist through the air, and hollered, "By crikey! We'll be able to go back and nip that blighter Gladstone in the bud!"

Burton shook his head and muttered, "There's a problem."

He knew the plan wouldn't work. In travelling back to alter the past, the rebels would simply create a new strand of history. This one, in which he now found himself, would remain unchanged.

Babbage misinterpreted the comment as a question. "There is. The helmet is almost drained of power. If you give me permission, I can transfer energy to it from the Nimtz generator. The process might possibly allow the intelligence to regain some measure of sanity, enabling it to repair itself and provide me with further information."

"Permission?"

"The suit is yours."

Burton sighed. He indicated his consent.

Babbage consulted his pocket watch and declared it to be nine o'clock on the fifteenth of February.

The king's agent suddenly knew exactly who, where, and when he was.

The wrong Burton.

In the wrong place.

On the wrong day.

Another repeat performance. Why?

Babbage ran his finger around the side of the Nimtz generator. The disk crackled and threw out a fountain of sparks. The old man recoiled with a cry of alarm.

Burton reached to either side, took Swinburne and Spencer by their arms, and started to pull them away from the bench.

Babbage stepped backward. "I hadn't anticipated—"

A bubble formed around the helmet, suit and boots. With a thunderous bang, it popped, and the time suit, most of the workbench, and a large chunk of Isambard Kingdom Brunel vanished. The engineer slumped and became motionless.

Spencer cried out, "Blimey! Where's it gone?"

"No! No! No!" Babbage wailed. "This is a disaster! We can't have lost it! It's impossible!" He stamped his feet and clapped his hands to his face. "How? How?"

Burton closed his eyes and massaged the sides of his head. "I've had enough of mysteries, and the light in this place always gives me a headache. I'm leaving."

Swinburne and Spencer joined him. They walked back across the workshop and out through its doors. Snow was falling from a pitch-black sky. It was white. The courtyard, swathed in it, glared brilliantly under the spotlights.

The men left the power station and approached the armadillidium. Burton ordered, "Open." It unrolled its considerable bulk. He climbed aboard, and his companions followed him up.

"The chaps are waiting for us at the Hog in the Pound," Swinburne said. "Let's see what plan Trounce and Slaughter have come up with. A means to rescue Miss Mayson from Gladstone's lustful groping, I hope."

Taking hold of the reins, Burton guided the woodlouse back through the gardens and out onto Nine Elms Lane.

He looked down at his hands. The scar on the left was no longer there. Brightness swept in from the corners of his eyes. He saw his fingers curled around the reins of his armadillidium; around the reins of a clockwork horse; around the handlebars of a velocipede.

In an instant, the snow stopped falling and it was daylight.

He lost control of his vehicle, hit the back of a hansom cab, careened into the kerb, and crashed to the ground. The penny-farthing's crankshaft snapped and went spinning high into the branches of the trees lining the riverside.

He lay sprawled on the ground.

The cab driver yelled, "You blithering idiot!" but didn't stop his vehicle.

A raggedly dressed match seller—a woman who lacked teeth but possessed an overabundance of facial hair—shuffled over and squinted down at the king's agent. "Is ye hurt, ducky?"

For a moment, he couldn't reply, then he managed to croak, "No. I'm all right."

"You look all battered. Better get yerself up off the pavemint afore the snow soaks into 'em smart togs o' yourn. Stain 'em scarlit, so it will. Would ye like t' buy a box o' lucifers?"

Burton pushed himself up. He thanked the woman for her concern and exchanged a few coins for a matchbook.

After dragging his broken velocipede out of the road, picking up his hat, and brushing himself down, he stood for a minute, utterly perplexed. He touched his head and found that his hair was short. There were scars on his scalp, a painful lump at the back of his skull, and a scabby cut on his chin. His left elbow hurt. In fact, *all* of him hurt.

Gradually, it dawned on him that he was on Cheyne Walk. He could see Battersea Power Station on the other side of the river. Fumbling for his chronometer, he flipped its lid. It was three o'clock in the afternoon.

Of what day?

He retrieved a cheroot from his pocket and smoked it while watching a creaking and clanking litter crab lumber past. The humped contraption was dragging itself along, its eight thick mechanical legs thumping against the impacted pink slush that covered the road, the twenty-four thin arms on its belly snatching this way and that, digging rubbish out of the mushy layer and throwing it through the machine's maw into the furnace.

Burton's hands were shaking.

He scraped at the ground with his heel and revealed a layer of bright red beneath. It appeared oddly fibrous, and he vaguely registered that the seeds had extended long hair-like roots.

Home?

The carriages and wagons that passed him were drawn either by real horses or by their steam-powered equivalents—small wheel-mounted engines that somewhat resembled the famous Stephenson's Rocket. People crowded the thoroughfare just as they always did, a mélange of the well-to-do and poverty-stricken, of the mannered and the uncouth.

A rotorchair chopped through the leaden sky. A hawker sang, "Hot chestnuts, hot chestnuts, penny a bag!" Three urchins raced past laughing and shouting and flinging snowballs at each other.

The final vestigial glow of Saltzmann's Tincture faded.

He looked back the way he'd come. The distant, blackened and ragged stump of Parliament's clock tower was visible over the rooftops.

All was as it should be, but he could sense on the inside of his legs, just above the knees, where the woodlouse's saddle had pressed against his legs, and when he closed his eyes he could hear the resentful tones of the mechanical horse.

Those experiences had been real.

He finished his cigar, flicked it away, and wheeled his clanking penny-farthing along the thoroughfare to Number 16. Just as he reached the house, its front door opened and Algernon Swinburne stepped out, dressed in a wide-brimmed floppy hat, overcoat, and an absurdly long striped scarf.

"What ho! What ho! What ho!" the poet shrilled. "Fancy finding you on my doorstep. I thought you'd be out for the count. Did you come to talk me into taking an afternoon tipple? I mustn't. I mustn't. Oh all right. Consider me persuaded. Have you slept? I say! Look at the state of your boneshaker. Surely you didn't ride it in this weather?"

"The crankshaft broke," Burton replied, "and, in truth, Algy, I have no notion of how or why I ended up here."

"Are you one over the eight already? Drinking to ease the pain, I suppose, though your wounds appear somewhat less gruesome by the light of day. Not your face. Just your wounds."

"I haven't touched a drop, but a drink sounds like a very good idea." Burton tested his left elbow, bending it cautiously. It hurt, but not as much as he expected. "Sister Raghavendra applied her miraculous salves?"

Swinburne looked surprised. "She was stitching and smearing for some considerable time. Have you forgotten?"

"After a fashion. Let's cross to Battersea. I'd like to take a look at the station. I'll explain on the way."

"We were there just yesterday. Explain what?"

"Yesterday? Is it Thursday?"

"The sixteenth, of course. Did that knock to your head scramble your wits?"

"A very good question."

Burton searched his memories and found them to be a confusing tangle, some fading quickly, while others suddenly emerged like the sun breaking through clouds. Experiences overlaid one another in palimpsestic contradictions.

He'd been at Battersea Power Station, where Raghavendra had treated his wounds. The recollection was clear. He could see her bending over him, her long black hair hanging down, her skin dark, and her eyes big, brown and beautiful.

"The ointment smells rather bad," she'd said, "but it will accelerate the healing provided you can avoid being hit again, which, knowing you, is very doubtful. I'm tempted to thump you myself."

As vivid as that scene was in his mind's eye, he knew that at exactly the moment it occurred he was also riding a clockwork horse from Buckingham Palace to the headquarters of the Department of Guided Science. Similarly, he'd watched Charles Babbage's experiment go awry at nine o'clock last night while he was, at the same time, sitting at his desk this morning writing up a report of Spring Heeled Jack's attack. He'd snatched three hours of sleep at exactly the moment he'd witnessed Babbage's actions repeated.

I left the station with Algy and Sadhvi. The cabriolet dropped him home first, then her, and took me to Montagu Place. I slept fitfully, woke early, wrote the report. I dozed. I ate lunch. I rode here.

As they pushed the penny-farthing through the narrow alleyway beside Swinburne's residence and into the back yard, he began to tell the poet about his lost, replaced, extended, repeated—he couldn't settle on an accurate description—hours.

He slid his cane from the velocipede's holder, and they returned to the pavement and started eastward toward Chelsea Bridge. Burton limped, feeling again the damage done to him by his assailant in Leicester Square.

"I can only conclude," he said, "that I somehow slipped into alternate Burtons in alternate histories and was, for some reason, twice drawn to Babbage's attempt to revive the damaged time suit."

"You went sideways, if I might put it like that? And a little back through time? How, Richard? Why?"

"I'm at a loss. Right now, I can hardly think straight."

They walked on in silence for a few minutes, crossing the Thames, wrinkling their noses.

"Are you sure you're not becoming malarial again?" Swinburne asked.

"No, Algy. It was all as real as—" Burton gestured at their bright-pink surroundings. "As this."

The perturbing thought occurred to him that this outlandish vista, too, was not the one to which Sir Richard Francis Burton properly belonged.

They reached the south bank of the river and continued on until they were at the edge of the land bordering the power station.

"I require but a moment," Burton said, drawing to a halt.

He spent two minutes gazing at the edifice; at its four copper towers, which vanished into the low cloud; at its many high-set windows; and its entrance gates and red brick walls. He could see in the snow the marks made by his, Swinburne's and Raghavendra's feet as they'd arrived and departed last night. Physical evidence of a certain truth.

"All as it should be," he murmured. "Let's find a watering hole."

He set off, with Swinburne scampering beside him. They strolled past Battersea Fields until they came to Dock Leaf Lane. The poet pointed his cane at a small half-timbered public house. "How about there?"

"The Tremors," Burton said. "Very apt."

"Indeed so," Swinburne enthused. "It's the place El Yezdi investigated in his own history when he was hunting for Spring Heeled Jack."

They crossed the road and entered the premises. Just as El Yezdi had described in his reports, it had smoke-blackened oak roof beams pitted with the fissures and cracks of age, tilting floors, and crazily slanted walls.

There were two rooms, both warmed by log fires. Passing through to the smaller of them, they settled on stools at the bar.

An ancient, bald and stooped man with a grey-bearded gnome-like face rounded a corner, wiping his hands on a cloth. A high collar encased his neck, and he wore an unfashionably long jacket.

"Evening gents," he said in a creaky but jovial voice. His eyes widened when he saw Burton's battered face. "Ow! Looks like you were on the wrong end of a bunch o' fives!"

"London," the king's agent said ruefully. "It's the most civilised city in the world."

"Aye. It's given me my fair share of punch-ups, that's for sure. Deer-stalker, sirs? Finest beer south of the river. Or would you prefer Alton Ale? I've a few bottles left. It'll be hard to come by until they rebuild the warehouse. You know it burned down?"

"Yes, we're aware of that," Burton said. "I've developed an aversion to Alton. A pint of Deerstalker will do just fine, thank you."

"For me, too," Swinburne added. "What a splendid old pub. Are you Joseph Robinson, sir?"

The publican took an empty tankard from a shelf, held it to a barrel, and twisted the tap. As the beer flowed, he said, "Aye, for me sins, though folks always calls me Bob. Dunno why." He placed a beer in front of the poet then took down a second glass and filled it for Burton. "You've heard of me, have you?"

"Yes," Swinburne answered. "From the Hog in the Pound."

Robinson looked surprised. "That old place! But I owned it well afore your time, youngster."

"My father had occasion to take a beverage there," Swinburne lied.

"Oh, I see. Lots did. It was popular in its day."

Burton searched himself for any sense of *déjà vu*. He found none, felt relieved, then was suddenly disoriented by the arrival of an elderly man who stood beside Swinburne and greeted the landlord. "All right, Bob?"

"Hallo, Ted," Robinson replied. "I'll be right with you just as soon as I've finished servin' these fine gents."

"I kin wait, so long as it ain't 'til the beer's run out."

The newcomer possessed weather-beaten skin and a bald pate, a huge beak-like nose and a long pointed chin. He resembled Punchinello, and when he spoke sounded like him, too—his tone sharp and snappy.

The king's agent paled. The coincidence was profound. The man was Ted Toppletree, who was described in El Yezdi's *The Strange Affair of Spring Heeled Jack*, and at his feet, eagerly sniffing at Swinburne's ankles, was the very same basset hound Burton had seen in his "other" study.

Toppletree noticed that his pet had attracted attention.

History began to repeat itself.

"Arternoon, sir," Punchinello said to Burton. "Ain't seen you around this way before. I reckon I'd remember a mug—er, I mean a face—like yours, if you don't mind me a-sayin' so. You looks like a regular fighter. A pugilist. No offence meant. The name is Toppletree, Ted Toppletree, an' the dog here is Fidget. He's the best tracker you'll ever find; can sniff out anything. He's fer sale if'n you're interested." He addressed Swinburne, "Blimey! He's taken a right shine to you, ain't he!"

The poet, whose trouser leg was now being pulled at by the hound, emitted an agonised groan. He'd also recognised the developing scene. Glaring at Burton, he hissed, "Don't you dare!"

Burton ignored him, cleared his throat, and stuttered, "May—may I offer you a drink, Mr.—Mr.—Mr. Toppletree?"

"Very good of you, sir. Very good indeed. Most generous. Deerstalker. Best ale south of the river."

Robinson, responding to a nod from Burton, poured the third pint.

Swinburne jerked his ankle away from Fidget only to have the dog lunge forward and bite his shoe.

"Ouch! I say!" he objected. "Confound it! Why won't he leave me alone?"

"Here, Fidget! Sit still!" Toppletree pulled the hound away. The animal settled, gazing longingly at the little poet's ankles. "You sure you wouldn't like to snap 'im up, sir?"

"I've never been surer of anything," Swinburne responded. He took a long gulp of ale. "I do believe you may be right about this beer, though. Very tasty! Perhaps little Fidget will calm down if we offer him a bowl?"

"How—how much?" Burton croaked.

"A pint should be enough to send him into a profound sleep," Swinburne said.

"I was addressing Mr. Toppletree. How much for the dog?"

"You surely can't mean to purchase the beast again," the poet groaned.

"Again?" Toppletree asked. "Wotcha mean again?"

"He doesn't mean anything," Burton said. "Two pounds?"

"Daylight robbery!" Swinburne objected.

"Two pounds," Toppletree quickly agreed, obviously surprised at the phenomenally high offer.

Swinburne moaned and said to Joseph Robinson, "I think I require a stiff brandy."

The landlord obliged and was paid by Burton, who then slid a couple of pound notes across the bar to Toppletree.

"Much obliged, sir," the man said. "You won't regret it. He's a fine animal."

"Then why have you sold him?" Swinburne asked.

"He's rather too fond of nipping me wife, sir. Doesn't like her, an' she can't stand the sight of 'im, the poor little fella."

"She's very discerning."

Toppletree bent and tickled Fidget under the chin. "Bye bye, old son. Suppose now I'll have to find another way to annoy the bloomin' missus!" He passed the animal's lead to Burton. "I'm off to join me mates in a game of dominoes, sirs. Been a pleasure meetin' yer both. All the best to yer."

He departed, taking his pint with him.

Robinson moved away to serve another customer.

Burton pulled the basset hound around so his stool blocked its route to Swinburne's ankles. He winced as his damaged elbow gave a pang.

"The dog again, Richard? Why?"

"You know how useful Fidget was to El Yezdi. The hound saved your life."

"A different history, a different beast, and a different Swinburne."

"Quite so, and during my visions—or whatever they were—I saw this very animal in a different Burton's home. Perhaps we belong together."

"You patently do. In an asylum."

"Maybe so. The intricacies of time are enough to send any man loopy. Don't you find it significant, though, that we just experienced an event that will be repeated, in another version of history, one year from now? Remember, El Yezdi purchased Fidget in 1861."

"Significant how?"

"Because it has demonstrated that, as my counterpart insisted, time has echoes and patterns. A great many events are common to a great many of the histories, though they don't always transpire in exactly the same manner or at exactly the same moment."

Swinburne shrugged. "What of it?"

"It occurs to me that what I have witnessed—to wit, Babbage's experiment in multiplicity—might be a rather unusual circumstance, for, in every case, it happened at precisely nine o'clock on Wednesday the fifteenth of February; a moment which, I remind you, the scientist himself emphasised."

Swinburne swigged back his brandy and followed it with a mouthful of beer. "An unusual circumstance," he echoed. "Heaven forbid we should encounter one of those."

They ordered a second pint each, and Burton went through his experiences again, this time describing as many details as he could remember.

Later, after they'd indulged in a third drink, he said, "By God, I'm wearied to the bone and hurt all over. I require the healing arms of Morpheus."

"But I've hardly touched a drop!"

Burton gave Fidget's lead a little more slack, and the dog edged closer to the poet's feet.

"Very well! Very well!" his friend cried out. "I concede!"

They bid Joseph Robinson farewell, nodded to Ted Toppletree, stepped out of the public house, and both immediately voiced cries of astonishment.

Initially, it appeared that a fresh layer of red snow had fallen, but they quickly recognised that, in fact, the vivid colour belonged to a dense mass of tiny shoots that had emerged from the icy layer. The little plants had taken root in every available space.

"This is beyond the bounds!" Burton exclaimed.

"You're not wrong. They are growing impossibly fast," Swinburne observed. "We were only in the pub for a couple of hours!"

They slowly followed the road back toward the river, observing the scene with awe. As they came abreast Battersea Fields, Swinburne said, "Is it my imagination or can I actually see them growing?"

He crouched and gently touched a tiny, tightly bunched, and as yet unfurled bloom. "I can. Look at this. It's visibly in motion!"

Burton squatted—with a slight groan as his bruised body objected—and gazed intently at the tiny blossom.

"Uncanny," he muttered.

"*Tempus flores.*"

Burton raised a questioning eyebrow. "Time flowers?"

"They appear to be transcending its limitations, and given the moment of their arrival, and the events you've experienced within the past twenty-four hours, I think the designation is suitable." Swinburne closed his eyes and declaimed:

> *One, who is not, we see: but one, whom we see not, is:*
> *Surely this is not that: but that is assuredly this.*

"The significance?" Burton asked.

Swinburne shrugged. "I don't know. The words came to me out of the blue."

"In connection with these flowers?"

"Yes."

Again, the diminutive poet closed his eyes and, after a long pause, continued:

> *What, and wherefore, and whence? for under is over and under:*
> *If thunder could be without lightning, lightning could be*
> *   without thunder.*
> *Doubt is faith in the main: but faith, on the whole, is doubt:*
> *We cannot believe by proof: but could we believe without?*

Burton stood and tightened his coat around himself. "It sounds like an objection to religion."

Swinburne also straightened. "To monotheism, perhaps. A yearning for the advent of a new paganism. How I rue the One who casts his veil of grey over us, Richard; who bids us contemplate death when all around us are the bright colours and vibrancies of glorious life. We have allowed ourselves to be crushed by a despotic deity who demands of us a lifetime of toil and service and promises in return a harsh judgement for most, and ambiguous rewards only for those who enforce His rule. I place all my hopes in Darwin. His wonderful insight can teach a far greater satisfaction and reassurance than blind faith can offer—a simple pleasure gained from the sheer exuberance and tenacity of existence. The human species should revel in a permanent state of delighted astonishment at this world, but instead we allow ourselves to be yoked to a tiresome and unyielding fear of it."

Fidget lunged forward and sank his teeth into Swinburne's ankle. The poet squawked and hopped away, arms flapping wildly. His long scarf became entangled around his ankles. He tripped and fell into the snow, rolling and squealing. Burton watched him but without amusement. Though he'd become familiar with his friend's propensity to go off at a tangent, Swinburne's words had been peculiarly out of context, and while he'd been speaking, Burton had noticed a glazed quality to the other's eyes, as if the poet had slipped into a trance.

The king's agent bent, plucked the flower out of the ground, and cautiously held it to his nose. It was discharging a pleasant but rather cloying perfume.

"Algy," he said. "How do you feel?"

Swinburne leaped to his feet and shook a fist. "Furious! I shall purchase a muzzle for that little devil."

They trudged on. When they reached Chelsea Bridge, the poet opted to cross it on foot and walk the short distance back to his digs. Promising to deliver Burton's penny-farthing back to Montagu Place on the morrow, he set off.

Burton hailed a hansom and was soon rattling northward with Fidget sitting between his feet. He felt as if he'd been awake more hours than his pocket watch could attest to, and his thought processes were becoming increasingly sluggish. His friend's odd outburst, the bizarre flowers, Spring Heeled Jack, the vanishing time suit, the other histories—they all blurred into a jumble of mismatched events. He could make no sense of them, and the more he tried, the more confused he felt.

He tried to quieten his restless thoughts by looking out of the window. It didn't help. He found himself anxiously scrutinising the city in case it had suddenly transformed into a near but not quite accurate copy of itself.

When he arrived home, he found Mrs. Angell dusting the bannisters. She gawped as he stumbled in and cried out, "Great heavens! You went out again! You've hardly slept! Look at the state of you! Your clothes are ruined! And—and you have a dog!"

"I fell off my velocipede. This is Fidget, a new addition to our household. You don't mind, Mother?"

The old dame clapped her hands together and beamed down at the basset hound. "Ooh no! I ain't had a dog since I were a little girl. He's a beauty! Just look at them big brown eyes o' his. An' you know how I hate wastin' scraps, sir. I'm sure he'll be more 'n' happy to swallow 'em up."

"Good show. Perhaps you'd put that to the test? I wouldn't mind a little something myself. I'm famished. An early supper would be much appreciated."

"There's a pot of lamb curry on the stove," she said, taking Fidget's lead. "It'll be ready in half an hour."

"Just the ticket."

His housekeeper gave his clothes a further disapproving inspection then, with the hound waddling behind her, descended to the kitchen.

A few minutes later, Burton was slouching in his armchair. He'd wrapped himself in his *jubbah*—the loose outer garment he'd worn during his pilgrimage to Mecca—and had wound a colourful turban around his head. A cheroot dangled from his lips. He glanced cautiously around the room.

There was no parakeet. Everything was in its proper place.

He moved his feet closer to the fire, feeling its heat penetrate the soles of his pointed Arabian slippers, and thought first of Abdu El Yezdi, then of the Burton who'd ridden the clockwork horse, and finally of the one who'd steered a giant woodlouse.

Multiple Richard Francis Burtons.

"There is no other me but I!" he told the room, though he knew the statement was erroneous.

At half seven, Mrs. Angell sent Bram Stoker up to summon him to the dining room. She'd cooked with her usual expertise, but as hungry as he was, the king's agent ate slowly and dazedly, hardly tasting the food. His muscles had stiffened so much that every movement pained him.

After the meal, he returned to the study for a postprandial drink. He stood before a small wall mirror. He saw two stitches in the gash in his chin. His old scars, on his cheek and scalp, were where they should be.

He stared into his own dark eyes.

The room was quiet but for the steady and persistent ticking of the mantel clock.

Traffic chugged past outside. Footsteps. Muffled snippets of conversation. A newsboy hawking the evening edition: "Terror in Leicester Square! Read all about it! Stilted ghost haunts the city!" Very faintly, Mr. Grub's singsong cry countered the headlines with: "Roasted corn! Come an' get it! On the cob! Nice 'n 'ot!"

In the hallway, the grandfather clock wheezed and chimed nine.

Time.

It flowed through Sir Richard Francis Burton and around him.

It emanated from him and was infused into him.

He saw its presence in the depth of his eyes, the past mocking, the present conspiring, and the inexorable future waiting with an icy and pitiless patience.

CHAPTER 5

THE JUNGLE

Mr. Galton says we can alter every part of an animal; that we can instil in them abilities that don't belong to their species at all. He proposes mice that glow like jellyfish, sheep the size of shire horses, and cats with long hair so static that it will function to lift dust from our carpets. He says he can create parakeets that have the ability to relay messages word for word, and swans that a man might ride through the air. His mind is filled with wild schemes and ungodly imaginings. I fear him, I fear his ideas, but most of all, I fear how enticing I find them. What if he were to apply them to the human species? What then? Dear Lord, do not let me fall under this man's spell.

—From the diary of Nurse Florence Nightingale

Burton awoke in his bed, though he couldn't remember having moved to it.

Daylight slanted through the crack in his curtains. He pushed back the sheets and swung his feet to the floor, crossed to the window, and yanked the drapes open. Outside, the yard and the mews beyond it were thick with vermillion flowers.

He turned back to the room and went to the washbasin to shave and sponge himself down. He was still sore all over, but his remarkable constitution had responded well to Sadhvi Raghavendra's ointments. His cuts were hard with puckering scabs, his bruises were already yellowed, and the swelling on the back of his skull had gone.

He wrapped his *jubbah* about himself with some difficulty—his left elbow, in particular, was very tight—and was descending the stairs when the doorbell jangled. Bram Stoker answered the summons just as Burton reached the landing outside his study. Maneesh Krishnamurthy and Shyamji Bhatti greeted the lad from the doorstep.

"Come on up, fellows," Burton called, and to Bram, "Would you bring us a pot of coffee, young 'un?"

The boy offered a snappy salute and scurried off as Krishnamurthy and Bhatti entered. Assistants to the minister of chronological affairs, they were both handsome young men, though currently grim-faced. Burton said no further word until he'd ushered them into chairs in his study.

"From your expressions, I fear you bring bad tidings."

Krishnamurthy nodded. "We do. Between nine and eleven last night, Spring Heeled Jacks caused havoc around the city."

"Jacks?"

"Four simultaneous manifestations—at the Royal Geographical Society, at the Athenaeum Club, at Oxford University, and again in Leicester Square."

"All places I frequent."

"Yes. And he was shouting for you at every location."

"Yet when he found me on Wednesday, he had nothing coherent to say." Burton frowned, and added, "We're referring to it as *he* now, Maneesh?"

"The Jacks were disoriented, disturbed, panicked and violent, as was Edward Oxford shortly before Abdu El Yezdi killed him. This, together with their repeated references to Queen Victoria and obvious obsession with you, has led the minister to suggest that the insane intelligence Babbage attempted to drive out of the damaged suit has somehow found its way into these stilted mechanisms."

"Which in form clearly resemble it," Bhatti added.

"So yes, Sir Richard," Krishnamurthy continued. "We think they are *he*, as in Oxford."

Burton rubbed his chin thoughtfully, feeling the roughness of the stitched laceration beneath his fingertips. "Hmm. One might advance the theory that Babbage's experiment somehow enabled the insane intelligence to flee back to the future it came from, there to advance and automate the time suit and send it to torment me. However, the proposition stumbles on the fact that the intelligence in the suit is synthetic and could not have instigated any such action. As Babbage observed, it has no capacity for independence. It can only respond to instructions."

Burton stood, turned away from his visitors, and stepped to one of the two windows. He gazed out at Montagu Place. The rooftops of the buildings on the other side of the road, the windowsills, the inner edge of the pavements, the gutters—every surface that hadn't been trodden down or driven over—every inch was densely crowded with flowers, all now the size of crocuses.

"But," he said, "the theory might be valid if we add to it a mind other than Oxford's, one that ordered the suit to escape our time the moment Babbage activated the Field Preserver."

"You suggest that someone took control of it?" Bhatti asked.

"And plucked it from right beneath our noses. It leaves us with three questions: who, from when, and why?"

They fell silent as Bram entered and quietly served them coffee. After he'd departed, Bhatti said, "It may be that Babbage holds the key to this mystery. Apparently the electrical pattern held within the damaged suit was imprinted into his Field Preserver at the instant the suit vanished. He's working on a means to analyse it. If there was some kind of communication from the future—an order—it might have been recorded."

"The power station is our next stop," Krishnamurthy said. He gulped his coffee and clattered the cup back onto its saucer. "We'd better push on. Will you accompany us?"

"No. I'm sick of the sight of the place. Besides, I have another line of inquiry to pursue."

"There's another?"

"The flora."

"The flowers? Because they and our hopping maniac arrived in unison?"

"Yes," Burton replied, "and Swinburne responded oddly to them. You know how I've come to trust his instincts."

"Phew!" Krishnamurthy exclaimed. "What extraordinary times we inhabit!"

Burton saw them out of the house then rang for Stoker. "Will you tell Mrs. Angell I'm ready for breakfast? Then I want you to get a message to Mr. Swinburne. Ask him to get here by noon."

"Right you are, sir."

The boy headed down to the kitchen while Burton entered the dining room. After a short wait, his housekeeper entered bearing a tray and served him bacon, sausages, eggs, grilled tomatoes, fried mushrooms, and buttered toast. He ate with uncharacteristic gusto, yelled his thanks from the hallway, and climbed the stairs to his bedroom, there to dress.

He was frustrated by his aches and pains and had to remind himself that only thirty-six hours or so had passed since he'd been thrown through a plate glass window. Sadhvi's lotions did nothing to soothe his impatience. Tiredness, weakness—there was no place for them in Burton's philosophy.

With his lip curled in self-disdain, he tugged open a bedside drawer and pulled from it a bottle of Saltzmann's Tincture.

"Blast you, Algy," he muttered. "I'll not spend the day hobbling about like a confounded invalid."

He twisted out the cork and drank.

"And to hell with all objections!"

He sat on the bed, leaned forward with his head hanging, and waited for the tincture to enter his circulation.

It hit him like an exploding sun.

He gave a quavering cry and toppled to the floor, holding himself up with his hands and knees.

He felt a cold gun barrel press into the back of his neck.

He heard Isabel Arundell's voice.

"If you move, I swear to God I'll put a bullet through your brain."

Dick Burton, spy, traitor to his native country, and Otto von Bismarck's strongest piece in the deadly chess game currently being played across Europe, was defeated.

He'd come so close. He'd discovered the existence of Spring Heeled Jack. He'd learned the truth about the apparition's identity and origin. He'd found where the British government's secretive Society of Science was keeping the time suit. And he'd almost snatched it from them.

The accursed king's agent! She'd been on his heels ever since he'd killed Krishnamurthy and Bhatti, and now, just as his victory seemed assured, she'd caught up with him.

Still dazed from the knock to his head, on his hands and knees, with pain searing through his skull, he tried desperately to gather his thoughts.

"Stay down," she advised. "Try anything and I'll not hesitate."

"Miss Arundell," he rasped. "Your sense of timing is immaculate—and exasperating."

He tried to push himself up, but her weapon jabbed into his neck again.

"Last chance. Believe me, I'm itching to pull this trigger."

Perhaps his attempt to move so soon after being clouted was a mistake anyway; it sent his senses spinning, and, for a moment, he couldn't remember where he was. In his bedroom, surely? No, else there'd be a carpet beneath his hands and knees. There was only one place he knew that possessed this harsh, unnatural illumination. Battersea Power Station.

As if to confirm it, he heard Babbage's characteristic rasp. "Have you quite finished, Madam? Am I to suffer these interruptions every time I'm on the verge of an important experiment?"

"Had I not interrupted, Charles," Isabel responded, "you'd have nothing to experiment with. He was about to steal the time suit."

Isabel. Alive. She's alive.

"Please," Burton croaked. "Let me stand. Let me look at you."

"Keep him in your sights, Algernon," she said.

"Rightie ho."

Swinburne. So he was here, too.

Burton put a hand to his face. It was clean-shaven.

He had thoughts overlaying thoughts, memories upon memories. One stratum clarified, the rest blurred.

He recognised himself.

Another side step.

"All right," Isabel said. "Get to your feet. Slowly. Any sudden movement and I'll shoot you dead."

Another voice, male: "Be careful. I know to my cost how dangerous the swine can be."

Burton raised his head and saw John Hanning Speke. The man had been killed in Berbera four years ago, but here he was, in nearly every respect as Burton remembered him, tall, thin, with a long, mousy brown beard and a weak, indecisive sort of face. The sole difference was that this Speke's left eye was missing, along with much of the skull above it, and had been replaced with a mechanism of glass and brass. Burton very slowly climbed to his feet, and the man's artificial eye whirred as the metal rings surrounding the black lens adjusted its focus.

"Run to earth, at last," Speke said. "You'll not escape this time, Dick. It's the noose for you."

Burton didn't respond. Very gradually, he turned. He saw Babbage, standing by a workbench with the damaged suit on it. He saw a hulking contraption of jointed legs and tool-bearing limbs, which he guessed was Isambard Kingdom Brunel. He saw Algernon Swinburne, short-haired, scar-faced, and despite his diminutive and somewhat effeminate form, looking surprisingly brutal. And he saw Isabel Arundell.

She was slender, elegant, beautiful, and aiming her pistol straight between his eyes.

"Isabel," he whispered, hardly able to resist rushing forward to take her into his arms.

"Shut up," she snapped. "Charles, please proceed. We'll allow our uninvited guest to witness the activation of the suit. I want him to go to the gallows knowing we have it, knowing it works, and knowing we'll use it to defeat his master's filthy empire." She flicked the end of the gun slightly and said to Burton, "Watch. This marks the end of all Bismarck's schemes."

Burton looked back at Babbage. The elderly scientist clapped his hands together. "Have you all quite finished? Interruption after interruption! Unacceptable! This is a place for science and the advancement of understanding, not for your ridiculous games of politics and one-upmanship. Now, be quiet and observe." He tapped the suit's helmet. "This, as I have already told you, has the ability to repair itself but currently lacks sufficient energy to do so. By reestablishing its connection to this," he pointed at the Nimtz generator, "I believe power enough will be transferred." He took a pocket watch from his waistcoat. "Isambard, please record that the experiment commences at nine o'clock on the evening of the fifteenth of February, 1860."

He reached down and traced a shape on the side of the generator. It glowed, crackled and let forth a shower of sparks.

"I'd move back if I was you," Burton advised.

A bubble swelled out of the suit. Babbage and Speke, standing closest to it, retreated hastily.

"And," Burton said, "hey presto."

The time suit vanished, taking half the bench and a chunk of Isambard Kingdom Brunel with it.

"How did you do that?" Isabel demanded. "Bring it back at once!"

Burton turned to face her. "Isabel, know this. I loved you from the very first moment I saw you."

She snarled at him. "You traitorous hound."

He saw her finger tighten on the trigger.

There was a loud report.

He felt himself explode out of his body.

Dying was like blinking.

He was sucked back into it.

When he opened his eyes, Burton was facing Babbage again, and the bench and the suit were back.

Isambard Kingdom Brunel, in human form except for an accordion-like apparatus creaking in and out on his chest, took a cigar from his mouth and said, in a gravelly voice, "Will it work, Charles?"

"Of course it will."

Brunel looked to Burton's right. "Should we do it, sir?"

"Yes."

Burton turned his head to see the man who'd spoken. It was Lord Elgin's former secretary, Laurence Oliphant. His skin and hair were alabaster white. His features were distorted, resembling those of a panther.

Babbage announced that it was nine o'clock on the fifteenth of February, 1860. He went through the identical routine with the identical result.

Burton waited silently while Babbage and Oliphant tied a tourniquet around Brunel's right arm, the engineer's hand having been taken by the bursting bubble.

Isabel is alive in at least one branch of history. My enemy, but alive. By God! To see her! To see her!

Grief tightened his chest. He closed his eyes, swayed, and thought he might fall.

Babbage said, "Mr. Lister, note that the experiment commences at nine o'clock, fifteenth of February, 1860."

Burton opened his eyes. The interior of Battersea Power Station had transformed into what appeared to be a nightmarish surgical ward. Vast pulsating monstrosities of flesh and tubes and organs humped up from the floor around him. Tentacled glowing organisms hung from the high ceiling. Cartilage and throbbing arteries stretched from wall to wall. He was standing in the midst of it, facing a workbench. Babbage and the surgeon Joseph Lister were on the opposite side. Charles Darwin and Francis Galton were whispering together to his left. Damien Burke and Gregory Hare—who in El Yezdi's history had been allies and in his own enemies—were to his right, both dressed, bizarrely, as Harlequin.

"I must confess, this procedure involves an unusual degree of unpredictability," Babbage said. "For if there's a time suit here, then there are time suits in the other realities, too, and if every Charles Babbage simultaneously connects every helmet to every Nimtz generator in every history, what then?"

Ah! Burton thought. *Is that it?*

Babbage reached toward the suit.

"Stop!" Burton shouted.

The scientist glanced up at him. "Don't interfere, sir! Know your place!"

He touched the generator.

Pause.

Pop.

Gone.

While Babbage and Lister squabbled, Burton walked over to Damien Burke and said, "Where's Brunel?"

Burke's lugubrious features creased into a frown. "Dead. Did you forget killing him, Mr. Burton?"

"Ah. And what about Isabel Arundell?"

"She's still on her honeymoon, isn't that right, Mr. Hare?"

"It is, Mr. Burke," Hare agreed.

"To whom is she married?"

"Why, to Mr. Bendyshe, of course."

"Bendyshe? Thomas Bendyshe?" Burton threw his head back and gave a bark of laughter. When he looked down, he was in front of the bench yet again, and the power station was an intricate structure of wrought iron and stained glass, like a baroque cathedral.

"Mr. Gooch," Babbage said, "make a note. It is nine o'clock on the fifteenth of February, 1860. We shall begin."

Burton felt a pistol in his waistband. He yanked it out and pointed it at Babbage.

"No. Step away from the suit. Don't touch it."

Babbage glared at him. "There is no time for games, Captain."

Burton shot him in the head.

As blood sprayed and Babbage fell backward to the floor, Burton yelled, "Everyone remain absolutely still or I swear I'll kill every one of you."

"My giddy aunt! Have you lost your mind?" Swinburne screeched from beside him.

"You've killed Charles!" Gooch cried out.

Burton heard Richard Monckton Milnes, behind him, say, "You'd better have a damned good explanation for this, Dick."

The time suit popped out of existence.

Gooch, Swinburne, and Monckton Milnes gaped at the indentation in the floor where the bench had been.

"What happened?" Monckton Milnes muttered.

Gooch said, "Impossible! Charles never touched it."

Burton lowered his gun. "Now *that*," he said, "is very interesting indeed."

"What is?" Swinburne asked.

Finding himself in mid-stride, the king's agent stumbled and stopped. There came a tug at his hand. He was holding a lead. Fidget, by his right ankle, looked up.

To his left, Swinburne drew to a halt.

"Algy? I—I—I beg your pardon?"

"I said, what is?" Swinburne replied. "You said something was interesting."

Burton placed a hand on his friend's shoulder to steady himself. The world buckled and distorted around him. It shimmered, solidified, and he saw they were in Whitehall Place, close to the Royal Geographical Society. The street's gutters were piled high with red blossoms, bright beneath an unbroken but thinning grey mantle of cloud.

"Um, the date?"

"The date is interesting?" Swinburne asked. "Why so?"

"No, I mean, what is it?"

The poet stared at him. "The seventeenth, of course. What's the matter? Surely not another hallucination? When? Just now?"

"It's Friday?"

"Yes. One o'clock-ish. Good Lord! I didn't notice a thing!"

"Wait. Tell me, what have we been doing? Where are we going?"

"You summoned me. I pushed your broken velocipede all the way to your place and arrived about an hour ago. You told me about last night's invasion of Spring Heeled Jacks and your conversation with Krishnamurthy and Bhatti, and then we hopped into a cab. It just dropped us off."

Burton looked at the RGS building. "We're here for Richard Spruce."

"You remember that?"

"No, I presume it. He's the only botanist we know. I don't recall a thing since—" He stopped and considered. "Since just after breakfast. The experiment—I keep returning to it. I've witnessed so many alternate versions of the bloody event that I'm giddy with it."

The king's agent massaged the back of his neck. He could still feel the Saltzmann's throbbing in his veins, though the sensation was fast fading.

"It was unusually rapid again," he murmured, referring to the fast onset of the tincture's effects and their unusual intensity.

Swinburne, mistaking his meaning, said, "Not really, if it lasted from breakfast to lunch. All morning in the grip of a mirage!"

The tincture.

The visions.

Of course!

Burton heaved a sigh. "Come on."

They strode the short distance to the Royal Geographical Society and went inside. Burton nodded to the portly man at the reception desk, who immediately came out from behind it, hurried over, and said in a hushed voice, "You'll not cause any bother?"

"Bother, Mr. Harris?" Burton asked.

"Sir Roderick is furious with you. Your monster caused a great deal of damage last night."

"It's not my monster," Burton protested. "I'm not responsible for what happened here."

"It was screaming your name and Sir Roderick holds you accountable. The Society doesn't welcome such disruption. You may be disbarred."

Burton snarled, "If that's his attitude, Sir Roderick can shove the Society right up his—"

"Harris," Swinburne interrupted. "We just want a word with Richard Spruce. We'll be but a moment."

Harris looked relieved. "He's not here."

"Where, then?" the poet asked.

"I don't know."

"We'll find someone who does," Burton said. He shouldered past Harris, who cried out, "But! But! But! I say! No dogs allowed!" and ascended the wide staircase with Fidget and Swinburne at his heels. To their left, portraits of the Empire's most celebrated explorers were hanging crookedly. Dr. Livingstone had a hole in his forehead and Mungo Park was upside down.

They passed along a wood-panelled hallway to the clubroom. The normally impressive chamber was in disarray. The mirror behind the bar was broken. The carpet was strewn with fragments of glasses and bottles. Tables and chairs were splintered and overturned.

There were only eight men present, three of them staff, who were assiduously cleaning the mess.

"No Spruce," Burton murmured, "but I see old Findlay by the window. Perhaps he can point us in the right direction."

Arthur Findlay, a lean-faced individual, was sitting in an armchair, reading a newspaper through *pince-nez* spectacles, apparently oblivious to the signs of chaos that surrounded him. He looked up as they approached, sprang to his feet, and clasped Burton's hand in greeting.

"I say! Beastly Burton! How the deuce are you, old fellow? Been brawling again, I see. Here, last night, was it? I've heard rumours of a wild animal on the rampage."

"Hallo, Arthur. I'll confess to a slight spat, but it wasn't here. Have you met Algernon Swinburne?"

"Hallo, lad. You're the poet, aren't you? Super! Simply super!"

"What ho! What ho! What ho!" Swinburne returned. He pointed down to the basset hound. "Have you met the mutt? His name is Beelzebub, Savage Fiend of Hell."

"Fidget," Burton corrected.

"Lovely breed," Findlay observed. "Bassett hound, what! Very placid. Wouldn't say boo to a goose."

"Ha!" Swinburne exclaimed.

The geographer grinned at him. "I say, your hair is as fiery as our new flora, lad. Baffling, the flowers, hey? Perfectly extraordinary. What the devil? What the very devil?"

Burton said, "On which subject, we're looking for Richard Spruce. Any idea where he might be?"

"The botanist fellow? In the Cauldron, I believe."

"The East End? Why?"

"Ashes, Burton! Ashes! A fine growth medium and the area offers no restriction, what!"

It made sense. The terrible slums and tenements of the crime-riddled

East End—the Cauldron—had, last November, been destroyed by the city's worst fire since 1666. Despite a particularly wet winter, the area had smouldered for weeks afterward. It was cool now, but rebuilding hadn't yet commenced.

"Join me for drinkies?" Findlay suggested.

"Certainly," Swinburne said.

"No," Burton countered. "We're on a mission, Arthur. We'll go straight to Spruce."

Minutes later, they were back out in Whitehall Place. Swinburne whistled piercingly for a cab—causing Fidget to bark and Burton to wince—then took off his hat and waved it at a hansom while jumping up and down. "Hey there! Hey! Cab! Over here! I say! Cabbie!"

The vehicle swerved and pulled to a stop beside them.

"No need ter get a bee in yer bonnet," the driver said. "I saw yer."

"The Cauldron!" Swinburne cried out. "And don't spare the blessed horses!"

"I ain't got no 'orses. It's a steam engine, see?" The driver jerked his chin at the machine chugging in front of him.

"Well, don't spare that then!" Swinburne shrilled.

He climbed aboard.

Burton gave the driver an apologetic look, lifted Fidget into the carriage, followed, and sat. As the conveyance jolted into motion, he said, "Why the histrionics, Algy?"

Swinburne clapped his hands in Burton's face. "To keep you in the here and now. By golly, to think we spent the past hour together and you didn't even know it. Don't you even recall my limerick?"

"Limerick?"

"An engineer by the name of John Kent, had a tool most remarkably bent, his wife bore the brunt, when it—"

"Stop! I assure you, I'm entirely in the present."

"This one?"

"Yes, this one."

Despite Burton's protest, Swinburne regaled him with bawdy poems and jokes all the way to Aldgate, where the hansom stopped, the hatch in the roof lifted, and the driver shouted down, "Can't go any farther, gents."

His passengers disembarked. Swinburne fished a shilling from his pocket and passed it up, his manner distracted, his eyes not straying from the heaped foliage that surrounded them.

"Two and six," the driver said.

"Here." Burton passed up the remainder of the fare. "Thank you, driver."

The man took the coins and gazed around. "I were here three days ago, an' all this weren't. Where'd the blessed things come from? What are they? Roses? Poppies? Gladioli?"

"I haven't the foggiest idea," Burton replied.

The carriage departed. Swinburne, throwing out his arms, twirled on the spot and laughed, "A red garden! London has become a red garden! Ouch! I say! Keep that blasted dog away from my feet, will you?"

"Sorry," Burton said.

They picked their way along the street, stepping through tangled growth, rounded a corner, and passed the fire-damaged skeleton of a tenement building.

They stopped. They stared.

The ruined Cauldron lay ahead.

Burton had expected to see a great plain of ash from which the stumps of burned buildings jutted. Instead, he saw a thick jungle of the brightest reds.

"My hat!" Swinburne whispered. "How has it grown so fast? We'll never find Spruce among that lot!"

Burton cupped his hands around his mouth and yelled, "Spruce! I say! Spruce! Are you there?"

After a moment, a faint voice sounded. "Hallo! Who's that?"

"I'm Burton! Where are you, old chap?"

"Over here!"

"Where?"

"Here!"

"Keep calling, we'll join you!"

They moved forward with Fidget squeezing through the undergrowth beside them. After a few steps, the plants closed overhead and progress became difficult.

"We?" came a faint cry. "We who?"

"I'm with the poet Algernon Swinburne!" Burton pushed into a tangle of leaves and twisting branches, exotic blooms and weird gourd-like fruits. Swinburne reached out and touched one of the latter. "Fruiting after just a few hours? I feel like I'm dreaming."

"I've never seen anything like it," the king's agent agreed. "Not even in Africa."

"Poet?" Spruce cried out. He sounded closer.

"Seeking inspiration!" Swinburne called. "I'm writing a verse entitled 'O Pruning Shears, Wherefore Art Thou When I Need Thee?'"

The chuckled response was plainly audible, and the next moment they broke through into a clearing and saw Spruce standing in its centre. "Hallo, Sir Richard, Mr. Swinburne."

Spruce was a long-limbed fellow with curly but receding hair and a beard peppered with grey. His manner, as he shook their hands, was friendly but reserved, his eyes evading theirs in a fashion that struck Burton as diffident rather than shifty.

"What do you make of it, old chap?" the king's agent asked. "Have you seen anything like this before?"

"Not at all. It's utterly fantastic. The rate of growth is simply staggering, yet the species—whatever it is—appears more suited to the humidity and heat of central Africa than to a cold British winter."

"Is that where the seeds have come from?"

"I would say so."

Spruce squatted and gestured for Burton and Swinburne to follow him down. The latter manoeuvred carefully to ensure that his buttocks were facing away from Fidget.

Spruce said, "Look at this." He used his right hand to scrape away snow until a layer of ash was revealed, then dug a little more, exposing a tangle of thin white roots.

"It has a fibrous and propagative root system with a plenitude of rhizomes, so that while one plant may sprout from the seed, a great many more will then sprout from the expanding roots. But here's the peculiar thing—" Spruce dug at the ash until he'd made a shallow trench between the trunks of two tall, thick bushes. "Do you see what I mean?"

Burton examined the exposed roots. "As you said, both plants have grown from a single artery."

"Ah," Spruce responded. "That's the thing. These particular ones haven't. I can see from their stage of development that they were both seedlings."

Burton used his forefinger to trace the path of one particular root. "But this joins them."

"Exactly. Every seed-born plant has extended roots to its fellows, and those roots have merged with one another. It's almost as if all of this—" He stood and held his arms out to encompass all the verdure, "is a single organism."

Swinburne asked, "And its growth? Have you an explanation? A theory?"

"None. Were I not witnessing it with my own eyes, I should say it's impossible. All this—in two days!"

Burton turned and gazed at the leaves, flowers and fruits.

Spruce asked, "Did you encounter anything like it during your expedition to the Central Lakes?"

"Nothing close," Burton answered. "Nothing even with this hue."

"Then, if you'll pardon the question, why are you here, Sir Richard? I wasn't aware that you counted botany among your interests."

"I'm a hobbyist, nothing more, but this phenomenon is so thoroughly outré that it's piqued my curiosity."

"I can certainly understand that."

"If you find out anything more, would you let me know? I live at fourteen Montagu Place."

"For sure."

"Thank you. We'll not interrupt your research any further."

After bidding the botanist farewell, Burton, Swinburne and Fidget headed back the way they'd come.

"We didn't learn much," Swinburne ruminated. "What now?"

"We'll drop in on my pharmacist, Mr. Shudders."

"Why?"

"He supplies me with Saltzmann's Tincture."

Swinburne screeched, "What? What? What? The drug Sadhvi

Raghavendra has repeatedly warned you against is sold by a man named *Shudders*—and still you gulp it down? I think you might be the most ridiculous fellow I've ever met!"

"That, Algernon, is because, unlike me, you've never had the advantage of encountering yourself."

"But—for crying out loud!—you're buying more of the foul poison? Your addiction is beyond the bounds! Must I gather the Cannibals and have them help me lock you away until the dependency has passed?"

"I simply want to know where he gets the tincture from."

"Why?"

"Because I think it's the cause of my visits to variant histories."

CHAPTER 6

THE SECOND EXPERIMENT

> My delicate health and retiring disposition have combined
> with my love of botanical pursuits to render me fond of soli-
> tary study, and I must confess that I feel a sort of shrinking
> at the idea of engaging in the turmoil of active life.
> —Richard Spruce

Burton and Swinburne emerged from the jungle-swathed Cauldron and strode westward along Leadenhall Street toward Cheapside. Fidget jogged along beside them, panting, his tongue flapping and his nose twitching as he detected a myriad of enthralling odours.

Swinburne asked, "Why do you think Saltzmann's the source of your hallucinations?"

"I've told you, Algy, they're *not* hallucinations. Initially, I thought the first incident was caused by my run-in with Spring Heeled Jack, but I took the tincture right afterward, and the next time I drank it, the second incident occurred. On that occasion, Jack wasn't involved."

At the Bank of England they flagged down a landau.

"Oxford Street," Burton directed.

They boarded, and the carriage got moving.

In contrast to their journey to the Cauldron, their ride away from it was conducted in silence. Burton was pondering the disparate mysteries, while Swinburne was fuming about his friend's dangerous addiction.

By the time they disembarked, it was snowing again, albeit lightly.

Swinburne jammed his floppy hat onto his springy hair, wound his long scarf around his neck, and dodged away from Fidget's eager teeth.

"That's the place," Burton said, pointing a little way ahead.

Despite the weather, the famous thoroughfare was crowded, and they had to push through the milling pedestrians, hawkers and ne'er-do-wells to reach the pharmacy. They entered. A bell clanked over the door. In response to it, an individual emerged from a back room and stood behind the counter. He was a lanky, grey haired, gaunt-faced and terribly stooped old man, wrapped in a thick coat and with fingerless woollen gloves on his hands.

"Good afternoon, Sir Richard," he said in a voice that sounded like creaking wood.

"Hello, Mr. Shudders," Burton said. "How's business?"

"Mustn't grumble. Mustn't grumble. Can I be of service? Saltzmann's, is it? My stock is low, but I think I have two or three bottles remaining."

"No," Burton replied, "I have sufficient, but could you tell me where it comes from?"

"The supplier? Locks Limited, sir."

"And where is that located?"

Shudders pushed out his lips, tugged at his right ear, and squinted his eyes. "I don't rightly know. I started selling the tincture some five years ago after being approached by a company representative. Other than that youth—"

"Youth?" Burton interrupted.

"Why, yes, a very young man. He convinced me of the efficaciousness of the potion and left with me a case of bottles, promising to deliver more if I sold them."

"Which you did?"

"The very next day. As a matter of fact, it was you who purchased them, and where they are concerned, you've been my principal customer."

"Have I indeed?" Burton tried to remember how he'd become acquainted with Saltzmann's. His normally excellent memory failed him. That, in itself, filled him with suspicion.

"By what method are the bottles delivered?" he asked.

"Whenever my stock is low, a wagon brings a new box and I pay for it on the spot."

Swinburne interjected, "But how do you inform them when you're running out?"

"I never have to. They always turn up at just the right time."

"And you only have two or three bottles left," Burton noted. "Which means you're expecting another delivery soon?"

"Yes. Later today or tomorrow, I should think."

The king's agent pondered this for a moment. "Do they stop in the street?"

"No. There's a delivery yard out back."

"Mr. Shudders, for reasons I cannot go into, I have to investigate Locks Limited. Can I count on your cooperation?"

The pharmacist looked worried and wrung his hands. "Has there been some problem with the tincture, sir? Should I stop selling it?"

"No problem other than the mystery of its ingredients. Concerns have been raised that it might be extremely addictive."

"So is laudanum, but there's no law against selling that. I don't think I'm in the wrong."

"Nor am I accusing you. I'm intrigued, that is all."

"Ah, well then. What can I do?"

"Do you happen to stock extract of anise?"

"Certainly."

"I'd like to purchase a bottle. Will you then show us the back yard?"

The decoction was handed over, and a minute later, after Burton had secured Fidget's lead to a chair in the shop, Shudders ushered the two men out of the back door and into a small cobbled area that opened onto an alleyway leading into Poland Street. It had been swept clean of snow, though a very thin layer had formed upon it since. Red flowers crowded around its edges.

"The wagon comes right into the yard?" Burton asked.

He received an affirmation.

"Are you expecting any other deliveries beside the one from Locks?"

Shudders shook his head. "Not until next Tuesday."

Burton gave a grunt of satisfaction. He stepped across the yard, uncorked the bottle, and started to spill the gooey liquid onto the ground, dribbling it in a wide arc just inside the gate.

Shudders, blowing on his fingertips to warm them, looked on curiously.

When the bottle was empty, Burton returned to the pharmacist. "The moment the delivery is made, will you get word to me? You know my address."

"Very well, Sir Richard. But what—?"

"I have my methods," Burton responded.

Shudders swallowed nervously and looked perplexed.

Swinburne grinned.

They bid the pharmacist farewell and left the shop.

Burton turned up his collar and looked at the darkening sky. "These short winter days make me long for Africa, Algy. Do you think this horrible climate is responsible for the British imperative for expansion? Is our empire built upon drizzle and chill?"

"It's a credible proposition," the poet replied. "At least, when held against that which suggests a tonic could send a man to witness a specific event in other histories. Great heavens, Richard! Saltzmann's is a sauce, not a sorcerer!"

"Where that mystery is concerned, I hope we've just placed a key in the *Lock*."

"Ouch! Balderdash for mains and the worst kind of quippery for afters!" Swinburne complained.

"On which note, I intend to work up an appetite by walking home, where I shall await word from Krishnamurthy and Bhatti. Let us see whether old Babbage has cast any light on our various mysteries."

"If you ask me, he's just as likely to conjure up new confusions as he is to provide answers. The man is as mad as a March hare and becoming madder by the moment." Swinburne jerked the end of his scarf from between Fidget's teeth and wrapped an extra loop around his neck. "I shall call upon you tomorrow morning." He took his leave and was quickly lost from view among the milling pedestrians, though Burton could hear him screeching for a cab.

The king's agent set off toward the end of Baker Street. The freshly lit street lamps were each forming a nimbus in the falling snow, and the hunched metal backs of street-crabs glimmered in the illumination as they clanked along the busy thoroughfare. The gutters, filled with a mulch of trodden and crushed snow and flowers, looked to be running with blood, which, together with the rapidly blackening sky and the uncannily rubicund quality of the light, gave everything a thoroughly infernal appearance.

Through it, Burton strode, his demonic features attracting disapproving and rather fearful glances from the more well-heeled passersby. To them, his gentleman's clothes were an incongruous affectation, as if a tiger had adorned itself with lace. He glowered back, silently railing against the judgements of so-called civilised society.

His mania for exploration had been steadily increasing these past few days. Restlessness boiled within. London was a confinement, its social rituals a bore. He yearned for the fresh stimuli of exotic lands.

However, he also sensed that events were accumulating around him and fast reaching a tipping point. This unnerved him, yet he also welcomed it. If there was an enemy, he wanted it out in the open. He wanted battle to commence.

"Come on," he whispered. "Show yourself."

Unfamiliar horizons or an implacable foe, either would suffice to fill the absence that gnawed at his heart, anything to distract him from the fact of Isabel's death.

He tipped his hat to Mr. Grub at the corner of Montagu Place and Gloucester Place, and a few paces later arrived home. Bram Stoker greeted him in the hallway. Burton said to him, "I have a job for you, young 'un."

As member of the Whispering Web—a remarkable communications system comprised of the empire's millions of orphans, ragamuffins and street Arabs—Stoker was able to send a message that, by word of mouth, would reach its destination with greater rapidity than the post office could offer. He also had access to a repository of practical knowledge that, in its field, was the equivalent to anything held in the British Library or British Museum.

"Sir?"

Burton divested himself of hat and coat.

"I need the location of a company called Locks Limited."

"Shouldn't take long," the youngster said. "I'll get the boys onto it at once."

"Good lad."

While Stoker slipped into his outdoor clothing, Burton went up to his study, lit its lamps, threw himself into his chair in front of the fireplace, rested his feet on the fender, lit a cheroot, and smoked.

He thought about Saltzmann's Tincture. He'd first used it five years ago during his initial foray into Africa. More recently, it had sustained him throughout his search for the source of the Nile, keeping malaria at bay until the final days of the expedition, when he'd finally succumbed. It was only since last November that his reliance on the potion had spun out of control, with him requiring larger and larger doses to smooth his jagged emotions and blunt the sharp edge of grief. Usage had become a dependency. The dependency had become an addiction.

He sighed and massaged his forehead with his fingertips.

Idiot, Burton. Idiot.

He considered the enhanced awareness the tincture instilled—the almost overwhelming cognisance that countless possible consequences extended outward from every circumstance—and realised the liquid had endowed him with this enriched perception even before he'd been made the king's agent, before he'd learned of the innumerable contemporaneous histories.

The correlation between the medicine's effects and his current knowledge couldn't be ignored.

"Mr. Shudders," he muttered. "Are you really a straightforward pharmacist, or maybe something more?"

An hour and a half later, there came a light tap at the door and, in response to Burton's hail, Stoker entered. Fidget padded in beside him, crossed the floor, collapsed onto the hearthrug, and started snoring.

"Hallo, young 'un," Burton said. "Did you find any answers?"

"To be sure, sir. There's four companies what is called Locks Limited, an' it ain't no surprise that two of ' em make locks. Of t'other two, one supplies materials to the building trade, an' one sells pianos."

"None providing pharmaceuticals as a sideline, then?"

"It's unlikely, so it is."

"Thank you, lad."

Stoker gave a nod and left the room.

Burton spent the next hour meditating. He allowed his thoughts to roam freely, dwelling for a time on this, for a while on that, following paths that trailed into nowhere, and others that led to the peripheries of an idea until, from the meanderings, the vaguest glimmer of a form emerged; the ghost of an incomplete conception.

Multiple Babbages. Multiple time suits. A single moment. A synchronous act.

On this he dwelled, neither judging nor accepting, but simply observing as one notion clicked into place beside another.

The grandfather clock in the hallway below, as if encouraging his nascent revelation, chimed nine.

A detonation rattled the windows.

Startled, Burton jumped to his feet.

There came a loud crash from downstairs.

In the street, people yelled and screamed.

"What now?" he muttered.

He heard Mrs. Angell cry out in alarm. Fidget woke up, dived beneath a table, and started to bark.

A voice roared, "Burton!"

Heavy footsteps thudded up the stairs, and the study door flew open, slamming against the bookshelf behind it, sending books spilling to the floor.

Spring Heeled Jack ducked through the opening and stalked in.

"Burton! Have I found you? Here? In this side note?"

Burton rapidly backed away until his heels bumped against the hearth. He thought fast and said, "Side note? Perhaps in a biography? A book written about me after my death? One that exists in the future? Is that how you know the places I frequent?"

He observed the intruder's smooth chest. No scratch. A different mechanism. Not the one he'd fought in Leicester Square.

"Why am I here?" the creature demanded. It shoved a desk aside and kicked a chair out of its way. "What have you done?"

"I don't—"

Before Burton could finish, Jack pounced forward, seized him by the lapels, and shook him until his teeth rattled. "Why are you significant?"

The king's agent felt his fingertips brush against a poker. He pulled it from its stand, swept it up, and whipped it against the side of his assailant's head.

"Get the hell off me!"

Spring Heeled Jack dropped him and staggered to the side, putting a hand to its dented cranium. "Where is the prime minister? What am I doing here? I'm lost! I'm lost!"

"Just stop!" Burton commanded. "Calm down. We can talk."

The figure crouched, and Burton was convinced that, had there been a face, it would be snarling.

"It's your fault!" Jack said.

Burton brandished the poker like a sword. "Stay back, I say! What is my fault? From where—and when—have you come?"

Disregarding the questions, the intruder took one slow step closer, its head waving from side to side like a cobra's. A shudder ran through it. "Prime Minister. Guide me. Please!"

"Which prime minister?" Burton asked. "Whom do you serve?"

Raising its blank face to the ceiling, Jack hollered, "I serve Queen Victoria!"

It lunged forward, knocked the poker from Burton's hand, and slapped the side of his head with such force that the king's agent was sent spinning across the room into a desk and to the floor.

Please. Not again.

He glimpsed Mrs. Angell standing in the doorway with Bram Stoker. They both had their hands clenched over their mouths. He cried out, "Stay back! Fetch the pol—"

He was grabbed by the neck, hauled upright, and struck again, viciously. His head jerked sideways, and blood sprayed from his mouth.

"Tell me! Tell me!" Jack screamed. "Why do I fear you?"

Burton rasped, "I have no idea what you're talking about."

He saw his housekeeper crossing the room behind his attacker, opened his mouth to warn her away, but hadn't a chance to utter a sound before a fist impacted against his eye. He clutched at Spring Heeled Jack's arms. His muscles, already weakened, were no match for the creature. It shoved him hard against the wall.

The wind knocked out of him, Burton slid to his knees and put a hand down to steady himself. A glutinous string of blood oozed from his mouth and nose. He looked up. "You insane bastard."

Jack loomed over him. "I want to go home."

There came a loud *thunk*. The white head fell from the shoulders and bounced onto the floor. The figure folded down on top of Burton. Blue sparks crackled from its severed neck. They sputtered and died.

He struggled from beneath it.

Mrs. Angell, with her hands clutched around the hilt of a scimitar, said, "It's kneading the bread and tenderising the meat what does it."

"Does what?" Burton croaked, as he struggled to his feet.

"Puts the strength in me arms, sir. Did I do the right thing? Panicked, I did. Grabbed this here sword off your wall and afore I knew what I was intending I'd chopped the head off the clockwork man. A new type, is it? I hope they haven't built many of 'em, not if they loses control of 'emselves like what this 'un did!"

"You were splendid, Mother Angell." Burton took her by the elbow as the weapon dropped from her hand, and she suddenly swayed. "Sit down, dear."

"My heart's all a flutter," she said tremulously. "It's lucky you keep your blades so sharp. Goodness gracious, but look at your poor face. Thumped again! You don't 'alf make an 'abit of it."

The king's agent pulled a handkerchief from his pocket and applied it to his mouth. His bottom lip was split, and the cut on his chin had reopened.

"Is our front door broken?" His voice sounded unsteady.

"The main lock, but it weren't bolted."

"Stay here. I'll go and make us a little more secure." He nudged his foot into the prone form of Spring Heeled Jack—it was completely lifeless—then walked to the door, stopped, and looked back. "That was a very brave thing you did."

"Oof!" she responded. "Oof!"

He lurched down the stairs, his legs almost giving way, went to the front door, and examined its splintered frame. The lock had been knocked out of the wood, but the bolts at the top and bottom of the portal were intact.

Bram Stoker appeared on the doorstep with two constables in tow.

"I fetched the coppers!" the lad exclaimed. "Crikey! What was it?"

Both policemen were familiar to Burton, and they, in turn, knew he was the king's agent. He greeted them. "Kapoor. Tamworth. I've just been assaulted. Can't go into details. I need you to stand sentry duty until further notice."

His authority was absolute. They asked no questions, but saluted and immediately positioned themselves at either side of his doorstep.

"Bram, will you get messages to Mr. Krishnamurthy and Mr. Bhatti. They're probably at Battersea Power Station. I need them to come here immediately with a wagon big enough to cart off our uninvited guest."

The boy raced away. Burton addressed P. C. Tamworth. "I'm leaving the door ajar. Let my guests through when they arrive, please."

Hearing the stairs creak, he turned and saw Mrs. Angell descending with Fidget behind her.

"He ain't much of a guard dog, is he?" she said.

"You should rest."

"Oh, don't fuss. I'm all right. I'm a policeman's widow, ain't I? Seen some things in my time, I have, though stilted men without faces takes the biscuit. Fair chills the blood. I'll fetch a raw steak for that eye an' me broom for your study."

"I'll clean the mess."

Mrs. Angell grumbled, "Well, see that you do. I don't care 'ow much time you've spent among them African head-hunters, I'll not 'ave stray noggins layin' around the house." She headed toward her basement domain, the dog following.

Burton went up to his bedroom, sponged his wounds, then returned to his study and closed the door. After placing the spilled books back onto the shelves, he crossed to Spring Heeled Jack and retrieved the creature's decapitated head from beneath a chair. He carried it to one of his desks, sat, and started to inspect it. What he saw unnerved him so much that he dropped it and had to pick it up again. The outer skin of the creature was a waxy, cold and pliable material that he couldn't identify, but inside, amid manufactured parts, there was pink flesh.

"Bismillah!" Burton muttered. "What are you? Man or machine?"

He had to wait until midnight for Krishnamurthy and Bhatti, and when they arrived, Burton was surprised to hear a third person piling up the stairs with them. They hurtled into the room without ceremony, and the addition proved to be Detective Inspector Trounce.

"Mayhem!" the Scotland Yard man thundered. "Bloody mayhem! Spring Heeled Jacks left, right and centre! By Jove, what the blazes has happened here?"

Burton removed the raw steak he'd been holding to his swollen eye and held up the severed head. "This did."

"You got one!"

"More the case that it got me."

The two Indians moved over to the stilted body and squatted down beside it. They each gave a cry of surprise at the exposed fleshy interior of its neck.

"How many, Trounce?" Burton asked.

"Hard to say. Six that I'm sure of, counting this one. Leicester Square again. The Royal Geographical Society again. Old Ford village. Marvel's Wood. Battersea Fields." He pointed a thick forefinger at Burton. "You. Without a doubt, they're hunting you. Why?"

"I don't think they themselves could answer that," Burton said. "As with the first encounter, this one found me but didn't know what to do about it."

Bhatti looked up. "The minister has received further reports about yesterday's manifestations, Sir Richard. Apparently, our friend here—" he patted the decapitated corpse, "or his brethren—also visited Lucca and Naples in Italy, and Boulogne in France."

"All places I've lived," Burton said. Inwardly, he flinched. It wasn't true that he'd lived in Boulogne, but he didn't want to explain that it was significant for being the place where he'd first met Isabel.

"It's obvious that a net is being cast with you as its prey," Bhatti went on, "but what is the point, when you've been twice caught with no consequence aside from a severe beating?"

"Consequence enough," Burton protested. Gingerly, he felt his eye. It had closed almost to a slit.

"And in the meantime people are being frightened witless," Trounce said. "I'll not have it! It has to stop!" He snatched his bowler hat from his head, dropped it, and kicked it at the fireplace. It narrowly missed the blaze, bounced from the hearth, and rolled beneath a desk.

Burton said, "We're doing what we can. Maneesh, what's the news from Babbage?"

"Probably that he'll be over the moon when we deliver this body to him. But, also, he needs you at the station straightaway. He thinks he may be able to locate our absconding time suit, but your assistance is required."

"Mine? What can I do? I'm no scientist."

"For sure, but you're the same man as Abdu El Yezdi, which apparently is of considerable significance." Krishnamurthy and Bhatti lifted the headless cadaver. "Let's put this into the carriage and get going."

"Lord help us, cover it with a sheet, at least," Trounce snapped. "We don't want to look like confounded body snatchers."

This was done, and a few minutes later the group squeezed into a steam horse–drawn vehicle, which then went trundling southward, Battersea bound. Trounce had elected to join them and watched as the king's agent dabbed an alcohol-soaked handkerchief against his latest facial injuries.

"I'm sure it looks worse than it is, Trounce."

"It looks hideous. Even your bruises have bruises. One more punch-up, and you'll be unrecognisable."

"That might prove advantageous."

There was insufficient light in the cabin to allow for further scrutiny of the Spring Heeled Jack, but Bhatti, who was holding the head upside-down on his lap, remarked, "The texture of its skin is exactly like the cloth of the time suit. More solid, but the same scaly feel."

It was the last thing said for the duration of the journey. A pensive silence fell upon them.

They travelled down Gloucester Street, past Hyde Park and Green Park, along Buckingham Palace Road, over Chelsea Bridge, and arrived at Battersea Power Station.

A guard opened the doors in response to their knock and ushered them through. "Mr. Babbage is in the workshop, sirs," he said, peering with interest at the limp, sheet-concealed figure.

They entered, crossed the quadrangle, and went into the workshop. A technician gestured for them to follow him. They did so, trailing between the machines to the central work area.

Yet again, Burton looked upon Charles Babbage, who, with Daniel Gooch, was attending to a throne-like chair beside which the Field Preserver was suspended. The undamaged time suit was on a bench beside it. The men were tinkering with a great mass of wires that stretched between the hanging box and a framework that surrounded the suit's helmet.

Isambard Kingdom Brunel was standing nearby, completely motionless. Trounce stood in front of him, peered at the metal face, and muttered, "Dead as a doornail."

Gooch looked up at them as they placed the Spring Heeled Jack on a worktop and removed the sheet. "Sir Richard! You've captured one of the mechanisms!"

"I have," Burton said. "Though I suffered a drubbing in the process."

"So I see. My goodness, you've certainly been in the wars lately." Gooch approached and started to examine the prone figure. "My stars! This looks like flesh."

"It is. How's Brunel?"

"In a total fugue. I checked his probability calculator and it seems fine. We're leaving him for a while to see whether he comes out of it naturally."

Burton looked at Babbage, who was so deeply engrossed in his work he had neither glanced up from it nor acknowledged the new arrivals. "I understand my presence is required, Daniel? Why?"

"Charles can explain it best." Gooch called to the scientist, waited a moment, then, when the old man failed to respond, shouted more loudly, "Charles!"

The elderly scientist finally tore his eyes from the box and looping wires. He clapped his hands together, cried out, "Ah! Burton! Excellent! Just the man!" but then saw the stilted figure and, for the next fifteen minutes, utterly ignored everyone while he pored over it.

Finally, he addressed Gooch. "Have this stored in ice. Send for Mr. Lister. His medical knowledge is required. This mechanism has biological components. Our investigation of it might be more autopsy than dismantlement. Incredible! Incredible!"

Gooch called over a group of technicians and issued orders. Three of them carted the corpse away. A fourth hurried off to summon Lister.

"We shall proceed with our experiment while we await his arrival," Babbage asserted. He jabbed a finger first at Burton then at the throne. "You. Sit."

The king's agent stayed put and folded his arms across his chest. "I'll not subject myself to anything before you explain it to my satisfaction."

Babbage gave a cackling laugh. "Ha! The primitive man views scientific processes as the darkest of sorceries, is that it? Don't you worry, sir. No harm shall come to you. All you have to do is wear the helmet for a few moments and issue an instruction that it will accept from only you."

Gooch added, "As you know, Sir Richard, Abdu El Yezdi allowed Mr. Babbage to ask questions of the functioning helmet but strictly forbade him to issue it with commands. We still follow that dictate."

"An absurd precaution," Babbage spat. "My research is needlessly crippled."

"My counterpart saw the suit give rise to unhealthy enthusiasms in certain scientists," Burton commented. "He no doubt intended that you be spared the same."

"I'm not subject to childish passions."

"I'm glad to hear it. To return to the matter in hand, what instruction?"

Babbage pressed his fingertips together. "Ah. The instruction. Yes. At the moment the outfit vanished, it broadcast its electromagnetic field with such strength that it was inscribed into my Field Preserver. The reverse of what I intended."

"The experiment was supposed to record the contents of the healthy headpiece, not the damaged," Maneesh Krishnamurthy clarified.

"That is what I just indicated, young man. Do you intend to add unnecessary observations to everything I say?"

"No, sir. My apologies."

Trounce leaned close to Burton and whispered, "By Jove! A tetchy old goat, isn't he?"

Gooch said, "We're pretty sure the same burst of energy is what incapacitated Isambard."

Babbage rapped his knuckles against the Field Preserver. "Thus what is imprinted is, in essence, a thought from the insane mind of Edward Oxford. Burton, I want you to order the functional helmet to access the recording then employ your own intellect to analyse it. You will experience it as an intention, a memory or perhaps an emotion, which you'll feel as if it's your own. I believe that, within that frozen thought, you may detect evidence of whoever issued the command that initiated the suit's disappearance. You might also discover where it has gone."

He lifted the pristine helmet and the framework that surrounded it. Burton regarded it for a moment. "Very well. Let's get it over and done with."

He moved to the throne-like chair and sat. Gooch stepped forward and gave assistance to Babbage, both pushing the headpiece down over Burton's cranium. The king's agent felt soft padding pressing against his hair and encasing his skull so completely that only his face was visible to the others.

Babbage leaned over his Field Amplifier, examining its dials.

Gooch asked Burton, "Do you hear it, sir?"

"Hear what?"

"The voice of the synthetic intelligence."

"I don't hear anything."

"You have to wake it. Wait. We need to make a few adjustments first."

The Field Preserver began to hum.

"Now, Sir Richard," Gooch said. "Think the words *engage interface*."

"What do they mean?"

Babbage growled, "Must you question every statement? Just do as Mr. Gooch says."

Burton did, and in his mind a male voice answered, "*Ready*," causing him to jump in surprise.

"Y-yes," he stammered. "Now I hear it."

Babbage rubbed his hands together. "Bravo! Tell it to search for external connections."

Burton thought, *Search for external connections*.

"*One found*," the voice declared immediately.

"It says it's found one."

"That's the Field Amplifier. Good. Order it to connect and display."

Burton issued the instruction.

"*Warning, the source is corrupted*," came the response.

The king's agent relayed the words to Babbage, who replied, "Tell it to disregard and proceed."

Disregard and proceed, Burton thought. He looked at William Trounce, who was observing the proceedings with his arms folded and a disapproving expression on his face. Suddenly, the Scotland Yard man faded, overlaid by a scene that materialised in front of Burton's eyes. The king's agent saw a woman standing in a garden, pregnant, holding a tea towel. She was pretty, with long black hair, large brown eyes, and a short, thick, but curvaceous and attractive body. She looked directly at him and smiled.

He loved her.

He wanted to return to her in time for supper.

He heard himself say, in a voice that wasn't his own, "Don't worry. Even if I'm gone for years, I'll be back in five minutes."

The woman disappeared into a blazing white inferno.

Pain seared into his mind.

He screamed.

CHAPTER 7

ECHOES OF OXFORD

THE MARK III PROBABILITY CALCULATOR

THE LATEST WONDER FROM
MR. CHARLES BABBAGE

ABLE TO MAKE MORE THAN A TRILLION CALCULATIONS PER SECOND.
ADVANCED INTELLIGENCE.
CONVERSES. ADVISES. ASSISTS.

THE DEPARTMENT OF GUIDED SCIENCE
FORGING A PATH INTO THE FUTURE

The interviewer asked, "Mr. Oxford, how does it feel to single-handedly change history?"

"I haven't changed history," Burton replied. "History is the past."

"Let me rephrase the question. How does it feel to have altered the *course* of human history? I refer to your inventing of the fish-scale battery, which so efficiently emulates photosynthesis, and which has given us the clean and free power that lies at the heart of all our current technologies."

"I don't really know how it makes me feel," Burton responded. "I'm an ordinary man, like any other. My concerns are with my family and with contributing whatever I can to society."

The interviewer chuckled. "Hardly ordinary, sir. Physicist, engineer, historian, philosopher—you are just thirty-five years old, and already your name is up there with geniuses like Galileo, Newton, Fleming, Darwin, Einstein, Temple, Clavius the Fourth, the Zhèng Sisterhood—"

"Stop, please!" Burton protested. "We're lucky enough to live in a world where those who want to explore to the limits of their abilities are encouraged and given the resources to do so. I work in my particular fields and others work in theirs. We have astounding musicians, engineers, artists, designers, architects, storytellers, athletes, chefs, and so forth. However, those people who are content to operate at a more sedate level are as extraordinary in their own right as anyone you might call a genius. The miracle of existence is that everyone is utterly unique. Each and every one of us should be equally celebrated."

"But don't you find it astonishing that it's your creation, in particular, that's arguably caused the biggest change to culture since the Industrial Revolution?"

"Why 'in particular'?"

"Because of where you come from."

"Aldershot?"

The interviewer smiled. "Not geographically. Genetically."

Burton frowned. "Genetically? To what are you referring?"

"You're a historian. You yourself have identified the Victorian Age as the beginning of the modern world. Have you not researched your own ancestry? If one of your forebears had succeeded in his perfidy, there'd have been no Victorian Age at all."

"Perfidy? That's a marvellously old-fashioned word. My partner would approve of it. She works at a language revivification centre."

The interviewer laughed. "It's funny how the language changes, isn't it? Like clothes, what was once outdated is now fashionable again. But to return to the question, I'm referring to your family tree. You are descended from another Edward Oxford, who lived from 1822 to 1900. When he was eighteen years old, he attempted to assassinate Queen Victoria. Fortunately, both the shots he fired missed her. Don't you find it fascinating that we have one Oxford who might have prevented the commencement of the modern age and another Oxford who has, through his genius, ended it by enabling the authentic freedoms of trans-modernity?"

"My studies of the period have been focused on industrial development, so no, I wasn't aware of this other Oxford," Burton answered. He felt a little uncomfortable. "And, to be honest, I don't find it particularly fascinating. It's a function of the human mind to link events into a narrative and to separate history into chapters, but those are conceptual impositions that don't necessarily reflect the true nature of time. There is no actual correlation between what I have done these past few years and what my ancestor did—or attempted to do—" He made an instantaneous mental calculation and continued, "three hundred and fifty-seven years ago."

"Then you don't think the Oxfords are genetically predisposed to change—or to attempt to change—history?"

"Like I said, history is the past. It can't be changed."

"Let us face in the other direction then, and look into the future. What next for Edward Oxford?"

"I expect my next projects to grow out of my current studies of the Tichborne diamond."

"Which is?"

"A large black gemstone discovered over a hundred years ago in a labyrinth beneath the old Tichborne estate in Hampshire. It has extraordinary electromagnetic properties, for which I hope to find a practical application."

"Such as?"

"It might be capable of storing brainwaves in such a fashion that they continue to function."

"Continue to—do you mean—to think?"

"Yes. A person's conscious mind could be stored within the structure of the stone."

"That's astonishing!"

"It is, but there are a lot of other possibilities, too. The research is at a very early stage, so I can't really tell you much more."

"Well, unfortunately we're out of time anyway. May I wish you continued success in your various endeavours, and I'd like to offer my gratitude, on behalf of the audience, for all that you've achieved. Thank you very much indeed for sharing your thoughts with us this morning."

"It was my pleasure. Thank you."

The interview ended, and Burton swiped the air-screen away. He turned to his partner, who was sitting at the breakfast table.

She raised her eyebrows and said, "That was peculiar."

"It was. Queen Victoria!"

"Didn't you know?"

"I had no idea, but I'll certainly look into it."

"Why bother?"

"I'm interested."

"Funny how all the Oxford men seem a little eccentric. It appears the characteristic goes back a long way."

"Are you suggesting we're inclined to madness?"

"Of course not, but imagine what it must have been like in those days. For the majority of people there was no freedom and no opportunities. If your ancestor had the same potential intelligence and passion as you do but was denied an education and outlet for them, might the frustration not have tipped him over the edge?"

"I suppose. Who knows what a person might be capable of in such circumstances?"

Burton stood and picked up his mug of coffee. "I'd better get to it. What are you doing today?"

"I have an art class in an hour. This afternoon, I'm teaching at the language centre."

He stepped over and planted a kiss on her forehead. "See you tonight?"

"If you don't work too late."

He smiled and left the kitchen.

In his laboratory, he sat at his desk, accessed the Aether, and called up information pertaining to the Victorian-era Oxford.

The facts were sparse.

Born on the ninth of April 1822 in Birmingham, his ancestor had moved to London with his mother and sister around 1832, and by '37 was living with them in lodgings at West Place, West Square, Lambeth. He was employed as a barman in various public houses, the last two of them being the Hat and Feathers in '39 and the Hog in the Pound in '40.

On the tenth of June 1840, while the queen, who'd been on the throne for just three years, was taking her daily carriage ride through

Green Park with her new husband, Prince Albert, Oxford stepped along-side the vehicle, drew two flintlocks, and shot at the monarch. His bullets flew wide. After being seized by onlookers, he was arrested, charged with treason, but ultimately found not guilty due to insanity. He was sent to Bethlem Royal Hospital—the infamous Bedlam—where he remained, a model patient, until being transferred to Broadmoor Hospital in 1864. Three years later, he was released on the provision that he'd immediately immigrate to Australia, which he did. He was married there to a girl much younger than him, fathered a son, and lived a respectable existence for a short while before turning to drink and thievery. The family broke up. After that, his life deteriorated, and he died a pauper.

"Sad," Burton muttered.

He called his great-grandfather, who, despite being 112 years old, was still possessed of all his faculties, though, like every male Oxford, he was a little idiosyncratic. The old man's lean, sharp-nosed face appeared almost immediately as the air-screen unfurled.

"Hello, Eddie. I thought you might call."

"Hi, Grampapa. How are you? You look well."

"Nonsense. I look like an Egyptian mummy. I'm nearing my termi-nation date. I have eleven years left. Eleven! Can you imagine that?"

"You know full well that DNA scans don't always accurately predict the moment of death."

"And you know full well that they usually do. It'll be heart failure."

"Easily avoided. When will you get repaired?"

"Never, lad. I'm content to slip away. No one should live beyond his or her time, and I've been around for long enough. In the old days, they were lucky to make it to eighty. You understand, I hope?"

"I do, and I respect your right to make the choice. Actually, it's the old days I'm calling about. What do you know about our ancestors?"

"Ha! That interviewer got you curious, did he? You did well, by the way—came across as clever but reasonable. Not many of the male Oxfords could've managed that. We tend to be an unbalanced crowd. What's the correct term nowadays?"

"Off-narrative."

"Ha ha! Bloody ridiculous! My grandfather would've used *off their rocker* if he were feeling generous. More likely *crackpot* or *crazy* or *nuts*. Language has no bite anymore. You kids emit nothing but a watery drone. Mind you, when I was a kid I never understood a bloody word the adults were saying. They all spoke in acronyms. English language restoration was the best policy the government ever introduced. That girl of yours is doing a good job. Heh! *Perfidy.* I liked that. Bravo the interviewer! What were we talking about?"

"Ancestors. The assassin. Did you know?"

"About our family embarrassment? Actually, I'd forgotten all about him until he was mentioned. But yes, I knew. I wonder if I still have the letter?"

"Letter?"

"It's the oldest relic we've got. Wait, let me look."

The lined face disappeared from the screen. A minute later, the image of a handwritten letter appeared on it.

"Sent to his wife," Grampapa said. "I'm afraid there's no record of her, but I vaguely recall my grandfather saying something about her being the daughter of a family Edward Oxford was acquainted with before he committed his crime. Do you want a hard copy?"

"Yes, please."

"It's coming through now." Grampapa reappeared. "But listen, don't get too caught up in all this nonsense. It was a long, long time ago. You know our DNA consultant recommended that you focus on what you do best, which is to make the future better. The past is no place for a genius like you. I'm very, very proud of everything you've achieved. When I think about that bloody assassin, I realise how much you've put the pride back into the Oxford name."

"Thank you, Grampapa. Can I come visit soon?"

"Whenever you like."

"I'll call again in a few days."

"I look forward to it."

Their conversation ended. Burton took the letter from the desk's printer and read it.

My Darling

There was never any other but you, and that I treated you badly has pained me more even than the treasonable act I committed back in '40. I desired nought but to give you and the little one a good home and that I failed and that I was a drinker and a thief instead of the good husband I intended, this I shall regret to the end of my days, which I feel is a time not far off, as I am sickly in body as well as in heart.

I do not blame you for what you do now. You are young and can make a good life for yourself and our child back in England with your parents and I would have brought more misery upon you had you stayed here, for I have been driven by the devil since he chose me as his own when I was a mere lad. I beg of you to believe that it is his evil influence that brought misery to our family and the true soul of me never wished you anything but happiness and contentment.

You remember, my wife, that I said the mark upon your breast was a sign to me of God's forgiveness for my treachery and that in you he was rewarding me for the work I had done in hospital to restore my wits and good judgment?

I pray now that he looks mercifully upon my failure and I ask him that the mark, which so resembles a rainbow in its shape, and which lays also upon our little son's breast, should adorn every of my descendants forevermore as a sign that the great wrong I committed shall call His vengeance upon no Oxford but myself, for I it was who pulled the triggers and no other. With my death, which as I say will soon be upon me, the affair shall end and the evil attached to my name shall be wiped away.

You have ever been the finest thing in my life. Be happy and remember only our earliest days.

Your loving husband
Edward Oxford

P.S. Remember me to your grandparents who were so kind to me when I was a lad and who, being among the first friends I ever had, I recall with immense fondness.

Burton called his mother. After a short wait, she responded. She looked younger than he did.

"Hi, Mum."

"Ed, I was just watching your interview. Why did that that horrible man bring up ancient history? What has it to do with you?"

"I know, he took me by surprise. Did you know about the Victorian?"

"No."

"I just spoke to Grampapa. He has a letter written by him."

"By the Oxford who tried to kill the queen?"

"Yes. It mentions a birthmark. The same as yours."

His mother pulled down the neck of her shirt. There was a small blemish on her skin, just above the heart. Bluish and yellow in colour, it was arc shaped and somewhat resembled a rainbow.

"My father didn't have it," she said, "but Grampapa does, and his father did, too. It misses occasional generations but always seems to reappear. What's the letter about?"

"The would-be assassin had been deported to Australia. He got married there and had a son, but it all went wrong. The letter was to his wife, who was leaving him and returning to England with the child."

"How wretched. The family DNA probably doesn't have much of that man left in it, though, so don't start getting fanatical about the past."

"That's what Grampapa said."

"You know what you're like. You get too obsessive about things."

"I suppose. It's got me thinking about the Oxfords, that's for sure. Why do you have the name? Why didn't you change it when you married?"

"Why follow such an outmoded tradition? Besides, none of the Oxford daughters ever adopted their husbands' surnames."

"But how come?"

"I don't know."

"And the children always took the Oxford name even if the father's surname was different?"

"Yes. That hasn't been a problem for many generations, but in earlier times it probably caused a few arguments."

"Hmm. So the family name has lasted through history better than most others. Peculiar." Burton looked at the safe in the laboratory wall. "Anyway, I'd better get back to work. Love you."

"Returned tenfold. Bye, son."

He dismissed the air-screen, stood, went to the safe, and retrieved the

Tichborne diamond from it. Holding it up to the skylight, he marvelled at its size and the way the illumination skittered across its black facets. There was something almost hypnotic about it.

Burton returned to his desk, activated the analysis plate, and put the gemstone on it. Immediately, information began to flow across the desk's surface. It kept coming. He'd seen it before but still found it incredible. The structure of the stone was utterly unique, unlike anything he'd ever encountered.

"Even more sensitive than a CellComp," he whispered to himself. "More efficient than a ClusterComp. More capacity than GenMem."

It didn't seem possible.

A peculiar notion occurred to him, obviously inspired by the revelation concerning his ancestor. He considered it for half a minute then pulled up a calculation grid and formulated a four-dimensional mathematical representation of the idea.

He employed his grandfather's favourite archaic expletive. "Bloody hell!"

The numbers and formulas created a shape around him that extended in every direction, both in space and time. He sank into it, was swallowed by it, and experienced an extraordinary sensation wherein the calculations mutated first into swirling colours then into a pulsating sound, which slowly stretched, twisted, and coalesced into a voice that exclaimed, "Hallo hallo hallo! Awake at last!"

Burton blinked and realised he was lying on a bed. Algernon Swinburne was sitting in a chair nearby. He was sporting an absurdly large red blossom in his buttonhole. Seeing Burton peering at it, the poet said, "It grew on my doorstep. Rather fetching, don't you think?"

"With the floppy hat and scarf?" Burton observed. His voice sounded gravelly. "You look like you've stepped out of a pantomime." He cleared his throat, noticed a glass of water on the bedside table, and reached for it. "What time is it?"

"Eight in the morning. You've been unconscious all night. Trounce called on me and sent me here. I've just arrived. Here, let me help you to sit."

Swinburne rose, stepped over, slid an arm under Burton's shoulders, and gave assistance as his friend struggled up. He took the glass, after Burton had swallowed its contents, and placed it back on the table.

The king's agent peered around with his good eye—the other was still slitted—and recognised one of Battersea Power Station's private rooms.

He leaned back, emitting a slight groan. His head was aching abominably. "What happened?"

"According to Gooch, you told the helmet to connect to Babbage's device, then screamed and passed out. How do you feel?"

"My skull is throbbing. By God! How many visions can a man endure? I saw through Edward Oxford's eyes, Algy."

"Which Oxford? The sane one or loopy one?"

"The sane, in the far future, at the moment when he realised that travelling backward through history might be possible."

Burton winced and pressed his hand against his temple. "For sure, I'll not be allowing Babbage to place anything on my head ever again. Did he gain anything?"

"Quite the opposite. But you did. Feel your scalp."

Burton ran his fingers through his hair. The scars on his head felt raised, gritty, and extremely tender. He winced. "What happened?"

"The helmet tattooed you. Wait, I'll fetch Babbage. He can explain it better than I."

"Tattooed?" Burton muttered, as his friend scampered from the room.

Minutes later, the poet returned with Babbage and Gooch.

"Are you in pain, Sir Richard?" the latter asked.

"A little. What's this about a tattoo?"

Babbage barked, "Adaptive application!"

"In English, if you please, Charles."

The scientist tut-tutted irascibly. "I told you before. The helmet's components can rearrange themselves to change their function. The Bio-Procs extracted black diamond dust from their own inner workings and injected it into your scalp, following the line of your scars."

Gooch added, "You may remember that Abdu El Yezdi's scalp was similarly tattooed by the Nāga at the Mountains of the Moon. In his case, it was required to enable a procedure that sent him through time independent of the suits, though other factors, of a complex nature, were involved. He never fully explained the process to us, which means we can't reproduce it."

"I wouldn't let you if you could," Burton growled. "So what is the point of this confounded liberty?"

"We don't know," Babbage said. "I shall have to keep you under observation. Run some tests."

"Most certainly not. I've been subjected to quite enough, thank you very much."

"Did the synthetic intelligence apprehend anything from the Field Amplifier?" Gooch asked.

Burton nodded—and immediately regretted it as pain lanced through his cranium. He said, "Perhaps," then recounted his visions, first of the woman, then of Oxford and the black diamond.

"The woman was his wife," he finished, "pregnant in the initial vision, which was overlaid onto my view of the workshop, but not in the more involved and vivid second, which took me to a period before they were married, and in which I was so utterly immersed that I thought myself him. My—that is to say, Oxford's—love for her was exceedingly strong."

He stopped and swallowed as an ache squeezed at his heart. He wanted to see Isabel. It was a torture to know that in some other versions of this world, she still lived.

Why can I not be one of those other Burtons? One of the more fortunate ones?

He went on, "But there was no trace of lunacy in the memory, so I wonder whether it came from the functioning helmet rather than from the imprint in the Field Preserver."

"You're probably correct," Babbage said. "The confounded headpiece erased all the data from my device, injected the diamond dust into you, and immediately ceased to function. We have nothing of Edward Oxford remaining except for what's in your scalp, and that won't last for long."

"The tattoo will come out?"

"No, it's too deep. What I mean to say is that the traces of Oxford inside it will soon be overwritten. Being in such proximity to your brain, the dust is within its electrical field. Your thoughts will quickly expunge the knowledge they contain. It's a tragedy. Genius is being replaced by the prosaic."

"Charmed, I'm sure," Burton muttered.

Swinburne said, "It appears that every time you conduct an experiment, Charles, we lose something."

Babbage bared his teeth.

Gooch made an observation. "For the second time, an intelligence to which we attribute no sentience has acted independently. There has to be interference. A meddler."

"No. I don't believe so," Burton said. He looked at Babbage. "Prior to the damaged suit's disappearance, you stated that if it had been the only one in our possession—if Abdu El Yezdi had never given you a pristine version—you would have transferred power from its Nimtz generator to its helmet, hoping to instigate self-repair mode."

Babbage put his fingertips to his chin and tapped it. "I did say that, yes. It would have been the obvious course of action."

"Well, what if all your counterparts in all the alternate histories—none of whom had a functional suit—did exactly that, all at precisely the same moment, nine o'clock on the fifteenth of February, 1860?"

The old man gazed at Burton, his mind obviously racing. His left eyebrow twitched upward. His mouth fell open. He put his hands together and rubbed them. "There—there—there would be the possibility that—that—by God!—that through means of resonance, the insane fragments of Edward Oxford's consciousness would—would link together across the parallel realities."

"And in consequence?"

Babbage suddenly clapped his hands and yelled, "By the Lord Harry! Active pathways!" He hugged himself and started to pace up and down at the foot of Burton's bed, his eyes focused inward.

"Active pathways," Swinburne said. "Oh, how you mingle incompatible words, Babbage. What are active pathways?"

Babbage answered as if addressing himself rather than the poet. "A thought is a burst of subtle electrical energy that flows through the brain, following paths between the cells. Every notion creates new routes. The damaged helmet couldn't function because only one route was imprinted into the diamond dust—Spring Heeled Jack's final thought. It is a static conceptual matrix, the frozen obsession of a dying madman. However—"

He stopped, frowned, placed his fingertips to his head and tapped away.

They waited.

"However. However. However. If a resonation spanned the different realities, then a potentially infinite number of—of—"

He stumbled to a halt again.

"I think I understand," Daniel Gooch murmured. He turned to Burton. "Consider it three-dimensionally. From above, you could look down and see a single path following one particular route. From ground level, though, you might see that it is actually countless paths laid one atop the other, opening up countless new avenues on the vertical."

"Enabling the synthetic intelligence to become conscious?" Burton asked.

"Trans-historically," Gooch confirmed.

"You just made that word up!" Swinburne protested.

"I mean it to suggest the notion that the intelligence, which lacked the capacity for independent action in any single history, might have gained it by extending itself across every iteration of reality."

Babbage whispered, "*Sentient*. But still insane!"

"So no one caused the damaged suit to vanish," Gooch mused. "It did it all by itself. But where did it go?"

Burton said, "Back to where—or rather, to *when*—it originally came from. The year 2202."

"You gleaned all this from the functioning helmet?" Swinburne asked. "Is it alive, too?"

Gooch answered, "Was, in a manner of speaking. Not now. Inevitably, it must have also been influenced by the resonance. Whatever intelligence has been formed by the multiple iterations of the suit, the sole undamaged helmet was probably the only sane element of it." He narrowed his eyes at the king's agent. "Now it appears to be a part of you. Intriguing!"

Babbage stopped pacing and peered at Burton. "Whence this theory? I demand to know!"

The king's agent climbed out of the bed and crossed to where his clothes were folded upon a chair. He started to dress. "I have witnessed your counterparts in other histories, Charles. In all of them, he did exactly what you've stated you would do. I watched him connect the damaged suit's helmet to the Nimtz generator and in every case the suit vanished."

"You witnessed?" Gooch interjected. "Did you visit a medium?"

"No, Daniel. My mind was projected into my other selves."

"By what means?"

"Through the influence of a medical tonic called Saltzmann's Tincture."

"Ridiculous!" Babbage barked. "A magical potion? Pure fantasy! And if it were true, it would imply that someone brewed the concoction specifically so you'd be warned of the advent of this new intelligence. Who? How is it possible?"

Burton buttoned his shirt. "The identity of our ally remains a mystery. It's one I intend to solve."

Accompanied by Swinburne, the king's agent took a cab home. The sky was clear and the day's cold had a sharp bite. In the hansom's cabin, they shivered and their breath clouded from their nostrils.

While his friend waited in the vehicle, Burton entered number 14 and, two minutes later, emerged with Fidget.

"Is the beast really necessary?" Swinburne huffed, folding his legs up onto the seat as Burton climbed in. "Haven't I suffered enough?"

"Correct me if I'm wrong," Burton said, "but you haven't been beaten black and blue, rendered unconscious, and tattooed against your will."

"Nevertheless, I value my ankles. They're a vital part of me. They keep my feet attached to my legs."

Burton bumped his cane against the roof of the cabin. The hansom jolted into motion.

"I say, Richard, are we caught up in a feud between two Edward Oxfords, one demented and the other with his marbles intact?"

"I posit but a single Oxford consciousness. One that betrayed itself when its single fragment of sanity indicated to me where the rest had fled."

"That's how you interpret what you saw?"

"With regard to the initial vision of Oxford's pregnant wife, certainly. The longing for her was overwhelming."

"So he's jumped back to 2202 to find her," Swinburne mused.

"The tragedy of it being that he won't arrive in the 2202 from which he came, for it no longer exists. He wiped it out of existence when he changed the past. That, I believe, is what the second part of the vision was attempting to show me."

"Surely he must know? Isn't it the very fact that sent him over the edge?"

"It is, but perhaps 2202 is the only point of reference remaining to him."

"No," Swinburne said. "There's another."

"What?"

"The man who killed him. Sir Richard Francis Burton. Which might explain why he's sending his henchmen back in time to beat seven bells out of you."

"I should consult with Doctor Monroe at Bethlem Hospital," Burton murmured. "He might offer useful insight into the workings of an unsound mind."

The king's agent looked out of the cab's window. Flowers crammed the city's every nook and cranny, clung to every untrodden surface. He murmured, "Are we to be overgrown? I wonder how this foliage fits into the picture?"

They travelled to Oxford Street and disembarked outside Shudders' Pharmacy.

"I just sent a boy with a message for you," the old man exclaimed as they entered his shop. "A box of two hundred bottles was dropped off an hour ago. An extraordinary amount. They normally only bring twenty at a time."

"Dropped off by whom, Mr. Shudders?"

"The usual young lads."

"By wagon?"

"Yes. Why such a large delivery, though? I'm most puzzled."

"Will you take us through to the back yard, please?"

The pharmacist gestured for them to follow and led them out into the little cobbled area.

"Did the wagon come in?" Burton asked.

"It did."

"Then it'll have some of that anise adhered to its wheels." Burton turned to Swinburne, "Let's see if Fidget can earn back the money I paid for him."

"And once he's done his job," the poet responded, "perhaps you'll return him to Mr. Toppletree?"

"I think not."

Burton pulled the basset hound across to the gates, squatted, and watched the dog as it snuffled around, tail wagging, obviously excited by the strong odour.

"Follow, Fidget! Follow!"

The hound strained at its lead and loosed a gruff bark.

"Come on!" Burton called. "He's caught the scent! Thank you, Mr. Shudders."

"My pleasure," Shudders mouthed, looking thoroughly perplexed.

Burton and Swinburne raced after Fidget as he plunged out of the gate and into Poland Street.

"He's taking us to the last piece of the puzzle!" Burton cried out. "I feel sure of it!"

CHAPTER 8

THE DREAMING ROSE

Today will die tomorrow.
—Algernon Charles Swinburne

It was quite the foot-slog. Fidget dragged them out into Oxford Street's traffic, and amid the cursing of indignant drivers they wove their way through panting vehicles and whinnying horses, in and out of billowing clouds of hot steam and gritty smoke, along to Holborn and up onto the Hackney Road. They arced around the northern border of the fire-ravaged and now overgrown Cauldron, then south down Saint Leonard Street all the way to Limehouse Cut Canal.

"Back into the East End!" Swinburne cried out.

The waterway marked a straight border at the edge of the vanished slums, the ruins of which were now completely buried beneath an amassed tangle of red. Facing the jungle, the flame-blackened sides of factories loomed over the channel.

All but one of the buildings were active, with fumes belching out of their towering chimneys and wagons arriving and departing from their loading bays. The exception was a seven-storeys-high derelict with nary a windowpane that wasn't either cracked or broken.

"My hat, Richard!" Swinburne said. "Isn't that the place Abdu El Yezdi wrote of in his first account? The home of the mysterious boy known as the Beetle?"

"It is. In the history El Yezdi came from, the lad was head of the League of Chimney Sweeps, which doesn't exist in our variant of reality."

"Yet we have Locks Limited," the poet murmured. "Without the K, I'll warrant. L.O.C.S.—League of Chimney Sweeps."

Fidget guided them around to the front of the abandoned factory, and there they found a wagon parked by a double door. The basset hound stopped by one of its wheels, pressed his nose against its rim, gave a bark, then cocked his leg and wetted it.

"Phew! There's nothing like a fast hike across the city to keep the cold at bay. We must have walked five miles, at least," Swinburne said. "What a nose the little devil possesses, to have followed the trail all that way."

He paced over to a dirty window and squinted through the fractured glass. "Have a look at this!"

Burton joined him and saw that thick scarlet leaves completely blocked the view. The jungle was inside the building.

The king's agent moved to the doors, tried them, and found them to be secured. He rapped on the portal with the head of his cane.

No response.

Swinburne hammered his knuckles against the window. "Hallo! Hallo! Anyone at home?" A narrow wedge of glass toppled from the pane and clinked onto the ground by his feet.

They waited. Nothing.

Burton bent and examined the door's keyhole. "It's a basic deadlock. I'll have it open in a jiffy."

He retrieved a set of picks from his pocket and got to work. It took him less than a minute. There came two clicks, a clunk, and a loud creak as he pulled the doors open.

His breath hissed out through his teeth in a little cloud.

Swinburne gave a squawk of surprise.

The doors opened onto a tunnel through dense vermilion vegetation. Very little light filtered in through the factory's dirty windows, but among the crowded leaves and tangled branches, strange fruits hung, glowing like little lanterns.

"A fairy grotto!" Swinburne exclaimed.

"A fiery grotto," Burton corrected. He took a cautious step forward. "This tunnel hasn't been cut or even cultivated. The plant appears to have grown into an arched pathway quite naturally. How thoroughly odd." He moved a little farther into the building. "Shall we see where it goes?"

He closed the door behind them and tied the end of his dog's lead to its latch. "Wait here, Fidget."

Very slowly, listening for any sound, they proceeded through the closely packed verdure.

The jungle's leaves showed enormous variety, some being smooth edged, others crinkly. Its flowers ranged from tightly bunched petals to splayed blooms, some as small as daisies, others wider than Burton's arm span. Branches went from bulky limbs to spindly twigs. All were contorted and twisted, curling this way and that, corkscrewing, bending and dividing in every direction, ending in buds and fruits and big gourd-like growths.

The scent was delicious, heady, and intoxicating. Burton started to feel—albeit faintly—the same euphoria that Saltzmann's gave him, and, as they moved forward into the factory, he noted that Swinburne appeared to be fast slipping into a state of reverie.

They rounded one tight bend after another.

"A labyrinth?" Swinburne whispered. His voice was slurred.

"A single path," Burton noted, "folding back and forth but gradually guiding us to the centre."

"What Minotaur awaits us, I wonder?"

They kept going.

Burton noted that the floor was carpeted with a springy layer of fibrous roots, all matted together, and that the plant was somehow generating heat, for the atmosphere felt warm and humid.

"I feel very peculiar," Swinburne mumbled.

"The aroma," the king's agent responded.

"It's affecting you the same way, Richard? You feel a sense of—of—?"

Burton glanced at his colleague. "Endless possibilities?"

"Yes, that's it. I find myself so relaxed that poetry is positively flooding from me. By golly! Such inspiration!"

Throwing his head back, he sleepily declaimed:

I hid my heart in a nest of roses,
Out of the sun's way, hidden apart;
In a softer bed than the soft white snow's is,
Under the roses I hid my heart.

He stopped and gave a dopey grin, then his eyes widened and he emitted a gasp as a voice whispered:

Why would it sleep not? Why should it start,
When never a leaf of the rose-tree stirred?
What made sleep flutter his wings and part?
Only the song of a secret bird.

"My hat! Who said that?"

Burton pointed up into the branches to their right. "There's someone there. A child, I think."

The voice, susurrating like leaves in a breeze, said, "Please. Don't look at me. Walk on. The path is nearly ended. You are expected and welcome."

"I can't make him out in the—in the—" Swinburne said. He suddenly yawned, before finishing, "in the gloom."

"Hey, lad!" Burton called. "Come out of there. We mean no harm."

"How did you finish my verse?" Swinburne added, speaking very slowly. "I only just thought of it."

"It is the song of the rose," came the reply. "Follow the path."

The king's agent looked at his companion, shrugged, and continued on. They walked, aware that the small figure was scrambling from branch to branch and keeping pace with them. Burton tried to catch sight of the boy, but the leaves were so densely packed, and the red light so deep and shadow-filled, that he could discern little of him.

Rounding a bend, they stepped out into a clearing; a domed space completely enclosed by foliage from which hundreds of glowing fruits dangled in clusters, like fat grapes. In its middle, a bush humped up from the floor, and at its top a single flower blossomed, a red rose of phenomenal proportions, almost three feet in circumference, with fat bees and colourful butterflies and bright motes drifting lazily in the air around it.

The perfume was thick and cloying. Burton staggered and sank to his knees.

Leaves rustled as their escort moved around the edge of the glade.

"Are you the Beetle?" Burton murmured.

"Yes," came the whispered reply.

"You manufacture Saltzmann's Tincture?"

"It comes from the gourds."

"Then this vegetation has been here for some considerable time?" Like Swinburne, Burton had to stop to yawn. "Long before the seeds fell?"

"It began to grow up through the planks of the floor a little more than five years ago. This Wednesday past, it produced the seeds and sent them out of the factory's chimneys to summon you here."

"To summon me?"

"To summon your companion. The poet is the key."

"Hallo? Excuse me? What? What?" Swinburne drawled.

From the amid the crowded leaves, and with much creaking and squeaking, two slim branches extended, heavy gourds drooping from each.

"Moving?" Swinburne slurred. "Is the jungle moving?"

The gourds dropped and cracked at Burton's and Swinburne's feet. Thick honey-coloured liquid oozed from them.

"Drink, Mr. Swinburne," the Beetle whispered. "You too, Sir Richard."

Swinburne sat cross-legged on the carpet of roots, between Burton and the rose, with the gourd in front of him. Burton, with his unswollen eye blurring, tried to focus on his friend. For a brief moment, he saw him clearly. Swinburne's green eyes were wide. His pupils were distended. He appeared to be in a trance. Pink butterflies were fluttering around him and settling on his shoulders. Burton thought he might be hallucinating. He looked up and felt sure that, in the small gaps between the vegetation above, he could glimpse a night sky milky with stars.

Impossible.

Swinburne closed his eyes, a slight smile on his face, raised the gourd, and drank from it.

Burton fought to make sense of what he was seeing. The poet resembled a dreaming Buddha, the red of his hair merging with the red of the rose behind him, until the poet and the blossom appeared to merge into one.

Though he didn't will them to do so, Burton's hands grasped the gourd and raised it to his mouth. He swallowed sweet viscous liquid.

A voice, like Swinburne's but reverberating as if spoken into an echoing cavern, sounded in his mind:

> *Time, thy name is sorrow, says the stricken*
> *Heart of life, laid waste with wasting flame*
> *Ere the change of things and thoughts requicken,*
> *Time, thy name.*

"Algy, get out of my damned head!" Burton moaned.

From the vegetation, the Beetle urged, "Don't resist it. The weight of ages is upon you."

What the hell does that mean?

The voice continued:

> *Girt about with shadow, blind and lame,*
> *Ghosts of things that smite and thoughts that sicken*
> *Hunt and hound thee down to death and shame.*

The unaccountable sense that he was not in an East London factory but deep in Central Africa swept through him. The Mountains of the Moon!

> *Eyes of hours whose paces halt or quicken*
> *Read in blood-red lines of loss and blame,*
> *Writ where cloud and darkness round it thicken,*
> *Time, thy name.*

Was the rose reciting the verse? A talking flower?

> *Nay, but rest is born of me for healing,*
> *—So might haply time, with voice represt,*
> *Speak: is grief the last gift of my dealing?*
> *Nay, but rest.*

Petals unfurling. Ages unfolding. Time, curling around itself, opening its secrets.

Petal layered upon petal. History layered upon history.

What am I seeing?

The Beetle's voice: "The world's narrative."

> *All the world is wearied, east and west,*
> *Tired with toil to watch the slow sun wheeling,*
> *Twelve loud hours of life's laborious quest.*

Burton tried to distinguish between his vision and his imagination. He couldn't. Jumbled sensations bubbled and swirled through him. A rose, a poet, a rhythm, an utterance that chanted through eternity, sprouting from within itself—the seed as the verbalisation, the shoot as the emerging verse, the blossom as signification, the pollination as cognisance, the fruit of understanding, again the seed.

Time is a form of expression? A language? A lyric? The words sung to a tune? A dance?

Pulsating colours. Stratified harmonies. Invasive fragrances.

> *Eyes forespent with vigil, faint and reeling,*
> *Find at last my comfort, and are blest,*
> *Not with rapturous light of life's revealing—*
> *Nay, but rest.*

Slowly, the words metamorphosed. They became flavours. The flavours became colours. The colours became sensations. The sensations became numbers.

An equation.

It pulsed away from him, and the farther it withdrew, the more of itself it revealed, until he could see the entirety; a megalithic, looping, paradoxical mathematical structure of such esoteric intricacy that, for a moment, he viewed it with an utter lack of comprehension.

Then it slotted into place, and he understood it as Edward Oxford had understood it.

He opened his eyes, looked at the bedroom ceiling, and thought about the attempted assassination. Turning his head, he gazed at the woman who lay sleeping beside him—the woman who'd been his wife for the past two years.

She was pregnant.

I must understand my roots, he thought. *Else the branches may bear bad fruit.*

Later, in his laboratory, he shaved thin slivers from the side of the black diamond, hooked them up to a BioProc, marvelled at the output, and gradually realised what the data meant. His equation may have been labyrinthine in its complexity, but filtered through a BioProc, it also became practical.

He could do it.

He could travel back.

He could watch.

Sir Richard Francis Burton momentarily opened his eye. He saw red jungle but didn't comprehend it.

Burton? Who is Burton? My name is Edward Oxford.

His eyelid slid shut, and it was six months later. During that period, he'd constructed a suit of fish-scale batteries; had connected the shards of diamond to a chain of CellComps and BioProcs, forming the heart of the main control unit—a device he named a *Nimtz generator*—and had embedded an AugCom and BioProcs enhanced with powdered black diamond into a helmet. It acted as an interface between his brain and the generator and would also protect him from the deep psychological shock he suspected might affect a person who stepped too far out of their native segment of history.

If the prototype worked as planned, its various elements could later be created at a cellular level and coded directly into his body. Such an augmentation could never be made public. There was only one black diamond—

There are three.

—and he could see no way to replicate its unique qualities. As it was, in order to integrate it with his biological functions, he'd have to powder some of the gem and tattoo it into his skin—a primitive solution and, obviously, one that couldn't be applied to the entire population.

Besides, what would happen if everyone in the world could travel through time?

So, no bio-integration for the moment. And no tattooing. Just the clunky old-school technology—a thing he would wear—and if the experiment worked, he'd consider the next step afterwards.

By now, the project had kept him out of the public eye for a considerable period, and journalists were clamouring for another interview. Not wanting to arouse their suspicions, he eventually conceded. After explaining that he was working on a new theory of botanic integration, he was asked the usual questions. Did the recording of information directly into individuals' DNA—which had commenced a century ago—mark a new step in evolution? With the old computer technologies now completely supplanted by cellular manipulation, could the human body itself be regarded as a machine? Had the replacement of the New Web with the Aether resulted in a new understanding of botanic sentience, and what were the implications? Might that sentience be incorporated into human consciousness?

He answered distractedly, his mind all the while considering the gravitational constants to which his calculations had to be tethered, else his jump through time would also become a disastrous jump into the far reaches of space.

Then it came again. "How does it feel to single-handedly change history?"

He offered exactly the same reply as before. "I haven't changed history. History is the past." Then he chuckled, and there was an edge to the sound, and the following day it was reported that Edward Oxford was obviously working too hard and needed a holiday.

Two weeks after everything else was complete, he hit upon a ridiculously simple solution to the last remaining difficulty. When the bubble of energy generated by the Nimtz formed around the suit, it was essential that it touched nothing but air, else it would carve a chunk out of whatever it was in contact with, and the shock of that could seriously injure him. Initially, Burton thought he'd have to jump off a bridge to achieve this, but then in a moment of mad inspiration, he designed boots fitted with two-foot-high spring-loaded stilts. Whimsical they may have been, but they solved the problem. Leap high into the air. Jump through time. Don't take anything with you.

On the first day of February in the year 2202, he told his wife what he intended to do.

She rested a hand on her distended belly and said, "I'd rather you waited until our child is born."

"Because you fear for me?"

"Yes, of course."

"There's no danger. If the coordinates I set are inside or contiguous with a solid object at the destination point, the device will automatically readjust them."

"But what if you do something that interferes with events as they happened?"

"I have no intention of doing anything except watch my ancestor attempt to kill Queen Victoria then move a day or so ahead of the event to chat with him. I'll listen to whatever he has to say but shan't attempt to dissuade him. Besides, if I was to do anything to alter history, then time must possess some sort of mechanism to correct the interference, else we'd know about it, wouldn't we?"

"How?"

"There would be an anomaly of some sort."

She voiced her doubt with a hum, and added, "And what if your ancestor attacks you? He's obviously capable of violence."

"I'll be careful. If he gets agitated, I'll make a rapid departure."

His wife chewed her lip and looked uncertain.

Burton experienced a pang of guilt. He'd told an unanticipated lie.

I'm not going to just watch him. I'm not going to just talk to him. I'm going to stop him. Yes! Stop him!

The intention was unexpected; it had come out of nowhere.

He shrugged it off and put a hand on his partner's knee. "It's all right. Really, it is. Nothing can possibly go wrong."

"When?" she whispered.

"In two weeks. On my birthday."

And so it was.

On the fifteenth of February, 2202, Burton completed his preparations. He dressed in mock Victorian clothing—with a copy of the letter from his ancestor in one of the pockets—pulled his time suit on over the outfit, affixed the Nimtz generator to his chest, strapped the boots over thinner leather ones, and lowered the round black helmet onto his head.

Intricate magnetic fields flooded through his skull. Information began to pass back and forth between his brain and the helmet's BioProcs. The structure of his brainwaves soaked into the diamond dust.

Bouncing on the stilts, and with a top hat in his hand, he left his laboratory and tottered out into his long garden. Three centuries ago, Aldershot had been a small town twenty-five miles or so from central London. Now it was a suburb of the sprawling metropolis, the glittering spires of which could be seen in the near distance. He stood and contemplated them for a moment. They were intrusive. The advertising that flickered and flashed upon their sides struck him as ugly and psychologically aggressive. But there was change in the air. The era of consumerism had long passed, and such remnants were fast disappearing. The human species, it was generally agreed, was on the brink of becoming something rather more elegant than it had ever been before—something that, perhaps, would integrate with its environment in a subtler manner. No one knew what or how. They just knew it was going to happen.

His wife came out of the kitchen and walked over to him, wiping her hands on a tea towel.

"You're going now?" she asked. "Supper is almost ready."

"Yes," he replied. "But don't worry. Even if I'm gone for years, I'll be back in five minutes."

"You won't return an old man, I hope," she grumbled, and placed a hand on her stomach. "This one will need an energetic young father."

He laughed. "Don't be silly. This won't take long."

Bending, he kissed her on her freckled nose.

He straightened and instructed the suit to take him to five-thirty on the afternoon of the tenth of June, 1840, location: the upper corner of Green Park, London.

He looked at the sky.

Am I really going to do this?

An inner voice that hardly felt a part of him urged, *Do it!*

In answer, Burton took three long strides, hit the ground with knees bent, and launched himself high into the air. A bubble formed around him. It popped. He fell, thudded onto grass, and bounced. Glancing around, he saw a rolling park surrounded by tall towers. In the near distance, there was the ancient form of the Monarchy Museum, once known as Buckingham Palace, where the relics of England's defunct royal families were displayed.

A thicket lay just ahead. Burton ran into it, ducking among the trees.

He reached up to his helmet and switched it off.

A foul stench assaulted his nostrils: a mix of raw sewage, rotting fish, and burning fossil fuels.

He started to cough. The air was thick and gritty. It irritated his eyes and scraped his windpipe. He fell to his knees and clutched at his throat, gasping for oxygen. Then he remembered he'd prepared for this and, after opening the suit's front, fumbled in his jacket pocket, pulling out a small instrument, which he applied to the side of his neck. He pressed the switch, it hissed, he felt a slight stinging sensation, and instantly could breathe again.

Burton put the instrument away and rested for a moment. His inability to catch his breath had been a perceptive disorder rather than a physical one. The helmet's AugMems had protected him from the idea that the atmosphere was unbreathable—now a sedative was doing the job.

He unclipped his boots, kicked them off, and quickly slipped out of the time suit. He stood and straightened his clothes, placed the top hat on his head, and made his way to the edge of the thicket. As he emerged from the trees, a transformed world assailed his senses, and he was immediately shaken by a profound uneasiness.

Only the grass was familiar.

Through air made hazy by burning fossil fuels, he saw a massive expanse of empty sky. The towers of his own time were absent—they'd been nothing but an illusion projected onto his senses by the headpiece. London appeared to be clinging to the ground and slumbering under a blanket of relative silence, though, from the nearby road, he could hear horses' hooves, the rumble of wheels, and the shouts of hawkers.

Ahead, Buckingham Palace, now partially hidden by a high wall, looked brand-new.

Quaintly costumed people were walking in the park.

No, not costumed. They always dress this way.

Burton started to walk down the slope toward the base of Constitution Hill, struggling to overcome his growing sense of dislocation.

"Steady, Edward," he muttered to himself. "Hang on, hang on. Don't let it overwhelm you. This is neither a dream nor an illusion, so stay focused, get the job done, then get back to your suit."

Job? What job? I am here to observe, that is all.

Again, it was as if a second voice existed inside him. It whispered, *Stop him! Stop your ancestor!*

Burton reached the wide path. The queen's carriage would pass this way soon.

My God! I'm going to see Queen Victoria!

He looked around. Every single person in sight was wearing a hat or bonnet. Most of the men were bearded or moustachioed. The women held parasols.

He examined faces. Which belonged to his forebear? He'd never seen a photograph of the original Edward Oxford, but he hoped to detect some sort of family resemblance. He stepped over the low fence lining the path, crossed to the other side, and loitered near a tree.

People started to gather along the route. He heard a remarkable range of accents, and they all sounded ridiculously exaggerated. Some, which he identified as working class, were incomprehensible, while the upper classes spoke with a precision and clarity that seemed wholly artificial.

Details kept catching his eye, holding his attention with hypnotic force: the prevalence of litter and dog faeces; the stains and worn patches on people's clothing; rotten teeth and rickets-twisted legs; accentuated mannerisms and lace-edged handkerchiefs; pockmarks and consumptive coughs.

"Focus!" he whispered.

A cheer went up. He looked to his right. The queen's carriage had just emerged from the palace gates, its horses guided by a postilion. Two outriders trotted along ahead of the vehicle, two more behind.

Where was his ancestor? Where was the gunman?

Ahead of him, a man wearing a top hat, blue frock coat, and white britches straightened, reached under his coat, and moved closer to the path.

Slowly, the royal carriage approached.

"Is it him?" Burton muttered, gazing at the back of the man's head.

Moments later, the forward outriders came alongside.

The blue-coated individual stepped over the fence and, as the queen and her husband passed, took three strides to keep up with their vehicle, then whipped out a flintlock pistol, aimed, and fired. He threw down the smoking weapon and drew a second.

Burton yelled, "No, Edward!" and ran forward.

What the hell am I doing?

The gunman glanced at him.

Burton vaulted over the fence and grabbed his ancestor's raised arm. If he could just disarm him and drag him away, tell him to flee and forget this stupid prank.

They struggled, locked together.

"Give it up!" Burton pleaded.

"Let go of me!" the would-be assassin yelled. "My name must be remembered. I must live through history!"

I must live through history. I must live through history.

The words throbbed into the future, echoed through time.

The second flintlock detonated, the recoil jolting both men.

The back of Queen Victoria's skull exploded.

Burton gripped the gunman, shook him, and heaved him off his feet.

His ancestor fell backward, and his head impacted against the low cast-iron fence. There was a crunch, and a spike suddenly emerged from the man's eye. He twitched and went limp.

"You're not dead!" Burton exclaimed, staggering back. "You're not dead! Stand up! Run for it! Don't let them catch you!"

The assassin lay on his back, his head impaled, blood pooling beneath him.

Burton stumbled away.

There were screams and cries, people pushing past him.

He saw Victoria. She was tiny, young, like a child's doll, and her shredded brain was oozing onto the ground.

No. No. No.

This isn't happening.

This can't happen.

This didn't happen.

Burton backed away, feeling terrified, fell, got up again, shoved his way out of the milling crowd, and ran.

"Get back to the suit," he mumbled as his legs pumped. "Try something else."

He raced up the slope and ran into the trees.

His heart was pounding.

He pushed through to where he'd left the time suit.

I'll go farther back. I'll change this.

He suddenly registered that someone was behind him. Before he could turn, an arm encircled his neck and squeezed with agonising force, crushing his throat. He saw his suit, the boots and headpiece, just feet away. He reached for them, but it was hopeless. He knew he was going to die.

A man hissed in his ear, "You don't deserve this, but I have to do it again. I'm sorry."

Do it again?

He felt his head being twisted.

My neck! My neck! Get off me!

His vertebrae crunched.

White light flared.

He felt suspended, as if time had halted.

He heard Charles Babbage's voice.

"It is nine o'clock on the fifteenth of February, 1860."

"It is nine o'clock on the fifteenth of February, 1860."

"It is nine o'clock on the fifteenth of February, 1860."

"It is nine o'clock on the fifteenth of February, 1860."

"It is nine o'clock on the fifteenth of February, 1860."

The voice overlaid itself again and again, as if thousands of Babbages were speaking at once.

Flee! Burton thought. *Get away from here! Back home! Back home in time for supper! Back home! Back home in time!*

CHAPTER 9

AN UNLIKELY EXPEDITION

Talk, talk, talk, and while you are talking, the Chinese are exacting yet another tax, undermining yet more of our trade agreements, imposing ever more restrictive practices, undermining our economy with increasingly ruthless cunning and guile. Talk as much as you wish, but I am taking action. I shall burn the Old Summer Palace. I shall bomb the Forbidden City. I shall line up supporters of the Qing Dynasty and shoot them in their heads. China shall feel my pitiless wrath, and China will capitulate. Then, you can stop talking. Instead, you can listen, and you will hear, "We concede. Lord Elgin has made us understand."
—James Bruce, Eighth Earl of Elgin

It was one o'clock in the afternoon on Monday the twentieth of February, and fourteen individuals were gathered in the library of suite five at the Royal Venetia Hotel. They were not particularly comfortable, for the room was bursting at the seams with books and the group had difficulty finding places to sit or stand among them. The volumes, which ranged from boys' adventure novels to esoteric tracts, from political memoirs to philosophical treatises, lined every wall from floor to ceiling, were stacked high on the deep red carpet, and were piled haphazardly in every corner.

Sir Richard Francis Burton's brother, Edward, presided over the meeting. Morbidly obese, with a face disfigured by scars, he was wrapped, as was his habit, in a threadbare red dressing gown and occupied an enormous wing-backed armchair of scuffed and cracked leather. There was a half-empty tankard of ale on the table beside him. His clockwork butler, Grumbles—with his canister-shaped head of brass cocked slightly to one side—was standing nearby, ready to refill the glass.

"So the jungle is dying?" Edward asked.

"*Withdrawing* might be the better term," Burton replied. "In a few days, nothing of it will remain except mulch. It has fulfilled its purpose. London will soon be clear of its unseasonal blooms."

"Sentient herbage. Utterly preposterous."

"That's not the least of it. The jungle and Algernon are one and the same."

Edward Burton glowered at the king's agent, then at Detective Inspectors William Trounce and Sidney Slaughter, Police Constable Thomas Honesty, Sadhvi Raghavendra, Daniel Gooch, Charles Babbage, Richard Monckton Milnes, Captain Nathaniel Lawless, Maneesh Krishnamurthy, Shyamji Bhatti and Montague Penniforth. Together, these individuals comprised the secretive Ministry of Chronological Affairs, of which he was the head.

"All of you give credence to this fantasy, I suppose?" he asked.

"I trust Sir Richard's judgement," Gooch said.

"Likewise," Trounce muttered. "Which means I may have to start doubting my own."

The others nodded, apart from Babbage, who appeared to be counting his fingers.

The minister addressed Swinburne. "And what do you make of it, young man?"

The poet kicked spasmodically, accidentally knocking over a stack of books, and shrilled, "It's delicious! The jungle is me and I am it and we are one and the same. Or some such."

"That isn't much help."

"May I partake of a bottle of your ale, Minister? I feel sure it will clarify my thoughts."

Edward Burton impatiently waved his permission.

Burton said, "We know that in Abdu El Yezdi's native history, when he trekked to the Mountains of the Moon, a version of Algy went with him. El Yezdi never explained what happened to his companion, but he does record that a Prussian agent, Count Zeppelin, followed them, and that the man possessed venomous talons—a product of eugenics. As fantastic as it sounds, the toxin caused an individual named Rigby to transform into vegetation. It appears that the same fate befell the poet."

From the sideboard to which he'd moved, and with a bottle in one hand and a glass in the other, Swinburne said, "The other jolly old Swinburne is now a plant-based consciousness. It possesses a unique perception of time and is aware of every variant of history. It was able to send its roots through into our world to warn us what has happened. Simply splendid! I feel thoroughly proud of it, him, and myself!"

Edward gave a puff of incredulity. He lifted his ale, gulped it down, and jabbed a fat forefinger toward his brother. "It inflicted the visions upon you?"

"They weren't visions exactly," Burton corrected. "The jungle worked with the Beetle and the children under his command to produce Saltzmann's Tincture from its fruits. Through a vague mesmeric influence, and over the course of half a decade, it introduced the decoction to me and slowly increased its potency. The most recent doses caused my awareness to slide from one iteration of history to another, drawing my attention to the advent of what we might term the Spring Heeled Jack consciousness, which was created when all the Charles Babbages across all the histories performed the same experiment at the same moment."

"It knew ahead of the event that it would occur?"

"As I say, the jungle has a unique perception."

"And what of your experiences as Edward Oxford?"

Burton paused to light a cheroot. "The one sane fragment of Spring Heeled Jack caused black diamond dust to be injected into my scalp. It was an act of suicide, for my own thoughts would soon overwrite it. However, before that occurred, I received from it memories of the time suit's construction and the final moments of its inventor. It was a message, or rather, it was the gift of an essential item of information."

"What information?"

"Before I answer that, I think you should hear what the jungle showed Algy."

The minister turned his eyes back to the poet.

"Well?"

Swinburne, who had a glass to his lips, swallowed hastily, coughed, spluttered, and dragged a sleeve across his mouth. "What? Pardon? Hello?"

"Your leafy counterpart," the king's agent said to him. "Give an account of your experience while under its influence."

"Ah, yes. I say! This is a fine beer, Your Maj—um—your ministery-ness. What! Er. Well. It happens to be the case, apparently, that our history is where the destiny of the human race will be played out. This, thanks to the efforts of Abdu El Yezdi—he having averted the next century's world wars, the ones that'll so afflict the other histories. Ours is the stage upon which Mr. Darwin's theories will be enacted." Swinburne moved back to his seat, sat, and crossed then uncrossed his legs. "In our distant future, the year 2202 should be one of transcendence and transformation. Perhaps Oxford's breakthrough, his overcoming of the limitations of time, is meant to be a part of it. Unfortunately, it has all gone completely arse over elbow."

"Because of Spring Heeled Jack, I presume," the minister said.

"Yes. The insane Oxford consciousness has fled back to that year and has there somehow blocked the evolutionary process."

"And the jungle knows this—?"

"Because it is—that is to say, I'm—it's there." Swinburne hiccupped.

Detective Inspector Slaughter, who had a tankard of milk in his hand, cleared his throat, smoothed his huge moustache, and said, "Forgive me for interrupting, and forgive me again if I seem a little cold-hearted, but need we be overly concerned about events that are occurring three and a half hundred years hence? We shall be long dead by 2202, after all."

Constable Honesty snapped, "Child on the way. One day, perhaps, grandchildren. So forth."

Slaughter held up a hand. "I concede your point, Constable. I myself have a daughter."

"With all due respect," Burton said, "the issue goes deeper even than protecting your descendants. Every evening since Charles performed his experiment, we have been invaded by stilted mechanisms."

"Eleven of the monstrosities last night," Trounce interjected.

"That the Oxford consciousness is sending them back to the year it was created implies what we might term a soul searching, a quest for identity."

"Why are the creatures so obsessed with you?" Monckton Milnes asked.

"Because Oxford has twice been killed by a Richard Burton, and those deaths, paradoxically, were integral to the creation of this Spring Heeled Jack intelligence."

Trounce snorted. "By Jove! Does it think you're its father?"

"I wouldn't go that far, old fellow, but it may well regard me as essential to its growing self-awareness, and I'm certain it fears me and has an irrational need to kill me."

"Patricide," Slaughter put in. He shook his head wonderingly. "Though—no offence intended—it isn't going about it in a very efficient manner, is it? Why are the stilt men so—"

"Nutty," Swinburne interjected. "Absolutely bonkers."

"I was going to say *disoriented*."

Burton drew on his cheroot and blew out a plume of blue smoke. "If the Spring Heeled Jack mind is still coalescing into a functioning entity, perhaps they reflect its incompleteness."

Edward Burton signed for Grumbles to refill his glass. "It has to be stopped."

"Yes," the king's agent replied.

"What, brother, do you suggest we do?"

Turning to Babbage, Burton said, "Charles?"

Daniel Gooch reached out and prodded the preoccupied scientist, who looked up, blinked, and said, "I'm not to blame. The probability of all my selves performing the experiment at the same moment is so low as to be virtually inconceivable. The only explanation is that time itself possesses an agenda."

"No one regards you as the source of the problem," Burton said. "But you might have the solution."

"How so?"

"In one of the alternate histories, you proposed to apply the principles of the time suit to a specially constructed vehicle in order to send a group of us through history."

"Did I, indeed?" Babbage exclaimed.

"Microscopic components reproduced in macroscopic form. Could you do it?"

"Hmm!" Babbage raised his fingers to his head—tap tap tap!—and muttered, "I've just finished designing the Mark Three probability calculator. It has nowhere near the power of the suit's helmet, but I daresay it could be adapted to the task. We also have plenty of the black diamond shards. However, without the mathematical formula that enables the procedure—"

Burton reached up and, aping the scientist's habitual gesture, tapped his own head. "I have the equation. That was the message given to me by the diamond dust, by the undamaged helmet. The jungle helped me to understand it."

Babbage gave a shout of excitement and leaped to his feet. "You can recall it?"

"If I put myself into a mesmeric trance, I should be able to retrieve the memory. I warn you, though, that writing out the formula will probably take some days. It is exceedingly complex."

"By the Lord Harry!" Babbage exclaimed. He wrung his hands eagerly then stopped and frowned. "Hmm. But it won't solve the principal difficulty, which is that to duplicate the suit's function I'd have to create a machine the size of a room. It would need to be inside a very large vehicle, and a flying one at that."

Burton addressed Nathaniel Lawless. "Captain?"

Lawless's face turned as white as his finely trimmed beard, and he stammered, "Surely—surely you don't mean to—to—to pilot the *Orpheus* into the future?"

"Yes!" Babbage shouted. "Yes! I could adapt your rotorship!"

"Pah!" Edward Burton barked. "Dick, this is an absurd notion! You mean to take the fight to Spring Heeled Jack? To the year 2202? What will you do when you get there? You'll be hopelessly lost. A fish out of water. A centuries-old antique!"

"Richard," Monckton Milnes added softly, "the shock of finding himself outside of his own era turned Oxford into a raving lunatic. What's to prevent the same from happening to you?"

"The jungle had two hundred bottles of Saltzmann's delivered to my pharmacist," Burton said. "A small dose each day will be sufficient to counter the deleterious effects."

Sadhvi Raghavendra protested, "On what do you base that supposition?"

"I've been using the tonic for five years. I'm well acquainted with its effects."

She gave a dismissive wave of a hand. "It turned you into an addict."

"A froth-mouthed gibbering imbecile," Swinburne added.

"Hardly that, Algy. And the addiction is already easing now that its purpose is achieved."

Raghavendra arched an eyebrow at him and said nothing more.

"I repeat," Edward Burton murmured. "What will you do?"

Burton smoked. He narrowed his eyes. He drawled, "Whatever is necessary. We'll work it out when we get there. The advantage is ours."

"And how, may I ask, do you draw that conclusion?"

"Because we can plan ahead." Burton nodded toward Thomas Honesty. "Tom has a baby on the way." He indicated Montague Penniforth and Detective Inspector Slaughter. "Monty already has a little boy, and Sidney a daughter. My Cannibal Club is populated by eligible bachelors. I propose that we transform it into a secret and elite organisation whose members will pass down to their descendants the details of our mission. We'll move forward through time in a series of jumps, stopping to meet with them along the way. They'll advise us with regard to social and technological developments. They'll keep their eyes open for Oxford's presence and will tell us if it manifests ahead of 2202, and will also assist us in avoiding detection." He spoke to Honesty, Slaughter and Penniforth. "How about it, gentlemen? Will you join the group? Will you become Cannibals?"

Honesty jerked his head in assent.

Slaughter wiped a line of milk from his moustache. "A family mission, is it? In for a penny, in for a pound, that's what I say."

Penniforth gave a thumbs-up.

Edward Burton said, "Brother, please tell me you're joking. By heavens, the whole endeavour is doomed from the start."

"If you have a better idea, let's hear it."

The minister picked at his fingernails for a moment before, in a quiet tone, saying, "How can it possibly work? Won't you simply create yet another alternate history?"

Burton turned to Babbage. "Charles?"

"You intend to make a change to the future, not to the past," the old man said. "Our reality is—from the present moment onward—thus suspended between two possibilities: you will come back from the future or you won't. For you, as you travel forward through time to 2202, the history you pass through will not be in any way defined by the answer, for you won't yet have provided it."

"What? What? What?" Swinburne screeched.

Ignoring him, Burton asked, "But if we ask someone from the future what became of us?"

"They simply won't know," Babbage replied. "Every consequence of your return—or consequence of your none return—will remain in an indefinite state until you actually do one or the other."

"And if we do return, will we be able to act on the knowledge gained from the future?"

"Yes."

"So we'd be creating yet another branch of history."

"From the perspective of the future you've returned from, yes, but subjectively, no."

"Aargh!" Swinburne shrieked. "How can time be subjective?"

"My dear boy!" Babbage exclaimed. "How can it not be?"

"I'm hearing words," Trounce grumbled, "but if you threw them into a bag, gave it a good shake, and poured them out, the results would make just as much sense to me."

The minister held up a hand to halt the discussion. "All right. All right. Let us suppose I finance the project. Who would you take with you, Dick?"

"A small company," the king's agent answered. "Volunteers only."

"Me," Swinburne said.

"And me," Sadhvi Raghavendra put in. "You'll need my medical expertise, especially if you're dosing yourselves with that horrible tincture."

"It's utterly preposterous," Detective Inspector Trounce declared. "Whatever it is. Nevertheless, you can count on me. Perhaps I'll eventually understand what I'm becoming involved with."

"The *Orpheus* is my ship," Lawless stated. "I'll not give her over to anyone else, so I'm in, too. But crew?"

"How much can be automated?" Burton asked Babbage.

"A lot. The Mark Three will fly her. I'll give the *Orpheus* a brain."

Lawless whistled. "That'll be interesting." He pursed his lips then said to Burton, "I suppose I can train you and your fellows for whatever duties remain."

"I'll come," Maneesh Krishnamurthy announced. He gripped his cousin, Bhatti, by the arm before he could also volunteer. "No, Shyamji. You've been romancing that charming young dressmaker. I have high hopes for you. Put a ring on her finger. Start a family. Throw your lot in with the Cannibal Club."

"But—"

"No argument."

Shyamji Bhatti frowned before offering a shrugged concession.

Gooch said, "You'll require an engineer to keep the airship in good order. Mr. Brunel is out of action and shows no sign of recovery. Take me."

Burton said, "Thank you, Daniel." He glanced at each of the volunteers in turn. "Seven of us, then. Let me remind all of you that even if we inadvertently cause further bifurcations in history, we can travel back along them. This world will still be here. We can return to it." He faced his brother. "Minister?"

Edward held his sibling's eyes for a second. "Very well. If only to save us from a plethora of stilted lunatics, I'll sanction this tomfoolery. I'll also see to it that the Cannibal Club receives whatever funding it requires, with one proviso; I shall lead it. The group's mission will need to be meticulously planned, its existence ingeniously concealed, its continuity assured for many generations. There is no man alive more suited to such a job than I."

"Agreed," Burton said with a slight smile.

Over the course of the next hour, the minister secured one of the hotel's private sitting rooms, and the core members of the Cannibal Club were summoned.

By seven o'clock, they were all present with the exception of Henry Murray, who'd left the city to visit friends in Somerset. Sir Richard Francis Burton, Edward Burton, Richard Monckton Milnes, Thomas

Bendyshe, Doctor James Hunt, Sir Edward Brabrooke and Charles Brad-laugh settled in the chamber, accepted drinks, and each lit a cigar or pipe.

"'Attend immediately by order of the king,'" Brabrooke quoted. "I've never before received such a peremptory invitation."

"Nor have you ever been requested to do what I am about to ask of you," the king's agent said. "We find ourselves in extraordinary circumstances, gentlemen. So strange, in fact, that you'll be required to swear an oath of absolute secrecy and loyalty to the crown before we continue."

The club members glanced at one another, eyebrows raised, but none objected, and, after the vows were made, full disclosure followed, causing the brows to rise even higher.

Once the briefing was over and the commission served, they sat in stunned silence, which was eventually broken by Bendyshe, who suddenly bellowed with laughter and cried out, "By all that's holy, you've assigned to us a mission to mate!"

Doctor James Hunt grinned. "I shall devote myself to it assiduously."

Sir Edward Brabrooke raised his glass. "Ladies of London beware."

"Tally ho!" Charles Bradlaugh cheered.

Monckton Milnes looked at Burton and winked.

Burton left his brother with the group to plan the future of the club. He returned to suite five. His colleagues there had divided into smaller groups, each discussing some specific aspect of the planned venture.

"I wish Brunel were with us," Gooch quietly said to him. "I don't doubt I can build Babbage's version of a Nimtz generator, but I'm certain Isambard would make a better job of it."

"You can't revive him?"

"I fear not. When the damaged time suit vanished, the burst of energy it transmitted appears to have erased his mind from the diamonds in his babbage calculator."

"But—" Burton's brow creased, "if that's the case, why did it not also erase the undamaged helmet?"

"I asked Babbage the very same question. He posits that it's because the helmet contained a healthy version of the same mind. What hit Brunel as something alien and overwhelming struck the helmet as a moment of disordered thought that it was able to quash with its own rationality. For poor Brunel, it was too unfamiliar. He had no way to resist. We've lost our friend and the world's most brilliant engineer. He's dead."

"I mourn with you, Daniel. He was a great man and a good friend. But I also have every faith that, even without him, you can fulfil what we require of you."

Gooch flexed his mechanical arms and folded his real ones across his chest. "I'll direct all the Department of Guided Science's resources to the design and construction of the Nimtz generator and to the refit of the *Orpheus*. Despite the complexity of the project, with so many people working on it, it won't take more than a few weeks. But what of the future, Sir Richard? Surely they'll have flying machines. Won't our nineteenth-century rotor-ship stick out like a sore thumb? How will we avoid detection?"

"We'll depend on the Cannibals," Burton answered. "Or, rather, on their descendants. Their remit will include the securing of up-to-date airships into which we can transfer the *Orpheus*'s machinery. We must replace her as we travel."

"Expensive."

"My brother intends to make careful investments to assure us adequate funds."

A thrill of unexpected excitement suddenly coursed through Burton's veins. He left Gooch, went to a window, and looked out at the Strand. The street lamps glowed unsteadily, glimmering through falling snow. Pedestrians crowded the pavements. Traffic pumped steam and smoke into the air.

A new expedition! A new journey into the unknown!

After so many extraordinary events, Burton felt almost immune to further surprises and, indeed, over the course of the following three weeks, though he was six times pounced on by Spring Heeled Jacks, he dealt with them in an almost perfunctory manner, by now aware that they succumbed easily to a bullet or a blow to the head. He sustained no further injuries. However, at the end of that period, the theory he'd formed to explain the creatures and the events associated with them was somewhat shaken by an occurrence that didn't fit into the picture.

It happened on a wet Thursday morning just a few yards from his house.

He'd breakfasted, gone to the mews at the rear of number 14, fired up the furnace in his steam sphere, and set off for Battersea Power Station.

Steering out of the alley that opened onto Montagu Place, he directed the vehicle toward the junction with Gloucester Place, drove past his front door, and pushed his toes down on the accelerator plate.

A bubble appeared in the air less than twenty feet ahead. It popped, and a woman fell into the road. She screamed. Bits of polished wood and a severed arm hit the ground around her.

Burton slammed his heels down, braking hard. It was too late. The sphere thudded into the woman, she was dragged under its drive band, and Burton was jolted as it bumped over her.

He threw himself out and ran to the back of the vehicle.

Nearby, on his corner, Mr. Grub yelled, "Bloody hell!"

The woman lay broken and bleeding. Her appearance was thoroughly bizarre; she possessed a preternaturally tall and attenuated body, a very narrow face, huge black eyes with no whites around the pupils, and a lipless mouth. She was colourfully attired, as if for a carnival.

She blinked at Burton and in a faint voice said, "Oh! It's you again! Where are we?"

A bubble formed around her. The king's agent stepped back.

The woman vanished with a loud bang, taking a bowl-shaped lump of macadam with her.

Grub ran over. "Blimey! Where'd she go?"

Burton said, "Back to wherever she came from, I suppose."

"And left a bloomin' great pothole behind her."

"I'll report it," Burton said. He sighed. "We live in strange times, Mr. Grub."

"Aye," Grub muttered, "I blame Disraeli. He's a bit of a dandy, ain't he? I reckons this world would make a lot more sense if an ordinary ol' geezer like me was in charge."

"You should run for parliament."

Grub shook his head sadly. "Nah. It's not me place to do so."

Six weeks later, Burton took lunch with Thomas Bendyshe in the Athenaeum. Despite being a palatial and tall-ceilinged chamber, the club's eatery had always been known by the rather more humble appellation of 'the Coffee Room.'

Bendyshe, as usual, was at full volume. Oblivious to the morsel of lamb chop lodged between his front teeth, he bellowed, "So you'll be off tomorrow then, old boy?"

"Keep your voice down," Burton urged. "For pity's sake, Tom, why must you always hoot like a confounded foghorn? And yes, the *Orpheus* is ready at last."

"My word!" his companion trumpeted. "What a rapid job they've made of it, hey? Bloomin' miracle workers!"

It was true, the Department of Guided Science, and especially Charles Babbage and Daniel Gooch, had worked at a phenomenal rate to prepare the vessel for its forthcoming voyage. Battersea Power Station had never been so crowded or so active. Its engineers, physicists, logicians, theoretical mathematicians, designers, inventors, chemists and metallurgists had worked night and day without pause. Even the venerable Michael Faraday had been called out of retirement to contribute his expertise to the project.

Bendyshe used his fork to stab the last potato on his plate, transferred it to his mouth and before he'd swallowed it, said, "I've not seen you since that extraordinary meeting at the Venetia. Lord, what a couple of months. How many times have you been assaulted by the jumping Jacks?"

"Eleven," Burton replied. "And look at this."

He took a quick gulp of wine then reached into his jacket and pulled out a folded letter, which he handed across the table.

Bendyshe put down his cutlery, took it, opened it, read it, and hollered, "From old George Herne on Zanzibar!"

"Shhh!" Burton hissed. "It is. He reports that the stilt men have been causing mayhem even there, and word has reached him from Kazeh that they've been seen in that far-flung town, too. The Africans consider them invading demons."

"They might be right," Bendyshe observed. He took a couple of minutes to scan through the missive. "So everywhere you've been, there the freakish creatures are. A veritable infestation. Poor old Bartolini has been forced to close his restaurant. You aren't his favourite customer, not by a long shot. I reckon he'd kick you in the seat of the pants if he dared."

Burton offered a regretful grimace. "I've been banished from the Royal Geographical Society, as well. Four times, the Spring Heeled Jacks have crashed into its lobby demanding to see me. I have a permanent police guard outside my home. Ten battles have been fought in Montagu Place. Though perhaps 'battle' is too strong a word."

"Eh? Why so?"

"They don't put up much of a fight. Grub, the vendor who plies his trade on the corner, saved me last week by clouting one of them over the head with his coal shovel."

"Ha! Good man!" Bendyshe frowned, applied a fingernail to his teeth, dug out the strand of meat, looked at it, put it back into his mouth, and said, "I read those crazy tales left by Abdu El Yezdi. So you really think these stilt-walkers are some aspect of Edward Oxford?"

"Yes, though they don't appear to realise it."

"Peculiar, hey?"

"It is."

A waiter stopped at their table and refilled their glasses. Burton turned down the offer of another bottle. When the man had gone, he said, "Are you comfortable with your new role, Tom? The Cannibal Club will soon become a very different prospect. There'll be no more horseplay."

"Apart from the hunt for a suitable spouse, hey?"

"Well, yes, I suppose."

"I'm ready, willing and able. Incidentally, your brother intends to combine my anthropological knowledge with his own financial *nous* in order to play the markets."

Burton rubbed the scar on his chin with his forefinger. "Anthropological stockbroking?"

"If I can accurately forecast the ebb and flow of human affairs, and the minister, based on those predictions, invests wisely, then we should be able to establish assets enough to fund the Cannibal Club for many generations to come."

"On what will you base your prognostications?"

"I shall consult with the Department of Guided Science to learn what varieties of machinery they think will develop in future years and how it might be employed by industry and society. I'll work with old Monkey Milnes to examine up-and-coming politicians, their philosophies and inclinations, and where they might take our world. I'll learn from the patterns of history, and will scrutinise current trends and project them forward. And I'll confer with the Empire's most talented mediums."

"A major project, Tom."

"I relish it. I hope that my—" He stopped and gaped as, somewhere behind Burton, a loud pop sounded, followed immediately by a crash and cries of alarm.

The king's agent jumped out of his seat and whirled, yanking a Beaumont-Adams revolver from his waistband.

A Spring Heeled Jack had materialised in the dining room and landed on a table. It was flailing about amid broken glasses and crockery, yelling, "Where is Burton? My neck! Don't break my neck! Prime Minister? Where are you?"

Burton raised his gun.

"Everybody stand clear!"

Patrons scattered. He aimed at the figure and, as it clambered to its feet, pulled the trigger, once, twice, three times, hitting it in the chest. The stilt man collapsed to its knees, a bubble peeled outward from its skin, and it vanished.

Tom Bendyshe, temporarily neglecting his atheism, cried out, "Mary mother of God! Won't they ever stop?"

Thirty minutes later, Burton's membership was rescinded and he was banished from the Athenaeum.

"Soon, I shan't be allowed anywhere," he complained, as he bid his friend farewell.

"Tomorrow, you won't *be* anywhere," Bendyshe observed. "At least, nowhere in *this* age."

THE VOYAGE

I want to go ahead of Father Time with a scythe of my own.
—H. G. Wells

CHAPTER 10

THE APATHY OF 1914

The day of small nations has long passed away; the day of
Empires has come.
—Joseph Chamberlain

The following day, the minister of chronological affairs said, "Whatever else you do during your visit to the future, will you please
prevent the Spring Heeled Jacks from making further visits to us? I'm
thoroughly irritated by the infernal pests."

Miraculously, Edward Burton had left the Royal Venetia Hotel and
was sitting in a growler at the foot of the *Orpheus*'s boarding ramp. Battersea Power Station towered in the background.

It was raining.

Sir Richard Francis Burton, standing beside the carriage and holding
an umbrella against which the water drummed, replied, "Must I remind
you, Edward, that while you've been hiding away in your hotel suite, it is
I who've borne the brunt of the intrusions?"

"A reminder isn't necessary," his brother said. "I'm exhausted by the
constant worry."

"About the disruption?"

"About you, you dolt."

Burton was silent for nearly a minute. Then he said, "It appears that
eugenics, or a similar science, will make a resurgence in the future."

"You base that assertion on what?"

"Joseph Lister has finally identified the flesh inside the Spring Heeled Jack mechanisms."

"And?"

"It appears to be a variation of pork."

"Pork? You're telling me they're pigs?"

"A pig machine hybrid."

"God in heaven! What nightmarish world does Oxford inhabit?"

"I'll soon find out." Burton hesitated, then added, "If I don't come back—"

"Do," Edward snapped.

The king's agent looked around at the rain-swept airfield and up at the station's four copper towers. "Just how much will it all change, I wonder?"

The minister grunted. "Babbage and Brunel have been the driving force behind the immense progress we've witnessed in our lifetime, but Babbage is old and increasingly eccentric, and as for Brunel, he's little more than a statue now." Raising his fat fingers to his face, Edward Burton stroked his stubbled jowls. "Your initial jump will be a mere fifty-four years; a tiny step by comparison with your ultimate destination. Surely the world will be recognisable?"

"If we went backward the same number of years, we'd be in 1806. Imagine what an inhabitant of that time would make of this."

His brother nodded. "You're right. Well, needless to say, I'll do all I can to ensure that members of the Cannibal Club meet you at your scheduled stops. I regret that I'm unlikely to be among them. Mortality—I find it such a terrible disappointment."

"Don't treat this as a good-bye, Edward. You know I can't bear such sentiment."

The minister looked away, cleared his throat, lifted his cane, and banged it on the growler's ceiling. "The Venetia, Mr. Penniforth."

Montagu Penniforth looked down from the driver's box and touched two fingers to the peak of his cap. "Good luck to yer, Sir Richard. Me little 'un's name is Clive. Three years of age now. He'll be there to meet yer, I 'ope. A mite older, though."

"Thank you, Monty."

A tremor shook the carriage. It coughed a plume of steam, rattled, and moved off. Burton watched it go, took a final look around, then spun on his heel and strode up into the *Orpheus*.

Daniel Gooch and Charles Babbage met him as he entered. He furled his umbrella and handed it to the elderly scientist.

"We're ready," Gooch said. The engineer had abandoned his auxiliary arms and appeared a little ill at ease with just his own natural pair.

Babbage cast his eyes over the dripping umbrella in his hand as if uncertain what it was, then glowered disapprovingly at Burton. "Can I trust you with my devices, sir? They are my masterpieces."

"I shan't go near them," Burton replied. "They are in Daniel's charge."

"Excellent." Babbage tapped the engineer's shoulder with the brolly's handle. "I want them returned to me undamaged, young man."

Gooch nodded. "Of course. I'll look after them. I give you my word."

Babbage made a sound that suggested he didn't believe the guarantee. He turned his attention back to Burton. "Remember, the equipment will move the ship through time but not instantaneously. She can't match Edward Oxford's suit for efficiency. For him, the transference from one date to another was like the blink of an eye. For you, there will be intervals between. They may be disorientating. You might even lose consciousness. Don't worry. The Mark Three calculator will function independently and will see you to your destination."

"Thank you."

The old man said to Gooch, "I'm relying on you to analyse the machinery of the future and bring me detailed reports."

"I'll do so."

Babbage gave a nod of satisfaction, peered again at Burton's brolly, then opened it, held it over his head, muttered, "Ah ha!" and descended the ramp to the ground.

Gooch said to the king's agent, "Will you help me to close her up?"

They pulled in the ramp, slid the double doors shut, and twisted the bolts into place.

"I have to go to the engine room, Sir Richard. Mr. Trounce is assisting me. Mr. Krishnamurthy and Miss Raghavendra are in what used to be the smoking lounge, overlooking the Nimtz generator. I've trained them both in its operation, which isn't nearly as complicated as Mr. Babbage would have you believe. You'll join Mr. Swinburne and Captain Lawless on the bridge?"

"I will. For heaven's sake, Daniel, drop all the 'misters' and 'misses' and just call me Richard. We've known each other long enough to dispense with formalities. First name basis, if you please. Has everyone taken their dose of Saltzmann's?"

"Yes."

"Good show."

Burton and Gooch set off in opposite directions.

As he traversed the passageway and ascended the stairs to the command deck, Burton marvelled at the brilliance and craftsmanship of the scientists and engineers. As predicted, Babbage had been unable to reproduce the microscopic workings of Oxford's suit, but that he'd created their functional equivalents, albeit on a much larger scale, in such little time, was astonishing. Of course, he'd been studying the suits for many years, so was well versed in the operations of its many components, but he'd lacked the mathematical principle at the heart of them. When Burton supplied it, Babbage for the first time saw with absolute clarity how Oxford's invention defied the strictures of time, and he was able with breathtaking rapidity to design a device that employed contemporaneous machinery to do the same. Where Oxford's genius had fitted it all into a helmet and small flat disk, Babbage required a double-sized Mark III probability calculator and a twenty-four-foot-long, twelve-foot-wide, and ten-foot-high contraption of cogs, levers, pistons, looms, barrels, sliding links, moveable arms, teeth, pegs, holes, warp beams, cranks, ratchets, gears, wheels, pipes, valves, cross heads, cylinders, regulators, inlets, outlets, flywheels, boilers, pumps, condensers, ducts, transmitter disks, field amplifiers, chronostatic coils and a loudly rumbling furnace.

All the remaining fragments of the Nāga diamonds had been fitted into it, each in a lead housing to prevent their slightly deleterious emanations from affecting the travellers. The resonation between the gems was known to give rise to mediumistic faculties. Far from being useful, these abilities tended to cause confusion, indecisiveness and headaches.

Work had not stopped at the manufacture and assembly of the generator's many parts. The weight of the machine was such that the *Orpheus* herself required an extensive overhaul, and it was here that the haste showed, for where her original trimmings were luxurious, the new additions were stark and basic. No influence of the Department of Arts and Culture here. Just bare, unpainted metal. Thus it was that when Burton entered the bridge he found himself in a room that, at eye level, possessed sumptuous fixtures and fittings but that, when one looked up, gave way to a new domed ceiling in the middle of which an unadorned—and, frankly, quite ugly—framework held the spherical Mark III; the ship's "brain."

"My poor *Orpheus*," Captain Lawless said, following Burton's gaze. "They've made of her a monster."

Swinburne, at his side, exclaimed, "Oh no, Captain! She's beautiful. Not in form anymore, perhaps, but without a doubt in purpose."

From above, a voice said, "At least someone appreciates me."

Burton groaned and looked at Lawless. "I take it you've become familiar with Babbage's so-called personality enhancements?"

"That's what I was referring to, Sir Richard. A monster."

"You should be grateful," *Orpheus* protested. "What other captain has ever had such a close working relationship with his ship?"

"What other captain would endure it?" Lawless countered. He said to Burton, "Ready?"

"The ramp is in and the hatch is locked."

"Good-oh. If you would, Mr. Swinburne?"

The poet nodded and crossed to a speaking tube. He blew into it and shrilled, "Trounce! I say, Pouncer, are you there?"

Putting the tube to his ear, he received an answer, then responded, "Fire up the engines, dear fellow! And three cheers for our jolly old escapade!"

Lawless arched an eyebrow at Burton and murmured, "Not the standard of discipline I'm used to."

"Whatever you do," Burton advised in a whisper, "don't get Algy going on discipline. You'll hear things you'd wish you could forget."

A deep grumble vibrated through the floor.

"I must admit, I've been thoroughly impressed by Trounce though," Lawless continued. "He rolled up his sleeves and took to the training like a fish takes to water."

"He's a practical sort," Burton confirmed. "Whereas Swinburne's head has always been where we are just about to go; that is to say, up in the clouds."

"Engines at optimum," *Orpheus* announced. "Are you going to stand around chin-wagging or shall we get on with it?"

"Take us to latitude north fifty-one, east one degree, altitude eight thousand feet," Lawless commanded. He explained to Burton, "As planned—opposite the mouth of the Thames and a little north of Margate. Far enough out to sea to avoid detection, I hope."

"Ascending," *Orpheus* said.

Swinburne whooped.

The floor lurched slightly as the ship left the ground, its engines thundering.

"I feel somewhat redundant," Lawless commented.

"Some judgements require more than cold calculations," Burton murmured. He stepped to the rain-spattered window and took a last look at the sprawling city before the ship was swallowed by the weather front.

"En route," *Orpheus* noted. "We'll reach the coordinates in twenty minutes. The Nimtz generator requires a pressure of one thousand and five hundred psi in order to achieve the necessary power by the time we get there. It is currently at one thousand and ten psi. I suggest you adjust valves twenty-two to twenty-eight to setting six so we might accelerate through time without any delay."

"On the other hand," Lawless said, "sometimes cold calculations are just the ticket. Mr. Swinburne, relay the *Orpheus*'s advice to Mr. Krishnamurthy, please."

"Aye aye, Captain Lawless, sir. Straightaway." Swinburne gave a snappy salute and clicked his heels.

"Just 'aye aye' will do."

Bright yellow light streamed through the windows as the airship emerged from the cloud and soared into the clear sky above it. With rotors thrumming, she sped eastward, leaving a trail of glaring white steam behind her.

Burton sat at a console and stared into space.

Initial destination: 1914. By that year, in every other variant of history, a world war was raging. In Abdu El Yezdi's native reality, the conflict was many years old and the Prussians had overrun the world. In others, hostilities were just commencing. However, here, uniquely, the Germanic nations were placated, had joined in an economic and political alliance with the British Empire, and were sharing the spoils of Anglo-Saxon hegemony.

Nineteen fourteen might be a small step, but Burton wanted to see how the Empire would develop without the devastating events that so slowed progress in its counterparts. Besides which, it would be wise to contact the immediate descendants of the Cannibal Club, just to be sure the purpose of their mission remained clear.

While the king's agent gave himself over to quiet meditation, the Mark III made intermittent observations pertaining to flight speed, course and altitude, Lawless gazed out at the blanket of cloud below, and Swinburne communicated the captain's occasional commands to the engine room.

An air of expectation and trepidation hung over all.

They waited.

"We are at north fifty-one, east one degree," *Orpheus* finally declared as the engines altered their tone. "Holding position. Flight duration twenty minutes, as anticipated. Rather good, if you ask me. I got it exactly right."

Burton blinked, took a deep breath, stood, entwined his fingers, and cracked his knuckles. "Has the Nimtz made the initial set of calculations?"

"It doesn't make the calculations," the ship replied. "I do. And I have. As always, at your service."

Swinburne placed a speaking tube back in its bracket and added, "Maneesh and Sadhvi are standing by."

Burton crossed to him and indicated another tube, this one marked *Shipwide*. He tapped it and said to Lawless, "Do you mind, Captain?"

"Go ahead."

Burton took up the tube and spoke into it. He could hear, beyond the bridge door, his voice echoing through the vessel.

"Sadhvi, William, Maneesh, Daniel, we're all set. In a moment, I'll command the *Orpheus* to move ahead through time. I have no idea how we'll be affected, but, whatever you experience, please remain at your posts." He hesitated, then added, "Thank you all, and—and may fortune favour us."

Replacing the tube, he glanced at Swinburne—who grinned broadly—then looked up at the ceiling and said, "*Orpheus*, take us to nine in the evening of December the first, 1914."

"Are you quite sure about this?" *Orpheus* responded. "I'm liable to become instantly outmoded. I don't relish the thought."

"Just do it, please."

"On your own head be it. You'll become antiquated too, you know. I'm engaging the generator. Hang on tight."

Outside, everything suddenly turned completely white.

Utter silence closed around Burton. He saw Swinburne look at him and move his mouth as if speaking, but there was no sound at all, not from anywhere.

The poet slowly became transparent. So did the walls. Suddenly Burton was floating in limbo.

He fragmented. All the decisions he'd ever made were undone and became choices. His every success and every failure reverted to opportunities and challenges. The characteristics that had grown and now defined him disengaged and withdrew to become influences. He lost cohesion until nothing remained except a potential, existing as coordinates, waiting to take form.

He was a nebulous, unarticulated question.

The possible answers were innumerable.

A decision.

A path chosen.

Manifestation.

A recognition of whiteness, of shapes emerging from it and darkening it, of Swinburne's face.

Burton swayed, stumbled backward, regained his balance, and looked around the bridge.

"Phew!" Swinburne exclaimed. "That felt like an instant and an eternity all rolled into one."

"It was fifty-four years," *Orpheus* said. "We have arrived."

Burton said, "Call down to the others, Algy. See how they are."

This was done, and the poet reported, "All's well."

Lawless said, "*Orpheus*, a systems check, please."

The ship responded, "Done. I'm perfectly fine, thank you for asking."

The captain crossed to a console and examined its dials. "It's a clear night, and windless according to the readings. Cold, though. I suggest we switch off all lights and descend to five hundred feet."

"Agreed."

"*Orpheus*, you heard that?"

"I'm not deaf."

"Then proceed."

The bridge's electrical lights clicked off, and the engines moaned.

Burton's stomach moved as he felt the drop in altitude. He strode to the window. Swinburne and Lawless joined him. They looked out. A full moon was riding low in a starry sky. In half a century, the heavens hadn't changed one jot.

The king's agent muttered, "I'm a fool. I should have taken the phases of the moon into account. We'll be visible."

"Why did you choose December?" Lawless asked.

"Because Abdu El Yezdi caused the Russian dictator, Rasputin, to die this year. That, however, was in a different history. I'm interested to know what happened to him in this one. I'm hoping that the three great wartime mediums were so prone to resonance that their death in one history caused their deaths in all the others."

"There's a yacht," Swinburne said, pointing downward. "I can just about make it out. See?"

Burton searched the silvered surface of the sea. Before he spotted the vessel, it drew his attention with a sequence of flashes.

"That's them," Lawless said.

"How do you know?" Burton asked.

"It's Morse code. A system created back in the forties. The Navy is in the process of adopting it. Um, that is to say, the Navy of 1860. That ship is sending the word 'Cannibal.'" Raising his voice, he ordered, "Steer twenty degrees to the southwest, forward half a mile, and descend to thirty feet above sea level."

"That's rather low," the ship noted.

"Weather's calm," the captain countered.

The floor shifted as the airship followed the command.

"Go get yourself ready, gents," Lawless said. "I'll call down to Trounce and Gooch. They'll meet you in the bay."

Burton made a sound of acknowledgement and, accompanied by Swinburne, exited the bridge. They traversed a stairwell down past the main deck to *Orpheus*'s cargo bay, where they found their friends waiting.

"Hell's bells!" the detective inspector grumbled. "That was a thoroughly unpleasant experience. I felt like I dissolved."

"Better get used to it," Burton advised. "Help me with the hatch."

The four of them unlatched the bay doors in the floor and pulled the portal open. Frigid night air swept in, bearing with it the salty tang of the sea. They looked out. The glittering water appeared dangerously close. As they watched, the small vessel that had signalled them glided into view. They saw figures standing on its deck, their pale moonlit faces gazing up at them. A voice shouted, "Hail fellows well met!"

"Who's there?" Burton called.

"The Cannibal Club circa 1914! Come on down. It's quite safe."

Gooch moved to a winch and rotated a handle. A small platform with handrails on three of its sides swung out from a corner of the hold until it was positioned over the hatch. He used another handle to lower it a little.

"All aboard," he instructed.

Burton, Swinburne and Trounce stepped carefully onto the swaying square of metal. They gripped the rail.

"Say hello from me to the denizens of the future," Gooch said, and started to wind the handle.

As the platform sank, Swinburne proclaimed, "Into the unknown, ta-rah, ta-rah!"

They emerged from the bay and dropped smoothly down to the boat. A cold breeze dug its fingers into their inadequate clothing. The platform clunked onto the wooden deck, and the cable looped around it as Gooch gave plenty of slack.

A slim white-haired and round-faced man with a pencil-thin moustache stepped forward from the gathering that awaited them. He shook them each by the hand and said, "Sir Richard, Mr. Swinburne, Mr. Trounce, I am James Arthur Honesty. Your colleague, Detective Inspector Thomas Honesty, was my father."

"By Jove!" Trounce exclaimed. "So he made detective inspector! Good man!"

James Honesty smiled. "He did, sir, and he always spoke very highly of you—said you were the best man on the entire force."

Trounce harrumphed and stuck out his chest a little. He suddenly deflated and said, "Spoke? You mean he's—he's—"

"Father passed away fourteen years ago, sir."

Burton touched Trounce's arm. "Remember, old chap, he's still alive where we've come from."

Honesty said, "Come belowdecks. I'll introduce you to the current Cannibals and tell you how things stand with the world. The *Orpheus* will be fine. Such ships, though old, are still in use and a common sight. She won't be disturbed."

He led them to a door, down a flight of steps, a short way along a narrow corridor, and into an undecorated room furnished with a table, sideboard and chairs. They sat and waited while Honesty's colleagues appeared and filed in. The chamber was soon crowded.

"You made it, then," Honesty said. "The chrononauts! Perfectly marvellous!"

"Chrononauts?" Burton queried. "Is that what you call us?"

"It is. So here we all are, thrilled beyond measure to meet you. I'll confess, not a few of us have secretly suspected the whole affair to be some sort of wild hoax, but there's one among us who's maintained the faith, so to speak, and whom you must thank for keeping us organised and committed. A friend of yours."

He gestured to a very elderly individual sitting two seats to his right. The old man was gazing at Burton with an amused twinkle in his eye. Burton looked at him. Slowly, recognition dawned.

"Bismillah!" he said huskily. "Brabrooke! Edward Brabrooke!"

"Great heavens!" Swinburne cried out.

Brabrooke laughed, his parchment-thin liver-spotted skin creasing into a myriad of wrinkles. He leaned across the table and extended a gnarled hand to the king's agent, who gripped it enthusiastically, and to the poet, who did likewise.

"I feel that I'm dreaming," Brabrooke said. His voice rustled like dry leaves. "Here am I, seventy-five years old, and there's you two, exactly as you were when we last got sloshed together, half a century ago. How are you, Richard? Algy? How the very devil are you?"

Burton responded, "As you say, my friend, I'm exactly as I was when we last met, which for me was just a couple of weeks ago. And the others?"

"All gone, I'm sad to say. We lost old—"

Burton interrupted. "Stop! Forgive me, but I shouldn't have asked. I think it best if you—if all of you—refrain from speaking of those who've passed. For me, they're still alive, though they currently occupy a different portion of time to this. Do you understand?"

The Cannibals nodded, and Brabrooke said, "Yes, I can see how that might be for the best." He paused. "But I expect you'll want to know what became of you—whether you returned from this voyage or not?"

"Can you tell me?" Burton asked cautiously.

"No. It's the most peculiar thing. I have vivid memories of you prior to your departure, but after that there's a thoroughly curious indecision. I feel, at one and the same time, that you returned but also that you didn't. If you did, whatever we got up to after 1860 is lost in a frustrating amnesia."

"Babbage warned us of such a phenomenon."

"His theories are in our records. Knowing the 'why' of it doesn't make it any the less odd." Brabrooke reached out and took a broad-shouldered man by the elbow, pulling him to his side. "Anyway, let's look forward, not back. This is my son, Edward John."

"I've heard so much about the three of you," the younger Brabrooke said. "It's an honour to meet you."

"I also have a grandson," Edward Brabrooke said. "Eddie. When he's older, he'll join our ranks. Perhaps he'll get to meet you, too."

James Honesty put in, "Suffice to say, Sir Richard, that all your friends dedicated themselves to the continuation of our little organisation, and many are here represented." He gestured to another, stockily built youngster. "This, for example, is Lieutenant Henry Bendyshe."

With an oddly familiar voice, the lieutenant bellowed, "By crikey! I'm very happy to be here, sirs. My grandfather always told tall tales of you, Sir Richard, and of you, Mr. Swinburne. He considered you the finest of friends."

"Gosh!" Swinburne muttered. "Tom found a wife. The poor girl."

"And this," Honesty continued, nodding toward a strikingly beautiful blonde-haired woman, "is Miss Eliza Murray, granddaughter of Admiral Henry Murray."

"Admiral!" Burton and Swinburne exclaimed.

Brabrooke cackled. "Who'd have thought such an utter rapscallion would rise so high, hey?"

Swinburne smiled at Miss Murray and exclaimed, "My hat! But you're the spitting image of him, except female, of course, and considerably better looking. In fact, you completely outshine him. There's barely any resemblance at all."

She laughed. "My mother says I have his face."

"Well," Swinburne said, "he was tremendously handsome, then. Apparently."

Burton turned his attention to a dark-complexioned middle-aged woman. "And you, madam, bear a distinct likeness to Shyamji Bhatti."

She bobbed. "His daughter. I am Patmanjari Richardson, née Bhatti."

"Your father's cousin, Maneesh Krishnamurthy, is up in the *Orpheus*. Perhaps you'd like to meet him?"

Honesty turned to her. "Go say hello, by all means."

"I should like that very much." She smiled and left the room.

Another woman, in her midfifties, was introduced as Catherine Jones, daughter of Detective Inspector Sidney Slaughter.

"We also have with us Clive Penniforth," James Honesty said, jerking a thumb toward a muscular fellow, "whose father was a cab driver of your acquaintance."

"Gents," Penniforth said. His voice was so deep it sounded like an avalanche. He touched his fingers to his temple. "Pops is still with us, but he don't get around much no more. Has a spot o' bother with his hips. He sends his best."

"Good old Monty!" Swinburne exclaimed.

"And finally, from the old crowd, we have Robert Crewe-Milnes, the first Marquess of Crewe."

The marquess, a handsome man with a wide moustache and a military bearing, said, "My father was Richard Monckton Milnes."

Unexpectedly, Burton felt overcome by emotion. The muscles to either side of his jaw worked spasmodically. He blinked at Crewe-Milnes, who gave a sad smile of understanding and said nothing more.

Swinburne sniffed, pulled out a handkerchief, and blew his nose.

After a moment's silence, Honesty said, "So that is nine of us, all descended from the original Cannibals, with the exception of Mr. Brabrooke, who *is* an original. However, as you can see, we are twelve in total. We have three new recruits, who we felt could contribute much to our cause, they being inclined toward considerations of the future, as well as possessing admirable insight into the present. The first is Mademoiselle Amélie Blanchet."

A rather coarse-featured, overweight and ostentatiously dressed woman of about fifty years murmured, "Welcome aboard, gentlemen. Bonjour. Bonjour."

"She wields considerable influence in high society. Few people better comprehend how an undercurrent of idle gossip influences cultural and political movements, and no one hears more of it than she."

The woman gave a somewhat sardonic smile.

Honesty went on, "Then we have Erik von Lessing, who has many connections in the German government."

Burton acknowledged the white-haired and smartly dressed man, who returned his nod with a sharp bow.

"And last but by no means least, our resident visionary." Honesty indicated a tubby little chap who was no taller than Swinburne. "Mr. Herbert Wells."

"I feel honoured to meet you, Sir Richard," Wells said. His voice was high-pitched and childlike. "And you, too, Mr. Swinburne."

Burton frowned. "Herbert Wells? Herbert *George* Wells?"

"Yes," Wells responded. "You're no doubt remembering the fellow Abdu El Yezdi wrote of in his account entitled 'Expedition to the Mountains of the Moon.' We are pretty certain that he was me, albeit a different me in a different version of history." He shuddered and added, "And thank goodness for that. My poor counterpart suffered the dreadful world war we ourselves have avoided."

"Perhaps, then, I should say it's nice to meet you *again*, Mr. Wells," Burton said, with a wry curl of his lips.

Wells chuckled.

"Shall we get to business?" Honesty asked. "Practicalities first?"

Burton nodded. "Let's. The *Orpheus*?"

"Penniforth and von Lessing are our resident experts in engineering. Gents?"

"Aye," Penniforth rumbled. "Airships ain't changed all that much since your time. The *Orpheus* can just about pass muster if no one looks too close, like. But we're goin' to fit her with a telemobiloscope afore you set off again."

"A telly-mo-billy-whatsit?" Swinburne enquired.

"Invented by a German," von Lessing put in. "Christian Hülsmeyer. It can detect other ships in your location through means of reflected radio waves."

The poet threw out his hands in a helpless shrug. "Radio?"

"Wireless telegraph signals."

"Good Lord!" Burton exclaimed. "Useful!"

"We even transmit entertainment shows through 'em," Penniforth added. "Music and suchlike. We 'ave a radio unit ready to add to the *Orpheus*. It will make it easier for the future Cannibals to contact you."

"Excellent. And what else?"

"There ain't much else."

"Really? Am I to take it that progress has slowed?"

Edward Brabrooke interjected, "Yes, it most certainly has. These youngsters refer to our time as the Steam Revolution, Richard, and rightfully recognise Isambard Kingdom Brunel and old Charles Babbage as the geniuses at its heart. You'll doubtlessly recall that Isambard ceased to function in 1860?"

"For us, it was just a couple of months ago," Burton noted. "He never recovered?"

"No."

"What became of him?"

"He was declared dead. There was a magnificent ceremony at St. Paul's Cathedral to mark his passing, and a stone was laid bearing his name, though there was no corpse to bury beneath it. His mechanical form is exhibited in the British Museum. As for Charles Babbage, he went into hiding for half a decade and—I'm sorry, but this is necessary information—lost his mind. They say he died a raving lunatic, though no one is sure exactly when."

"Why the uncertainty?"

Brabrooke shrugged and made a gesture that incorporated the room. "Perhaps his close association with this endeavour has cast the same veil over him that confounds our post-1860 memories of you."

"Odd."

"It is. The sixties are regarded as a mysterious period. Significant events were left unrecorded, were hushed up, and have been inexplicably forgotten. Whatever occurred, it marked the end of the Steam Revolution, and those few who knew him generally agree that Babbage was somehow at the heart of it. All I can tell you for certain is that, on the twenty-eighth of September, 1861, he destroyed all his prototypes, all the devices he had in his possession, and incinerated his every plan, blueprint, and diary. He left no trace of his work at all, other than the Mark Two probability calculators that occupied the heads of existing clockwork men, and as you know, those calculators were notoriously booby-trapped, so any unauthorised infiltration caused them to self-destruct. Very few of them still exist. Put simply, we lost Babbage and his knowledge. It was the death-knell of the Department of Guided Science. By the 1880s, it had been incorporated into the Department of Industry and all the great names associated with it were gone."

Swinburne said, "What about the blueprint for our time mechanism—the Nimtz generator? Didn't he give it over to the Cannibal Club?"

"Destroyed," Brabrooke said. "We don't know how it works. We'll never be able to reproduce it, or modernise it, or even mend it if it breaks down."

Burton murmured, "Then I must depend on Daniel Gooch." He

frowned. "Twenty-eighth of September, 'sixty-one, you say? Why does that date ring a bell?"

Herbert Wells answered, "You read it in 'The Strange Affair of Spring Heeled Jack,' Sir Richard. That date, in El Yezdi's native history, was when your counterpart first encountered Edward Oxford."

Burton murmured, "Ah yes, of course." He raised a hand to his head and ran his fingertips through his hair, feeling his scars and the grittiness of the diamond dust etched into them. It was becoming a habitual gesture. "Charles placed great faith in El Yezdi's obsession with timing and coincidences. Perhaps that explains the *when* of his actions, but it doesn't explain the *why*."

Wells said, "His motive remains a mystery, but his actions certainly slowed our progress, as did our lack of participation in the wars."

Burton frowned at him. "Wars, Mr. Wells? Did Abdu El Yezdi fail to avert the disaster he predicted?"

The little man shook his head. "No, no. If, in all the other histories, a worldwide conflict has broken out, then we have, thanks to his efforts, been spared it. In our world, the conflict has for the most part confined itself to Russia and China."

"In what manner?"

"It started with Russian expansionism. In 1877, that country declared war on, and obliterated, the old Ottoman Empire, advancing westward to occupy a number of Eastern European territories. In 1900, it turned its attention to the south and ventured into the northern provinces of China, sparking a fierce war with the Qing Dynasty. Initially, this didn't go so well for the Russians, and five years later its people rose in revolution and overthrew the ruling aristocracy. They united under a new leader. A man Abdu El Yezdi encountered."

"Grigori Rasputin."

"Yes. Under his mesmeric leadership, Russia renewed its assault on China, which by now was weakening rapidly due to the trade embargoes inflicted upon it by our own empire, they being a legacy of the bad relations caused in your time by the actions of Lord Elgin. The situation reached crisis point three years ago, when the Qing Dynasty collapsed. China is currently re-forming itself as a socialist republic. As for Russia, it received a terrible blow earlier this year when Rasputin suffered a brain haemorrhage and died."

"Ah. I was curious to know whether that would happen."

Swinburne said, "And the British Empire, Mr. Wells?"

"Now known as the Anglo-Saxon Empire. It's steered clear of conflict and continues to consolidate its strength. It has now incorporated all of Western Europe, most of Africa, India, the Caribbean, and Australia. We also have a strong economic alliance with the United States."

"The united states of where?" William Trounce asked.

"America," Wells said. "The year after your departure, a civil war erupted between the North and South of that country. It lasted from 1861 until 1865. The North won. The U.S.A., as it is commonly called, is currently expanding its manufacturing infrastructure and rapidly growing in power. I fear we are being left behind. As I mentioned, without the incentive of battle, where the sciences and engineering are concerned, the pace of change has become ever more sedate in the A.S.E."

A.S.E., Burton thought. *Anglo-Saxon Empire. U.S.A. United States of America. Just as Edward Oxford's grandfather mentioned, the world is being abbreviated.*

Henry Bendyshe took a thick binder from the sideboard and handed it to Brabrooke, who then passed it to Burton, saying, "Your brother left this for you. It covers all the principal developments in every field of endeavour."

Burton gave a snort of amusement. "Typical of the minister. He thinks that, because we're travelling three hundred and forty-two years into the future, I'll have plenty of time for reading."

Brabrooke laughed. "You'll be getting another such file at your next stop. We intend to chronicle world events for you. When you return to 1860, you'll have a guide to the future."

"Which may well become an extravagant work of fiction the moment we act upon the information in it," Burton mused. "Nevertheless, useful. Thank you." He put the book down and patted it thoughtfully. "So, to the most pertinent question. What of Spring Heeled Jack? We know 2202 is his ultimate destination, but is the Oxford intelligence influencing history as he moves forward through it?"

"We have no evidence to suggest so," Brabrooke replied.

Burton considered the back of his hands for a few moments. He looked up at Brabrooke, said softly, "Thank you, old friend," then met the eyes of each of the others in turn. "My gratitude to each and every one of you. Your predecessors were my friends. I have no doubt they would be proud of you. Much as I'd like to remain here and get to know each of you, the fact is, my companions and I are on a mission, and I feel it necessary to press on. It's an incongruous sensation to know that all the time in the world is at our disposal yet to also feel that time is pressing."

James Honesty said, "We quite understand, sir. There are two points of business remaining before we get to work modernising the *Orpheus*. The first is that, during the months before Mr. Michael Faraday passed away, when it was obvious that we could no longer rely on Mr. Babbage, he created a device for us. It is a beacon that can signal to your ship while it is speeding through time. We know your next scheduled stop is the year 2000. However, if the beacon functions as he promised, then the Cannibal Club can summon you to an earlier date should we deem it necessary. If we detect any sign of Edward Oxford, and if you now give us permission, we shall do so."

"Permission is enthusiastically granted," Burton said. "That's an excellent development."

Honesty continued, "The second matter is this, Sir Richard: we feel it wise that a member of our group join you. We all have half a century's worth of knowledge that you and your associates lack. What you encounter and may not understand at your next stop might be somewhat more familiar to a person from the year 1914."

Burton pondered this. "I can't disagree, Mr. Honesty. Whom have you elected?"

Herbert Wells stood up. "Me, sir."

"Then welcome aboard the time machine, Mr. Wells."

CHAPTER 11

THE SQUARES, CATS AND DEVIANTS OF 1968

What is history? An echo of the past in the future; a reflex from the future on the past.

—Victor Hugo

They emerged from whiteness.

Herbert Wells put his hands to his head. "Ouch! What a ghastly sensation."

The *Orpheus* said, "We have been waylaid. This is not the year 2000."

"What happened?" Nathaniel Lawless demanded.

"The Cannibals have used their Faraday beacon. It is ten o'clock on Sunday morning, the seventeenth of March, 1968."

"Another jump of fifty-four years," Burton murmured. "Coincidence?"

"My hat! We're over a century into the future!" Swinburne exclaimed.

"Marvellous!" Wells cried out. "Though it's just half the time for me, of course. Nevertheless, marvellous!"

"There is an incoming radio transmission," *Orpheus* said.

Lawless and Burton crossed to the box-like contraption the 1914 Cannibals had added to the bridge.

"It was this, wasn't it?" Burton asked, lifting a fist-sized semicircular object from the side of the device.

"Yes," Lawless said. "Blue to receive, green to send."

The king's agent pressed a blue button. Immediately, a female voice filled the bridge. *"Orpheus? Hello, Orpheus? Respond, please."*

"Now the green, and answer," Lawless instructed.

Burton did as directed. The voice was cut off. He spoke into the object in his hand. "This is Burton, aboard the *Orpheus*. Can you hear me?"

Blue button.

"Sir Richard! Hi. Right on. You made it. Welcome to 1968. Listen, this is important. Fly your ship twenty miles to the east. You're too exposed there and badly outdated. You'll be noticed. We have a replacement vessel waiting for you."

"Understood. We're on our way. To whom am I speaking?"

"My name is Jane Packard, daughter of Eliza Teed, née Murray. I'm Admiral Henry Murray's great-granddaughter. I have with me an Honesty, a Penniforth, a Slaughter, a Bhatti and a Brabrooke. The Cannibals are still going strong, sir."

"Splendid! We look forward to meeting you, Miss Packard. I assume you have news for us?"

"We do. I'd prefer to tell you face to face, if that's cool with you."

"Cool? Er, all right? Yes, it's fine. We'll rendezvous with you in—" He looked at Lawless, who said, "Fifteen minutes." Burton relayed this before breaking contact.

"A replacement?" the *Orpheus* said. "What do they mean, a replacement? I'm in fine fettle. I don't want to be replaced."

"Don't worry," Lawless replied. "You'll be transferred to the new ship."

"I should hope so."

"I say," Swinburne announced. "That Miss Packard sounded rather— um—*casual*, didn't she?"

"An alteration in tonal communication," Burton observed. "We must expect such modifications over the years. Language is flexible. It adapts."

Wells said, "It might be an indication of her social standing. Such matters were in upheaval during my time. There was a rapidly expanding middle class."

"It being?" Burton asked.

"The bourgeoisie and petite bourgeoisie."

"I think I understand the reference. There were signs of such a phenomenon in the eighteen sixties. No doubt, had this middle class been better established in the mid-nineteenth century, I would have been labelled as such. I never quite made the grade as far as the gentry were concerned."

Lawless consulted the meteorological console and murmured, "Exceptionally mild for the time of year, by the looks of it." He joined Burton, Swinburne and Wells at the window and peered ahead at the horizon. After a while, they discerned two objects brightly reflecting the spring sunshine, one in the air and the other on the water.

A couple of minutes later, *Orpheus* said, "They're calling us again."

Burton went to the radio, clicked the switch, and listened as Jane Packard said, "We have you in sight, *Orpheus*."

"Acknowledged, Miss Packard. We can see you, too. What do you want us to do?"

"Have yourself, Mr. Swinburne, Mr. Trounce, Miss Raghavendra and Mr. Wells lowered onto the yacht. We'll take you to London. You'll be staying with us for a couple of days. Captain Lawless, Mr. Gooch and Mr. Krishnamurthy should follow our airship in the *Orpheus*. They'll be escorted to a secluded cove on the coast of Holland, where your babbage devices will be transferred from the old ship into the new and your people will be instructed in the piloting of the updated vessel."

"We're in your hands, Miss Packard."

A few moments later, the other flying ship drew alongside. It was a streamlined affair, with a white tubular body, sharply pointed at the front but flaring into a vertical sail-shape at the rear. Two spinning rotors, each enclosed in a flat circular housing, were inset into wide triangular wings, which made the entirety of the vessel a horizontal V-shape. Steam was blasting out from beneath it, rolling out across the water's surface and half obscuring the yacht.

"My goodness!" Wells exclaimed. "Will you look at that!"

"She's a Concorde class jump jet," Jane Packard transmitted. "Created by British and French engineers and just coming into service."

Nathaniel Lawless glanced at Swinburne and whispered, "Jump jet?"

"Machines will soon seem like magic to cavemen like us," the poet muttered. "I fear they're already far beyond our comprehension."

Half an hour later, all but Lawless, Gooch and Krishnamurthy had been lowered onto the deck of the large and extraordinarily luxurious yacht. They stood beside Jane Packard and watched—their hair whipped about by the sea breeze—as the two airships receded into the east.

Wells whispered, "Adapt or perish, now as ever, is nature's inexorable imperative. And my goodness, *how* we humans adapt!"

"The Concorde is a real beauty, Mr. Wells," Packard conceded. "And futuristic in design. We hope she won't appear too out of place at your next destination."

She was the only person, aside from them, on the deck. Perhaps in her late forties but young-looking, she was slim and athletic, with very long blonde hair and a freckled face free of cosmetics, though adorned with spectacles. She was clothed in such a shocking outfit that Burton hardly knew where to look. Her upper body was scarcely covered by a sleeveless, buttonless and collarless thin white shirt upon which the face of an African was depicted along with the mysterious word *Hendrix*. Over this, she had what was either a sleeveless coat or an absurdly long waistcoat of fringed suede leather. Her legs were encased in—of all things—trousers, tailored from some manner of light canvas, faded blue in colour, and breathtakingly tight around the knees, thighs and loins but wide and flappy at the ankles. She had a string of beads around her neck, another around her left wrist, and wore moccasins, or something very similar, on her feet.

As mild as the weather was, she was underdressed for it and plainly cold.

"Come below," she said as the yacht's engine growled and the vessel started westward. "The club has a lot more members since 1914. A few of my comrades are aboard, but you'll meet others in London, including Mick, who we've selected to join your expedition."

"Is he related to one of the originals?" Swinburne asked.

"Nope."

She guided them down and into a lounge room that was furnished in garishly bright colours with its fittings and decor moulded from a waxy material similar to the skin of the Spring Heeled Jacks. In response to Burton's query, she informed him that it was "plastic."

A small group rose from sofas to greet them. All were garbed, like

Packard, in such an informal manner they might as well have just got out of their beds.

"Wow!" one of them said. "Sir Richard Francis Burton—in the flesh! And Algernon Swinburne! This is way out there!" He stepped forward and extended his hand. "Mark Packard."

"My younger brother," Jane added.

Burton took the hand and shook it. "Pleased to meet you, Mr. Packard. Long hair has come back into fashion for gentlemen, I see. I noticed it was worn rather short in 1914."

"Still is among the straights," Packard replied.

"Straights?"

Jane Packard interjected, "We'll explain all that in a minute. Let's get everyone acquainted first."

She introduced the rest, who'd all been gaping as if Burton and his friends were ghosts. The Cannibals were Patricia Honesty, Trevor Penniforth, Eddie Brabrooke, Jimmy Richardson—who bore an uncanny resemblance to Shyamji Bhatti—and Miranda Kingsland of the Slaughter family, plus Karl von Lessing, grandson of Erik, and a new recruit named Jason Griffith.

Everyone settled on seats and sofas. Penniforth and Kingsland served coffee. Mark Packard and Jason Griffith lit what initially appeared to be roughly rolled white *cigarillos* but which, once their fumes reached his nostrils, Burton instantly recognised as hashish. Brabrooke offered him a tobacco *cigarette*.

"Manufactured in France?" Burton asked the young man.

"Made and smoked everywhere now," Brabrooke responded.

Burton couldn't help but give a grunt of shock as Miranda Kingsland and Patricia Honesty both started to smoke. Women did so in his own time, of course, but rarely in company with gentlemen.

Kingsland, noticing his expression, grinned. "My gender is making great progress in liberating ourselves from the restrictions yours has imposed on us throughout history."

"Glad to hear it," Burton said. He drew on the cigarette, coughed, made a face, muttered, "Bismillah!" and took a gulp of coffee, which tasted even worse.

Sadhvi Raghavendra—dressed in a loose Indian smock and looking surprisingly contemporaneous with the Cannibals—addressed Jane Packard, "If I may ask, you said the Cannibal Club has expanded. How many more are there?"

"Phew!" Packard answered. "Thing is, you see, we've kind of become a social movement."

Burton frowned. "Our mission is supposed to be secret."

"Oh yeah, man!" Jason Griffith interjected. "Still is. We're in on it, and Mick and the Deviants know the game, but the rest are like, kicking against the straights without knowing the full story, if you dig what I'm saying."

Trounce shifted in his seat and looked at his companions in utter bafflement.

"Deviants?" Swinburne asked. "Straights? Dig?"

"We should start at the beginning," Miranda Kingsland put in.

"And in English," Trounce muttered.

"Yeah, but when was that?" Griffith asked her.

"1950s," Karl von Lessing said decisively.

"Sir," the king's agent said to him, "perhaps we have too many speaking at once. With due deference to your friends, may I suggest you take centre stage and recount to us what has occurred during the course of the past fifty-four years, who Mick is, what these 'deviants' and 'straights' are, and why you and your colleagues felt the *Orpheus* should be summoned to 1968?"

Von Lessing looked at the others. They each gave words of consent:

"Sweet."

"Sure thing."

"Fine with me."

"I can dig it."

"Okay, so here's the scene," von Lessing said. "First, secrecy. Your brother was a genius. He created an investments company that, for years, has been like, *thriving*, man. The Bendyshe family runs it—" He broke off as Burton laughed.

"Sir Richard?"

"Good old Bendyshe! I'd never have predicted his line to be so responsible!"

"The original, the Thomas you knew, gave really—what's the word?"

"Prescient," Mark Packard put in.

"Yeah—*prescient* advice to the old minister of chronological affairs. This yacht and our Concorde are privately owned by the Bendyshe Foundation, which has offices in Bombay and is currently headed by Joseph and James Bendyshe. So, you see, the Cannibal Club is well financed and, as I said, thriving, but still completely hidden."

"We'll keep it that way," Jason Griffith added. "You can be sure."

Burton gave a grunt of approval.

"So," von Lessing continued, "on to the history lesson. I guess things started to get a bit flaky back in the 1930s. Real bad famines had been weakening Russia since Rasputin's death, and China was winning the war. Then, from 1935 to '40, led by Poland, the Eastern European countries—Bulgaria, Hungary, Romania, Ukraine, and the Baltic states—ousted their occupying governments and declared independence. Russia was on the brink of total collapse until, in 1940, assistance came from an unexpected quarter."

Burton raised an eyebrow enquiringly.

"China," von Lessing said. "It declared a complete ceasefire, handed back captured territory, and flooded the country with aid. It then rebuilt its former enemy's industrial infrastructure and established exclusive trade relations. In 1949, they merged and became the United Republics of Eurasia."

"That's rather a startling turnaround," Swinburne observed.

"Too right. For sure, it caught us—and the Yanks—on the hop. So now the world had three superpowers: the A.S.E., the U.S.A., and the U.R.E."

"My hat! What a badly curtailed vocabulary you have."

"Yeah. Maybe the abbreviations reflect our politicians' tiny minds. Anyway, the Anglo-Saxon Empire and the United Republics are separated by a belt comprised of Slavic Eastern Europe, the Middle East, British India—which is the A.S.E.'s only direct border with the U.R.E.— and the South East Asian countries of Burma, Thailand, Cambodia and Vietnam."

"Thailand?" Burton asked.

"You knew it as Siam. The belt countries are stable and at peace except for South East Asia, which is currently the scene of a bloody conflict between the U.R.E. and U.S.A."

"America? Why America?"

"Ideology. East Eurasia has adopted socialist principles. America is concerned that if these are imposed on South East Asia, which China lays claim to, they'll easily spread through India and into the Anglo-Saxon Empire, which actually isn't as crazy as it sounds, since many of the kids—particularly in France—are already socialists."

"Or, at least, say they are," Patricia Honesty murmured.

"Bravo!" Herbert Wells said quietly. "I'm convinced that socialism has the potential to lead us to a more humane system than capitalism allows. Through it, we can destroy false ideas of property and self, eliminate unjust laws and poisonous and hateful suggestions and prejudices, create a system of social right-dealing and a tradition of right-feeling and action. I believe it to be the schoolroom of true and noble Anarchism, wherein by training and restraint we shall make free men."

"And women, Mr. Wells," Honesty put in.

"Of course! Of course! Forgive me my antiquated methods of reference."

"Forgiven. You're obviously ahead of your time."

Wells laughed. "I most certainly am!" He slapped his thigh. "Corporeally!"

"But why is America doing the fighting and not us—not the A.S.E.?" Swinburne asked.

Von Lessing answered, "Firstly, because America's prosperity has come about largely through its alliance with us; an alliance it suspects might crumble if we lose our enthusiasm for the frenzied capitalism it so fervently preaches. Secondly, because there's a strong independence movement in India, and if we made that country the front line in a war, for sure it would leave the A.S.E., taking our strongest manufacturing regions with it and depriving America of its principal source of trade. And thirdly, because with the U.S.A. doing the fighting, the conflict has a better chance of being contained. If we participated, the hostilities would undoubtedly spread. China detests us, and has done since your time."

"Thanks to Lord Elgin," Burton said. "But surely your politicians have tried to make amends for his ill-judged actions? His vandalism occurred over a century ago."

"Squares don't apologise. They just make excuses."

"Squares?"

"The straights."

Swinburne squealed and flapped his arms. "What in blue blazes are you talking about? Straight squares? Have you ever heard of bent ones?"

"Yeah, man. There are plenty."

"What? What? What?"

Sadhvi Raghavendra said, "Perhaps you could endeavour to employ rather more traditional language, Mr. von Lessing?"

"Yes, please," William Trounce grumbled.

"I must confess," Wells added, "I'm a bit lost."

Von Lessing held up a hand. "Sure. Sure. I'm trying. Um. So, like, remember how, back in your day, the politicians either came through Oxford or Cambridge universities or were, at least, aristocrats, yeah?"

"Yes," Burton and Wells chorused.

"That never changed, and those people have increasingly bungled it on the political scene. They're stuck in their ways, man. Completely out of touch. Following outdated traditions. They don't know how to work with East Eurasia, whose people they regard as savages."

"Ah," Wells said. "You mean the Anglo-Saxon genius for parliamentary government continues to assert itself; there is a great deal of talk and no decisive action?"

"Right on! Exactly that! And it's like, the middle classes respected these people, 'cos that's the traditional way of things, so there's been no challenge to 'em."

Patricia Honesty added, "The people we refer to as straights or squares, Mr. Swinburne, are the ones who blindly stick with the status quo even if it's plainly festering and useless; the ones who're incapable of changing course; who haven't the guts or imagination to do so. They have no ability to adapt and evolve."

"And the deviants?" Burton asked.

"Rock 'n' roll, man!" von Lessing enthused.

"Good Lord!" Wells exclaimed. "What is *rocking role?*"

"Rock and roll," Mark Packard clarified, "is where it's at, and we reckon it's going to change the world."

Burton's brow creased. He looked at von Lessing, who explained, "It's fast rhythmic music. It came out of the States—America—having evolved from the blues, jazz and swing."

The chrononauts all stared at him blankly.

Von Lessing continued, "Styles of music that can all be traced back to America's slave population, which brought from Africa a storytelling tradition accompanied by an intense beat and a sort of call-and-response chant."

"At last," Burton murmured "Something I'm familiar with. The musical storytelling you refer to is—according to legend—said to have originated in the Lake Regions of Central Africa." He looked first at Swinburne and then at Wells. "The Mountains of the Moon. Significant."

"Those peaks appear to have an inordinate involvement with human affairs," the poet noted.

"What?" von Lessing asked.

"We're piecing together a jigsaw," Burton told him. "Please continue. What bearing does this music have on the political situation?"

"So, uh, yeah, rock and roll really took off in the fifties and it kinda galvanised the kids, gave them a sort of independent identity, I guess. Made them rebellious."

"Created the teenager," Patricia Honesty put in.

"What is a teenager?"

She smiled. "In your day, Mr. Burton—um, I mean, Sir Richard—there was no transition from childhood to adulthood. You were a kid until you got a job, and then you were an adult, whatever your age. Nowadays, between thirteen and twenty, there's a sort of rite of passage. Teenagers have their own culture, their own music, their own fashion."

"They think for themselves," von Lessing said. "And now this free-thinking is extending into some of the older generation, too. We're sick of the establishment, the straights, and we're making plenty of noise about it."

Herbert Wells asked, "And that's the deviation you spoke of?"

Von Lessing laughed. "Yeah, man. You see, this is what happened;

the government saw the people were getting restless and losing respect for their so-called 'betters.' By sixty-four, Harold Wilson was elected as prime minister. This dude reckoned the only way to keep the populace happy was by making the weakening Empire strong again, to prove our superiority. To do that, he revived a banished technology; one that only the British had knowledge of. He made eugenics legal, and it quickly developed into what's now called *genetics*."

Burton gasped. "Eugenics! We'd seen signs that it would return. Had this Wilson fellow no idea of the dangers?"

"I don't think he cared," von Lessing responded.

"Interfering with nature," Jason Griffith muttered. "It stinks, man. Really stinks."

Wells said to Burton, "I believe it was banished in your age because the early experiments were bedevilled by unexpected consequences?"

"They were," Burton confirmed. "For every advantage the science's founder, Francis Galton, bred into his subjects, a counterweight occurred quite spontaneously. He once created a stingless bee. He didn't anticipate that it would also develop such speed of flight that, when it collided with his assistant, it went through him like a bullet, killing him instantly."

"No wonder it was outlawed," Wells muttered.

"And now it's back," von Lessing said, "as a part of the futile manoeuvrings of a stagnant leadership. The kids have had enough. They've started to protest. They want a revolution. Most don't know anything about Spring Heeled Jack or your mission to find him, but we Cannibals have started to see signs of him in the new genetically altered—er—*products*. So we recruited this guy, Mick Farren, 'cos he's a strong voice in the underground movement. He runs an antiestablishment newspaper and keeps careful track of what the government is up to. He's also in a band, so has influence with the freaks. If it comes to it, we want to be prepared and able to offer some sort of resistance against the mad intelligence."

"In a band? You mean like a brass band?" Swinburne asked. "How can that possibly work? And what are freaks? Eugenic creations?"

"Ha! No, man. It's all guitars and drums and singing now. The freaks—the turned-on kids—dig it. Mick's respected and he has insight. He's a good cat to have on our side. People would follow him."

"Literally a cat?" Swinburne asked. "Medically raised to a human degree of evolution?"

"No. Cat. Dude. Bloke. Chap. Fellow."

"Oh."

With a glance, Burton and Swinburne made a silent pact to allow certain peculiarities of the future's language pass them by without further comment.

Burton said, "And Spring Heeled Jack?"

Von Lessing replied, "Today, in London, there's going to be a mass demonstration against our alliance with America and against American aggression in South East Asia. The police are expected to show up in force. I want you to see them."

"Why?" Burton asked.

Von Lessing glanced around at his colleagues. "We—we want your opinion of them."

Detective Inspector Trounce looked puzzled. "Of the police?"

"Yeah."

"Without preconceptions, I take it," Burton said. "Except you've already indicated that you've detected Spring Heeled Jack's influence. In the police?"

"Yep."

"You have me intrigued."

"Yeah, well, I don't want to put any ideas in your head, so what say we finish for now and get some grub? Are you hungry?"

Burton wasn't but felt it impolite to refuse, so the meeting broke up and the chrononauts were served an early—and thankfully small—lunch. Burton wasn't sure what it consisted of. Some elements of it were laden with salt, others with sugar, and it all left a nasty chemical aftertaste.

Jane Packard told them, "Eddie, Karl and I will go ashore with you at Margate to meet with Mick and travel into London. You have a little while to hang loose before we arrive."

"Hang loose," Sadhvi Raghavendra said when they were left alone. "How unpleasantly descriptive."

"I wonder what their poetry is like?" Swinburne mused.

"I dread to think," Wells said. "Will we understand a word anyone says when we reach 2202?"

Burton said, "In my visions of Oxford's native time, everything was perfectly comprehensible and there was some mention of language rehabilitation. New words are introduced as time passes, others go in and out of style, but the foundations remain. In my opinion, it's the form of society itself that's more likely to mystify us."

"It's already doing so," Trounce muttered. "Music as a political force? Children defying the government? By Jove! What a madhouse!"

For a further half hour, they discussed what they'd learned from the current crop of Cannibals. Burton felt pride that his brother and Tom Bendyshe had secretly amassed—and so wisely invested—such funds that the organisation could afford the Concorde jump jet. It impressed him beyond measure. Too, he was gratified that his friends, the original club members, had so efficiently passed their cause down to their descendants. This new generation struck him as strange, strikingly unceremonious in attitude, scruffy in appearance, but undoubtedly committed and trustworthy.

After a while, Eddie Brabrooke poked his head into the cabin. "Time to go ashore, folks."

They put on their coats—but were told to leave their hats, which had gone out of fashion—and followed him up onto the deck. A motorboat was bobbing on the water next to the yacht. Burton looked toward the shore and Margate's seafront. He'd known the town as a major holiday destination, and it had hardly changed at all except that, even from this distance, it had obviously lost its gloss and become shabby and neglected.

Bidding adieu to those who were remaining behind, Burton and his companions followed Brabrooke, Karl von Lessing and Jane Packard down a rope ladder and into the boat. The woman at its tiller greeted them and introduced herself as distantly related to Richard Monckton Milnes.

She steered them to the side of the town's promenade and, as they ascended a slippery set of stone steps, said, "See you when you get back."

Burton stood and examined with interest the people who were strolling along the seafront. Though many of the men were suited, the overall impression was of a major drop in the standards he was used to, both in terms of attire and manner. As for the women, there was a scandalous amount of flesh on display. Dresses and skirts, which never revealed even an ankle in his era, had diminished in size so radically that even naked thighs were unashamedly exposed for all to see.

"Hardly the Utopia I was hoping for," Wells muttered. "It smacks more of Sodom and Gomorrah."

"Indeed," the king's agent agreed.

Don't be judgemental, he told himself. *Don't think of them as English. Be the ethnologist.*

"There's Mick," von Lessing said, waving at man who was striding toward them.

"Lord help us," Trounce muttered.

Mick Farren was all hair. It framed his face in a great bushy nimbus. The detective inspector couldn't take his eyes off it.

Burton, whose travels had exposed him to an endless variety of strange sights, was able to look beyond the extravagant halo. He saw a slim youth of medium height, dressed in worn blue canvas trousers—perhaps the uniform of his generation—a black shirt, a short black jacket made from leather, and boots that reminded the king's agent of those worn by Spain's *vaqueros*. Farren's long and, by the looks of it, oft-broken nose might have dominated the face of another man, but in him it was eclipsed by the eyes, which, as he came closer, were revealed to be direct, sullen and challenging.

"Sir Richard," he said, shaking Burton's hand.

"Mr. Farren."

Few people could meet and hold Burton's gaze. Farren did. The king's agent felt himself being assessed.

He passed the test.

In a surprisingly soft and cultured tone—Burton was half expecting a cockney accent—Farren continued, "The *Orpheus* was called to 1968 because I recommended it. I hope what you see today will justify my decision." He turned to the others. "Miss Raghavendra, Mr. Swinburne, Mr. Trounce, Mr. Wells—I'm honoured to meet you all. I expect this time period will strike you as lurid and uncultured. That's because it is." He smiled slightly. "If you'll follow me, I have a couple of cars parked around the corner. We'll drive you to London."

"What are cars?" Trounce asked as they followed Farren away from the promenade and into a street lined with shops.

"Diminutive of 'autocarriage,'" Herbert Wells put in. "They were invented during my childhood as an alternative to the old steam spheres." He pointed to a yellow metal box at the side of the road a little way ahead. It was mounted on four wheels and had glass windows. "By the looks of it they've become rather more sophisticated than the rickety contraptions of 1914."

As they emerged onto a wider thoroughfare, five of the vehicles whipped past at a tremendous velocity, steam whistling from pipes at their rear.

"Like a landau," Swinburne observed, "but with the driver and the engine inside."

It being Sunday, the town was fairly quiet and the shops were closed. Burton examined the contents of their display windows and only understood half of what he saw. Everything appeared garish, plentiful, and cheaply manufactured.

"What are those rods?" Sadhvi enquired, pointing at the rooftops.

Karl von Lessing answered, "Television aerials, Miss Raghavendra. Television is like radio but with moving pictures, a little theatre in your sitting room. The aerials pick up the signals."

"Moving pictures?" Swinburne exclaimed. "You mean, like a zoetrope?"

"A what?" von Lessing asked.

The poet cried out and aimed a kick at thin air. "How are we ever to communicate?"

The group came to two parked cars. Trounce and Raghavendra joined Eddie Brabrooke and Karl von Lessing in one, while Swinburne, Wells and Jane Packard squeezed into the back of the other, with Burton in the front beside Farren. The king's agent watched closely as Farren manipulated steering rods and a footplate—a very similar arrangement to that of the old steam spheres and rotorchairs.

"Steam?" Burton asked, as the car rolled out into the road.

"Yep," Farren responded. "The Yanks favour petroleum engines, but they're unreliable as hell. Anglo-Saxon steam technology is still where it's at. Over the past century or so, we've learned how to squeeze the most out of the least. It was Formby coal in your day, wasn't it?"

"Yes."

"We use a process called muon-catalysation now, which is powered by an extension of the Formby treatment. We can make a marble-sized lump of coal blaze like a sun for a whole day, and a vehicle can run on twelve gallons of heavy water for almost two hundred miles at speeds of up to sixty miles an hour."

"Heavy water?"

"Yeah, man. That'd take me a week to explain."

The car accelerated, and Margate was quickly left behind. As the vehicle swept westward, Burton and Swinburne saw that the little seaside towns—Herne Bay and Whitstable—which had flourished in the mid-1800s, were now, like Margate, in a sad state of dilapidation, while the countryside between them had been rendered a characterless patchwork by intensive farming.

Further inland, the Kentish towns of Faversham, Sittingbourne and Gillingham were vastly expanded, but the new buildings struck the chrononauts as soulless and unprepossessing, and by the time they reached Gravesend they were shocked to find themselves already on the outskirts of the capital. London was immensely expanded.

As they swept into the densely built-up outer reaches of the city, with other vehicles flowing around them, Burton asked, "You are a musician, Mr. Farren?"

"Mick, please. I'm a singer and songwriter, among other things."

"In a band?"

"The Deviants."

"And music has become a political force?"

"Uh-huh."

Farren reached down to a knob on the control panel in front of him and gave it a twist. The car's cabin was immediately filled with a harsh blend of trumpets, guitars and other instruments that Burton couldn't identify. The cacophony sounded vaguely Spanish and was accompanied by three or four male voices singing in harmony.

"Ouch!" Swinburne exclaimed. "What a racket!"

"The song is called 'The Legend of Xanadu,' Mr Swinburne," Farren said. "By Dave, Dee, Dozy, Beaky, Mick and Tich."

"My hat! What are they? Dwarfs? What happened to the seventh?"
Farren gave a throaty chuckle.

"I presume the song refers to the Empire's difficulties with China,"
Burton said. "Though I fail to understand the Spanish motif."

Farren shook his bushy head. "No, Sir Richard. This is what's known
as pop music—pop, short for *popular*. Its only function is as commercial
entertainment. It has very little meaning. I doubt the kids even know
where Xanadu is. Let's try a different station."

Keeping his eyes on the road ahead, Farren twisted another control
knob. The music dissolved into crackles, whines, howls and snatches
of conversation before settling into an urgent and primitive-sounding
rhythm over which an American-accented voice sang about "breaking on
through to the other side."

"Rock music," Farren revealed. "This band is called *The Doors*."

"How is it different to pop?" Burton asked.

Farren thought for a moment. "I guess rock music is less about com-
merce and more about cutting through the surface of civilisation to find
an authenticity within each of us."

Burton considered this and said, "That was one of the aims of the
original Cannibal Club when Doctor James Hunt and I first founded it. I
must admit, we didn't much pursue the objective."

"We were too busy getting three sheets to the wind," Swinburne
added.

"Nevertheless, it's yet another curious coincidence," the king's agent
muttered.

Farren said, "What you intended at the club's inception is now more
important than you ever envisioned. The people are so distracted by
bread and circuses they've lost any sense of themselves. They don't realise
they're being enslaved by the system."

Swinburne leaned forward. "By which you mean the system of governance established and run by the upper classes?"

"Exactly," Farren answered. "Except, if you scrape away the layers of
illusion, I'm pretty sure you'll find a single presence at the rotten core of it."

Burton looked at him. "Edward Oxford?"

"Yep."

> The Britain that is going to be forged in the white heat of
> this revolution will be no place for restrictive practices or
> for outdated methods on either side of industry.
> —Harold Wilson, 1963

T hey caught their first glimpse of police constables at the junction
of Oxford Street and Tottenham Court Road. A tower—the tallest
any of the chrononauts had ever seen—dominated the area, an unsightly
edifice of concrete and glass.

"Centre Point," Mick Farren said. "Completed last year. Thirty-two
storeys, all completely empty. An eyesore and total waste of money."

It was a dramatic example of how the capital had altered. Buildings
crowded against each other, pushed upward into the sky, and appeared
to occupy every available space. Here and there among their ill-designed
and blocky facades, segments of the nineteenth century could occasionally be spotted, like broken memories clinging to existence, but little of
Burton and Swinburne's world remained beyond the major monuments,
and to the king's agent, even the dome of St. Paul's Cathedral—which
bulged up into the crystal-clear air—looked suddenly small, helpless and
insignificant.

After leaving the cars in Bedford Place, the Cannibals had walked to
the southern end of Tottenham Court Road where they'd joined an enor-

mous crowd of demonstrators. Farren told them an even larger crowd was gathered in Trafalgar Square, the two groups slowly working their way toward Grosvenor Square. Burton had witnessed protests in the 1850s, but nothing to match this. People were present in their thousands, long-haired, colourfully dressed, many holding banners and placards, and all chanting, "Ho! Ho! Ho Chi Minh! Ho! Ho! Ho Chi Minh! Ho! Ho! Ho Chi Minh!"

Farren put his mouth to Burton's ear and shouted above the din, "Ho Chi Minh. Former president of Vietnam. He represents what the people of South East Asia desire for their region, as opposed to what the U.S.A. or U.R.E. wants."

Following his lead, they pushed into the crowd, taking up position behind a group of youths holding a banner bearing the words "Mersey-side Anarchist Group."

Burton felt completely out of his depth. He obviously wasn't alone in his sense of vulnerability; Sadhvi Raghavendra was clinging to his left elbow for security, Wells was looking nervously this way and that, and Trounce was staying very close, too, and was visibly trembling. Only Swinburne appeared at ease amid the uproar. He twitched and danced and laughed and added his shrill voice to the chanting.

Raghavendra tugged at Burton's arm, nodded toward Trounce, and yelled, "Richard! I don't approve of the stuff, but you have to give William another dose of Saltzmann's. This is all too much for him."

Burton nodded, drew a bottle from his jacket pocket, and at that moment saw the police constables. He dropped the tincture, and the glass shattered at his feet.

"Bismillah!"

There were twenty policemen standing in a row on the pavement.

But they weren't men.

Swinburne shrieked and pointed. Trounce staggered against the king's agent. Raghavendra put a hand to her mouth. Wells swore.

"Don't stare at them," Eddie Brabrooke advised. "Believe me, you don't want them to notice you."

"You understand now why I activated the beacon?" Farren asked.

"Yes," Burton croaked. "By God, yes!"

The constables were humanoid in form, standing upright, with bulky torsos and short, thin limbs, but they possessed the heads of pigs. Dressed in black uniforms with silver buttons, they wore round helmets and had long boots encasing the lower part of their legs. The boots were mounted on spring-loaded, two-foot-high stilts.

"The genetically altered pigs were first introduced to the force a couple of years ago," Farren said. "They're strong and vicious but lack height and speed. The new uniforms were introduced last month to address that problem. The moment I saw them, I thought of Spring Heeled Jack."

"The similarity is striking," Burton responded. "Undoubtedly, Oxford's influence is at work. Has the genetic manipulation resulted in the usual side effects?"

"Yes," Farren answered. "They possess an unanticipated degree of aggression."

The police creatures were lost to view as the crowd suddenly surged forward.

Taking their cue from some of the groups around them, the Cannibals and chrononauts linked arms—Wells, Farren, Burton and Trounce leading, with Jane Packard, Karl von Lessing, Raghavendra and Swinburne following behind.

Leaning close to Trounce, Burton shouted, "William, are you all right?"

Trounce looked at him with glazed eyes. "Too many people. Too many people."

Burton disengaged his arm and checked his pockets. Silently, he cursed himself for not bringing more Saltzmann's from the ship. A stupid mistake. He hooked his hand back around Trounce's elbow. "Stay with us, old chap."

Like a tidal wave, the crowd swept along Oxford Street.

"We're heading to the American Embassy," Farren announced. "A show of strength."

For the next hour, conversation was almost impossible. The chanting increased in volume and vehemence, and an ominous air of smouldering violence pressed down upon them like a brewing storm.

Burton retreated into his role of detached observer. He took in every detail of people's attire, of their gestures and expressions, and of the words he heard spoken—or more often shouted—around him. He recognised that the England he knew was in the grip of a deep transformation, driven by a powerful zeitgeist, and rapidly becoming almost unrecognisable to him. Individuals who thought they were in control of their actions were, he perceived, actually motivated by an almost primordial passion, something chthonic and incomprehensible, though vaguely sensed. He could see it in Mick Farren's eyes. The songwriter appeared almost mesmerised, as if participating in a war of gods without being fully cognisant of it.

And where was the insane Edward Oxford in all of this? How much of the apparent madness Burton observed was that of the Spring Heeled Jack consciousness? Had the man from 2202 infected history like a virulent disease?

Jane Packard yelled, "This is more than we anticipated, Sir Richard. Follow us. We're going to slip into a side street and get away from here."

It immediately proved more easily said than done. The sheer weight of numbers made the demonstration almost impossible to navigate, and over the course of the next thirty minutes they were shoved helplessly along with it all the way to North Audley Street, forced left, and driven into Grosvenor Square. Here, the furore was overwhelming and the crush of bodies immense.

Burton managed to manoeuvre to Raghavendra's side. He shouted into her ear, "Stay close to William, Sadhvi."

She said something he couldn't hear and squeezed past Packard to join the Scotland Yard man.

Farren caught Burton's eye and nodded toward the right. Following the gesture, the king's agent saw, through the many banners and waving placards, a huddled mass of uniformed pig men, all mounted on horses. The creatures were holding sword-length batons, and their steeds were draped with light chain mail and wore horned headpieces, making them resemble unicorns.

The more Burton looked, the more constables he noticed, and every one of them had a wicked glint in its eyes.

He barged past two furiously chanting men to reach Farren. "Is there any law against protesting?"

"In theory, no. In practice—man, we're in trouble. Everyone knows a confrontation is inevitable, but I didn't think it'd be today." He pointed at a large blocky building, the focus of the protesters' anger. Burton could see pieces of fencing—obviously torn up by the crowd—being thrown toward it.

"The American Embassy," Farren said. "If its perimeter is breached, all hell will break loose."

No sooner had he spoken than a series of detonations sounded. Burton saw small canisters spinning through the air, trailing smoke as they arced from the cluster of uniformed pig men into the middle of the crowd.

"Tear gas!" Farren shouted.

Grey fumes billowed up, casting a swirling veil over all. People crouched and clung to each other. A voice blared into the square, "Disperse immediately! Disperse immediately! Return to your homes!"

Burton's eyes started to burn. He squinted through the thickening cloud and pushed past Farren to Swinburne, Trounce, Raghavendra and Wells. "Stay together," he bellowed, but his voice was lost in a cacophony of screams and shouts and the repeating demand, "Disperse immediately! Disperse immediately!"

Bottles and the poles used for placards started to rain down on the police, flung by the increasingly enraged demonstrators.

"Disperse immediately! This is your final warning! Disperse immediately!"

Goaded into ungovernable rage and considerable panic, the mob heaved and eddied like a boiling liquid, with individuals breaking off as small spaces appeared among them, only to then be engulfed again. Burton recognised, however, that some must have been escaping into side streets, for increasingly he and his companions were able to force their way southward.

Suddenly, without any perceivable prompt, the mounted constables let loose ferocious squeals and surged forward. Men and women fell beneath their horses' hooves. The pigs swiped their batons indiscriminately, cracking heads, breaking arms, bruising ribs. Others, on foot, bounded high into the air, propelled by their spring-loaded stilts. They came flying out of the caustic gas, crashing down on people, attacking them brutally and, it appeared, with glee.

Burton staggered and coughed. He felt like he was breathing in fire. With blurred vision, he saw Jane Packard's head spray blood as a baton crunched into the back of it. She fell and was immediately trampled by her assailant's horse. The king's agent lurched toward her but found his way blocked when a constable landed in front of him. The pig man snorted and laughed wickedly. Its snout wrinkled into an expression of unmitigated savagery as its beady eyes fixed on him and it raised its weapon to strike.

Mick Farren came careening into it, knocking it to the ground. He slammed a fist into its face, snatched the baton from its hand and, gripping the staff at either end, crushed it into the pig's neck. He screamed at Burton, "Get away! Wait for us by the cars!"

Another constable hurtled down. It grabbed Farren by his bushy hair and yanked him backward. Burton swore, then pounced onto it and, acting on instinct alone, applied a Thuggee wrestling hold to its head and twisted until he felt the neck snap.

Farren raised the baton and hammered its end between the eyes of the pig beneath him. He rose from the unconscious body. "We have to get the hell out of here!"

Burton couldn't answer. He struggled to draw breath. Vaguely, he was aware that Brabrooke was bent over Jane Packard's broken body; that Swinburne was with Wells, who had blood streaming down his face; that Raghavendra, Trounce and von Lessing were nowhere in sight; and that the main line of mounted police had swept by and was now crashing through the crowd to his left.

Brabrooke shouted, "She's dead! Oh God! I think Jane's dead!"

Farren hesitated. "We have to get Burton's lot to safety."

"Then go. I'll stay with her."

"Eddie, it's not—"

"Beat it!"

Farren stepped to Burton's side and took hold of his arm. They were jostled as protesters seethed around them. Burton cried hoarsely, "This damned gas has me blinded! Where are Sadhvi and William?"

"I saw Karl with them," Farren said. "He'll get them to the cars. We have to split before the pigs head back this way."

They elbowed through to Swinburne and Wells, grabbed them, and pushed on toward the southwestern corner of the square. The Cannibal from 1914 was in a bad way, dripping blood and fighting to remain conscious, depending on the poet for support.

"What has happened to the world?" Swinburne shrieked. "This is worse than Bethlem Hospital!"

The amplified voice blared, "Disperse immediately! All those who resist will be arrested!"

The group flinched back as another constable hit the ground just feet away. It immediately bounced onward, without sparing them a glance.

Swinburne pushed Wells at Burton and Farren. "Quick! Take him."

Burton caught Wells. A riderless police horse came thundering out of the steam. Swinburne ran at it, seized the flapping reins, and swung himself up into the saddle. He yelled, "Follow!"

People scattered out of the horse's way as Swinburne expertly took control of the animal and, despite it being skittish, nudged it harmlessly through the protesters, forging a path toward South Audley Street. Burton and Farren walked behind, holding Wells upright.

Finally, they broke free of the throng, staggered out of the square, and found further progress blocked by three constables.

"Under arrest!" one growled. "Stealing horse!"

"Assault!" the second announced.

"Resisting!" the third added.

"I confess!" Swinburne exclaimed. "Yes, yes, and yes!"

He yanked on the reins, and the horse reared up lashing out with its front legs. One hoof caught a pig under the chin. The creature flopped to the pavement, out cold. The other hoof thudded into a constable's stomach. The pig folded, dropped to its knees, and instantly turned a nasty shade of green.

Burton let go of Wells, took three long strides, crouched under the remaining constable's swinging baton, and delivered a devastating right hook. The beast spun a near-complete revolution and crumpled.

"Lucky," Burton murmured. "I couldn't see what I was hitting."

Swinburne dismounted. "How'd you know when to duck?"

"Instinct. How are your eyes, Algy?"

"Stinging like blazes, but I'm all right."

"Then guide me, please. Mick, you have Herbert?"

"Yep. Let's head for Piccadilly. Maybe we can hop on a bus and make it back to the cars."

It didn't work out that way. By the time they'd staggered to the northern edge of Green Park, their eyes had cleared, but when they tried to board a bus—a two-storey-high, bright-red, steam-driven contraption—its conductor glared at Farren's hair, looked disgustedly at the state of Wells, gaped in bemusement at Burton and Swinburne, and snapped, "Not you, sweeties!" before ringing the bell that signalled the driver to get going.

They tried two more buses with similar results.

So they walked all the way to Piccadilly Circus, along Shaftesbury Avenue and High Holborn, then up Southampton Row to Bedford Place. By the time they reached the cars, Herbert Wells was somewhat recovered. All, though, were footsore and exhausted.

Burton's scientific detachment had become rather more pathological. He felt as if a thick pane of glass separated him from the environment, and, increasingly, when anyone addressed him, an expanding distance inserted itself between him and them. Remotely, he recognised that Swinburne was starting to experience the same, and when von Lessing and Raghavendra greeted them at the vehicles, he saw that the latter, too, was suffering this insidious entrancement. As for Trounce, he was virtually catatonic, sitting in the back of one of the cars with wide, fixed eyes and a slack mouth.

"It's too much," Sadhvi mumbled. "We're losing our minds."

Burton turned to Farren. "Mick, we can't hold out for another day. Not without a dose of Saltzmann's. You have to get us back to the *Orpheus*. We'll stay aboard her until the refit is completed."

Farren gave a curt nod. "I'll drive you back to the yacht." He addressed von Lessing. "Karl, Eddie's with Jane. She's badly hurt. Maybe even—maybe even dead. Will you stay and track them down?"

Von Lessing paled. "Yeah. I'll check the hospitals. What a bloody mess."

They bid him farewell. Raghavendra and Wells joined Trounce in the back of the car while Burton climbed into the front with Farren. They set off back toward Margate. No one spoke. Farren was lost in his own thoughts, and as for the chrononauts—

They just felt lost.

It was evening by the time they boarded the yacht. Burton and his companions had little idea of where they were or what they were doing. The Cannibals guided them to bunks, and they all fell into an instant and profound sleep.

Burton awoke at noon on the following day in an unfamiliar room and with the taste of Saltzmann's haunting the back of his throat. He was lying on a bed—more like a shelf projecting from a concave wall—and still wearing yesterday's clothes, which were torn and stained with blood and dust.

He sat up, looked at his hands, and noted that the knuckles were cut and bruised. Slowly, recent memories seeped back into his conscious mind.

Standing, he looked out of a porthole and saw a broad triangular wing beyond which, past a narrow strip of coastline, the sea sparkled brightly. He was obviously on the Concorde—the new *Orpheus*—and when he turned to face the tiny cabin, he saw that his suitcases had been transferred to it from the old ship. He opened an inner door and found an en suite bathroom. Forty minutes later, he was clean, dressed in fresh clothes, and feeling a great deal better.

Burton exited into a very narrow corridor with doors running down either side of it. He'd asserted from the shape of the wing that the prow was to his left, so he followed the passage along to a door. It opened onto a long, narrow tubular lounge. A group rose to greet him: Captain Lawless, Gooch, Krishnamurthy, Raghavendra, Mick Farren, Patricia Honesty, Trevor Penniforth, and Jason Griffith.

"How do you feel?" Sadhvi asked.

"Fair to middling," he answered, taking a seat and fishing a cheroot from his pocket. "Much more myself. The others?"

"Still in their beds. Algy is in good shape. Mr. Wells required stitches and will need to rest a while. William had a hard time of it. I've sedated him and dosed him with more of that accursed Saltzmann's than my principles should allow, but without it I'm concerned he might lose his sanity."

"And with it?"

"After plenty of sleep, I think he'll return to us."

"I'm sorry, man," Farren murmured. "My fault. I could have summoned the *Orpheus* to any day, and I went and picked the day of a bloody riot."

"We couldn't have known, Mick," Patricia Honesty put in.

"It doesn't matter," Burton said, lighting his Manila. "What's important is that we saw evidence of Spring Heeled Jack's presence."

Krishnamurthy frowned. "I don't understand. If he's here in 1968, how and why and *where?*"

Burton gave a nod of thanks to Griffith, who'd placed a plate of sandwiches and a cup of coffee before him.

"Conspiracy theory," Farren muttered.

"Mr. Farren?" Burton said.

"The Automatic Computing Engine."

"And what is that?"

"There was this dude, Alan Turing, who I guess you could call Charles Babbage's successor. He was a genius mathematician who, in 1950, is rumoured to have invented an equivalent to one of the old babbage probability calculators, except using a different and more powerful technology. Turing claimed great things for his machine, and for a few years he was the toast of the Anglo-Saxon Empire. His device would return to us the global dominance we enjoyed back in your age, and which we'd been steadily losing to our allies, the Americans. It would lead to the total mechanisation of our industries, allowing each and every one of us to live comfortably, pursuing our individual interests. No more drudgery. No more working classes being oppressed by the system." He finished sarcastically, "Yeah, right on!"

"It didn't happen?"

"In 1952, he was prosecuted for being a homosexual."

Burton raised an eyebrow. "The state takes an interest in people's sexual preferences?"

"Obsessively. He was publicly humiliated, experimented on, and two years later died from cyanide poisoning. Suicide, apparently, but there are those—the Cannibal Club among them—who think he was murdered."

"Because?"

"Because the Automatic Computing Engine never appeared. The

government claimed they examined it and found nothing but a prototype based on dodgy theoretical work. It was unsound and unworkable."

Gooch interjected, "But you have other ideas?"

"Too right. I think the government lied and continued to develop it in secret. I think fourteen years after its inventor's death, the Automatic Computing Engine is something quite different to what he intended. He envisioned a Utopia. The government, I suspect, has plans for exactly the opposite. If the machine really exists, I don't know how it's being used, but something very bad is happening behind the scenes, and if you discover that the crazy presence of Edward Oxford has somehow infiltrated the device, and that it's manipulating government policies, then I won't be the slightest bit surprised."

"By God," Krishnamurthy muttered. "How can we fight something we can't see?"

Burton responded, "By moving forward through time until it's in plain sight."

Sadhvi Raghavendra sighed and held up a hand, palm toward him. "I understand your impatience and the sense of urgency, but remember, Richard, that the advantage of our ability to transcend the limitations of time is that we aren't required to hurry. I insist that we all rest for another day. We have casualties."

Nathaniel Lawless added, "To be frank, I'm not confident I'm sufficiently *au fait* with this new ship's systems, either. I'd like to study her for a while longer before our next hop."

Penniforth smiled and rumbled, "Your Mark Three ain't comfortable, neither, Cap'n. Without Mr. Gooch, we wouldn't 'ave known how to connect the thing, an' we certainly don't know how to tell it what's what."

Gooch added, "The babbage will work it out for itself, but it'll have to experiment for a bit, so yes, I agree, we should stay put for another day."

"We're still on the Dutch coast?" Burton asked.

Patricia Honesty answered, "Yep. This is Bendyshe Bay—private land owned by the Foundation. We're secluded and perfectly safe."

"Good. In that case, by all means, we'll rest before we make our next foray into the future."

"The year 2000?" Lawless asked.

Burton shook his head. "No. Change of plan. Our first two legs consisted of fifty-four years each. Let's add another fifty-four. Next stop, 2022."

Jason Griffith stood and fetched a file from a bookshelf. He handed it to Burton. "A little something to keep you occupied. *The History of the Future*, volume two."

Burton groaned. "I haven't read a single page of volume one, yet."

"Karl is our historian," Griffith said, "but he's not as meticulous as your brother was, which is why the second chunk of history you jumped through has made for a slimmer file. Easier to read, man."

Burton hummed his acknowledgement and asked, "Where is Mr. von Lessing?"

The group became silent. Farren broke it. "Still in London. He got word to us. Jane was killed by that bloody pig."

Henry Murray's great-granddaughter, Burton thought. *Dead*.

It was Henry who'd introduced Burton to Richard Monckton Milnes. Both men were—had been?—a decade older than him and had greatly influenced his decision to make the famous pilgrimage to Mecca. By God!—how different might Burton's life be had he never met the man!

Suddenly, the warmth of Saltzmann's throbbed in his temples, and the lounge appeared to drop away from him. He envisioned the path his life had taken as a shimmering ribbon of light. It wound through an infinite tangle of other ribbons; crossing some; running parallel to others for short and long distances; coiling around and even knotting with a few. It weaved in and out, and as his imagination—or was it his insight?—gained clarity, he sank into it until the ribbon streamed through and around him, and he saw that it was comprised of mathematical formulae.

Tumbling helplessly, he was inundated by outlandish algebraic geometries; he folded into obtuse equations; he sped along lines of esoteric calculus. He dissolved into such contorted topologies that for an instant and an eternity, he was nowhere and everywhere.

Burton reconstituted around a bunched segment of probabilities that he somehow recognised as personality traits. They manifested as an utterly unique individual. He collided with its dazzling nucleus, his own cluster of singularities ploughing into those of the other, and they exploded outward in an incandescent blaze of newly forming potentials.

The birth of further equations.

The forging of new paths.

The creation of a friendship.

Burton possessed no knowledge of the woman who'd borne Henry Murray's child. Where he had come from, that event existed in the future. However, such were the intricacies of cause and effect, that he realised his mere presence in Murray's life had been enough to contribute to the existence of Jane Murray, for he'd influenced his friend's preferences and behaviour, caused him to make certain choices and to be at certain locations at certain times. He'd been the stimulus for steps taken, and subsequent ones had led his friend to that unknown woman, with whom Murray had created a child.

Converging ribbons.

Actions and consequences.

A child.

Descendants.

Jane Packard.

Dead.

Wordlessly, Burton jumped up and hurriedly left the lounge. He entered the passage that led to his cabin but had only just passed into it when he stumbled and was forced to lean against the bulkhead for support.

Sadhvi Raghavendra followed. She placed a hand on his shoulder and said quietly, "Richard, are you all right?"

He drew in a deep shuddering breath, fished a handkerchief from his pocket, and wiped a tear from his cheek.

"I never properly mourned Isabel," he whispered. "She was to be my wife, but she was killed, and there will never be a woman to replace her. I shall have no children. When I die, everything I am will die with me. Nothing of Richard Francis Burton will continue. I'll have no representation in the future."

She smiled sadly. "You've overlooked the obvious."

"Which is what?"

"You don't require representation. Where the future is concerned, you are very much in it."

CHAPTER 13

AN OLD FRIEND IN 2022

**FREEDOM IS A REWARD NOT A RIGHT.
FREEDOM IS ATTAINED NOT INTRINSIC.
YOU ARE A PRESUMED THREAT
UNTIL YOU DEMONSTRATE OTHERWISE.
EARN THE TRUST OF THE STATE.
WORK. CONTRIBUTE. OBEY.**

"Oops!" *Orpheus* said. "Watch out!"

Burton, blinking the whiteness out of his eyes, fell across the sloping cockpit and slammed into a control panel. Nathaniel Lawless landed on top of him.

The floor heaved upward, sending the two men tumbling in the other direction.

Algernon Swinburne let loose a piercing shriek. Mick Farren swore.

"Wait! Wait!" *Orpheus* demanded. "I'm getting the hang of it now!"

The ship lurched again.

"Stop it!" Swinburne hollered, somersaulting into Lawless.

"I'm trying! Do you think it's easy controlling a new vessel without any practice?" *Orpheus* protested. "You should be singing my praises!"

Finally, the Concorde levelled out. Burton, Swinburne, Lawless and Farren got to their feet.

"Report!" the captain barked.

"Give me a moment," *Orpheus* replied. "It's rather more intricate than before. Ah. No. Yes. All right, we're fine. We're at five thousand feet, directly above our starting point."

"Bendyshe Bay?" Lawless demanded.

"That's what I said, isn't it? I should warn you, there's a lot of air traffic around us. I recommend an immediate landing."

"Do it."

"The date?" Burton asked.

"As you ordered," *Orpheus* answered. "Four o'clock in the morning on Tuesday the first of February in the year 2022."

Farren looked out of the windows. "It's as black as pitch out there."

Burton felt suddenly lighter as the airship sank toward the ground. "I learned my lesson," he said. "It's a winter new moon. It was likely to be overcast, so running without lights, as we are, makes us harder to spot."

"Not to telemobiloscopes," Swinburne pointed out.

"Radar," Farren said, reminding the poet of the technology's new name. "Getting out of the sky is a very good idea."

"Someone's calling," *Orpheus* announced. "Really! This isn't a good time for interruptions. How many things am I supposed to do at once?"

"Let's hear it," Lawless said.

The *Concorde's* radio system was more sophisticated than the equipment they'd gained in 1914 and didn't require Burton or any of the others to hold the equivalent of a speaking tube. It projected a female voice directly into the bridge.

"Captain Lawless?"

"Hello," Lawless replied.

"Incredible! You just appeared out of thin air!"

"We're coming down. Is it safe?"

"Yes. Is Sir Richard with you?"

"I'm here," Burton said.

"Hello. Marianne Smith. Just a small party to meet you. We'll come aboard."

"Very well. We'll see you in a moment."

He'd hardly finished speaking before their descent slowed dramatically.

"Brace yourselves," *Orpheus* warned. "I've not landed a Concorde before. This might be disastrous."

"Cripes!" Swinburne muttered.

The ship bumped to a halt. The whining of its engines deepened in tone as they slowed to a stop.

"I'll gladly accept a round of applause," the Mark III said.

"Miss Smith?" Burton queried.

"Still here."

"We'll open the doors in a couple of minutes."

"Thank you."

The radio cut off.

"I'll stay here," Lawless said. "I want to get the hang of the manual controls. Just in case."

Burton nodded and gestured for the others to follow. They exited. The exterior hatch was just behind the bridge and in front of the lounge. Krishnamurthy and Gooch met them by it.

"Sadhvi's staying with Herbert and William," Krishnamurthy said. "They both require more time to recuperate."

Burton took hold of the hatch's right handle. He indicated that Krishnamurthy should take the left. In unison, they pulled and twisted, then pushed the portal open and slid it aside. A staircase automatically emerged from the base of the opening and glided down to the ground below.

Three shadowy figures were waiting. They mounted the steps, ascending to the chrononauts. The first of them to enter the ship was a short middle-aged woman with cropped grey hair and sharp features.

"Marianne," she said, and turning, gestured an elderly woman forward. "And you know my mother, Patricia."

"Miss Hon-Honesty!" Burton said, unable to fully disguise his shock. "We only just said good-bye."

"It's all right. Don't try to hide it," she replied. "For you, just minutes ago, I was twenty-two. For me, half a century has passed. I was Mrs. Smith for much of it, and now I'm a seventy-six-year-old widow." She gave a cackling laugh. "Life sucks."

"Sucks?" Swinburne interjected.

"Hello again, Mr. Swinburne. And hello, Mr. Gooch, Mr. Krishna-murthy. Yes, sucks. I'm afraid language is still degenerating."

She turned to Farren. "Mick, you bastard."

He gaped at her, his lips moving wordlessly.

"Look at you!" she exclaimed. "Exactly the same. My old friend, the revolutionary." She laughed. "But not as old as me!"

They embraced, and Farren muttered, "Bloody hell! Bloody hell!"

She pushed him to arm's length and smiled up at him. "I have excellent news for you."

"Wh-what?" he stammered.

"Your hairstyle is back in fashion."

Farren grinned, but Burton noticed pain in the young man's eyes—the same pain he himself had experienced upon meeting the elderly Edward Brabrooke in 1914. There was an agonising sorrow in seeing one's friends decay while you remained the same. Even more so, a vicious guilt.

Patricia Honesty moved aside and pulled forward the third person, a tall and gawky young woman, about eighteen years old, with fascinatingly misaligned features and a large gap between her front teeth. "This is Lorena Brabrooke."

The introduction swept away Burton's ruminations. Here was his old friend, again renewed, again refreshed, and again reborn.

Isabel, he thought. *Ah, who might we have become together?*

"Hey," the girl said, by way of a greeting.

Burton took an instant liking to her. He smiled when she fumbled his handshake. "Young lady, I'm delighted to see the Brabrookes are still going strong."

"Um. Thanks. I mean—wow!—it's like, you're a legend."

The king's agent chuckled. "No, I'm all too human."

"Aren't we all," Patricia Honesty put in ruefully.

"I was just with your father's friends," Burton told Brabrooke, "back in 1968."

"You mean my grandfather."

"Oh. My mistake." Burton threw out his hands. "How time flies!" He addressed Marianne Smith. "Just the three of you?"

"Yes," she replied. "We'll explain, but first—Lori?"

Brabrooke took something from a bag slung over her shoulder and quickly clamped it shut around Burton's forearm. While he was still uttering, "What the devil—?" the girl administered the same treatment to Swinburne, Farren, Gooch and Krishnamurthy. The men all examined the plain black bands that now encircled their wrists.

"I can't take it off!" Gooch grumbled.

"A blasted liberty!" Swinburne complained. "What's the meaning of it, Miss Brabrooke?"

"T-bands," came her mumbled response. "T for Turing."

"Turing!" Farren cried out. "I knew it!"

"Trust us," Patricia Honesty said. "They're necessary. Now, Sir Richard, it's absurdly early in the morning, we're standing in an open doorway, and there's a chill wind blowing on my neck. Invite us in or throw us out, one or the other."

Burton bowed politely and waved the three visitors in. They moved through to the lounge—Gooch and Krishnamurthy followed after securing the door—and settled on the sofas. Farren got to work at the coffeepot. Burton asked Honesty, "So, ma'am, how stands the Cannibal Club?"

"Ma'am? How quaint. I like it." The old woman gestured toward her daughter. "My child has taken the reins."

Burton turned his eyes to Marianne, who said, "We are fewer. Twelve of us. Secrecy has become a matter of life or death. The world is vastly changed since sixty-eight." She held up an arm to reveal that she, too, wore one of the bracelets. "These are to protect you."

"From what?" Burton asked.

"From the government."

"What on earth has happened?" Swinburne exclaimed.

"The Turing Fulcrum."

Patricia Honesty, jerking her chin toward Farren, interjected, "You remember—when we last met—Mick told you about the Automatic Computing Engine? What we suspected then was true; the government was developing it in secret. During the 1980s, the technology finally saw the light of day. Turings went into mass production. Now, everybody has one."

Krishnamurthy held up his arm and examined his bangle.

"No, Mr. Krishnamurthy," Honesty said. "I'm not referring to T-bands."

"Then what?" he asked.

From her bag, Lorena Brabrooke produced a thin eight-inch-long tube of what looked to Burton like brushed steel. She gave it a slight shake, and the chrononauts uttered sounds of amazement as, emitting a chime, it unfolded and, seemingly with a life of its own, snapped into a flat sheet, eight inches wide by ten long, and the thickness of a book cover. One side of it lit up, displaying colours and shapes that, when Brabrooke turned it to face them, they didn't comprehend at all.

"This is a Turing," she said. "It—um—I suppose it's a bit like one of your old babbages except, rather than being a distinct device, it exists in connection with all the other Turings, forming a network. It can give you any public information you require. Look."

Burton and the others leaned forward and watched as she moved her fingers across the screen and conjured up a mass of movement that, for a few moments, meant nothing to the king's agent. Then he suddenly realised he was looking through a window and, amid a great deal he didn't understand, he recognised the British Museum.

Brabrooke slid her fingertips across the screen, a little above it, and, dizzyingly, the scene rushed forward, as if the window was flying up the steps of the building. Doors whipped past. The entrance lobby—and the people in it—went blurring by. The viewpoint shot up the still-magnificent staircase.

Burton felt both absorbed and disoriented as Brabrooke moved the window through corridor after corridor, past exhibit after exhibit, until it slid into place beside a group of visitors who were standing in front of a plinth upon which there knelt a familiar figure.

"Brunel!" the chrononauts chorused.

Brabrooke touched a small circle on the screen, and a voice sounded from the device. "Isambard Kingdom Brunel, born on the ninth of April 1806, was an English mechanical and civil engineer and the founder of the Department of Guided Science. His designs, which revolutionised public transport, also allowed for the rapid expansion of the Anglo-Saxon Empire, and are generally regarded as—"

A flick of Brabrooke's finger caused the volume to decrease until it was barely audible.

"Magic!" Swinburne whispered. "Utterly impossible!"

The girl gave a small smile. "The devices are used for work, study, communication and entertainment, and—like I said—they can access any public information. That's the problem."

"Ah," Burton said. "Public."

Farren, who'd paused in his distribution of coffee to watch the display, said, "Information is controlled?"

Marianne Smith gave confirmation. "Yes. Tightly. Extreme restrictions. Also, all activity on Turings is monitored."

"All?" Burton asked. "But you said everybody has one. How can sense be made out of so much information?"

"By a central machine. The Turing Fulcrum. It reports to the authorities anything it interprets as illegal or suspicious activity."

Brabrooke said, "If I used my Turing to write T-mail to a friend—"

"T-mail?" Farren interrupted.

"A message. Like a letter but without any physical existence."

Patricia Honesty interrupted, "And you should know that there's no longer any other way to send a written communiqué."

"—and in it," Brabrooke continued, "I criticised government policies, I'd soon find the authorities knocking at my door."

"A police state?" Farren asked.

"Very much so."

"With pigs on stilts?"

"Yes. The constables."

Burton raised his arm. "And these bracelets?"

"They generate power from the motion of your arm and transmit it to the nearest Turing. They're also used for communication, to transfer funds when making a purchase, and they monitor your health and location."

"So why do I find myself with one on my wrist?"

"Because it's illegal for any citizen of the Empire to *not* wear one. Anyone seen without a bracelet is immediately arrested."

Patricia Honesty patted Brabrooke's arm. "Lori is our technical expert, Sir Richard. She's given each of you a false identity and a credible background. Every member of the Cannibal Club has the same. Our Turings are altered, too. They hide themselves. We—and our activities—are all invisible. That's a far more complicated achievement than it sounds. If it wasn't for her, you'd not be able to leave the *Orpheus*."

"By which statement," Burton said, "I presume you feel it apposite that we do."

"Yes." The old woman entwined her gnarled fingers and rested them on her lap. "The intelligence in each Turing is contained within microscopic squares of crystalline silicon."

"Got him!" Daniel Gooch cried out. "Silicon crystallises in the same pattern as diamond. If it's resonating at the same frequency as the gems in the time suits, the Oxford consciousness could easily enter it."

She nodded. "Precisely. Silicon is at the heart of the technology Alan Turing created, so it's quite possible that the insane intelligence which vanished from beneath your noses in 1860 has gradually been gaining influence since the 1950s."

Mick Farren pressed a hand down onto his great bush of hair and shook his head. He glared at Patricia. "How could you have let this happen, Pat? We were meant to overthrow the straights. Now they've got shackles on the whole population!"

"Consumerism conquers all," she answered. "Everything threatening was repackaged as something bright and cheerful and harmless. Whenever there's a challenge to the system, the system transforms it into a product and uses it as a weapon to keep the people distracted. We create our own oppression. Even the war has been reduced to entertainment."

"Whose war?" Burton asked. "America's, still?"

"Yes. Since your last visit, it has expanded into South China. The U.S.A. and United Republics of Eurasia are at it hammer and tongs. Their economies are suffering badly."

"And the Anglo-Saxon Empire?"

"During the seventies, the A.S.E. continued to offer cautious support to the States while managing to avoid any direct involvement with the conflict. Then Thatcher happened." The old woman produced a handkerchief and wiped her nose. "Our politicians are entirely lacking in ethics. It's a problem that has magnified with each subsequent generation, and it achieved its apotheosis in the last of our prime ministers, Margaret Thatcher. She came to power in 1979. Seven years later, she announced the cessation of the Empire's trade alliance with the States. The declaration came on the same day the first Turings went on sale—the day after, we suspect, the Fulcrum was activated. In fact, we think the withdrawal from the alliance was probably its first recommendation."

"Why?" Farren asked.

"Because it was such a contradictory turnaround. Rather than taking any notice of the people's opposition to America's aggression in South East Asia, the government, especially under Thatcher, had been ruthlessly curtailing the public's right to express it. By the eighties, the authorities had the power to limit how many people could gather, where, and for how long. Protest marches were made illegal. Why then, the sudden change of policy, the sudden bowing to the will of the populace? The answer wasn't clear until about twenty years ago, when one of our own people—a Cannibal descended from your friend, James Hunt—discovered that the British government was secretly supplying arms to both sides, to the U.S.A. and to the U.R.E."

"Despicable!" Swinburne shrilled.

Burton slid his fingers into his hair and felt his scars. "Abdu El Yezdi worked tirelessly to create a history free of world wars. Spring Heeled Jack appears to be working equally hard to undo everything he strove for."

"It seems so. And while we assist in our neighbours' destruction of one another, we've been steadily increasing our own power, based on an industrial and agricultural foundation of genetically enhanced animals and adapted human workers. Our global dominance is rotten and immoral through and through, but, of course, we are told a different story. According to the government, we're the bastions of civilisation, while the Americans and East Eurasians are little better than barbarians."

"That sounds familiar," Burton murmured. "My contemporaries depicted the Africans in the same light. It made it easier for us to justify the theft of their lands and resources."

Honesty nodded. "The A.S.E. has consolidated its grip on almost a third of the Earth's surface and a quarter of its total population. Its citizens are constantly warned of the threat posed by the U.S.A. and U.R.E.

while also kept occupied by an endless supply of trivial entertainments and meaningless pleasures. Consumerism and war. Extremes of indulgence and fear. No one can think straight. No one has the will to muster resistance. The government can sneak in any policy it likes, and people don't even notice."

Burton sighed and shook his head sadly. "What did you mean by the *last* prime minister? What have you now? A president?"

"I meant the last of the *human* prime ministers," Honesty replied. "These days, the government is formed by, and follows, the Turing Fulcrum."

"You've given over governance to a machine? How could it have come to this so rapidly?"

"It may feel rapid to you, but it crept up on us like a patient and cunning predator."

"Bloody hell," Daniel Gooch muttered. "Spring Heeled Jack is in control."

Krishnamurthy said, "This Turing Fulcrum—where is it?"

"Nobody knows. It's the most closely guarded secret in the world. I sometimes think we'd have a better chance at locating the Ark of the Covenant. Nevertheless, we must do our best, which is exactly why we want you to leave the ship and come with us to London."

"With the intention of destroying the bloody thing, I hope," Farren growled.

"Ultimately, yes, Mick. But one thing at a time, hey? First, let's find it."

"What do you propose?" Burton asked.

Patricia Honesty turned to Lorena Brabrooke, who, responding to the prompt, said, "We believe the Turing Fulcrum was first activated at nine o'clock in the evening on the fifteenth of February 1986."

Burton started slightly. *That date again! Nine on the fifteenth of February!*

"Based on what evidence?" he asked.

Brabrooke held up her Turing, the flat panel of which still bore the image of the Brunel exhibit in the British Museum. "Based on Isambard Kingdom Brunel. There'd been no sign of life from him since 1860, but at that precise instant, he said two words."

The chrononauts recoiled in surprise.

"What?" Krishnamurthy whispered. "He's alive?"

Gooch slapped his right fist into his left palm and cried out, "Good old Brunel!"

Brabrooke shrugged. "He didn't move and he's never spoken since. Repeated examinations have found nothing—no activity at all in his babbage." She shrugged again. "Just two words in nearly two centuries."

"What did he say?" Burton asked.

"*I am.*"

The king's agent frowned. "I am? I am what?"

"We don't know, but our theory is that when the Turing Fulcrum was activated it sent out a pulse of energy that resonated with the Nāga diamond fragments in Brunel's babbage. The words might have been an echo of the machine's first moment of self-awareness. That's why we regard Brunel as a possible key to the Fulcrum's location. If there's anything of him remaining, if we could possibly wake him up, he might be able to tell us what direction and distance the pulse came from."

"A long shot, admittedly," Patricia Honesty murmured. "But worth a try."

"Miss Brabrooke," Gooch interjected. "I'm an engineer. The thing you have in your hand—the Turing—is so far beyond my understanding that I can't even properly focus my eyes on it. What they tell me I'm seeing, my brain is trying very hard to reject. With progress having achieved such miracles, how is it you can't revive Mr. Brunel yourselves, yet you believe that we nigh on two-hundred-year-old fossils can?"

"Fossils!" Honesty protested. "You're younger than I am!"

"Shock," her daughter Marianne interjected.

Gooch looked puzzled. "Pardon?"

Burton muttered, "Yes, I see it." He addressed the engineer. "Daniel, Isambard has no notion of our mission. We'd lost him before even conceiving of it. If he has any sense of the time that's passed, the very last thing he'll be expecting to see is us. The surprise of it might knock the wits back into him."

"Fair enough," Gooch replied, after a moment's thought. "I suppose it might work, though personally I still think it more likely that his personality was completely erased. Beyond that, however, I have another, rather more serious reservation."

"It being?"

"That if we are so bedazzled by *that*," he jabbed a finger toward Brabrooke's Turing device, "then I fear whatever else we see might be so staggering that, before we can knock sense into Brunel, it'll knock all the sense out of us!"

With the world having changed so dramatically, they decided to keep their expedition to London small. A large party was more liable to attract attention, and, as Gooch had suggested, the excursion could be disrupted by an occurrence of mental instability. Fewer personnel meant a lesser chance that one of them would, as Swinburne put it, "start rolling his eyes and spitting foam."

The poet, Burton, Gooch and Farren—all well dosed with Saltzmann's —departed Bendyshe Bay in a small boat piloted by a Penniforth. Lorena Brabrooke went with them. During the voyage across the northern stretch of the Channel, she told them about the current Cannibal Club, revealing that, though the group was still funded by Bendyshe investments—currently run by two sisters and a brother—the Foundation itself had been broken up into a large number of much smaller organisations. They were more likely to evade scrutiny than the megalithic institution the original body had become.

Membership had grown more exclusive, currently consisting only of direct descendants. Those who hadn't been "blood members"—such as the Blanchets, von Lessings and Griffiths—were now absent.

"The younger ones in the group have all adopted the original surnames," she said, "even those that weren't born with them. It's a matter of pride."

"But why the dwindling numbers?" Burton asked.

"It got dangerously bloated back in the seventies." She addressed Farren. "Your lot were full of zeal, but you weren't exactly subtle."

"We didn't know we needed to be," he protested.

"The system is cunning, Mr. Farren. It manipulates people's fears and hopes, their insecurities and aspirations, and it ensures that all opposition is bogged down in a quagmire of prejudice, stupidity, propaganda and selfish motives. In your era, resistance was fun. In mine, it's potentially a death sentence."

"In my era?" Farren said. "The sixties weren't so long ago. How old do you think I am?"

"In your seventies, I guess."

"Christ! I'm twenty-five!"

"Anyway, like I was saying, the methodology the Cannibal Club employs to evade detection and keep an objective eye on developing history has had to change. It's all digital now."

"Something to do with fingers?" Gooch said. "The way you used your Turing device?"

"It's technical term. It refers to an extension of the systems your Mr. Babbage devised. Thanks to him, nowadays oppression and resistance do battle in the same arena, it being the realm of information, which he, after a fashion, created."

"Do you regard Babbage as a villain, then?" Gooch asked. "I've always thought of him as a hero, if a rather unpredictable one."

"I think of him as a genius, sir. If he knew how his systems were eventually employed, I expect he'd be horrified." An expression of pain crossed her features. "But I wish I'd never read Abdu El Yezdi's second report."

Burton, who'd been listening to the conversation with interest, said, *The Curious Case of the Clockwork Man*. I can understand your reservation. The affair was initiated when a different iteration of Charles Babbage, in a variant history, attempted to achieve immortality in order to pursue his intention to eliminate the working classes. He wanted to replace them with machines. The idea might not have been wholly villainous, but it was certainly inhumane."

Gooch looked thoughtful and muttered, "If we return, perhaps we should refrain from telling him about the path his work has taken. It might send him over the edge."

"We already know something will," Burton observed.

Swinburne, who was gazing ahead with Saltzmann's dilated pupils at the east coast of England—grey beneath a grey dawn—said, "He's already loopy, if you ask me. But Babbage aside, you say there's a sort of information war being waged, Miss Brabrooke? Surely, if this horrible government of yours is to be overthrown, there'll be a need for something more substantial. Armed revolutionaries."

"*I'm* an armed revolutionary," Brabrooke replied. "But people like me don't shoot anymore, we just aim."

Burton frowned. "Aim?"

"Access. Infiltrate. Manipulate." Brabrooke offered a crooked and gappy smile. "I acquire information I'm not supposed to have, I alter it without being detected, and I withdraw leaving no evidence that anything untoward has occurred. That's how I registered you all with the Department of Citizenship." The boat bounced and she put a hand to her midriff. "Ugh! I hate the sea. Would that Saltzmann's stuff of yours settle my stomach?"

The king's agent curled his upper lip, exposing a long canine in what might have been a smile but more resembled a sneer. "Do you know what it is?"

"Oh. Yes. It's—" she swallowed and went very pale. "Swinburne juice."

Mick Farren groaned. "Yeah, what was all that about? A red jungle?"

Burton gestured toward the poet. "You can ask it in person."

Swinburne smiled happily and winked. "Alternate futures! Strange events! Ripping adventures!"

"And in one of them you turned into a gigantic plant," Farren said flatly. "Weird."

"Indeed so," Burton agreed. "But my companions and I are here—and on our way to 2202—at the jungle's behest."

"Okay," Farren replied. "Weirder."

Perhaps appropriately, that was the last word the chrononauts were properly aware of for the duration of the next ninety minutes. From the moment the boat docked at Gravesend, time passed in an unintelligible smudge of sensations that overburdened them to the point where the king's agent—in a brief interval of near clarity—had no option but to dazedly pass around a bottle of the tincture that they might further dose themselves.

As the liquid radiated through him, he found himself gradually able to separate one thing from another, dragging from his jumbled senses first sound—mainly the roar of traffic—then smell, which delivered oily odours, and finally sight. This latter, a fragmentary mass, slowly congealed into the shape of the British Museum, though the blocky structure appeared to be floating amid a whirling storm of utterly indecipherable objects.

He realised that Lorena Brabrooke was peering up at him. "Sir?" She clapped her hands in front of his face. "Please. Say something. Snap out of it. I don't think I can do this for much longer."

He turned his head aside, coughed, closed and opened his eyes, looked back at her, and said, "Do what?"

"Lead you around like you're a pack of zombies."

"Zombie. Haitian. Supposedly an animated—" He stopped and blinked again. "Miss Brabrooke. We were on a train."

"Yes, we were. From Gravesend. Then we took the London Underground."

He shuddered. "Underground? No. I won't go underground. I can't bear to be enclosed."

She displayed the gap in her teeth. "We've already done it. Look, you see? We're at the museum."

Burton heard Swinburne's voice. "My hat! Where's a good peasouper when you need one? My eyes are too full. Look at all these people. How did the city become so overcrowded?"

Algernon. And Daniel Gooch. Mick Farren, too.

The latter shook his head at Burton. "It's doing my head in, man. I can't imagine what it's like for you."

The king's agent straightened and squared his shoulders. "I'm quite all right, Mr. Farren. Quite all right. Shall we proceed?"

"Yes!" Swinburne and Gooch pleaded in unison.

Lorena Brabrooke led them up the museum's steps and into the entrance hall. It was like reliving the scene they'd earlier viewed on her Turing—an eerie repetition—and it continued as they ascended the stairs and navigated through corridors toward the Isambard Kingdom Brunel display.

And there he was.

The great engineer.

The brass man.

Suddenly, Burton felt perfectly fine.

It was a winter Tuesday, and early in the morning, so there were few other people around, and none near this particular exhibit.

Burton, Swinburne and Gooch stood and gazed at their old friend. Acting on an instinctive respect, Farren and Brabrooke withdrew a little.

Brunel, kneeling on one knee, was posed on a plinth in such a manner as to appear deep in contemplation. His hulking body was clean, polished, and glinting beneath a spotlight, which threw the eye sockets of his mask into deep shadow, serving to emphasise his stillness, as if his mind was so far withdrawn that a void had taken its place.

The big Gatling gun was raised up.

Tools extended from his wrists and fingers.

One of his arms ended in a stump.

He was just as he'd been a hundred and sixty-two years ago.

Brunel! The man around whom a cult of science and engineering had grown; the man they called "the Empire Builder," who upon receiving hints of future technologies had used his boundless imagination and the materials of his era to reproduce ingenious approximations of them, transforming the civilised world, initiating the Great Age of Steam.

"He's regarded as a national treasure," Lorena Brabrooke said.

Burton glanced back at her. "The Anglo-Saxon Empire wouldn't have existed without him, Miss Brabrooke. He was there at its inception, fighting alongside us to prevent the sabotage of the alliance between Britain and the Central German Confederation."

She nodded, her eyes fixed on the exhibit.

The king's agent stepped closer to the plinth. He leaned forward and peered up into Brunel's eyes.

"Hello, my friend. It's been quite some time."

Nothing.

Swinburne asked, "Shall I kick him?"

Farren whispered, "Look to your right."

The poet did so. Burton followed his gaze. On the other side of the large chamber, a constable was standing guard beside a door, its hands clasped behind its back, its small glittering black eyes upon the visitors.

The pig creature was identical to the ones they'd seen in 1968, except that its stilted uniform was white.

They hastily turned their faces away from it.

Swinburne mumbled, "All right. No kicking."

Brabrooke said, "Try again, Sir Richard."

Conscious of the guard's scrutiny, Burton kept his voice low. "Isambard, do you recognise me? It's Burton. I'm here with Algernon Swinburne and Daniel Gooch. You remember Gooch, don't you? All those projects you worked on together? The transatlantic liners? The atmospheric railways? Hydroham City? By heavens, man, he built your body!"

Gooch moved to Burton's side. "Mr. Brunel, what happened to you? Won't you speak? We've come a long way to see you. Do you know what year it is? 2022!"

"Babbage helped us," Burton went on. "He designed a Nimtz generator. It allows the *Orpheus* to travel in time. What an undertaking that project was! The whole of the Department of Guided Science was given over to the job. All of your people laboured on it night and day, every man and every woman; that's the measure of their loyalty to you, old man."

Brunel didn't respond, didn't move. Not even a click emerged from him.

Swinburne pushed between them, stood on tiptoe, reached up, and snapped his fingers inches from the brass face. "Wake up, you confounded lazybones!" he demanded. "Get off your metal arse. We need your help."

The chamber suddenly echoed with the *tock tock tock* of stilts as the guard crossed it.

"Now you've done it," Lorena Brabrooke said. Under her breath, she continued, "Just follow its orders and, without incriminating yourselves, agree with whatever it says. Be careful."

As the pig man drew closer, Burton whispered, "Behave, Algy."

The constable stopped in front of them and snarled, "Don't touch the exhibit."

"I didn't," Swinburne objected. "I was just seeing how my hand reflected in its face."

"T-bands," the pig said. "All of you."

Lorena Brabrooke stretched out her arm, showing the bracelet. Burton, Swinburne, Gooch and Farren followed her lead.

The guard reached out and knocked his own bracelet against theirs, one after the other.

"Jeremy Swinburne," he stated. "Scriptwriter. Bendyshe Entertainments."

"Um. Yes," Swinburne agreed.

"Richard Burton. Actor. Bendyshe Entertainments."

"Yes," Burton said.

"Daniel Gooch. Director. Bendyshe Entertainments."

"That's me."

"Michael Farren. Producer. Bendyshe Entertainments."

Farren coughed. "Yeah."

"Lorena Brabrooke. Production Assistant. Bendyshe Entertainments."

"Yes, sir. We're doing the initial research for a docudrama about Isambard Kingdom Brunel. We have to study him closely, but we won't interfere with the display."

The guard wrinkled its snout. "Shut up. I'm doing a background check." Its beadlike eyes focused inward for a couple of seconds. "All right. You're clear. Continue. Don't touch."

It turned and stalked back to its post. *Tock tock tock.*

"Phew!" Swinburne said. "What a perfectly dreadful brute." He addressed Brabrooke. "Bendyshe Entertainments? We're doing what with the what for the what?"

"Never mind," she said. "It's all a fiction." She frowned at Burton, who was staring wide-eyed at Brunel. "Sir Richard?"

He didn't reply.

She touched his arm. "Sir Richard?"

"It's really over," Burton murmured. "My world. The time I inhabited. He built it and now it's all ended."

They considered Brunel.

"A brief span and then we are gone," Burton said. "Time is cruel." He straightened and sighed. "I thought he, of all of us, would live forever."

They remained in the museum for a further thirty minutes, standing close to Brunel, discussing his many projects and the people he'd known, hoping that Gooch was wrong and a spark of life remained, that the reminiscing would sink into the engineer and hook a memory, something to bring him out of his long, long fugue.

It didn't work, and when the guard showed signs of renewed suspicion, they gave up.

Led by Brabrooke, the chrononauts left the exhibition hall.

Behind them, Brunel remained silent and frozen.

When Burton glanced back before passing through a doorway, it was from such an angle that, due to the spotlight reflecting into the engineer's shadowed eye sockets, it almost appeared as if two little glowing pupils were watching them depart.

An illusion.

Isambard Kingdom Brunel was dead.

CHAPTER 14

THE ILLUSORY WORLD OF 2130

> Just because it makes no sense doesn't mean it's not good advice.
>
> —Mick Farren

"**W**hat's your opinion, Sadhvi?" Burton asked.

The king's agent was sitting in the lounge of the *Orpheus* with Raghavendra, Swinburne, Gooch, Trounce, Krishnamurthy, Lawless, Wells, Farren, and the Cannibals—Patricia Honesty, Marianne Smith and Lorena Brabrooke.

"Daniel was worst affected," Raghavendra said. "You, Richard, considerably less so, while Algy and Mick were dazed but remained coherent." She patted Swinburne's knee. "Our resident poet appears to have a strong resistance to what Mr. Wells has dubbed *time shock*."

Wells said, "I compare it to the disorientation one experiences when travelling in an exotic culture, but it's far more pernicious."

Raghavendra said to Burton, "Your history as an explorer has given you a degree of resilience—"

"Not enough," he interrupted. "I don't recall a damned thing about our return from the museum."

"Whereas Mick," she pressed on, "is only fifty-four years ahead of his native time period, so 2022 feels a little more familiar to him."

Farren blew cigarette smoke out through his nostrils, obviously not in full agreement.

"On this occasion, poor Daniel bore the brunt," Raghavendra said.

Trounce looked across to Gooch and muttered, "And I know exactly how you felt."

Gooch compressed his lips, nodded at the detective inspector, and asked Raghavendra, "What makes Algernon more resilient, do you think?"

"He has a unique brain," she responded. "He's extremely odd."

"Steady on!" the poet squealed. He jerked his leg, convulsed an elbow, and crossed his eyes.

"It's apparent to us all," Burton observed, "that his brain is arranged in a different manner to the normal."

"Disarranged, I should say," Trounce muttered.

"I say! Let's settle with *unique*, shall we?"

Burton continued, "My fear is that, for the rest of us, the effects are liable to get worse and the recovery time—providing we *can* recover—considerably extended. On this occasion, it's taken five days for us to properly regain our faculties. We've been safe enough, cooped up aboard this Concorde, hidden away in Bendyshe Bay—but what will we find at our next stop? What if the bay no longer belongs to the Cannibal Club?"

"The groundwork laid by your brother and Thomas Bendyshe back in the 1860s was pure genius," Patricia Honesty said. "It's endured all this time, and, with each successive generation, the Bendyshes have developed it and adjusted it to suit the period. I'm pretty certain the bay will stay in our hands, and if it doesn't, the Cannibals will have plenty of time to find another means to keep you safe."

"Be that as it may, we need our wits about us, and we've come to the point where the doses of Saltzmann's required to counter the time shock are almost as ruinous as the condition itself. The bottles delivered in the Beetle's final shipment aren't nearly as addictive as those that preceded them, but we still have to be cautious with the medicine."

"Ha!" Swinburne cried out. "You've changed your tune."

Sadhvi Raghavendra nodded her agreement.

"Nevertheless," Burton said.

"We're not even halfway through our voyage," Trounce observed. "How are we to endure the rest?"

"Nine years away from the halfway mark," Krishnamurthy added.

"A hundred and eighty years until 2202, and I doubt our stay there will be brief."

"Give me a bottle of the tincture," Patricia Honesty interrupted. "I should have thought of this before. Chemistry has advanced. We'll analyse it. Reproduce it. Or something similar."

Her daughter gave a gesture of approval. "In the space of fifty-four years, we'll probably create something considerably more effective and without any addictive qualities."

"You'll have twice as long," Burton said. "I intend just one more stop before our target date. If Spring Heeled Jack has integrated himself with this Turing Fulcrum of yours, he has power over a considerable portion of the world. Let's see what he makes of it by 2130. Will one of your number join us?"

"Not this time," Patricia Honesty said. She handed him *The History of the Future*, volume three. "We haven't the personnel to spare. Besides, there's a little something we've been experimenting with that makes it unnecessary for us to supplement your crew. Hopefully, you'll see what I mean a hundred and eight years from now."

A little over a century later, the chrononauts gathered by the ship's hatch and welcomed a single Cannibal aboard. His name was Thomas Bendyshe.

"You're the spitting image of your ancestor!" Burton exclaimed as he shook the man's hand.

"Hallo!" Bendyshe said. "I'm a great deal of him, but explanations must wait until later. First, let's replace your bracelets and transfer you to the new *Orpheus*."

Though he didn't appear to do anything to prompt it, the bands around the chrononauts' wrists instantly snapped open and slid down to their knuckles. Bendyshe collected the bracelets and put them into a cloth bag. Setting this aside, he then took a small container of pills from his pocket and distributed them among the chrononauts, two each, a blue one and a yellow one. "Swallow. They'll release AugMems, CellComps, BioProcs and other nanomechs into your bloodstream."

From his visions of Edward Oxford, Burton vaguely comprehended these terms. He knew that AugMems were capable of overlaying a man's perception of reality with an artifice. Oxford had used them in his suit's helmet, so when he arrived in 1840 to observe the attempt on Queen Victoria's life, it would initially resemble his own time. He'd planned to slowly reduce the AugMems' influence, revealing the reality of the past little by little. In the event, he'd acted too eagerly, removing his headpiece moments after his arrival, exposing himself to the past all at once. Burton was sure the resultant shock played its part in Oxford's subsequent decision to interfere with his ancestor's assassination attempt.

"Nanomechs," he said, testing the word. Its meaning played at the peripheries of his mind; Oxford's knowledge, not his own.

"Molecular-sized technology," Bendyshe said, "blending biological and artificial components."

"By Jove!" Trounce muttered in a sarcastic tone. "I'm glad you've cleared that up."

"Are they safe?" Herbert Wells—now fully recovered—asked.

"Perfectly," Bendyshe responded. "They'll integrate without any ill effects. They'll carry your false identities, in case the authorities check, and will also enhance your senses."

"I'm in," Mick Farren announced. He swallowed the pills.

"Ah yes, the 1960s," Bendyshe said. He laughed. "I'm afraid they're not recreational pharmaceuticals, Mr. Farren."

"No? Enhance in what way, then?"

"They'll show you whatever the government wants you to see."

Farren made a noise as if choking and stuck out his tongue, trying to regurgitate the pills. He spat an epithet that caused Sadhvi Raghavendra's eyes to widen. "Now you bloody well tell me!"

"Mr. Farren, your misgivings are entirely justified," Bendyshe said. "Fortunately, we Cannibals have developed a means to intercede with the nanomechs' functioning and turn them to our advantage. Provided you behave normally, nothing about you will raise suspicion. In addition, you'll not register on any surveillance net, your movements will be cloaked, and communications between us will evade all monitoring."

"That," Farren replied, "I like."

"Providing we behave normally," Swinburne echoed doubtfully.

"Algy has a point," Burton said. "To us, what you might regard as normal becomes ever more abnormal the farther forward into history we travel. There is also the matter of our behaviour being affected by the environment. Will the AugMems cause us to perceive this future world as a copy of our own? Do they render Saltzmann's Tincture unnecessary?"

"No, Sir Richard, there's a very good reason why they can't give you an illusion of 1860s London. You'll understand why later. However, there's a compound in the yellow pill that'll act much like Saltzmann's, only without the side effects. You'll need to take one every twenty-fours hours. I'll leave you with a supply."

"Then Patricia Honesty was true to her word," Burton noted.

"She was always the most reliable of us," Farren murmured. A strange expression crossed his face. Burton sympathised. It was difficult to process the notion that people who were alive yesterday were now long gone.

"If you all follow my lead," Bendyshe said, "you'll be fine."

Sadhvi Raghavendra sighed. "I'm not wildly enthused by the prospect, gentlemen, but nothing ventured—" She swallowed the pills. Her colleagues followed suit.

Bendyshe stepped back to the hatch. He signalled to a group waiting outside the Concorde. They responded by ascending the stairs, entering the ship, and silently filing past the chrononauts.

"My team will carry your luggage to the new ship before transplanting the Nimtz generator and the babbage. Captain Lawless, Mr. Gooch, Mr. Krishnamurthy, will you assist with the engineering?"

"Of course," Lawless said. "We're becoming rather adept at it."

"For the rest of you, it's off to London we go."

"Our third visit to the capital of the future," Burton commented. "What shall we find there this time?"

"You'll see indisputable evidence that Spring Heeled Jack is manipulating history. It will, I hope, give you some idea of what you'll face when you reach 2202. As for whether it's safe or not, we've done everything we can to disguise your presence. You should be able to move around freely and undisturbed. I do urge you, though, to watch your words in any circumstance where you might be overheard. Information is currency, and informers are everywhere."

Burton gestured for Bendyshe to proceed. The Cannibal led them outside. It was an overcast night, and Bendyshe Bay was ill lit. They could see nothing beyond the field in which the Concorde had landed, though, in truth, they didn't try, for their eyes were fixed in incredulity upon the two flying vessels beside which their own had landed.

"Rotorships!" Captain Lawless exclaimed.

Bendyshe pointed to the vessel on their left. "The *Orpheus*."

"But it looks identical my old ship," the airman observed.

"It *is* your old ship, sir. We have preserved it all these years. And it's a good thing we did. Nowadays, that is the standard of technology available to the masses."

Burton and Lawless exchanged a puzzled look. The king's agent said, "Has there been some manner of reversal?"

"There has—a result of the failed uprising of the 2080s," the Cannibal responded. They started across the grass toward the vessel. "The Empire was torn apart by seven years of rioting and civil disobedience. The people attempted to throw off the shackles imposed on them—literally, in the form of the bracelets—by the government. They failed. As a consequence of their actions, the division between the privileged minority and the underprivileged masses widened even farther. The latter were denied most of the advanced technologies. For them, it went retrograde. The more primitive varieties of steam machines were resurrected. The underclass has become very much like the workers of your own period, except they hardly know it."

"Do you mean they're drugged?" Wells asked.

"After a fashion. AugMems, which are injected at birth, enforce upon them an illusion of contentment. Their gruel tastes to them like honey, their relentless toil is imbued with false meaning, the filth in which they exist is perceived as comfort, and their empty lives are filled with distracting entertainments. They are happy because they are unable to recognise the severity of the limitations under which they labour."

A man and three women met them at the foot of the old *Orpheus*'s boarding ramp. Bendyshe turned to Lawless, Gooch and Krishnamurthy.

"You three will not witness the truth. Think yourselves lucky. May I introduce Jacob Hunt, Carolyn Slaughter, and Rebecca and Ben Murray? They're overseeing the refit of the ship. If you'll accompany them, please."

"You won't have any problems understanding the *Orpheus*, sirs," Carolyn Slaughter said. "She's hardly changed. Just a few additions." She smiled at Lawless. "It'll feel like coming home for you, I expect, Captain."

Lawless, Gooch and Krishnamurthy bid their colleagues farewell and followed the Cannibals into the familiar ship. Bendyshe led the rest toward the other. "The *Mary Seacole*. We'll fly her to the Battersea airfield."

"It's still there?" Detective Inspector Trounce exclaimed.

"Greatly expanded."

"Mr. Bendyshe," Wells said. "What did you mean by that comment, *think yourselves lucky?*"

"Only that the truth is rather disturbing."

They ascended the ramp, entered the ship, and were escorted to its lounge where they settled on chairs and sofas and were served food and beverages by Bendyshe. Burton felt uncomfortable eating once again in such an informal manner, and suddenly longed for Mrs. Angell. *You'll not take your supper in the study, sir! Not again! If you want to eat, you'll find your plate on the table in the dining room, where it bloomin' well belongs!*

"You spoke of the privileged and the underprivileged," Wells said to Bendyshe, "but what has become of the middle class? Back in 1914, I thought they were poised to take over the Empire."

"They were a relatively brief phenomenon," Bendyshe answered. "They grew throughout the twentieth and twenty-first centuries but proved ungovernable. Before, in Sir Richard's time, when there were simply the 'Haves' and 'Have Nots,' each individual knew his or her place in the world, and society, though not in the slightest bit fair, was at least stable. The middle classes were problematical. They always wanted more. They developed the notion that they could better themselves. They sought control. They felt they could be raised to the level of the elite, though they were rather less supportive of the idea that the lower classes might be raised to the middle. Such aspirations led them to instigate the failed revolution of the 2080s. Victory, they thought, was assured, for surely the minority wouldn't employ brute force against a vast majority."

Burton said, "They miscalculated?"

"Very. They didn't know what we know, that those in power were under the sway of Spring Heeled Jack. The crackdown, when it came, was ferocious beyond belief. The constables killed millions. Literally millions."

"Still stilted pigs?" Farren asked.

"Yes. Rather more mechanised than they were when they made their debut in the 1960s but essentially the same. They overwhelmed the rebellion, AugMems were employed to control the population, and the middle classes were forcibly thrust into the lower."

"I don't mean any offence," Sadhvi said, "but to which class do you belong, Mr. Bendyshe?"

Bendyshe grinned and for an instant looked almost identical to his ancestor. "By virtue of our ability to evade government influence, the members of the Cannibal Club cannot be classified. We are fugitives. Ghosts. We inhabit the cracks in the system."

The floor vibrated, and a rumble signified the starting of the ship's engines.

Having been reminded of the original Thomas Bendyshe, Burton said, "You hinted at some reason for your resemblance to your—what?— great-great-great-grandfather?"

"Seven greats."

"By my Aunt Gwendolyn's woefully woven wig!" Swinburne cried out. "Have we really come so far?"

"You are two hundred and seventy years from home. Yes, Sir Richard, I resemble him because my father's DNA was manipulated to accentuate the Bendyshe inheritance, and I am his—my father's, I mean—clone."

The floor tilted slightly as the *Mary Seacole* rose into the air and turned.

"You've lost me," Burton said. "I understand what DNA is, having briefly inhabited the mind of the sane Edward Oxford, but—"

"That doesn't help me," Trounce grumbled. "I hardly understand a bloody word. You might as well speak in Greek."

Burton looked at his friend, thought for a moment, then said, "DNA is a component of the cells in your body. It dictates how you will grow, what you will look like, what strengths and weaknesses you possess, and to some extent, how you will behave." He turned back to Bendyshe. "Correct?"

"In a nutshell."

"But clone?"

"Cloning involves the exact reproduction of DNA. I am not my father's son. I am his replica, as he was of his father. All the current Cannibals are identical to their immediate forebears. You see, it was discovered during the twenty-first century that memories are inscribed into DNA and can be passed on to clones, though it requires medical intercession to make those from earlier generations available. My father had many of his ancestors' recollections brought to the fore. They've been passed on to me. The Cannibal Club's mission is one that spans centuries, so we felt it would be advantageous to have this continuity." He stopped, peered at Burton, and went on, "For example, I vaguely recall your last meeting with my namesake. I believe we—I mean, you and he—took lunch at the Athenaeum and were interrupted by the arrival of a constable?"

"Bismillah! How is it possible?"

"It must seem miraculous, I know, but it's only science."

"Only!" Herbert Wells cried out. "What miracles Man has achieved!"

"Woman, actually," Bendyshe corrected. "The inscription of memory and character on DNA was proven by Doctor Hildegunn Skogstad in 2093. She then went on to develop the techniques we use to retrieve it."

Swinburne scratched his head vigorously, crossed his legs, and uncrossed them. "I must say, old chap, despite the similarity of appearance, you're considerably more subdued than the Tom Bendyshe I knew. You must count yourself fortunate. He was an utter ass. Loveable. But an ass. My goodness, I saw him—what?—last week and suddenly miss him terribly!"

"I'm my own man," Bendyshe said. "I'm writing my own memories."

"This must be what Patricia Honesty was referring to when she said we'd no longer need to take a new Cannibal aboard at each stop," Burton murmured. "You're better placed to advise us."

"Yes, because I have the history you hopped over stored away in here," Bendyshe said with a tap to his head.

"I'm tripping," Mick Farren declared, then clarified, "Hallucinating. You're talking about stuff that's so far out there it's like, y'know, just plain crazy, man. And suddenly you're all wearing the same clothes. What's up with that?"

"Democratic greys," Bendyshe said. "Your AugMems are taking effect. We won't block the government's broadcast yet. I want you to see what they want you to see before you're exposed to the truth."

"Riddles," Trounce murmured. "I bloody hate them. It's why I became a detective. To solve the bloody things until there were none left."

Burton blinked. A moment ago, the Scotland Yard man had been wearing a dark suit. Now he was in a grey and very utilitarian one. The chrononauts uttered cries of astonishment as they, too, experienced the odd transition. In a matter of moments, they were all attired in identical outfits. Yet they discovered that, when they looked down at themselves, they perceived their own clothes.

"Much of the Empire is in the same way illusory," Bendyshe explained. He stood and stepped over to a porthole. "We're crossing the Channel. The *Mary Seacole* is registered as a freighter. She'll not raise suspicion. We'll land in fifteen minutes or so."

"Our agenda?" Burton asked.

"I understand you were involved in the Grosvenor Square riot of 1968?"

"We were, unfortunately."

"We'll revisit the scene. Don't worry. There won't be any trouble this time. I simply want you to compare the present with what you've already experienced. On the way there, you'll be exposed to the lie generated by the Turing Fulcrum. On the way back, I'll reveal to you the reality of the world."

Fifteen minutes later, the chrononauts crowded around the portholes and gazed in wonder as dawn broke over the substantially expanded London of 2130. The city sprawled from horizon to horizon and stretched its thousands of towers high into the sky. It was a glittering, shining, blinking, reflecting, dazzling, multifaceted jewel cut through by the meandering Thames, the only part of it instantly recognisable to the travellers, though they eventually spotted the tiny-looking but apparently timeless landmarks of St. Paul's Cathedral, the Tower of London, Tower Bridge, and the parks—Hyde, Green, Regent's, and Hampstead Heath.

Gone, though, was the Battersea Power Station. Where it had once stood, and extending across all of Battersea Fields, there was now a massive aerodrome. As the *Mary Seacole* sank toward it, Bendyshe said, "The station was demolished in 2040. It had been standing derelict since the old Department of Guided Science was disbanded in the 1880s."

"I thought it a permanent fixture," Burton murmured.

"Nothing is," Bendyshe responded. "Only Time has dominion."

The rotors moaned, and the ship settled with a slight bump.

Bendyshe ushered the chrononauts toward the hatch. "We'll drive to New Centre Point then walk from there to Grosvenor Square. We're sightseeing, nothing more. When we're on foot, keep your voices low. Try not to be overheard. If any citizen hears you say something that can be regarded as suspicious or unusual, they will report it. Informing is a means to earn credit. The citizens of the Anglo-Saxon Empire are eager to denounce one another. Careless talk costs lives."

He opened the hatch. A vehicle was parked at the end of the ramp, a six-wheeled contraption of smooth curves and black glass.

"Straight into the minibus, please," Bendyshe said. "Our driver's name is Odessa Penniforth."

He hurried them down and into the conveyance. As they settled on the soft, well-upholstered seats, a slightly built young woman with cropped blonde hair and wide brown eyes looked back at them and said, "Hallo! I can't believe it. Are you really from the past?"

"Miss Penniforth," Burton replied. "We are practically dinosaurs."

Bendyshe pulled the door shut. "Let's go."

Smoothly and silently, the car pulled away and headed toward Chelsea Bridge, which proved to be a different and much wider structure to the one Burton and his friends had known. It was clogged with crawling traffic.

"Your cars appear more efficient than those from my time," Farren noted, "but why are they moving so slowly?"

"You'll see," Bendyshe said mysteriously.

They crossed the river and drove in a north-easterly direction. Though the vehicle's windows were opaque from the outside, they were transparent from within, and its passengers stared out in awe at the buildings that soared to either side of the road. High above the city, a network of thin bridges and walkways spanned the distances between the spindly towers, and many were hung with garish flags, vaguely reminiscent of the Union Jack but made much more complex by additional stripes and colours.

The king's agent gazed out of the window and wondered how he could fight an intelligence around which a whole society was forming. This London was virtually unrecognisable to him. Its citizens, who thronged the pavements in astonishing numbers—the population appeared to have increased tenfold—were all dressed in grey. The streets along which they moved, illuminated by electric lights despite it being early morning, were drab and characterless. There were none of the hawkers and performers of his time, no stalls or braziers, no dollymops or beggars, no ragamuffins or newsboys. It was all steel and glass and crowds of grey, grey, grey.

And there were constables everywhere, tottering along on their stilts, their pig faces now hidden behind blank white masks, their limbs longer and more human in form than their 1968 or 2022 counterparts, so they much more resembled the Spring Heeled Jacks who'd assaulted him back in 1860.

"It's a nightmare," he murmured.

"You're not wrong," Farren agreed.

They steered into Buckingham Palace Road, drove between Hyde and Green Parks—the whole area struck Burton as being oddly dark despite the clear sky and open spaces—and proceeded along the Mall. The thoroughfare, once the tree-lined haunt of the well-to-do, was now made distinct only by virtue of the park on the right. On its left, there were the same towers, the same glass, the same grey, and the same patrolling pig men.

Burton shook his head in disbelief.

This isn't real. It doesn't feel real. It doesn't look real. It's like a desert mirage, seemingly solid, seemingly close, but when you try to reach it, it moves away from you. What is going on here? What kind of Jahannam *has the Empire become?*

Up Charing Cross Road to Tottenham Court Road, and there the vehicle came to a halt, stopping among many similar machines in a rectangular plot of land beside an extraordinarily tall cylindrical edifice that appeared to have been constructed from diamond-shaped windows and little else.

"What ho! What ho! This all feels oddly familiar," Swinburne noted as he clambered out.

"New Centre Point," Bendyshe said. "Built on the site of the old one, which was bombed during the uprisings. It's a monitoring station."

"What does it monitor?" the poet asked.

"People."

Odessa Penniforth leaned out of the vehicle and said, "I'll wait for you here. Enjoy the revelation, everyone."

"I wish I knew what was going on," Swinburne exclaimed. "My hat! Do they still have public houses in 2130?"

"They do," Bendyshe confirmed. "The government came close to making them illegal but then realised that people speak before they think when under the influence."

"Must you keep calling upon your hat, Algernon?" Trounce complained. "Confound it! Why does no one wear them anymore? I feel naked without my bowler."

Farren looked this way and that, frowned at the hissing traffic, and muttered, "Is that music?"

"I hear it too," Herbert Wells said. "In the background."

"Muzak," Bendyshe said. "Ubiquitous, bland and characterless." He said to Farren, "You thought rock and roll would conquer the world. It didn't. Muzak did. It's the universal temper suppressant. An insidious tranquilliser."

"A horrendous hum," Swinburne added. "A detrimental drone."

Bendyshe nodded his agreement. "A puerile pacifier."

Farren gritted his teeth and fisted his hands. "Oh man," he growled. "What I wouldn't give for a Deviants gig, right here, right now!"

"You'd be shot dead on the spot," Bendyshe said.

Farren suddenly relaxed and chuckled. "Yeah, that was always the risk when I got on stage."

Staying close together they moved away from the minibus and joined the pedestrians flocking into Oxford Street. To Burton, it felt just as if they were joining the protest again, except the people—rather than being a noisy and colourful gathering with a purpose—were nothing more than innumerable and near-silent citizens squeezing along a highway too narrow for such a dense crowd.

Sadhvi walked at his side. Wells and Swinburne were just in front; both small, both squeaky-voiced, both looking eagerly back and forth, weathering the assault on their senses. Behind the king's agent, Trounce and Farren made quiet comments to one another; an odd combination, a police detective and a proto-revolutionary, united by a mutual disapproval of this confusing future world.

Guided by Thomas Bendyshe and jostled by the city's denizens, they shouldered past glass-faced shop fronts and comprehended nothing of what was displayed within, saw peculiar vehicles slide by and had no understanding of what their function might be, read signs and posters the words of which signified nothing to them, and were, without respite, subjected to the steady beat and sinuous melodies of soft and relentlessly insipid "Muzak."

Burton looked into the faces of the people and observed an incongruous mix of contented smiles and shifty eyes. Some, who were either tall or short or thin or fat, somehow left him with the impression they were just the opposite of what they appeared, as if a slender passerby was secretly obese, or a diminutive person a covert giant. This, together with the unaccustomed cleanliness of the city, gave the sense that he was among actors and moving amid a stage's cardboard scenery. There was no depth. No connection. No meaning.

Why was the traffic moving at such a sluggish velocity? Why did the quiet hiss of the vehicles, the subdued murmur of the pedestrians, and the steady low drone of the Muzak, amount to so much silence? Where was the life?

"The shadows," Sadhvi whispered.

"What about them?" he asked.

"They don't match."

She was right. The many electric street lamps, cutting through the permanent gloom at the base of the towers, endowed every individual with multiple shadows. For the most part, due to the crush of people, these couldn't be seen separately, but occasionally there came a break in the crowd and the shadows were made visible. Burton saw them and was horrified. Most were normal but many were misshapen blots or spiked puddles or stringy smears or snarled scribbles—not at all the contours of human beings.

"By Allah's beard!" he hissed. "What are we looking at?"

Wells glanced back at him and made a gesture, obviously having noticed the same. Burton responded with a curt nod and swallowed nervously.

They walked on. The king's agent kept feeling things bumping against his boots, as if the pavement was as littered as those of the old East End, but when he looked down, there was nothing there.

Now and then, he became aware of apparently sourceless sounds—creaks and snaps and groans, the clip clop of horses' hooves, the clank of a misaligned crankshaft, a hiss of pressurised steam—as though noises from his own London were somehow penetrating into this.

It's my expectations, he thought. *They're imposing what I'm familiar with onto this wholly unfamiliar city.*

He was unnerved and disoriented. There was a lump in his throat. He longed to see top hats and canes, parasols and bonnets, hansom cabs and horses, chugging steam engines and wobbling velocipedes.

Where has my London gone?

That struck him as a very uncharacteristic thought.

For all his life he'd felt an outsider. He'd cursed the ways and mores of his native land. It had rejected him, considered him too unorthodox, too untamed, and too unsophisticated. Society damned him for admiring the Arab and condemned him for mixing with African savages. Ruffian Dick! Beastly Burton!

Yet, how he wanted to be back there.

For perhaps the first time in his life, he felt helpless, and he felt humility. He realised that he had, in the past, conducted himself from a position of self-appointed superiority. Yes, he'd been an unwavering proponent of Arabic culture; yes, he'd dispassionately observed tribal societies; but he'd done so as a wayward son of the Empire, knowing that, though it looked askance upon him, it was always there as a measure by which to judge.

Fool! he thought. *Fool to think that you somehow existed outside of its confines. It made you!*

And now he was, at one and the same time, home but as far from it as he'd ever been.

As they shoved their way around the corner into North Audley Street—a much different junction to the one he'd seen in '68—he remembered his parents, how they'd dragged him from one place to the next, from Torquay to Tours, from Tours to Richmond, from Richmond to Blois, from Blois to Naples, from Naples to Pau, from Pau to Lucca, always moving, always compulsively restless, never giving him a moment to stop and form attachments, never a moment in which to simply belong.

He felt anger and sadness, resentment and self-pity.

Isabel. Isabel. Isabel. You were my hope, my foundation, my stability. Only through you could I be me. Why did you have to die?

In his mind's eye, he saw her, waiting in a garden, with a tea cloth over her arm.

You're going now? she asked. *Supper is almost ready.*

Yes, he replied. *But don't worry—even if I'm gone for years, I'll be back in five minutes.*

"Damnation!" Burton muttered to himself. "Are my memories no longer my own?"

CHAPTER 15

THE TRUTH OF 2130 REVEALED

WORK AND BE HAPPY.
THOSE WHO WORK, THRIVE.
FULFILMENT IS FOUND IN FUNCTIONALITY.

The Ministry of Genetic Enhancement

T he chrononauts, led by Thomas Bendyshe, arrived once again in Grosvenor Square, the middle of which was, thankfully, a great deal less congested than last time. From here, the travellers gained a better view of the upper reaches of the city. London had achieved phenomenal heights. Its towers ascended to such a level their top storeys faded into the atmosphere and their internal heat generated clouds, which streamed from them in wispy trails.

The many walkways and—Burton now noticed—monorails were of such a multitude that it looked as if the city was entangled. Small flying machines buzzed hither and thither, and, at a higher altitude, massive airships floated. Many were like the *Orpheus* and *Mary Seacole*, airborne antiques, appearing entirely out of place. Others were smooth disks of silver or gold, their mode of propulsion invisible and mysterious.

"I see nothing of my own time," Mick Farren said. "I might as well be on another planet."

"I see the same shaped plot of land," Detective Inspector Trounce observed, pointing around them. "This is still Grosvenor Square." He shuddered. "I didn't much enjoy what little I remember of my last visit."

Farren indicated a tall pyramidal structure. "That's where the American Embassy used to be."

"It's still the embassy," Bendyshe said. He looked around, and when he was satisfied no one was close enough to eavesdrop, he continued, "It's inhabited only by a few technicians nowadays. They oversee the equipment that broadcasts to your AugMems. The building is a part of an inner circle of establishments. From it and the others, a web of deception expands."

"Inner circle," Wells said. "And what is at its centre? The Turing Fulcrum?"

Bendyshe gazed at the embassy. "We think so."

He waved the chrononauts across to an area beneath a leafy tree, which, when Burton placed his hand against its bark, proved to be of the material called plastic.

Nothing is real.

The king's agent struggled to maintain a connection. His mind kept wandering, his attention being attracted by first one thing then another. His powers of analysis failed. Automatically, his hand went to his pocket, seeking Saltzmann's. There was none.

"What you've seen so far is but a single layer of the illusion under which the population labours," Bendyshe said. "I'll now give you a taste of the rest. I'm adjusting your AugMems."

He put his finger to his right earlobe and muttered, "Okay. Proceed." Suddenly, he was enveloped by a colourful aura. Burton looked at his friends and saw that they, too, appeared to be generating beautiful halos.

"We are masquerading as the elite," the Cannibal explained. "Thus we glow with the light of the upper classes. However, what we see is what the general populace sees. Look at the city's citizens."

Burton gazed across to the pavement. He saw, amongst the shuffling crowd, three people who were also surrounded by light. The rest were not. His eyes rested on a pedestrian. A calm voice whispered in his ear and caused him to jump in surprise. He heard the others utter sounds of astonishment.

John Thresher, cook, thirty-two years old. Three thousand two hundred and twenty-nine credits in debt. He plays poker. His wife has a lover. John hopes to win a fortune and lure her back, but he's lost money eleven games in a row.

The king's agent looked from person to person.

Teresa Chowdhury, child minder, nineteen years old. She is learning to read so she can train as a nurse. Her father tells her she has ideas above her station.

Cecilia Sanz Garcia, cleaner, forty-seven years old. She has pre-diabetes and a glandular disorder that causes extreme mood swings. She struggles with relationships.

Steven Powell, clerk, thirty-three years old. He suffers from shyness and has a tendency to stutter.

Blake Cresswell, baker, seventy-one years old. He's never held a job for more than two years. He's a convicted felon. His last crime, burglary, was committed twenty-seven years ago.

Mary Suzanne Clayton, metalsmith, twenty-four years old. She owns a small allotment from which vegetables are frequently stolen. She has hidden homemade wiretraps around its perimeter to catch the thieves.

"What's this?" Sadhvi Raghavendra exclaimed.

"In your time," Bendyshe replied, "I believe it was called *tittle tattle*."

"Gossip?" she said.

"Yes. Everyone knows everyone else's business. Only the upper classes are immune to the intrusion."

"It's a blasted liberty!" Trounce cried out. "By God! Has no one any privacy?"

"Only in their thoughts, and they have to be extremely cautious in expressing those, else they'll certainly fall foul of informants. Anything that can possibly be interpreted as seditious is reported, and the punishments are brutal."

"How can anyone think at all with all this horrible chattering in their ears?" Swinburne objected. "Can't they turn it off?"

"Only the elite have that privilege. As for thinking, I suspect the system is expressly designed to discourage it."

"Stop it, please," Burton said. "It's too much."

Bendyshe touched his ear again and mumbled something. The whispering voice fell silent. The auras faded. "That," he said, "is what the majority of the population must endure. Maximum distraction. Minimum meaning. Their existence is overflowing with inconsequential information. They drown in it. They are mesmerised by the trivial minutia of one another's lives, and so the really big issues evade them. Questions pertaining to justice and human rights and the distribution of wealth, the preoccupations of the nineteenth and twentieth centuries are no longer asked."

"This is perfectly foul," Herbert Wells cried out.

"Shhh!" Bendyshe urged. "You'll have the constables onto us."

"But he's right," Mick Farren said. "How could it have happened?"

"People were seduced," Bendyshe said. "The Turing devices and other technologies gave them an endless choice of entertainments, but the corporations that made those entertainments, in competing with each other for customers, rapidly reduced everything to its lowest common denominator. What might once have carried philosophical weight became nothing but empty spectacle; what stimulated the intellect now did nothing but titillate superficial emotions. By 2100, *intellectual* had become a pejorative term." He stood. "Come with me. It's time to show you the truth of the Anglo-Saxon Empire."

They followed him across the square to the mouth of South Audley Street, coming to a halt on the exact spot where, a hundred and sixty-two years ago, they'd fought off three constables.

Bendyshe pointed along the length of the thoroughfare. "Watch the street. I'm going to temporarily deactivate your AugMems. I'll give you a full minute of unadjusted reality. It's risky."

"Risky how?" Wells asked.

"AugMems work in both directions. They accept the government transmissions but also send out a signal that holds your personal details— false information in your case. If the latter is interrupted, the loss will be noted and constables will be sent to investigate. They'll hunt for any individuals who aren't broadcasting. It's therefore vital that we keep moving. I should be able to restore the AugMems' function before we're located."

"Is it worth endangering our mission?" Burton asked doubtfully.

"I think so. You need to see this."

"Very well. Please proceed."

"Start walking. Try not to react. We're going down to Green Park to take a look at the palace grounds."

They set off.

"Brace yourselves," Bendyshe said. He put a hand to his ear, quietly muttered a few words, then announced, "The AugMems will disengage in three, two, one—"

Burton gasped as the world around him flexed and suddenly took on an entirely different aspect. The blazingly reflective towers still soared above him, but now they were supported upon titanic legs and arches, so that the great vertical mass of the city was raised above the ground-level structures, which were now revealed to be shabby, dilapidated, and in many cases derelict buildings. Burton saw broken and boarded-up windows, cracked doors slumping on rusty hinges, peeled paint and crumbled brickwork, collapsed walls and piles of debris. The pavements were strewn with refuse. Malodorous air assaulted his nostrils.

He realised why the traffic was moving so slowly. The polished silver vehicles, which had filled the roads, were now in the minority. Most had transformed into ramshackle steam-driven carriages—there were even a few being drawn by mangy horses—all of which appeared even less developed than those of his era.

And the people. Bismillah! The people!

Attired in ragged, patched and mismatched outfits, pock-marked, rickets-twisted, lank-haired and brutish, the population of this London reminded Burton of the very worst disease-ridden enclaves of Africa—of the places where the Empire had intruded and devastated cultures, leaving only hopelessness, starvation, and a lack of identity in their place. Shambling along streets that now struck him as being the gutters and drains of the upper city, the denizens of this—literal—lower level of society were bowed beneath the weight of palpable fear. They flinched away from the constables who strode arrogantly among them, bouncing on their stilts, white and masked and fearsome; they avoided eye contact, though they were forever casting surreptitious and cunning glances at one another. They were as close to the feral state as he'd ever seen in his own species.

In countenance, all were repellent, but some were worse than others, even to the point where Burton felt himself go cold with horror. He saw lumbering giants, tiny-eyed, massive-boned, and bloated with muscle. He saw slight little things, so small they might have been fairy folk. He saw a woman from whom spines extended, like a porcupine; a man whose lower face bulged into an exaggerated snout, his jaws like rock, his teeth huge and flat; an elderly lady with twelve-inch-long multi-jointed fingers, seven on each hand; a group of boys with freakishly enormous ears; an aged man with four legs; a young girl with innumerable spider-like eyes.

"Genetic manipulation," Bendyshe whispered. "People artificially adapted to suit particular functions."

"I shall faint," Sadhvi said, her voice quavering. "Or lose the contents of my stomach."

The few elite who moved through the crowds were unmistakable. People looked away from them, moved out of their path, hunched into pathetic servility. Tall and willowy, dressed in colourful clothes, their faces haughty and disdainful, these privileged few all carried switches, which they employed with lazy contempt to strike at those who passed too close, causing little yelps of pain followed by hastily mumbled apologies.

"The upper class," Bendyshe said. "They inhabit the towers but sometimes venture down here on recreational jaunts and to remind them-selves of their status.

"This is atrocious," Swinburne said. "How can the Empire be so divided?"

"Empires are formed by a minority who gain a parasitical dominance over the majority. That applies inside, as well as outside of its borders."

Burton looked ahead and saw many more overarching walkways than he'd noticed before, so numerous they appeared to blend together, forming a large platform over the centre of the city. "That explains why it became so dark when we passed between the parks," he said.

"The parks are regarded as exclusive," Bendyshe responded. "So they're gradually being raised up out of the social mire. Do you see that huge framework in the middle of them? One day it will be New Buckingham Palace, the tallest building in the world. They started building it twenty-eight years ago and say it will take another seventy-two to complete."

"Why so long?" Wells asked.

"Because every brick of it will be uniquely decorated, and because the technology built into it will make it the Parliament building and the monitoring station for the entire empire, the nucleus of a web that inter-connects nodes—the American Embassy will become one such—that communicate with every existing BioProc and AugMem. Total control, all extending from that edifice."

"Seventy-two years," Swinburne said. "Meaning it will be completed in 2202. Interesting."

"And in its shadow an underworld," Wells commented. He watched an apish individual shuffle past. "Inhabited by troglodytes."

"Who see it through rose-tinted spectacles," Sadhvi added. "We suspected that Spring Heeled Jack might create an insane world. We were correct."

Quietly, Farren added, "If it's like this now, what the hell will we find at our final destination?"

They arrived at Piccadilly and started north-eastward, following the same route they'd taken after failing to catch a bus back in '68. The sky was almost completely obscured by the heights of the metropolis, but, as Burton gazed up, a great many of the walkways suddenly vanished and the illumination increased. He looked down and saw cleanliness and glass, gleaming cars and grey-uniformed pedestrians.

"I've restored the AugMems," Bendyshe said. "And not a moment too soon. There's activity on the police channel. We've been noticed. No need for panic; the constables will be alerted to an anomaly that matches the size of our group, so if we split up, we'll be fine. Mick, Sir Richard, William, Algernon, the principal streets of the lower city haven't much altered their topology since your time—you won't get lost—so I suggest you head along Regent Street to Oxford Circus, and from there to New Centre Point. I'll take Sadhvi and Herbert via Shaftsbury Avenue. We'll meet back at the minibus."

Farren paled slightly. He dug his fingers into his bushy hair. "Look, man, I'm all for it, but what if we're stopped by the pigs? Things didn't go too well last time."

"Don't worry. Members of the Cannibal Club are lurking nearby, ready to intercede should anything go wrong. They'll be shadowing you." Bendyshe tapped his ear. "CellComps have gathered in your earlobes and jawbones. It's how I contact my colleagues, and through them I can also communicate with you. If the Cannibals have to move in and get you to safety, they will, and I'll alert you."

Farren looked at Burton for encouragement. The king's agent gave him a nod and said, "North then east, straightforward and not much of a distance. I think we can manage."

The two groups divided.

As Burton, Swinburne, Trounce and Farren entered Regent Street, Burton moved close to the Scotland Yard man. "Are you coping, William?"

Trounce grunted. "I'm still with you. These nanny-whatsits they've dosed us with do a better job than that Saltzmann's of yours. By Jove, though, this world! What has the Police Force become? I joined to protect people. All I've seen as we've travelled forward through time is increasing intimidation." He rubbed his thick fingers over his square chin. "Not that I can trust my senses anymore." He made an all-encompassing gesture. "None of this is real."

"I wonder," Burton said. "How much of the world you and I have come from was real? We operated under the assumption that we were the most civilised country in the world, but I personally witnessed the destruction we wrought in India and Africa, and we know what senseless vandalism Lord Elgin inflicted upon China." He paused and watched a very large dome-shaped vehicle pass by. What was its real form? A creaking stagecoach? A rumbling pantechnicon?

"Humph!" Trounce said. "And I saw too much of the Cauldron to believe in our claims of superiority. I see your point."

"Perhaps Charles Darwin was too optimistic. Perhaps this world is different from ours only in that it's cloaked in a more pervasive illusion. The only thing that's evolved is our ability to fool ourselves."

The four men pushed on. Two constables click-clacked past, their smooth featureless faces slowly turning toward the group before, thankfully, looking away.

"It's weird," Farren said. "I truly can't believe my eyes."

They came to Oxford Circus and bore right into Oxford Street. As in their own ages, the thoroughfare was lined with shops, and Burton and Swinburne were both astonished to see Shudders' Pharmacy among them.

"Surely not!" the poet cried out.

"Generated by our AugMems, perhaps?" Burton theorised.

Unable to resist it, they went in. The chimeric neatness of the exterior didn't extend to the inside. The shop was shabby and in serious disrepair. Damp plaster sagged from its walls, and its ceiling had collapsed in one corner. Makeshift shelves supported a sparse stock of bottles and cartons.

A stooped white-haired old man in a grubby laboratory coat greeted them. He smiled. His eyes were filmy and unfocused. He rubbed his hands together and bowed obsequiously. "Can I help you, my lords?" He gave an uncertain cough that sounded like "a-hoof!"

"My lords?" Swinburne whispered.

"Your name?" Burton asked.

The man looked afraid. "I'm Martin Ocean Englebert Shudders, citizen number eight triple-four seven six three nine eight. Is there—*a-hoof!*—a problem? My paperwork is up to date. My payments are made. My accounts are—*a-hoof!*—in order. I've re-registered my citizenship promptly every month. I've never spoken out of turn."

"We haven't any concerns about you," Burton said. "We just wanted to see your shop. Has it been here for long?"

"Fifteen years. Perfectly legal and—*a-hoof!*—aboveboard. The regulations have always been adhered to. My family's loyalty has never been in question. None of us are socialists or objectors. I hate the U.R.E. and the U.S.A. I deplore their savagery. I wish those barbarians were all dead."

"It's all right. As I said, we don't doubt you. What was it before it was a pharmacy?"

"I don't know, my lord. It was empty when I started to—*a-hoof!*—rent it. But my grandfather held that it was in the family many generations ago, and was a pharmacy then, too. Many of my family have been in the trade. Legally."

"Thank you," Burton said. "I'm sorry to have disturbed you." He moved toward the door, the others following.

"You don't want to take anything?" Shudders asked. "Please."

"No. I'm sorry. Unless—do you stock Saltzmann's Tincture?"

"Saltzmann's, my lord? Saltzmann's. Saltzmann's. No—*a-hoof!*—I don't think I've ever heard of that. I have tranquillisers. Plenty of tranquillisers. Would you like tranquillisers? Please, have a bottle. Two bottles."

"No thank you."

They exited, looked back, and suddenly the windows were clean, and, through them, neat well-stocked shelves were vaguely visible.

They continued along the street.

"How very curious," Swinburne muttered.

"Echoes, rhythms and repetitions," Burton said. "Time is exceedingly strange."

They hastened forward, all suddenly feeling the need for the safety of the minibus, worried by their separation from Bendyshe, Wells and Raghavendra.

"Don't look back," Farren said, "but those pigs that passed us earlier are following."

"Why?" Trounce asked. "We haven't done anything."

"Two more on the other side of the road," Swinburne said. "Watching."

A third pair of constables dropped out of the sky and bounced on their stilts ahead of the group.

"Damn," Trounce muttered. "We're in trouble."

"Stay calm, ignore them, and keep moving," Burton ordered. He flinched and uttered a small cry of surprise as Bendyshe's voice sounded in his ear.

"Sir Richard. Don't be alarmed. You entered a shop?"

Burton murmured, "Yes."

"But didn't take anything. That's not done. When the elite enter the establishments of the poor, it's customary to remove something without paying. Your failure to do so aroused suspicion. The shopkeeper immediately reported you. Constables are now closing in on your position. Two of my colleagues are on their way to extract you. Kat Bradlaugh and Maxwell Monckton Milnes. Do whatever they say, please, without question or hesitation."

Burton turned to address his companions, but Swinburne tapped his own ear and said, "We heard. We're in trouble with the law because we failed to steal."

"I wish I had my revolver," Trounce mumbled.

New Centre Point was just ahead, but so were more constables.

"They'll take us before we can reach the minibus," Farren observed.

Bendyshe's voice: *"Turn right and start running. Kat will land a flier in*

Soho Square. Sir Richard, Algernon, get into it. The moment it departs, Maxwell will arrive in a second machine. Mick, William, that one's for you."

"The square's not far," Farren noted. "Unless it's been moved."

They rounded the corner into Soho Street and took to their heels. People scattered out of their path. A siren started to wail.

A constable flew through the air and landed in front of them, lowering a hand to the paving as it skidded across it. The pig creature stood, viciously swatted a young woman out of the way, and pounced onto Swinburne. The poet shrieked as solid arms clamped hard around him, catching him in mid-stride. He was lifted, legs kicking.

"Halt!" the constable commanded. "You are detained under Section Nine of the Public Order Act."

"I don't think so, chum," Trounce shouted. He slammed his heel into the back of the creature's knee. As the constable buckled, Burton piled into it and pulled it down. He ruthlessly hammered its head into the ground. The pig man went limp. Swinburne jumped to his feet.

"Run!" Burton bellowed. He saw constables springing in from all sides. One landed in front of him. He delivered a right hook to the side of its face. It staggered. He whirled away from it and sprinted after his companions.

The air vibrated, and, with a loud thrumming, a small wedge-shaped flying machine swept down between the gleaming towers and thudded into the square, landing just in front of them. Immediately, a shadow fell over it and a strong wind gusted down as a far larger vessel slid overhead. It was a white disk with six rotors set into its hull and a black-and-white chequered band decorating its outer edge. A menacing cannon-like array bulged from its underside. A deafening voice thundered from the machine. "Stay where you are. Do not resist. You are in violation of Sections Nine to Thirteen of the Public Order Act. You must submit to interrogation or forfeit your lives."

A door in the side of the small flier hinged upward. A middle-aged woman leaned out and yelled, "Burton! Swinburne! In! Now!" She pointed a pistol and fired three shots. Three constables, on the point of grabbing Farren, Trounce and Swinburne, were thrown backward and lay twitching in the road.

Burton pushed Trounce toward the vehicle. "Go."

In his ear, Bendyshe shouted, *"No! You and Swinburne first!"*

"Do as he says!" Trounce snapped. He took a pace backward and gave the king's agent a hefty shove. Burton fell against the flier. Kat Bradlaugh grabbed him by the elbow and hauled him in. The king's agent spat an epithet and reached out of the vehicle toward Swinburne. The poet extended his right hand. His fingertips touched Burton's. A constable dropped down behind him. It raised a truncheon. With a loud *snick*, a blade slid out of the end of the weapon.

"Algy!" Burton hollered.

The stilted figure thrust the baton into the back of Swinburne's neck. The poet opened his mouth in shock. The blade slipped out of it like a pointed tongue. Blood gushed. Swinburne's green eyes rolled up. He crumpled to the ground.

"No!" Burton screamed. "No!"

"Kat, get him clear!"

The door dropped shut. Burton hammered his fists against it and hollered, "Let me out! Let me out!"

The flier lurched upward.

"I have to help Algy!" Burton rounded on Bradlaugh. "Take me back down, damn you!"

Through gritted teeth, she snarled, "Don't be a fool."

The flier tilted to the left as she turned it. Through its side window, Burton saw constables teeming around Trounce and Farren. One lashed out at the detective inspector, its truncheon cracking ferociously across his eyes. Trounce's head snapped back, blood spraying from it. He collapsed, kicked, and lay still.

A second flier plummeted past and landed.

Kat Bradlaugh uttered a cry of dismay and grappled with the steering levers. Burton felt his stomach churning as the vehicle skewed and twisted. She shouted, "The police ship is trying to access our controls. Tom, can you help?"

"Maxwell, get Farren. Kat, I'm going to switch you to full manual."

"I'm ready."

"There are police ships approaching from the north and west. You'll have to stay low to evade them. Get going."

"We can't leave!" Burton cried out. "My friends are injured."

"Their nanomechs aren't transmitting life signs, Sir Richard. I'm sorry."

"No!" He grabbed Bradlaugh's shoulder. "Wait! Wait! I can't leave them! They can't be dead!"

She ignored him. The flier suddenly fell, jerked to a stop some fifteen feet from the ground, and started to slide sideways.

"Got it!" Bradlaugh exclaimed. "Which way out?"

A constable thumped onto the front of the vehicle, causing it to rock. The creature's fingers screeched against metal as it scrabbled for a hold.

"Off! Off!" Bradlaugh shouted.

The pig man squealed and scraped to the right. It fell out of sight.

"Follow Greek Street south," Bendyshe instructed.

Burton glimpsed Farren at the door of the landed vessel, engulfed by constables. He was fighting like a madman, punching, kicking, somehow resisting though vastly outnumbered. Behind the Deviant, the Cannibal, Maxwell Monckton Milnes, was being dragged from the driver's seat. His head was seized and forced all the way around. He went down.

"You bloody animals!" Burton cried out.

Farren broke free, dived into the parked flier, and yanked down the door.

"Mick," Bendyshe said. *"I've locked you in. Are you all right?"*

Burton heard Farren panting. *"No. Stabbed. Bleeding. It's bad."*

"Can you stay conscious?"

"Not for—not for long."

"You have to fly manually. Pull the joystick back to get her off the ground, side to side to steer, push it to descend. The footplate controls forward momentum and braking. Same as in your day."

"Got it."

"Hold on tight," Kat Bradlaugh said to Burton.

He was pressed into his seat as the flier suddenly shot forward then was thrown against the Cannibal as it veered sharply. A thin beam of light sizzled past the side window just inches from his head. He felt its heat on his face. The glass blistered and cracked.

Bradlaugh cried out, "They're firing at us!"

The second flier rose into view, weaving and bobbing as Farren struggled with the controls.

A voice blared from the police ship. "We have you contained. Land your vehicles immediately or we'll shoot you down. You have ten seconds to comply. No further warnings."

"Tom?" Bradlaugh asked.

"*Damn it. I'm helpless. You'll have to outmanoeuvre them.*"

"I can't."

Mick Farren's voice whispered in Burton's ear. "*I guess it's time for one last gesture of defiance. It's been fun, Sir Richard. A real pleasure to meet you. Good luck.*"

"Farren!" Burton called. "What are you—?"

Before he could finish, Farren's flying machine shot upward at a tremendous velocity, slammed into the bottom of the police vessel, and disappeared in a ball of flame. Bradlaugh screamed as the shockwave hit and the steering levers were wrenched out of her hands. Burning material rained down. The noise of tortured metal filled Soho Square, like the wails of a mortally wounded leviathan.

Bradlaugh snatched at the levers and regained control. "Let's get the hell out of here."

She steered the flier into Greek Street and accelerated to such a breakneck velocity that Burton couldn't draw breath. He twisted and looked to the rear just as the burning police disk went angling into a glass tower, ripped downward through its facade, broke in half, and disintegrated into the square amid a torrential downpour of fire, metal and broken glass. Then it was out of sight, and they were hurtling along, perilously close to the ground, through Charing Cross Road and into Long Acre.

"*Kat, safe house eight,*" Bendyshe ordered.

"Endell Street, yes?"

"*Yes.*"

"Got you. Half a minute."

The flier pitched onto its side and plummeted into a narrow alleyway. Burton, unable to think, held on tightly and moaned with fright as brick walls streaked past just inches away. The machine rocketed out into a lengthy back yard, flipped to the horizontal, hit the ground, screeched along in a shower of sparks, and smacked into a wall, its nose crumpling.

"Out!" Bradlaugh barked.

Blood dribbled into Burton's eyes. His head had impacted against the windscreen. He couldn't move.

"Out!" the Cannibal repeated. She hit a switch, his door swung upward, and she pushed him into waiting hands.

"This way, Sir Richard," Tom Bendyshe said. "Lean on me."

Burton had little choice. His legs were like rubber.

Bendyshe half-dragged him across the yard, through a door, over rotting floorboards, out of another door, and into a quiet street where the minibus waited.

Sadhvi Raghavendra and Herbert Wells hauled him into the vehicle. Kat Bradlaugh followed and collapsed onto its floor. The door slid shut. Bendyshe clambered in next to Odessa Penniforth and said, "Not too fast. Don't attract attention."

The king's agent felt the minibus move forward. Sadhvi applied a cloth to his forehead. He heard Wells say, "Are we going to make it, Mr Bendyshe?"

"My colleagues are laying a false trail. Irregular BioProc signals racing westward. We, in the meantime, will be at Battersea Airfield in a few minutes."

Sadhvi put a hand on Burton's shoulder. "Richard?"

Sadhvi is alive. Wells is alive. Lawless is alive. Krishnamurthy is alive. Gooch is alive.

He sucked in a shuddering breath.

But Mick Farren and—

He couldn't think it. Couldn't allow any acknowledgment of the fact. It came anyway.

William Trounce is dead.

Algernon Swinburne is dead.

THE FUTURE

A desire to resist oppression is implanted in the nature of man.
                    —Tacitus

CHAPTER 16

ARRIVAL: 2202

Society exists for the benefit of its members, not the members for the benefit of society.
—Herbert Spencer

ays went by. Sir Richard Francis Burton lost track of them. He and the surviving chrononauts were safe aboard the *Orpheus* in Bendyshe Bay, but their mission had come to a disastrous halt. The king's agent remained in his quarters. He refused to speak to his colleagues. He didn't eat. He didn't drink. He didn't smoke. He didn't sleep.

He sat.

Cross-legged on the floor, eyes fixed straight ahead, for hour upon hour, he sat.

Not a thing went through his head. His thoughts were utterly paralysed.

Sadhvi Raghavendra did what she could for him. She brought food and took it away untouched. She sat beside him and spoke of the things she and the others had learned from the Cannibal Club, of the plutocracy that now ruled the Anglo-Saxon Empire, of the rapid physical and mental degeneration of the lower classes, of the many techniques employed by their overlords to keep them subservient and pliable, of the terrible destruction wrought during the failed revolution of the 2080s.

"The British Museum was among the many establishments destroyed," she said. "Access to it had long been denied to the general public. It became a symbol of everything that was being withheld. As we saw in 2022, knowledge was distributed through the Turing devices, but it was strictly controlled, and that control became so increasingly draconian that by the 2070s even the Turings were discontinued. Not surprising, then, that the museum became, at one point, the focus of protestations. In 2083, the people, in their fury, determined that if they were to be denied the knowledge it held then the government would be, too. They blew it up. Isambard Kingdom Brunel was buried beneath the rubble." She placed her hand on his forearm and gave it a squeeze. "It's peculiar—I'd come to regard him as a point of consistency, an old friend who never changed. But I must contrast his loss with our encountering of all these new Bendyshes and Bradlaughs, Murrays and Monckton Milneses, Brabrookes and Hunts, Bhattis and Honestys, Slaughters and Penniforths. How oddly touching it is to see our old friends peeking out from behind all the new faces. Life goes on, Richard. Life goes on."

This latter sentiment, expressed during her most recent visit, caused something deep inside him to stir. A thought whispered as if from an immense distance:

Not Algy's life.

Not William's.

Not Isabel's.

Emotion stirred. It wasn't grief or self-pity or despair but a black and iron-hard anger that settled upon him with such subtlety that when Raghavendra next visited she didn't notice it at all, though she saw his dark eyes had become strangely shielded, as if he were looking out through them from much farther inside himself.

He started to take a little water, a little brandy.

Gradually, he regained awareness of who he was, where he was, and what he was supposed to be doing.

He ate a meal. He smoked a Manila cheroot. He stood, stretched his stiff legs, and regarded himself in the mirror over the basin. His internal silence was broken by two words:

King's agent.

He snorted disdainfully.

Burton washed and started to shave, pausing frequently to gaze at his reflection.

Like an aged steam engine, his mind slowly built up heat, fuelled by his rage, its gears creakingly engaging, motion returning to it.

You failed. They were under your command and they died. You failed.

It wasn't my fault.

Everything that makes you, you lose. Whenever you value a person, it's their death sentence. Wherever you settle, that place will change. The things you hold dear forever slip out of your grasp.

I cannot endure such loss!

Whenever you feel certain of something, the only certainty is that it will become something else.

No!

There is only one truth, and that truth is Time, and Death is Time's agent.

No! No! No!

He dropped the cutthroat razor and leaned with his fists against the bulkhead to either side of the mirror. He glowered at himself, one side of his jaw still frothy with shaving soap, water dripping from his moustache.

John Speke. William Stroyan. John Steinhaueser. Isabel Arundell. Algernon Swinburne. William Trounce.

He leaned forward until his forehead rested against the cool glass, shut his eyes, clenched his teeth and drew back his lips. Suddenly he was shaking and his respiration became strained. He wanted to find Edward Oxford and strangle him, hammer his face until he felt the bones fracturing beneath his knuckles, rip him apart until there was nothing remaining, but in his mind's eye, the man he envisioned himself battering with such ferocious brutality, the man he called Oxford, possessed his own features and was named Sir Richard Francis Burton.

With an inarticulate cry, the king's agent reeled from the basin, stumbled to a chest of drawers, snatched up a decanter, and poured himself a generous measure of brandy. He swallowed it in one and stood leaning on the furniture until he stopped trembling.

He returned to the basin to finish shaving.

He felt acutely aware of the edge of the blade as it slid across the skin of his throat.

I met Swinburne and Trounce just over half a year ago. How can I be so broken by their loss?

It felt as if he'd known them forever. They were family.

"Half a year?" he mumbled. "Nearly three hundred, more like."

Had the attachments formed across multiple histories? Were they so important to him because they had been important to Abdu El Yezdi?

After changing his clothes, Burton crossed to a Saratoga trunk, opened it, lifted out its top tray, and took a small bottle from one of the inner compartments. He pulled the cork, downed the tincture, moved to the middle of the floor, lowered himself, and sat cross-legged again.

He didn't need Saltzmann's anymore. His addiction had completely left him. But he wanted it.

Closing his eyes, he focused his attention on his scalp, sensing the scars that curved through the roots of his hair, feeling the diamond dust that was etched into them.

The tincture's glow eased him into a meditative trance. He filled his mind with a repetitive chant:

> *Allāhu Allāhu Allāhu Haqq.*
> *Allāhu Allāhu Allāhu Haqq.*
> *Allāhu Allāhu Allāhu Haqq.*
> *Allāhu Allāhu Allāhu Haqq.*

He sought the Swinburne jungle, prayed that it would hear him, transcend histories, and communicate.

> *Allāhu Allāhu Allāhu Haqq.*
> *Allāhu Allāhu Allāhu Haqq.*
> *Algy Algy Algy talk!*
> *Algy Algy Algy talk!*

Steady and persistent, like a heartbeat, the words throbbed through him until, very slightly, he started to rock backward and forward to their rhythm.

The tempo divided time—into seconds, into minutes, into hours, into days, into weeks, into months, into years, into decades, into generations, into centuries, into millennia, into ages, into epochs, into eras, into eons, into vast cycles of repetition through which the universe itself expanded and contracted like a beating heart.

Each division possessed a birth and a death, so there were births within births and deaths within deaths, from the infinitude of the microscopic to the boundlessness of the macroscopic. He recognised life as a commencement, life as a termination, life contained within a wave pattern, a vibration, a tone; a syllable through which intelligence was made manifest at every level.

The great paradox: everything in existence was imbued with intelligence, yet everything existed only because it was discerned by that intelligence. Matter, space, time and mind inextricably intertwined, creating themselves through self-recognition.

The insight blossomed in Burton like an unfurling red rose.

The jungle, its roots extending through histories, touched him for the briefest instant and delivered a truth—a stunning clarification of his earlier visions—that caused him to cry out in wonder.

"Bismillah! We have it reversed! The universe does not create life! Life creates the universe!"

The sound of his own voice intruded upon his trance. He opened his eyes but continued to sit quietly.

Twelve years ago—subjective years—he'd become a Master Sufi. Since that time, he'd been using the phrase *Allāhu Allāhu Allāhu Haqq* as a mantra to aid in meditation. Now, for the first time, he considered its meaning.

God Is Truth.

He didn't believe in God—not in one that responded to prayer and intervened in human affairs. However, if intelligence was the core and cause of reality, imagining it into existence and separating it into coherent parts, then might not the religious myths of a fall from "Grace" followed by a spiritual striving to return to "Him" be an allegory of humanity's tendency to lose itself in its own narrative structures, becoming so deeply attached to its signifiers that full awareness of the signified was lost?

Burton sighed and climbed to his feet. Crossing to the mirror, he once again considered himself. He gazed into his own eyes, saw the anger in them and, beyond it, something else, something new. What was it? A deep spiritual shock? A suspension of disbelief? An abandonment of the convictions and attitudes through which he'd defined himself?

I am unmade.

He squared his shoulders, curled his fingers into fists, and left his quarters.

He found Gooch, Wells and Bendyshe in the ship's lounge. They jumped up as he entered.

"Sir Richard!" Gooch exclaimed. "You are recovered?"

He gave a curt nod. "What's our status?"

"We're secure," Bendyshe answered. "No danger of detection."

Burton turned back to Gooch. "The *Orpheus*?"

"All shipshape and Bristol fashion."

"Then we'll get moving. Is everyone rested?"

They made sounds of affirmation.

Wells, apparently unnerved by Burton's abrupt attitude, said in a thin voice, "Um. We can—we can certainly depart immediately if you order it, but if you—if you require more time—"

"Time? No, Herbert. Time is the last thing I need."

Time is my enemy. Time leads only to death.

He turned back to Gooch. "The order is given. Tom, will you be coming with us?"

"No," Bendyshe answered. "The Cannibal Club needs to be a resourceful presence in 2202 that it may support you properly when you arrive there. We have three generations in which to strengthen the organisation. I will be cloned, and I'll see that everything that's necessary is done." He stood. "Sadhvi, Daniel, Herbert, it's been a pleasure to meet you. Sir Richard, will you walk me to the hatch?"

"Certainly."

Hands were shaken. Burton and Bendyshe left the room.

"I'm sorry for your losses," Bendyshe said. "I feel responsible."

"You're not. I am. I should never have entered the pharmacy. But enough self-recrimination. The mission will continue. We're a single step away from our destination. I'll not be deflected from our purpose. The reckoning with Spring Heeled Jack must come. Frankly, I look forward to it."

They reached the hatch. Bendyshe stopped and appraised Burton for a moment. "You seem somehow harder. More ruthless. I feel a little afraid of you."

The king's agent said nothing. He helped the Cannibal to slide open the portal. The air that gusted in was damp and bore the scent of wet grass.

Bendyshe stepped out then turned back.

"Sir Richard, we're fighting for humanity. Don't lose yours."

After a slight pause, Burton answered, "I may have no option. I sense an inevitability about it."

Suddenly, the other couldn't meet his eyes. Bendyshe looked down at the boarding ramp, up at the clouded afternoon sky, across to the *Mary Seacole*. He mumbled, "My ancestor—the Thomas Bendyshe you knew—he really loved you. He's a part of me and I can feel it."

Burton gave a slight nod. "He's a part of me, too."

They said no more.

After drawing in the ramp and securing the hatch, Burton went up to the bridge and was greeted by Captain Lawless and Maneesh Krishnamurthy.

"Let's prepare for departure, gentlemen."

From above, the Mark III babbage said, "At last! I feared rust might set in. I've been bored senseless."

Krishnamurthy, after momentarily gazing at Burton, said, "I'm glad to see you up and about," then set off toward the generator room, leaving Lawless and Burton alone.

"Fifteen days, give or take a few hours," the airman said. "That's how long our voyage has taken so far, though calculating duration when you're travelling through time is rather like trying to measure how much water a fish drinks."

"I'm sorry I've delayed us," Burton said.

"Don't be. You had every reason. Besides, we can linger for as long as we like. It makes no difference. We'll still arrive at nine in the evening on the fifteenth of February, 2202." Lawless rubbed his neatly trimmed beard. "But what's the plan? What will we do when we get there?"

"As her principal crew, you, Daniel and Maneesh will remain aboard the *Orpheus*. Myself, Herbert and Sadhvi will attempt to locate and destroy the Turing Fulcrum or whatever might have superseded it. If the Cannibals report to you that we've failed and lost our lives, then command of the expedition will fall to you. You'll have to decide whether to make another attempt or retreat back to our native time."

"We'll not flee," Lawless said.

Orpheus interrupted. "My apologies, Captain Lawless, Sir Richard. I have been readying the systems for flight."

"Good," Lawless responded. He looked up. "Why apologise?"

"Because I obviously misunderstood. When you said 'prepare for departure,' I thought you meant we might be going somewhere, not that you intended to stand around chatting."

The airman snorted his amusement. He touched his right earlobe and said, "Mr. Wells? Would you assist us on the bridge, please?" Upon receiving a reply, he shook his head wonderingly and said to Burton, "I feel as if these CellComp thingamajigs have made me clairvoyant. Microscopic biological machines. Lord have mercy. Science or sorcery, I ask you."

Wells arrived and took up position at the meteorological equipment. Burton moved to the Nimtz console, from which he could monitor the output of the generator.

Krishnamurthy whispered in his ear, *"Captain, Sir Richard, ready when you are."*

"Are we all set, *Orpheus*?" Lawless asked.

"I believe I've already made it perfectly clear that I am," the Mark III replied. "You're the one who's dawdling."

"Then proceed, please. You know the routine."

The familiar rumble of engines vibrated through the floor as the rotors whirled into a blur and lifted the ship.

"Now to once again discover the shape of things to come," Wells murmured.

A minute later, *Orpheus* announced that the vessel was in position and ready to jump through time. Lawless issued the command.

They entered and exited whiteness.

"I've received instructions," the Mark III immediately declared. "We are to set course for Battersea Airfield."

"Go ahead," Lawless said. "Top speed, please. Everyone all right?"

Burton and Wells nodded. The king's agent addressed the man from 1914. "Herbert, go get yourself prepared."

"Pistol?"

"Yes."

Wells left the bridge. Burton looked out at the thickly clouded night sky then crossed to the console Wells had just abandoned and examined its panel. "Snow is forecast over London," he murmured.

"Shouldn't be a problem," Lawless said.

"Not for me," *Orpheus* confirmed.

Burton made a sound of acknowledgement. "I'd better get ready."

He stepped through the door and descended to the main deck, walked along the corridor, through the lounge, and carried on until he came to Sadhvi Raghavendra's quarters. He tapped on the door and entered at her called invitation. She was wearing baggy trousers and a loose shirt—men's clothing.

"Richard!" she exclaimed. "How are you?"

"The walking wounded."

He lowered himself into a chair beside her bunk. She sat on the mattress and placed a hand over his.

"As are we all."

He rubbed his forehead and closed his eyes. "I don't know how much more I can take. Last year I lost my friends Stroyan and Steinhaueser. I lost—I lost Isabel. Now Algy and William. And seeing all these descendants of my friends, of Monckton Milnes and Bendyshe and Brabrooke and the rest, only serves to remind me of my own mortality and that, when I am gone, nothing of me will remain."

"It's not too late. What are you, thirty-nine years old?"

He snorted. "Three hundred and eighty-one by another reckoning."

She smiled. "My point is that you might still, one day, father a child."

"And see my own face somewhere in its features? An assurance of immortality? No, Sadhvi, that will never happen."

"Your pain will subside."

"If it does, it will make no difference. I was a young man in India. I was ravaged by fevers and subject to innumerable tropical infections. It has left me incapable of—of fathering a child."

She nodded slowly. "Ah. I see. My native country is an unforgiving one."

Sliding from the bunk, she squatted down in front of him so that her eyes were at a lower level than his, looked up at him, put her hands on his knees, and said, "You know the Hindu faith well."

"I do. What of it?"

"You are aware, then, that we believe a cycle of creation, preservation and dissolution is at the heart of all things, at every level of existence."

"It has been much on my mind. Have you been reading my thoughts?"

She smiled. "I wouldn't dare to, even if I could."

"Hmm. Cycles? What of them?"

"Just that, at a personal level, when one is in the midst of dissolution, when everything appears lost, there is still the promise of rebirth, of a new cycle to come, of fresh creation."

"If one survives," Burton rasped.

"The concept of survival exists only because we place fences around ourselves. It is easy to think that when the physical body dies, there is nothing beyond it. But that's because we depend on our senses to tell us what's real. Those senses are a part of the body. When it dies, so do they. They aren't the truth, Richard. That lies outside of us. Whatever suffering you're enduring, if you push it into a wider context, perhaps it will appear a little less overwhelming."

"What context?"

"Think of what we're doing. We've travelled many generations into the future. We should all be long dead and gone. Yet, here we are, on a voyage to help the entire human race fulfil its destiny."

He gazed into her eyes, saw in them compassion and faith and unshakable friendship. He clicked his teeth together then gave a sharp exhalation and said, "You're right. Of course, you're right. What is Richard Burton in the greater scheme of things? I am but a pawn in a game far too complex for me to understand."

"No," she said. "You're more than a pawn. Your life may not be what you hoped, but it is still yours. You have willpower. And you know better, perhaps, than any other man, how the actions of one person can alter the entire world."

Burton put his hand to his scalp, felt the scars. "That's for certain."

He came to a decision, stood, and gave a hand to Raghavendra as she rose.

"Let's go and discover what it is we must do."

They left the cabin and walked to the bridge, where they found Wells waiting.

"How long to Battersea, Captain?" Burton asked.

"Twelve minutes," Lawless responded. "We're just passing Whitstable. Descending through the cloud cover now."

"By heavens!" Wells exclaimed. He pointed out of the window. "Red snow!"

It was true. Bright scarlet flakes swirled thickly outside and speckled the window's glass.

Bismillah! Did I somehow summon the jungle?

Burton stepped closer to the glass.

Algy?

He said, "Nine o'clock, same day, same month, separated by three hundred and forty-two years. Red snow on both occasions. Had I any doubts about this mission, this would have swept them away."

The *Orpheus* lurched as the Mark III steered it sharply to the left. Burton and the others staggered. "Oops! Sorry about that!" the babbage said. "The conditions are interfering with my radar, and I didn't anticipate there being towers in the clouds."

"Towers?" Lawless asked. "At this altitude? This far out from the city? What do you— ?" He fell silent as the rotorship emerged from the dense canopy into a forest of brightly illuminated obelisks.

"My word!" Wells cried out. "London must cover the whole of the southeast!"

They gazed out at what had once been Whitstable, a small and sleepy coastal town, now apparently a borough of the capital, having been engulfed by the ever-spreading metropolis.

"I'm reducing speed," *Orpheus* said. "Some of those towers are touching three and a half thousand feet. I have to steer us between them."

"Do it!" Lawless snapped.

"I am," the Mark III replied testily. "Didn't I just say so?"

"It's incredible," Raghavendra exclaimed. "I could never have imagined such a city. The size of it! The height!"

The engines hummed as the rotorship weaved back and forth between the vertical edifices, moving through the mammoth metropolis, travelling in a westerly direction.

"I can barely take it all in," Lawless said. "Is it possible that people built such a marvel? It's the eighth wonder of the world!"

They saw the mouth of the Thames, but of the river itself there was no sign.

"Gone!" Wells cried out.

"Maybe not gone," Burton said. "Perhaps just built over. Even in the nineteenth century many of the city's waterways had been forced beneath the streets. The Tyburn, Fleet and Effra, for example, were all incorporated into Bazalgette's sewer system." He shivered, recalling bad experiences in those subterranean burrows.

They marvelled at the columns, which loomed out of the falling curtain of snow, all spanned by walkways, making London resemble a great hive through which many more flying machines floated, glimmering like fireflies.

"There's something ablaze," Lawless noted. He pointed. "Down there."

As the *Orpheus* altered course, swinging southward, Sadhvi drew their attention to three large lesser-lit areas, like linked hollows in the dazzling display.

"Hyde Park, Green Park and Saint James Park," Burton observed. "Still there and still the same shape after all these years." He grunted. "Which, if I'm judging it correctly, means that fire is in, or close to, Grosvenor Square."

Recurrences. Patterns.

"Descending," the Mark III announced. "Battersea Airfield ahead. I should warn you that I'm having problems with my altitude sensors. There's a peculiar echo."

"Clarify, please," Lawless demanded.

"A double reading. I'm not certain which of them is accurate."

"Everyone stay by the window," Lawless ordered. "We'll give visual assistance."

They saw other rotorships gliding past. In design, they differed little to their own vessel. If anything, they were slightly more primitive. However, as in 2130, there were also other flying craft—disks and needles and cones—that were obviously far more advanced.

"Apparently the divide continues," Wells said. "Progress for some, retrogression for others."

Burton felt a lightness as the *Orpheus* dropped, increased weight as it slowed and stopped.

"Is the ground fifty feet below us or a thousand?" the Mark III asked.

Lawless peered down and said, "Fifty."

The ship dropped, and they were all jogged slightly as it landed.

"Elegantly done as usual, despite the confusion," the babbage declared. "You may congratulate me."

"Consider your back patted," Lawless replied.

"Cannibal Club representatives are waiting outside."

"Thank you, *Orpheus*. Sir Richard, Herbert, Sadhvi, I wish you every success in your mission. Daniel, Maneesh and I will keep the ship ticking over, ready to respond in an instant should you require our assistance."

Burton said, "Thank you, Captain."

They clasped hands.

Burton, Wells and Raghavendra left the bridge and were met by Gooch and Krishnamurthy at the hatch.

"Ready?" Gooch asked.

Burton jerked his head in affirmation.

"A new Thomas Bendyshe," Wells mused. "I wonder how identical he'll be to the other?"

Gooch took hold of one hatch lever while Krishnamurthy gripped the other. They pulled, the portal opened, and the ramp slid down. A flurry of scarlet snow billowed in. They stood back.

Burton watched as two figures ascended toward him, an adult—male, to judge by the gait—and a child, both wrapped in ankle-length cloaks with wide cowls that kept their faces shielded from the downpour.

The visitors stopped in front of him. The adult snapped, "Government inspection. Do not resist. Let us aboard."

"We're a cargo ship," Burton said. "Empty."

"Nonsense. You're a vessel from the distant past and you're carrying enemies of the state."

"From the past?" Burton replied. "What do you mean by that?"

"You are chrononauts from the year 1860. And you, old son, are Sir Richard Francis Burton, the famous explorer."

"Old son?"

The figure gave a bark of laughter. He and his companion reached up and pulled back their hoods.

"I've always been absolutely hopeless at playacting," said Detective Inspector William Trounce.

"What ho! What ho! What ho!" cheered Algernon Charles Swinburne.

CHAPTER 17

THE UPPERS AND THE LOWLIES

Friends of my youth, a last adieu! haply some day we meet
    again;
Yet ne'er the self-same men shall meet; the years shall make
    us other men.
          —Sir Richard Francis Burton,
           The Kasîdah of Hâjî Abdû El-Yezdî

"Cloned!" Swinburne declared with an extravagant wave of his arms. "We were jolly well cloned!"

Sadhvi stammered, "But—but are you the same?"

Trounce tapped his head. "Humph! Memories and personalities intact. We recall everything. Is my bowler aboard? I still miss it."

Bemusedly, unable to stop staring, Burton nodded.

Trounce reached up to smooth his moustache, even though it wasn't there anymore. "By Jove, it's good to see you after all this time."

"Death defied," Wells whispered in awe.

"To the lounge!" Swinburne exclaimed, stepping forward and giving a mighty jerk of his left elbow. "A toast to old friendships renewed. Nineteenth-century brandy, hurrah! Believe me, they don't make it like they used to. By golly, I've missed it terribly. And all of you, too, of course. How the very devil are you?"

Burton suddenly pounced forward, caught the poet under the arms, yanked him off his feet, and whirled him around. "Algy! Algy! Bismillah!

Algy!" He dropped him and lunged at Trounce, embracing him in a bear hug. "William, you old goat!"

"Steady on!" Trounce protested.

Swinburne screeched with laughter. "Three hundred and forty-two years!" he crowed. "That's how long it's taken!"

"To get here?" Sadhvi asked.

"No! For Beastly Burton to go soft!"

"Idiot!" Burton protested. "By Allah's beard! Exactly the *same* idiot!"

"At your service," Swinburne said with a melodramatic curtsey. "I say! Did someone mention a toast?"

"You did. And I wholeheartedly second the motion."

Grinning helplessly, the reunited chrononauts closed the hatch and reconvened in the ship's lounge where, to Swinburne's evident delight, a decanter of brandy was produced. Swallowing his measure, the poet smacked his lips, gave a sigh of pleasure, and said, "At last. There are chemicals in everything, these days. Ruins the taste." He sat back in his chair, crossed his legs, uncrossed them, kicked out the right, twitched his shoulders, raised his glass, and added, "I appear to be empty."

Gooch provided a refill.

"Cloned," Burton said. "Are you, then, your own son, Algy? Grandson?"

"Neither. I'm me. The same person, the same memories, an exact copy of the body. The only difference is that I've lived a second childhood and have a brother I never had before."

"Brother?"

"This old duffer," Swinburne said, cocking a thumb at Trounce.

Burton's right eyebrow went up.

Trounce said, "Back in 2130, the Cannibals indulged in a little body snatching. Just like the old days, hey? Resurrectionists! DNA from our corpses was put on ice. Thirty-eight years ago, mine was used to create yours truly. Thus you now find me exactly the age I was when you last saw me. My great-grandfather was the Thomas Bendyshe you met; my father his clone, also named Thomas. My mother is Marianne Monckton Milnes. Of course, they're not strictly speaking my biological parents, but she bore me and they both raised me. In 2179, this scallywag was created—" He indicated Swinburne. "Fifteen years my junior. Same surrogate parents. The timing was carefully arranged so that he, too, would today be the age he was when you saw him last."

Burton pulled a cigar from his pocket, fumbled and dropped it into his lap, retrieved it, looked at it, then blinked at Trounce and said, "You—you spent a childhood together?"

"Yes!" Swinburne said. "You should have seen how skinny he was. And stubborn. An absolute mule."

"As you can see," Trounce said. "Carrots is every bit as loony as his previous incarnation."

Burton smiled at the nickname, which he'd heard used before in reference to his redheaded friend, though never by Trounce.

"I was somewhat past my childhood when he was born," the ex-detective went on, "but, yes, we were raised together, and for a specific purpose."

"It being our arrival?" Krishnamurthy ventured.

"Exactly. Algy and I are now the leaders of the Cannibal Club."

Sadhvi said, "What of Mick Farren, William. Was he also—um—reborn?"

Trounce sighed. "I'm afraid not. There was nothing left of him. I heard what he did. Brave chap! Funny, back in 1968, he scared me silly with that wild hair of his, but I came to like him more and more. A bad loss."

"And Thomas Bendyshe?" Burton asked.

An expression of uneasiness passed across Trounce's and Swinburne's faces.

The poet said, "Offshoots of the family still oversee our finances. As for the direct line, Father—"

"A distraction was necessary," Trounce put in.

"Distraction?"

"Spring Heeled Jack is in control of the Empire, there can be no doubt about it. You arrived at nine tonight, the fifteenth of February 2202, which as we know is a significant moment for him. For reasons that will become clear to you, we were concerned that he might be watching out for your arrival. Father gave him something else to think about."

"What?" Burton asked.

"The destruction of the American Embassy. The Cannibals have bombed it."

The king's agent again looked at his unlit cigar. He bit his lip and returned it to his pocket. "William, don't tell me the club is resorting to violence."

"Humph! The embassy has been a fully automated affair for many years. There was no one in it. Even so, it's a crucial hub in New Buckingham Palace's surveillance network, and its destruction will have caused considerable disruption throughout the city."

Burton said, "I see." He considered his old friend. Trounce looked the same, though clean-shaven and with slightly longer hair, but his manner was rather less gruff, and his diction a little different. The king's agent found it disconcerting.

Daniel Gooch poured Swinburne a third brandy and said, "I take it the Turing Fulcrum is still in operation?"

"It is," Trounce confirmed. "There's been no real progress for well over a century. Everyone is watched. Everything is recorded. Creativity is suppressed. Fortunately, we Cannibals have Lorena Brabrooke."

"We met her ancestor in 2022," Burton said.

"The same. Cloned. A bloomin' prodigy. Her ability to evade detection and construct false identities borders on the artistic. Your nanomechs were automatically updated the moment you appeared over Bendyshe Bay. By now, the Turing Fulcrum has already registered you as non-threats. If we exercise due caution, we can leave the ship and proceed with the mission."

"To locate and destroy the damn thing," Burton said.

"Quite so. There's no question that Spring Heeled Jack has infiltrated it, exists within it, and through it has taken complete control of the Empire, yet for all Lorena's ability to interfere with what the Fulcrum does, she's never been able to identify exactly where it is. It, on the other hand, has on a number of occasions got dangerously close to locating her, which is why we've until now hesitated to mount an all-out assault against it. Tonight will be different. She'll employ her talents to the full to confuse it while we set out to finally run Spring Heeled Jack to ground."

"By what means are we to do that?"

The detective opened his mouth to continue, but before he could utter a further word, Swinburne leaped up, punched the air, and shouted, "We're going to kidnap Queen Victoria! Hurrah!"

Sir Richard Francis Burton, Algernon Swinburne, Sadhvi Raghavendra and Herbert Wells were sitting in a medium-sized flier, a tubular craft with four flat disk-shaped wings. William Trounce was at the controls. They were in the air two miles west of Battersea Airfield on the other side of the now subterranean River Thames.

"Look down," Swinburne said. He pointed out of the window. "Cheyne Walk. That's where I lived in 1860."

"I don't recognise it at all," Burton said.

The poet explained that London now existed on two distinct levels, thus *Orpheus*'s confusion. Walkways and platforms had melded together, been layered with soil, and planted with well-lit lawns and prettily landscaped gardens—all currently being coated with red snow. They separated slender towers of such height that the upper reaches of the city disappeared into the cloud cover and soared so far beyond it they came close to scraping the stratosphere. The overall effect was one of cleanliness and spaciousness, a luxurious environment unimaginable in Burton's age.

Despite the thousands of towers, the upper level appeared to be sparsely populated. The king's agent had never seen London so quiet. By comparison to what he was used to—and, especially, to what he'd witnessed during the journey to this time period—very few people were strolling around below, even taking into account the weather. Those he saw were wearing the same cloaks and voluminous hoods in which Trounce and Swinburne, and now he and his fellow chrononauts, were attired.

"You're looking upon the city of the Uppers," Swinburne said. "The elite. The privileged. Below it, there exists the second city, the overcrowded domain of the Lowlies."

"The working classes, I presume," Wells said.

"Yes, Bertie. They exist in dire poverty and are so terribly deformed by genetic manipulations that they barely qualify as human. The London Underground is a place of horror, and I'm afraid we have to go down there."

"Why?" Burton asked. He could feel perspiration starting to bead his forehead.

Swinburne pointed to the northeast, where, at a high altitude, the edge of a platform—a third level—could be made out, its lights shining well above the upper city.

"That's the New Buckingham Palace complex; what used to be Hyde Park, Green Park and Saint James Park. It's inhabited by Queen Victoria and by government ministers and their staff and is exceedingly well guarded. However, water is pumped up to it from the River Tyburn, which flows beneath the lower lever. There are access conduits running parallel to the pipes that lead up from the depths to the heights."

Burton groaned. "Please don't say it."

"I know, Richard. You hate enclosed spaces and you have bad memories of the Tyburn tunnel—but there's no option. You have to go down there again."

The flier veered northward, skirting around the western edge of the parks.

Trounce said, "In 2138, when the new palace was still being built, Lorena's grandmother—the daughter of the Lorena Brabrooke you met in 2022—was able to access the architectural blueprints. We know from them that the conduits are connected by a lift to the upper pump room, which opens onto the palace roof where the palace greenhouses are located. They will be our point of entry."

"I'm still confused," Sadhvi said. "Queen Victoria?"

"Humph! I suppose it makes a crooked kind of sense that Oxford would re-create the monarch who lies at the heart of his madness," Trounce answered.

"Is she a clone, too?"

"I very much doubt it. DNA doesn't survive forever, and the original Victoria died three hundred and sixty-two years ago. Nor are there any descendants of the old monarchy who could convincingly claim the throne. No. I don't know who she is or where she comes from, but, for certain, she is Spring Heeled Jack's puppet, a figurehead enforced upon us to give a human face to his inhuman dictatorship."

"So she has direct communication with him?" Burton asked. "She receives her instructions from the Turing Fulcrum?"

"I don't see how she can perform her role otherwise."

"But kidnapping?" The king's agent shook his head. "It doesn't sit well with me."

"Nor me. If there was any other way—" Trounce fell silent.

He steered the flier between towers, and Swinburne marked off districts as they passed over them. "Earl's Court. Kensington. Notting Hill." The vessel veered to the east. "Bayswater. Edgware Road."

Smoothly, they descended and landed in a long and narrow lamp-lit public garden. As they disembarked, Wells shivered and said, "This snow is extraordinary."

"Blame my brother," Trounce muttered. He raised his hood and gave a grunt of satisfaction as the others did likewise. "Even when we're below, it'll be best if we keep our faces covered, especially you, Richard."

"Why me in particular?" the king's agent asked.

Swinburne giggled. "You might scare the natives. Have you looked in a mirror lately?"

Burton glared at him, then his face softened and he muttered, "The same old Algy."

Trounce pointed at the glowing glass frontage of a tall edifice. "Does the position of that tower ring any bells?"

"No," Burton said. "Should it?"

"Its foundations are rooted in the spot once occupied by fourteen Montagu Place."

"Home! By God!"

Swinburne grinned and nudged him with an elbow. "Good old Mother Angell, hey! Never fear, you'll be back there soon enough."

They fell silent as three "Uppers" walked by. Though the trio was enveloped in cloaks, sufficient of them was visible for Burton to see they were thin and willowy in stature.

Trounce waited until they'd passed then said to Burton, Wells and Raghavendra, "Hand over your guns. They're rather too antique for our requirements."

This was done, and he put them into a small compartment inside the vehicle, drawing from it five replacement pistols, which he distributed.

"The Underground is heavily patrolled by constables. They're identical to the creatures that attacked you in 1860, Richard. You'll remember how we fought them off with truncheons and revolvers. These pistols will make a better job of it."

"How does it load?" Burton asked, examining his gun with interest. "I've never seen anything like it."

"It's a Penniforth Mark Two," the detective inspector explained. "Invented by one of Monty's descendants. The bullets are stored in compressed form inside the grip. There are five hundred. You're unlikely to need more."

"Five hundred? How is that possible?"

"Humph! A nanotech thing. Quite beyond me. All I know is that after each shot a fresh bullet is squirted into the chamber where it instantaneously expands to its full form." Raising the weapon, he continued, "The gun has a small measure of intelligence. Watch."

He aimed at the flier. A small red dot of light slid across the vehicle.

"That marks the target, and, as you can see, I can aim just like normal. However, I can also do this. Front end."

The dot snapped across to the flier's prow.

"Rear nearside window."

In a blink, the dot moved to the vehicle's rear window.

"Ground, ten inches in front of the middle of the flier."

The point of illumination instantly snapped to the quoted position.

"If you need to shoot a weapon out of an opponent's hand, just tell the pistol to do so and it will take care of the aiming."

"Impressive!" Burton exclaimed.

"Better even than that," Trounce said. "You can instruct the bullets to kill or to stun or to explode."

Trounce pushed the weapon into his waistband and gestured toward an oddly shaped structure. "Our access point is over there. It leads down to the corner of Gloucester Place. Up here, we're safe enough. Down there, we won't be. Watch what you say and keep your faces shadowed by your hoods. Your BioProcs will work to divert attention away from you, but if you're seen to do—or heard to say—anything suspicious, the constables will be on us before you can say Jack Robinson." Trounce started, his eyebrows going up. "By Jove! I've not said 'Jack Robinson' for nigh on three and a half centuries! Funny how memory works when you're a clone."

They followed him to the structure, which proved to be the top of a spiral staircase.

"What's to stop the people down there from coming up here?" Sadhvi Raghavendra asked.

"Superstitious dread," Trounce answered. "The maxim 'know your place' has been drummed into them for nigh on a century."

"Will we attract attention by going down?"

"We're Uppers. We can go anywhere." He checked that their faces were all sufficiently shadowed by the hoods, gave a nod of satisfaction, and started down the metal stairs. Burton followed, Raghavendra was next, then Wells, and lastly, Swinburne.

The stairwell—a plain metal tube—was lit by a strip of light that spiralled down anticlockwise just above the handrail to their right. The illumination served only to accentuate the narrowness of the cylinder, and, as they descended, Burton's respiration became increasingly laboured, his claustrophobia gripping him like a vice.

Their footsteps clanged and echoed.

After five minutes, an orange radiance began to swell from below.

"Is the air getting thicker?" Burton mumbled.

"Actually, yes," Trounce said. "The Underground is hotter, made humid by steam-powered vehicles, and is pretty much a soup of nanomechs."

"That do what?"

"That keep the Lowlies placid."

They suddenly emerged from the tube into an open space. As they continued down the steps, Burton and his fellow chrononauts looked around in amazement. They were in Montagu Place, not far from the corner of Gloucester Place, but aside from the configuration of the roads the area was completely unrecognisable. Where Burton's house had once stood, there was now a row of derelict—but obviously inhabited—two-storey buildings. Toward Gloucester Place, and across it, visible along Dorset Street, much larger tenement buildings huddled. They were ill-built ramshackle affairs, mostly of wood, with upper storeys that overhung the streets. They were very similar to the old "rookeries" that had once existed in the East End, reflecting the same dire poverty and hellish conditions that had made of the Cauldron such a crime- and disease-ridden district.

In stark contrast to the overground, the streets here were densely populated. Slow-moving crowds were jammed to either side of a band of clanking, growling, hissing, chugging, popping, grinding, clattering traffic. The vehicles were more primitive than those of Burton's age, for the most part comprised of leaking boilers, smoking furnaces, chopping crankshafts, wobbling drive bands, and belching funnels. Some were pulled by horses or donkeys or, unnervingly, by gigantic dogs. That such methods of transport existed contemporaneously with the saucer-like fliers of upper London was extraordinary.

From all these contraptions, steam billowed into the air, making the atmosphere, which reeked of sweat and filth and fossil fuels, so foggy that the far ends of Montagu Place and Dorset Street were lost in the haze.

Hanging high over the thoroughfares, suspended with no visible means of support, a multitude of large flat panels glowed with letters and disturbing images. The closest, right next to the spiral staircase, portrayed a ferocious and Brobdingnagian slant-eyed panda rampaging across a city, crushing towers beneath its clawed feet, and with hundreds of tiny people dribbling from the corners of its snarling, fanged and blood-wetted mouth. "ONLY YOU CAN SAVE THE UNITED REPUBLICS OF EURASIA FROM ITS OWN BARBARISM!" the floating placard urged.

Farther along Montagu Place, another showed horned demons holding up a "monthly report" and laughing at its contents, which read, "MURDERED: BABIES . . . 2,019; CHILDREN . . . 3,345; WOMEN . . . 12,367; NONCOMBATANTS . . . 67,832. A GOOD MONTH'S BUSINESS FOR THE U.S.A.! STOP THIS HORROR!"

Over the junction with Gloucester Place, a third panel showed a man facing a Chinese firing squad. Behind him, bodies were piled so high they disappeared from view. "SERVE THE EMPIRE. MAINTAIN OUR CIVILISATION. RESIST SOCIALISM. WE ARE SUPERIOR."

Others panels read, "ONLY ANGLO-SAXON ENLIGHTEN-MENT CAN SAVE THE WORLD!" and "THE HUMAN SPECIES

DEPENDS ON YOUR LABOURS!" and "MUST WE ENDURE SUCH BARBARISM ON OUR DOORSTEP?" and "SOCIALISM CAUSES SPIRITUAL DECAY!"

Higher even than this floating propaganda, curving out and up from the many massive supports of the upper world's towers, red brick ceilings arched, enclosing everything, so that the London Underground resembled a humungous series of groin vaults, lit only by the gas lamps that lined the thoroughfares and the watery illumination that leaked from many windows. At the peak of each of the arched sections, fitted into dark holes, enormous fans were spinning, sucking out sufficient pollution to render the air breathable, but not enough to adequately clear it.

The whole domain was half sunk in shadow. It was filled with dark corners and fleeting movements; a place of furtive and crafty activities; of things caught by the corner of the eye but gone when looked at square on.

The chrononauts descended down from the ceiling, turning around and around on the spiral staircase, gazing in horror first at sagging rooftops upon which occasional scuttlings could be glimpsed, as if small burglars were fleeing from those who might bear witness, then into upper-storey windows that opened onto bare rooms in which figures lay starving or drunk or exhausted or dead.

Finally, they reached the pavement, where Burton stumbled and was caught by Trounce, who murmured, "All right?"

"Yes," Burton said. "Bismillah, William, have you brought us to Hell?"

"I'm afraid I have."

The passing crowd recoiled from them, giving them a wide berth, for the chrononauts were obviously Uppers and thus better, thus to be respected, thus to be feared.

"Oh my God!" Sadhvi whispered.

The people weren't people. They were less human even than the freakish pedestrians they'd seen in 2130. Shambling past, some were tall and attenuated; others short and bulbous, or bulky like boulders, or small, wispy and wraith-like, or multi-limbed, or half animal, or amoebic as if lacking skeletal structure, or padding along on all fours, or winged, or covered from head to foot in matted hair, or just so thoroughly grotesque that the senses could hardly make sense of them. Many were naked. More were dressed in rags. Most were in Army or Navy uniforms. Their language was the same rough variety of English that Burton knew from the shadier districts of his own London, though quite a few simply grunted or whined or barked or mewled.

The king's agent turned his eyes to Trounce and they were wide with horror.

"Genetic manipulation continues," the Cannibal said. "It's uncontrolled. Follow me. Stay close."

They began to move toward Gloucester Place.

Suddenly, blaring like a foghorn above the din of the traffic and clamour of voices, there came a thunderous bellowing. "Hot taters! Hot taters! Hot taters! Freshly baked for 'em what wants 'em!"

Burton peered ahead and saw, squatting on the corner, a short bulbous form in baggy garments with a flat cap upon its broad head. The creature's face projected in a peculiar manner, thrusting forward and flat like a frog's, with a mouth so wide that it touched the tiny lobeless ears to either side. Was it human? It appeared little more than a blob, with no visible legs or identifiable skeletal structure, and pudgy, apparently boneless arms.

The man—if it could be so classified—suddenly expanded his neck, throat and cheeks, puffing them out tremendously, like a balloon, so that he even more resembled a bullfrog, and opened that phenomenal mouth to once again blast, "Hot taters! Hot taters! Hot taters! Freshly baked for 'em what wants 'em!"

The chrononauts, their ears ringing, came abreast of him, and Burton clutched at Trounce's arm. "Wait!"

"Don't—" Trounce began, but it was too late.

Burton, though painfully aware of the disaster his impulsive visit to Shudders had caused, couldn't help himself. He addressed the potato seller.

"Good evening, sir."

"I ain't done nuffink, yer lordship. I swears to it," the man exclaimed, his tiny little eyes widening with fear.

"I'm not accusing you of anything."

"But, all the same, I ain't done a blessed thing. I'm innocent."

"How much for a potato?"

"What? I mean, pardon? How much?"

"For a potato."

The fellow smiled, his mouth widening to such a degree that Burton feared everything above it would be sliced off.

"Ah! I see! It's a test, is it, yer lordship?" The man reached behind him to a brazier and pulled from it a baked potato. He wrapped it in newspaper and, with a courteous bow, held it out to Burton. "On the 'ouse, yer lordship, as is good an' proper. Wiv me blessing."

Burton took it. "May I ask your name?"

The other looked up and swallowed and blinked. "Please don't report me. I really ain't done nuffink wrong."

"I have no intention of reporting you, my friend. I simply want to—I want to *recommend* you."

A ripple passed through the globular body, and the man again grinned. "Ah! Well! Bloomin' 'eck! That's bloody marvellous, if you'll pardon me language. The name's Grub, sir. Grub the Tater Man."

Burton turned and looked at Swinburne. The poet raised his eyebrows.

"And—and has your family traded on this corner for long?"

"Oh, forever! Since time immem—imum—"

"Immemorial."

"Aye, immaterial! That's the word, guvnor! It's our patch, yer see. We was 'ere even back when there were sky." Grub looked startled, as if realising he'd said something wrong. "Sorry, I didn't mean anyfink by it. I knows me place."

"Thank you, Mr. Grub," Burton said. "I shall enjoy my potato later."

He slipped the hot food into his pocket and, with the others, started to move away. They were stopped by Swinburne.

"Hold on," he said, and turned to Trounce. "Pouncer, the embassy is destroyed. No doubt the palace will transfer its functions to New Centre Point or somewhere similar, but that'll take time. This might be the perfect opportunity."

"Humph!" Trounce grunted thoughtfully. "The city is unmonitored. You may be right, Carrots."

The detective inspector addressed Burton. "Richard, show Mr. Grub your face."

Grub looked from Trounce to Burton, his eyes wide. "Steady on," he muttered in a worried tone. "I don't want no trouble, gents."

"My face?" Burton asked.

"Just momentarily," Trounce said.

Puzzled, the king's agent turned to face the potato seller. He reached up and pulled back his hood.

Grub's eyes practically popped from his head. His huge mouth gaped open. "Bloody 'ell! Bloody 'ell! I'm goin' to die! Oh no! I'm goin' to die!"

"No, Mr. Grub," Trounce said. "You'll be quite alright. Hood up, Richard."

Burton complied.

"But—but—but—" Grub stammered.

"Those who watch have been blinded," Trounce said. "The moment is upon us, Mr. Grub."

"But—you—aren't you—?"

"We are not. We're with you, sir."

"Bloomin' 'eck! Is it—is it that—I 'eard a whisper that the roof 'as fallen in not far from 'ere, m'lord. Is that it?"

"Yes. Certain measures have been taken. Soon, you'll feel it. A sense of release. A need to take action. Follow the impulse."

"Blimey."

"You'll spread the word? You understand who the true enemy is?"

"I does. We all does. We always 'ave done, ain't we? But I'll—won't I?—I'll not—"

"You won't be detected."

Grub made an indecisive movement, checked himself, then stiffened and saluted. "I'll do me bit, sir!"

"Good man."

Trounce returned the salute and led the chrononauts away.

"What the blazes was that all about?" Burton asked.

"You'll soon see," Trounce replied. He stepped out into the road. The traffic jerked to a stop. A few vehicles away, a boiler detonated and a cloud of white steam expanded from it.

They crossed Gloucester Place and moved into Dorset Street. Tenements leaned precariously over them, almost forming a tunnel. The shadows felt dirty and dangerous.

From behind came a further bellow, "Hot taters! Hot taters! Hot taters! As personally recommended by the Uppers! Come and buy and hear the word! Hear the word! Hot taters an' hear the word!"

"A Grub," Burton said to Swinburne. "Still there, on the same corner!"

"It's perfectly marvellous," the poet enthused. "Time has a little consistency, after all." He shrieked and jumped back as a mountainous cyclopean individual lumbered past, his huge leathery hands dragging along the pavement.

Behind the beast, two constables came click-clacking on their stilts. The crowd recoiled away from them. The policemen passed the chrononauts without giving them any attention. Burton saw that, as Trounce had noted, they were exactly the same as those that attacked him in 1860.

"Sent back through history," he whispered to himself. "And who could do that but Edward Oxford?"

Sadhvi Raghavendra stopped and knocked something unspeakable from the heel of her left boot. "Are there no street-crabs in the twenty-third century, William?"

"The nanomechs are supposed to consume waste material and use it for fuel," Trounce responded. "Unfortunately, down here it accrues faster than even they can manage."

"I suspect," Swinburne added, "that Spring Heeled Jack purposely allows a measure of waste matter to accumulate. Having the inhabitants of the Underground wallow in their own detritus gives them a constant reminder of their status."

They rounded the corner and entered Baker Street.

IT IS UP TO YOU TO RESCUE HUMANITY! TOIL FOR THE ANGLO-SAXON EMPIRE! WE MUST MARCH FORTH AND LIBERATE THE WORLD FROM THE SAVAGERY OF SOCIALISM!

"Was the world similar to this in the original 2202, Richard?" Herbert Wells asked. "In the single history that existed before time bifurcated?"

"As shown to me by the sane fragment of Oxford?" Burton responded. "No, it wasn't like this at all. Certainly, London had greatly expanded and was filled with tall towers, but I received no impression of such an atrocious divide, no sense of this inequality."

"Hmm. Curious. Insanity aside, if the Spring Heeled Jack intelligence has its origins in a considerably more pleasant future than this, why has he created such a dreadful alternative? Whence this twisted vision?"

"Perhaps it has its roots in my time," Burton answered. "It was in the nineteenth century that he lost his mind. He appears to have taken what he saw there and developed it along such abhorrent lines that this," he gestured around them, "is the result."

"Did our world really have such evil potential in it?" Raghavendra asked. "I thought us enlightened."

"You believed what you were told," Burton said, "but consider the Cauldron. Was it not an aspect of London that could easily be the progenitor of this?" He glanced at a thin ten-foot-tall, six-armed, four-legged figure that came tottering by like a tumbling stack of broom handles. It was wearing Army reds and an officer's hat, which it doffed flamboyantly to him, murmuring, "My lord."

Burton pulled his hood more tightly over his head. From its depths, he examined the crowd as it parted in front of his group, trudging past to his left and right. He saw dull, suffering eyes and gaunt faces. A great many of the Lowlies bobbed their heads or touched their foreheads in respect. All appeared disconcerted by the presence of these "Uppers."

Stilted figures prowled among them. The crowd shied away from the constables as they approached and cast hard looks at their backs after they'd passed. The Underground, Burton felt, was a pressure cooker, ready to explode.

"William!" he said.

Trounce halted. "What is it?"

Burton pointed across to the middle of Baker Street where a tall plinth divided the thoroughfare. It bore a large statue of a young woman. A plaque, attached to the base, declared, *Her Majesty Queen Victoria, of the United Kingdoms of Europe, Africa and Australia, Defender of the Faith, Empress of India.*

"Yes," Trounce said. "That's her. She took the throne five years ago, our first monarch since the death of King George the Fifth in 1905."

"I know who she is," Burton said. "I've seen her before. She appeared before me when I donned the time suit's helmet."

"I say!" Swinburne exclaimed. "Really?"

"She is—was—Edward Oxford's wife." Burton rubbed the sides of his head, his brow furrowing. "I should know her name. I'm positive it isn't Victoria, but it escapes me."

"Whatever it is," Trounce said, "Spring Heeled Jack obviously sought her out."

"And has literally put her on a pedestal," Swinburne quipped. "Would she have known what—who—he was?"

"No," Burton said. "Remember, Oxford wiped himself out of history. From her perspective, he has never existed."

"It must have come as quite a shock to her when she ascended to the throne, then."

"Shhh!" Trounce hissed. With his eyes, he indicated a group of constables who'd just rounded the corner from Blandford Street.

Following the former detective inspector's lead, the chrononauts stood casually and listened while he explained to them that "the Lowlies are the workhorses of the Empire. They take pride in their practicality, in their uncompromising ability to get a job done, and benefit from the spiritual cleansing that comes with hard toil." He continued in this vein until the stilt men had passed, then chuckled and said, "Trounce of the Yard, deceiving the police. Who'd have thought?"

"And indulging in pure fantasy, too," Swinburne added. "Spiritual cleansing, my foot!"

"Let's push on," Trounce said.

"Workhorses," Raghavendra echoed, as they resumed walking, "but why so many in military uniform?"

"The Empire is mobilising," Swinburne answered. "We are soon to move against what used to be the United States of America and the United Republics of Eurasia."

"War?"

"My hat! Hardly that, Sadhvi! The U.S.A. and U.R.E. are in no condition to resist. They battled each other for so long, with us supplying the munitions, that their various countries are utterly ruined. Their populations are decimated, and the old borders have gone."

"Are they still fighting each other?"

"If you believe the propaganda."

"Which you shouldn't," Trounce put in. "The Cannibal Club has infiltrated our government's records, which offer a story far different to that given the public."

Burton looked up at a billboard. SOCIALISM IS THE DEATH OF CIVILISATION.

Trounce followed his eyes. "There's no socialism. There's no longer any conflict. There hasn't been for a long time. Those vast regions of the Earth are now occupied by countless small communities, which somehow manage to survive in unutterably harsh conditions. They function under a self-regulating anarchism somewhat similar to that which existed in Africa before the Europeans and Arabs destroyed it."

"Why the lies?" Raghavendra asked. "Why is the Anglo-Saxon Empire telling its people that the rest of the world is filled with—with—"

"Savage socialists," Swinburne offered. "Permanently at each other's throats."

She nodded.

"Simply to mesmerise everyone into believing that this—" Trounce made an all-encompassing gesture, "is the superior civilisation and that it's threatened from without."

Swinburne added, "And also to justify our forthcoming invasions of America and Eurasia and our subjugation of their inhabitants."

"If we don't destroy the Turing Fulcrum," Trounce said, "Spring Heeled Jack will conquer the world."

"Bloody hell!" Burton responded.

"That," Swinburne said, "is exactly what it will be."

The lower end of Baker Street was lined by much higher buildings than they'd seen so far in this subterranean world, some of them almost touching the brick ceiling, and was teeming with even more of the hideously deformed Lowlies. When a pack of naked goat men bundled past, drunk, rowdy, stinking, and unashamedly aroused, Sadhvi Raghavendra said, "Can't you enable our AugMems, William, so we can share their illusion of a better world?"

Trounce looked surprised. "Like in 2130, you mean? Did I not say? This is what they see. The real world. The illusion of cleanliness was slowly phased out during the later twenty-one hundreds. It had done its job. The policy of 'know your place' has, through various methods, been so consistently and insidiously driven into the population over the course of three centuries that it's now instinctive and can be maintained with just basic propaganda and mildly tranquillising BioProcs."

"It's—it's repugnant!" Wells spluttered.

"But there's hope, Bertie," Swinburne said. "Look."

He pointed ahead at a large placard that had emerged from the mist ahead.

Burton stumbled to a halt and gazed in shock at it.

Floating over the street, it declared, "THE ENEMY IS AMONG US! THIS IS THE FACE OF THE SOCIALIST FIEND!" Beneath the glowing words, there was a portrait of a brutal and scarred face.

It was Burton's own.

The chrononauts uttered sounds of incredulity.

"It's what I've hinted at," Trounce said. "Spring Heeled Jack obviously remembers you, Richard. Fears you."

"I don't understand," Burton said. He looked down at Swinburne. "How does this offer hope?"

The poet gave a happy smile and a compulsive jerk of his shoulder. "By nature, the human race is very, very naughty."

"What?" The king's agent turned to Trounce, seeking a more cogent explanation.

Trounce said, "What Algy means is that if you tell a child not to do something without properly explaining why it mustn't be done, you can be sure that, the moment your back is turned, the child will test the prohibition."

"Spring Heeled Jack has overplayed his hand," Trounce continued. "It requires only a spark to light the fuse." He pointed up at the placard. "That face is the spark."

"I think I understand," Wells said softly, "When the government is perceived as the people's enemy, the enemy of the government is perceived as the people's friend."

Swinburne reached out and squeezed Burton's arm. "And when Bio-Procs stop tranquillising because, for example, the local transmitting station has been blown up by a dastardly member of the Cannibal Club, then—"

Burton cleared his throat. "I see."

Trounce said, "No doubt your Mr. Grub is now busily making your presence known. It adds greater urgency to our mission. We have to destroy the Fulcrum before the people drive themselves into sufficient a frenzy to take action, else there's little doubt that wholesale slaughter will ensue, first when the government attempts to quell our own insurgents, and then when it sends them to enslave the remains of our neighbouring empires."

"By God, Trounce. Have you loaded so much onto my shoulders? I'm just an explorer, an anthropologist, a writer."

"You've become a figurehead, too."

I just want to go home.

Burton looked at his friends, his eyes clouded with distress, aware that he'd just thought the words that had driven his enemy over the brink and into madness.

He felt his heart throbbing, moved his tongue against the roof of his mouth, and exhaled with an audible shudder.

Burton had often regarded emotions as a phenomenon of the body rather than of the mind. It was the body that instilled fear when destruction threatened and joy when survival was assured. To now achieve what was expected of him, he knew he'd have to transcend those corporeal impulses. He must become all intellect. He must be as hard and as cold as metal.

He glanced once again at the placard before saying to Trounce in a flat tone, "Let's get going."

They waited while a group of spiderish women herded a flock of geese past, then moved on to the junction with Oxford Street, the whole length of which appeared to be a teeming marketplace. Over the rooftops opposite, dark smoke stained the atmosphere. There was much shouting, a few screams, and many people running, scampering, hopping or scuttling back and forth.

Gesturing at the mouth of a road on the other side of the thoroughfare, Trounce said, "Here we are again. North Audley Street. If we continue straight on, we'll be back in old Grosvenor Square, with New Grosvenor Square overhead."

"Bad memories," Swinburne said. "Though they belong to my predecessor."

"I suppose the commotion is what Grub was referring to?" Wells asked.

"Yes. Aboveground, the American Embassy is a burning wreck. Beneath it, some of the Underground's ceiling has obviously fallen in. I hope there weren't too many casualties. We'll skirt around it. A little way eastward through the market then south into alleyways that'll take us to Berkeley Square."

"I've had unfortunate experiences in alleyways," Burton grumbled. "Being held at gunpoint by you being one of them."

Trounce laughed. "I recall I was masquerading as a fictional detective named Macallister Fogg at the time. A ridiculous farce. Did I ever apologise?"

"You didn't need to. I thumped you on the chin."

They walked through the market, passing stalls selling fruit and vegetables, meat and fish, clothes both newly made and second hand, pots and pans, brushes and cloths, tools and furniture; passing vendors of milk and tea and coffee, mulled wine and frothy ales, tinctures and pick-me-ups; passing tarot card readers and crystal ball gazers, palmists and phrenologists, astrologers who couldn't see the sky and numerologists who probably couldn't add up; passing four-armed jugglers and one-legged balancing acts, swan-necked singers and multi-limbed dancers, accordionists and violinists, deep-chested trombonists and bone-fisted drummers; passing emaciated beggars and obscenely curvaceous prostitutes, tousle-haired ragamuffins and shuffling oldsters, sad-faced young women and flint-eyed young men; passing vendors of corn on the cob and baked potatoes, winkles, mussels and jellied eels, roasted nuts and toffee apples.

It was as if Burton's London had been revived in an outrageously distorted form and buried beneath the surface of the Earth.

They walked on until they were almost opposite the spot where Shudders' Pharmacy had once been. There was no sign of it now, a slumping tenement having occupied the site.

"Here," Trounce said, and led them into a narrow alley between two immense arching pylons.

Rats scampered out of their path.

Trounce used the heel of his boot to shove a pile of rotting wooden crates out of the way.

They moved on in silence.

Rounding a corner, they were brought up short when a headless man jumped out of a shadowed niche and brandished a knife at them. He was naked from the waist up and had a coarse-featured face in his chest. "I durn't bloody care. I durn't. I'd rather cop it wiv summick in me pockits than nuffink. Give me what yer got. Anyfink. Give me. Give me, or I'll slice the bleedin' lot a yer."

Swinburne stepped forward. "My dear fellow," he said. "You have been liberated. We are your saviours, not your enemy. Do not misdirect your newfound discontent."

"Shut yer mouth yer bleedin' midget an' hand summick over."

The poet sighed. "Then with regret, I have no choice but to give you this."

He drew his pistol from his waistband. "Between the eyes. Stun."

The weapon made a spitting sound—*ptooff!*

The man flopped to the ground.

"Well done, Carrots," Trounce muttered.

"Poor blighter," Swinburne said.

Trounce led them around the prone form.

"He'll wake up in due course," the poet noted. "I can't blame him for his actions. He's waking from a BioProc haze; realising the unadulterated truth of his existence. There'll be anger and violence before the people identify, and move against, their true enemy."

They filed through a maze of twisting and turning rubbish-strewn passages, traversing a district that, in Burton's time, had been among the most prosperous in the city, but that was now much how he imagined Hades to be: confined, hot, dangerous and seedy.

Finally, the group emerged into Berkeley Square. Once a smart area filled with the well-off, it now resembled a mist-veiled crater in the middle of a shantytown.

"You'll recall this," Swinburne said to the king's agent as they reached the centre of the paved space. "Though not fondly." He kicked the toe of his left boot against a metal manhole. "Not exactly the same one, but close enough."

Burton remembered and felt himself go pale. Last year, or rather, three hundred and forty-three years ago, he'd climbed down through a very similar metal lid into Bazalgette's sewers, there to have a final showdown with an invader from a parallel history.

"The sewer was rebuilt and greatly expanded many years ago," Swinburne said, "but it still follows the course of the Tyburn River. This hatch leads down to a maintenance tunnel that runs alongside it. It's a lot drier than the sewer but also a lot narrower."

"We—we have to go—to go even farther underground?" Burton stammered.

"I'm afraid so."

"We'll be all right," Trounce said. "As long as we don't run into any spider sweeps."

CHAPTER 18

HER MAJESTY QUEEN VICTORIA

THE EMPIRE EXPECTS YOU TO DO YOUR DUTY
THE PENALTY FOR NOT DOING SO IS DEATH

The diameter of the tube was such that Burton, the tallest of the group, had to bend his back in order to pass along it. The physical discomfort only added to his distress. He felt like he was in his grave. The weight of the double-layered city pressed down, liable to crush the conduit at any moment.

His jaw was clamped shut. The muscles at its sides flexed spasmodically. Sweat trickled from his brow, and his legs were trembling so much he felt sure his companions must notice.

He said nothing, just followed Trounce, putting one foot in front of the other, holding his arms out and letting his fingertips slide along the inner surface, keeping his eyes half shut and mentally chanting, *Allāhu Allāhu Allāhu Haqq*, which, unfortunately, quickly turned into, *I am I am I am trapped.*

The maintenance tunnel was dark. Trounce had produced a small mechanical torch from his pocket and with this was illuminating their path, but the blackness retreated only a little way ahead and rushed in to follow closely at their heels.

Don't let that light go out! Don't let it happen!

Finally, Burton couldn't hold his curiosity at bay any longer and had to ask, "Algy, what are spider sweeps?"

"Children who've been genetically adapted for the purpose of keeping pipes such as this clean," Swinburne answered.

"Children," Burton murmured. "Good."

"Good at their job, yes," the poet agreed, "on account of the venom they spray to dissolve whatever dirt their coat of razor-sharp spines can't scrape off."

Burton's mouth went dry. "Nevertheless, they're just children."

"Oh yes. There's none above the age of ten."

"Excellent."

"Because the younger ones eat the elders."

"Oh."

"They're extremely aggressive."

"Uh-huh."

"And territorial."

"I see."

"And, I daresay, with the effect of the nanomechs wearing off, they won't hesitate to attack us."

"Thank you for alerting me."

"Beneath their spines, they're armour-plated. I should think our bullets would just bounce off them."

"That's unfortunate."

"I'm thankful to be as small as I am, really. I'm just a morsel. A crumb. I wouldn't want to encounter them if I was a big lump of juicy meat like, for example, you are."

"That's quite enough, thank you."

"Don't you want to hear about their extendible mandibles?"

"No, I think I get the picture."

They continued on through the cramped tunnel.

Burton tried to imagine open skies, wide Arabian vistas, and distant mountains. Instead, his mind delivered a remembrance of Boulogne and Isabel. He tried to dismiss it, but each wave of claustrophobia brought it closer.

I shouldn't be walking through a tunnel in the future. I should be strolling along a promenade with her. She should be my wife.

He felt brittle and taut, needed a distraction, something to divert his attention from the hollowness within and the constriction without.

He asked, "Algy, do you remain an atheist?"

"My hat! Of course! Why do you ask?"

"Because you died and were resurrected."

"Must you remind me of my murder? It hurt."

"You were dead for nearly fifty years."

"I know. What a thoroughly beastly waste of time."

"But do you remember anything of it?"

"Nothing at all. Except—"

The poet was quiet for a moment, and the silence of the tunnel was broken only by their footsteps and Burton's laboured respiration.

Trounce said, "Blinkers."

"Yes!" Swinburne cried out. His voice echoed. "Yes. Blinkers. That's exactly it, Pouncer."

"Don't call me Pouncer. And keep your voice down, Carrots."

"Blinkers?" Burton asked.

"Like racehorses wear," Trounce said. "So they aren't distracted by anything; so they see only the track ahead of them."

"Intriguing," Herbert Wells put in. "Or it would be if it made any sense. Would you explain, William?"

"Um. Blinkers is as far as I can get."

"Algy?" Burton asked.

"Soho Square," the poet said. "2130. I was running toward the flier, I reached out to grab your hand, there was a terrible pain, then nothing. My next memories are of my childhood, of my mother and father and old Pouncer, here and—as I matured—of a growing awareness of who I'd been before and, in fact, still was. It's very peculiar, I can tell you, to recollect yourself as an older person in the distant past. My early teens were very difficult—"

"Teens?" Burton interrupted, then immediately remembered what Mick Farren had told him. "Ah, yes, I'm sorry. Go on."

"I felt oddly divided," Swinburne said.

"It was the same for me," Trounce added.

The maintenance tunnel was curving toward their left. From the right, the muffled sound of flowing water could be heard. It sounded as if it was moving at great pressure.

Not water. Sewerage. I am trapped. I am trapped.

Swinburne continued, "But the mixed recollections were soon reconciled by the awareness of our mission. It helped to keep me on the straight and narrow."

"Plus," Trounce said, "we were both carefully fostered by Father—Tom Bendyshe—and knew from an early age that we'd find our purpose on the fifteenth of February, 2202—today—with the arrival of the *Orpheus*."

"That must have been strange," Raghavendra murmured.

"Oh, it hasn't been so bad," Swinburne responded. "Of course, we looked forward to seeing you all again, and I must confess, I've felt rather a fish out of water in this age. The nineteenth century always felt more like home, and I've missed it."

"Likewise," Trounce grunted.

"But the blinkers?" Burton asked.

"An impression that William and I never possessed before we died," the poet answered. "A constant suspicion that what we sense is only a fraction of the full picture. That there's a greater truth."

"A feeling that we've forgotten something," Trounce said. He raised a hand and slowed his pace. "Stay quiet now. We're coming to a monitoring station. There may be someone in it."

They crept ahead in silence until they were brought to a halt by a round metal door. Trounce put his ear to it and was motionless for two minutes. He stepped back, said softly, "I can't hear anyone," then turned the handle and pushed the portal open.

The room beyond was empty. It was also small but nevertheless came as a relief to Burton. Little more than a metal box, with a second door leading to the next section of the tunnel, it was at least well lit. In one wall—the one closest to the sewer—there were mounted a number of flat screens from which unfathomable displays glowed, charts and diagrams and rows of numbers.

Trounce started slightly, put his finger to his ear, motioned them all to stay silent, and murmured, "It's Lorena. This must be important. We're supposed to maintain network silence."

He listened, his head cocked to the side, his eyebrows low over his eyes.

Slowly, the colour drained from his face.

"Bloody hell," he mumbled. "You're certain?"

His lips whitened as he received the reply.

"Confound it! Do what you can, all right?"

He lowered his hand. It was shaking. He used the edge of his cloak to wipe his forehead and glanced at Swinburne, who said, "What's happened?"

"Father has been captured."

Swinburne gasped.

"Bendyshe?" Burton asked.

Trounce nodded. "After planting the bomb in the Embassy. He ran straight into a group of constables."

"Where have they taken him?" Swinburne asked.

Trounce reached up as if feeling for his bowler hat and looked irritated when he failed to find it. He sighed. "We don't know. She's lost track of him."

Burton asked, "She can't locate his position via his nanomechs?"

"They must have realised his nanomechs aren't under government control, so they'll have passed a nonlethal but very painful electric current through him to destroy them all prior to interrogation. It's left him totally isolated."

"Interrogation? Where would that occur? At police headquarters? Is there still a Scotland Yard?"

"No headquarters. There aren't even police stations. The constables don't require them."

"Then where are crime suspects held?"

"Suspects aren't held. They're executed. Immediately. Without trial."

"So—I'm sorry, William, Algy, I know he's your father—" Burton blinked rapidly. He still couldn't get to grips with that idea. "But if this age has such a barbaric policy, why do you think Tom Bendyshe will be interrogated rather than killed?"

Trounce and Swinburne exchanged a glance.

"I told you Lorena Brabrooke is a genius," Trounce said. "And she is. With her every successive clone, she's increased her skills. But the problem with keeping the Cannibal Club off the surveillance net—with making us invisible—is that it creates holes. Lorena can't fill those holes, but she can relocate them, so what you might term 'the absences we make' are not in the same places as we are. That's how we evade detection."

The king's agent dwelled on this for a moment, struggling slightly with concepts that remained highly abstruse to his nineteenth-century intellect. Before he'd properly formulated his next question, Raghavendra asked it. "Does Spring Heeled Jack suspect the existence of the Cannibal Club?"

"Until nine o'clock this evening, for all these years, we've resisted taking any action against him," Trounce replied. "We've been wary of drawing attention to ourselves. Had we done so, he might have hunted us to extinction, and your mission would be jeopardised. Nevertheless, he's known for some considerable time that *something* was evading him, and tonight—the date being what it is—we suspected his paranoia would be at its most extreme. That's why we feared your arrival would be detected and why we finally made a move."

"So where will they take Bendyshe?" Burton asked.

"I don't know," Trounce said. Frustrated, he slapped his right fist into his left palm. "Let's get going. Not a word in this next section. The pump room at its end is almost certainly occupied by a technician." He turned to the door that opened onto the second length of tunnel, twisted its handle, swung it wide, and holding his torch before him, led the way in.

Burton, Swinburne, Wells and Raghavendra followed.

This stretch proved longer than the first. They traversed it as rapidly as they could until they neared the pump room, at which point they slowed down and trod with care so their footfalls wouldn't echo. By the time the light shone upon another door, Burton's clothes were damp with perspiration and his eyes were slightly wild. He'd been clenching his teeth so hard that his whole face ached, and he felt as if his sanity might break at any moment.

Get me out. Get me out. Get me out.

Trounce looked back and put a finger to his lips. He passed the torch to the king's agent, but Burton's hand was trembling so much that the illumination shuddered back and forth until Swinburne reached out and took hold of the device.

Pulling his pistol from his waistband, the cloned Scotland Yard man wrapped his fingers around the door handle, clicked it down, and put his shoulder to the portal. It swept open and he hurtled in, brandishing his gun.

The room beyond was large and humming with machinery. The wall to the right of the door was entirely covered with buttons, screens, levers and projecting valve wheels. A woman with pale, wormy blue skin was sitting on a high stool facing it. Her limbs—two legs and eight arms—were exceedingly long, thin and multi-jointed. Her slender hands bore fingers of outlandish length, extending across different sections of the control panel.

She turned her head as Trounce barrelled in. Her skull, horribly narrow and drawn upward into a pointed cranium, was dotted with a plethora of glittering black eyes. Her mouth, packed with crooked and spiny teeth, opened and produced an uncanny whistling as the detective inspector, having misjudged the force of his entry, collided with her and knocked her from her seat. She hit the floor with Trounce on top of her but immediately thrust him off with such force that he flew into the air, hit the low ceiling, and crashed back down with a loud grunt, the breath thumped out of him. His Penniforth Mark II went skittering across the floor into a corner. The woman scrabbled up, employing her arms as extra legs to quickly back away, like a monstrous arachnid.

"I ain't doin' nuthin' but me job, m'lords," she hissed. "I keep to the law, so I does."

Burton stepped in and drew his weapon. "I have to render you unconscious, madam. It won't hurt and you'll recover in a little while."

"Unconscious? Unconscious? I doesn't want to be unconscious, m'lord, and I ain't no madam." Shook her head and put her hands to it. "I'm confused. Scared. Me head hurts."

"The nanomechs in your system have stopped working," Swinburne told her. "You can think freely."

"I doesn't want to think. You shouldn't be 'ere. It's the rules, m'lords." She looked at Burton, at his uncovered face. "Oh gawd 'elp me, it's you, ain't it! I dunno what to do. I dunno. I dunno. I ain't ready fer no revolution. I'm just a simple girl. I does me job an' nuffink else. What should I do, m'lord?"

"Just sleep," Burton said. He pointed his pistol and added, "Stun."

Ptooff!

The technician fell backward. Her limbs spread outward. She twitched and became still.

"Poor thing," Raghavendra said.

"The Lowlies are getting muddle-headed," Swinburne observed. "We have to work as fast as we can. If we gain control of the Turing Fulcrum, maybe Lorena will find a way to use it to broadcast an encouraging message to them, something to calm them down."

"And if we have to destroy it?" Burton asked.

"Then we'll have to employ the old-fashioned method of word of mouth. We'll recruit Mr. Grub. His was big and loud enough."

Trounce retrieved his pistol. They moved past the prone woman and walked between two horizontal groupings of pipes to where a flat platform was positioned beneath a square hole in the ceiling.

Trounce said, "This lift will take us straight up to the second pump room on the palace roof. Inside, the air is heated and pressurised, but when we exit we'll find the atmosphere too thin to breathe and freezing cold. Lorena will cause our BioProcs to compensate, but we'll have to move fast, else the strain on our bodies will kill us."

"It's one thrill after another, isn't it?" Swinburne commented.

The chrononauts mounted the platform, Trounce depressed a switch, and it rose through the opening into a dimly lit shaft. Looking up, Burton saw its four sides converging toward a far-distant vanishing point.

"It's quite a way," Trounce warned them all.

"And bloody slow," Swinburne complained.

"When this is all over and done with," Burton muttered, "I shall return to the desert where, in every direction, there'll be nothing between me and the horizon."

"Do you mean that?" Raghavendra asked. "Will you really go back?"

Burton looked into her eyes and felt a strange sensation in the middle of his chest, as if the lift was sinking rather than rising. "No," he whispered. "I don't suppose I ever will."

He turned away from her.

Up and up the lift rose. After a while, the chrononauts became tired of standing, so sat and waited, glancing up frequently, hoping they'd see the top of the shaft.

"We must have travelled for miles," Wells exclaimed after what felt like hours had passed.

"Up through the Underground," Trounce said, "then out over the upper city, through the level of the royal parks, and on to the top of the palace. I doubt we've travelled a third of that distance yet, and we've been going for about thirty minutes, I'll wager."

"Just half an hour?" Swinburne protested. "Half a day, more like!"

"Funny," Wells said, "how time feels different for everyone. I might say the day has dragged by, while you'll say it's raced. One man of fifty might feel sprightly, another feel that he's in his dotage. I often wonder whether Chronos exists at all. Might it not be a figment of our imagination?"

"Could our imagination be the seed of all existence?" Burton added, remembering his earlier meditation—though it had occurred seventy-two years ago. "Is there any reality outside of it?"

"Is it possible," Swinburne mused, "that the altitude is making you both delirious?"

Trounce chuckled. "And so the conversation is brought down to earth."

"Great heavens!" Sadhvi Raghavendra cried out. "That's a singularly inappropriate expression to use under our current circumstances." She looked up. "No sign of our destination. It's well past midnight already. It'll be the small hours by the time we get to the roof. What can we expect, William?"

"We're unlikely to find the greenhouse occupied at this time of night, so we'll use it as our base of operations. Once we're inside, I suggest you hold the fort, Sadhvi, while Carrots and I, and Richard and Bertie, split up and reconnoitre with the aim of establishing Her Majesty's where-abouts. We may have to abduct a member of staff and drag them back for questioning."

Raghavendra used her forefinger to give Trounce's arm a hard prod. "So despite your childhood here in the twenty-third century, your nineteenth-century sensibilities haven't seen any advancement. You still feel it necessary to deny the woman a meaningful role. Really, you're thoroughly backward."

"Not at all," Trounce protested. "Any good general will tell you that the path of retreat must remain well guarded. If I were a chauvinist, I wouldn't trust to leave the responsibility to you alone. If you want to exchange places with Carrots, I'll be just as confident with you at my side."

Raghavendra eyed Swinburne, who was compulsively drumming his left foot and wiggling his fingers.

"Thank you," she said somewhat wryly. "I accept."

The minutes ticked by, their number impossible to judge.

Burton squeezed his eyes shut.

You're not underground. You're rising high above it.

But I'm enclosed.

Not for much longer.

What if the lift mechanism freezes? What if we get stuck?

It won't. This will end soon.

"The roof!" Wells exclaimed.

Praise Allah. Praise Jehovah. Praise Zeus. Praise every god that has or hasn't ever existed.

The chrononauts got to their feet.

"Be ready," Trounce whispered. "There might be another technician ahead of us."

The platform slowed, slid up level with a floor, and came to a halt. They found themselves in a room very similar to the one they'd departed. It was unoccupied.

"Luck is with us," Trounce muttered. He led them past heavy pipes, past a glowing control panel, and to a door. "This opens onto the roof. There's a short distance to cross to the greenhouse." He drew his pistol and put his finger to his earlobe. "Lorena?" then, after a pause, "We're on the roof." He listened to her reply then addressed his companions. "Our BioProcs are about to drive up our body temperatures and maximise our lung efficiency. It won't feel pleasant. Follow my instructions exactly."

Swinburne pulled his handgun from his waistband. Burton raised an eyebrow at him. "Are you sure, Algy? You're a rotten shot."

"Not with a pistol that does whatever I tell it."

Suddenly, Burton felt overheated. His heart hammered. Dizziness and exhilaration gripped him. Too much oxygen!

Trounce eased open the door and led them through it. The roof beyond was clear of snow, being well above the clouds, and was illuminated by the lamps of the nearby greenhouse. The structure's various angles and planes stood out with startling clarity in the frigid, still, and thin air.

"Softly, softly," Trounce whispered.

Slowly, they proceeded toward the large rectangular block of glass. The light that shone from within it dazzled them, and Burton found himself squinting and averting his eyes. Nevertheless, he noticed that a plume of what appeared to be dense smoke was rising from the greenhouse's roof.

Burton's skin was burning, and his chest rose and fell with great rapidity, as if he was struggling for breath, though he felt no discomfort.

Swinburne whispered to him, "The upper city isn't as closely monitored as the Underground and, as far as Lorena has been able to ascertain, the palace complex even less so. One of the benefits of elitism is that you're granted a measure of privacy. Nevertheless, we'd be triggering alarms right now were it not for the destruction of the Embassy. Also, a full-scale information war has just commenced."

"Information war? You mean Miss Brabrooke is accessing, infiltrating and manipulating?"

"Exactly that. She and her people are hard at work. Communications are being disrupted, reports falsified, files corrupted, diversions planted. If she's judged it correctly—and I don't doubt that she has—even a synthetic intelligence as powerful as the Turing Fulcrum will be thrown into confusion."

"If the Fulcrum and Spring Heeled Jack are one and the same," Burton responded, "then there's a deal of confusion in it, anyway."

"Yet still it has managed to create this ghastly world," Wells interjected.

Trounce signalled for them to be quiet as they reached the side of the greenhouse. Crouching down, they peered through the glass.

"My hat!" Swinburne hissed. "I'm already here."

Inside, from the waist-high growing troughs up to the high ceiling, from one side of the interior space to the other, there was a mass of red foliage, a great aggregation of fleshy leaves, tangled branches, exotic flowers, bulging pods, heavy gourds, luminescent fruits, and—especially in the upper reaches—thousands of huge fluffy seed heads. These were noticeably disintegrating, bits of them breaking off and floating out though ventilation grills to form the cloud Burton had noticed—not smoke, but seeds, red but rendered black by the starlight.

"I suppose we shouldn't be surprised by its presence," the king's agent murmured. "After all, it was the jungle that brought Spring Heeled Jack's dictatorship to my attention. We wouldn't be here were it not for the experiences it foisted upon me."

"I don't see anyone inside," Trounce said.

He moved to the right until he came to a door, opened it, and quietly entered. Burton and the others filed in after him, senses alert. The change from frigid cloud to humid steam caused them to gasp and breathe heavily. Burton's dizziness increased, and he felt blackness pressing in at the edges of his vision.

Trounce put his finger to his ear and murmured, "We're in."

Burton clutched his chest as his heart skipped arrhythmically. He sucked damp air into his lungs and fought to stay on his feet.

The discomfort passed. His body stabilised. The chrononauts glanced at one another, satisfying themselves that all were well. They discarded their robes.

"Let's make certain we're alone," Trounce whispered.

Carefully, without a sound, they spread out and moved through the verdant corridors, passing back and forth between the troughs. Pungent fragrances filled their lungs, and Burton felt a slight headiness, though it wasn't nearly as overwhelming as that which he'd experienced in the Beetle's factory.

No one else was present.

The king's agent found a door that, when he cracked it open an inch, proved to be at the top of a stairwell. He closed it and turned to Trounce. "Here's our route in."

"A preliminary survey then. Agreed?"

"Agreed."

"We'll go down to the next floor, split into two teams, and separate. Let's assess how populated it is downstairs. If you can render a member of the queen's staff unconscious without detection, do so and bring them back here." Trounce said to Swinburne, "You stay here, Carrots. If anyone enters, stun 'em."

"Rightio."

Burton turned and reached for the door handle again, but before he could grasp it, it suddenly moved and the door swung inward, bumping against him. With an exclamation, he stepped back and fumbled for his pistol. Before he could retrieve it, a young woman stepped in. She uttered a small exclamation and stared at them bemusedly.

"Hallo, hallo!" Swinburne cried out. "What ho!"

Burton gasped. His mouth fell open. He was overcome by an urge to rush forward and embrace her. His heart filled with love. Tears blurred his vision.

Isabel! he thought. *Isabel!*

But it wasn't Isabel. The girl was short and broad rather than tall and graceful, dark rather than golden-haired. Though curvaceous and attractive, she couldn't match his fiancée's beauty.

This love isn't mine. It's Oxford's.

A name popped into his mind.

"Jessica," he said.

Her eyes widened. "You—you know me, sir? My real name?"

"Jessica," he repeated. "Jessica Cornish."

"But—but—I haven't been called that for—for—" She moved forward, put her hands out toward him and hesitated, her expression alternating between fear and wonder. "How?"

Trounce said gruffly, "Queen Victoria."

"Yes." Tears spilled onto her cheeks. "They—*he*—calls me Victoria. But I'm—I'm Jessica Cornish. How do you know me? Who are you people? Why are you here?"

Trounce slipped behind her and pushed the door shut. He levelled his pistol and muttered, "This is a spot of luck. But be careful, Richard."

"Lower your weapon," Burton said. He looked down at the queen. "For how long have you been the monarch, Miss Cornish—Your Majesty?"

"Jessica, please. Just Jessica. It feels—it's so good to hear that name again. I was chosen five years ago."

"And prior to that?"

"I lived in Aldershot. I was nobody. A nanny." She clenched her hands beneath her chin. "Who are you? Can you help me?"

"Help you?"

"I never wanted to be the queen. I don't know why I am."

"Miss Cornish," Swinburne said. "The proclamations. The ones you issue. Might I ask where they come from?"

"Him."

"Him?"

"The prime minister."

Swinburne looked at Trounce. "A prime minister? I didn't know we had one."

"It's news to me," Trounce said. "What of the Turing Fulcrum, Miss Cornish?"

"The—what?"

"The device that guides the government. Perhaps it advises the prime minister?"

"I don't know what you're talking about."

Trounce's eyes moved from Jessica Cornish to Swinburne to Burton.

The queen stepped closer to Sadhvi Raghavendra, instinctively seeking the support of her own gender. Raghavendra smiled at her, laid a hand gently on her upper arm, and said to Trounce, "She's innocent, William. A victim. It's plain to see."

The queen nodded. There was an almost childish pleading in her eyes, helplessness.

Burton asked, "This prime minster, when was he elected?"

"He never was."

"I mean, when did he assume his position?"

The queen leaned closer to Raghavendra. "Um. Forty years ago, I think."

"2162?"

"Yes."

"The year the original Edward Oxford was born," Burton mused.

"He'll be angry," the queen said. "You shouldn't be here. When they finish with that poor man, he'll come looking."

"Who are they?" Burton asked. "And what man?"

"The ministers. The traitor."

"I don't understand you."

She put her hands over her face and emitted a quavering moan. "Oh. Oh. They are terrible. Terrible! Their entertainments. So cruel. Torture!"

Trounce reached out and gripped her wrist, not gently. "They have a captive?" he rasped. "What are they doing to him? Tell me!"

"Steady," Burton murmured.

Recoiling from Trounce, the queen said, "He blew up the American Embassy."

"Father!" Swinburne croaked.

"They injected him with nanomechs. The machines are eating him from the inside."

"And they call it entertainment?" Trounce snarled. "By God! Where?"

"In the House of Lords. Five floors down."

Trounce's eyes blazed. Jessica Cornish moaned. "I have to go. I shouldn't be talking to you. I'll be punished. Let me go. Let me go."

"It's all right," Raghavendra said soothingly. "We're here to help you, Jessica. Will you trust us? Perhaps we can give you your freedom."

"He won't let you. He'll kill you all. He'll punish me for speaking with you. You don't understand. The prime minister is dangerous. Very dangerous."

"Miss Cornish," Swinburne said. "What happens here tonight will be the culmination of events that date all the way back to 1837. No danger will dissuade us from doing what must be done."

Burton turned to speak to Trounce but stopped when he saw his friend's eyes. The former detective appeared to be almost paralysed by anger, as if he could think only of charging down the stairs with his pistol blazing, yet knew this would be a fatal error. He stood battling with himself, trembling with fury, his mouth opening and closing.

Since being reunited with him, Burton had allowed Trounce to take the lead, conceding to his greater knowledge of this future world. Burton, though, was the commander of the mission, and he saw that he must now reassert himself in that position.

"Sadhvi," he said, "Miss Cornish will feel undoubtedly more comfortable with you. Take her across to the pump room and wait for us there. We'll either join you or send for you when our business is done. If neither of those happens and you judge that you've waited long enough, make your way back, with our guest, to the *Orpheus*. In the meantime, describe to her who we are and why we are here."

The queen moaned and shook her head. "They'll send equerries to search for me."

"We'll take care of that. Sadhvi, go."

Swinburne added, "Cross the roof as rapidly as possible. Remember, the queen has no adapted nanomechs in her system. Miss Cornish, you'll experience considerable discomfort outside. It's extremely cold and the air is thin. Have courage. You'll only have to traverse a short distance."

With a brusque nod of acknowledgment, Raghavendra pulled the queen away through the foliage and toward the door to the palace roof.

Swinburne put his finger to his ear and muttered instructions to Lorena Brabrooke. Sadhvi Raghavendra, at least, would be protected out there.

"It'll be a while before we can speak with Lorena again," he told them when he'd finished. "She's now setting out to disrupt all the palace's internal communications. Our BioProcs won't escape the effects."

Burton raised his pistol. "We four shall stay together. The Turing Fulcrum may have been using the faux queen as its public mouthpiece, but apparently a prime minister is providing a rather more assertive one, too. We need to get at him. First, though, let's rescue Tom Bendyshe."

Trounce growled, "And if anyone stands in our way, by God, I'll kill them."

CHAPTER 19

A PLEA TO PARLIAMENT

**WHAT YOU DO
IS WHAT YOU ARE DESIGNED TO DO
BE CONTENT
DO NOT COMPLAIN
DO NOT IMAGINE THERE IS ANYTHING BETTER**

Burton, Swinburne, Trounce and Wells quietly descended from the rooftop greenhouse to Buckingham Palace's uppermost storey. The staircase, being more of a service route than a feature of the palace's opulent interior, did not go down any farther. In order to reach the next floors, they needed to find the grand central stairwell. There were lifts, of course, but these were more often used by the palace's inhabitants and thus presented the chrononauts with a greater danger of discovery and entrapment.

Trounce and Swinburne both recalled from the architectural plans that the main staircase ran through the middle of the building and was located somewhere to their left. It was more for show than function, so they hoped to use it without being detected.

They moved out of the shadows at the end of the stairs and along a corridor, past the entrance to an elevator, and on to a junction with a much larger and more elegantly decorated passageway. There was a purple carpet running along its floor, its walls bore countless portraits— all of Jessica Cornish—and crystal chandeliers hung from its ceiling every twenty feet along its length. Doors gave way to rooms on either side. Narrow, baroquely carved sideboards stood between them, holding vases of red flowers, small statuettes and framed pictures, all of the queen.

Burton put his head around the corner and looked to the right. Far away, the hallway ended at double doors. He looked to the left. A white stilted figure was striding toward him.

"Stay where you are!" it shouted. "You are not recognised. Your presence is unauthorised."

"Damn!" Burton cursed. "We're discovered."

Swinburne stepped past him and raised his Penniforth Mark II.

"Head. Kill."

The pistol spat—*ptooff!*—and the stilted figure fell to the floor. They ran to it, and Burton saw a round hole exactly between where its eyes would be had it a human face. He stepped to a door and, holding his own weapon ready, opened it, revealing an unoccupied bedchamber.

"Drag it in here, we'll hide it under the bed."

While this was being done, he asked, "So constables patrol the palace, William?"

"This isn't a constable," Trounce responded. "It's an equerry, one of her majesty's personal attendants. Basically, it's exactly the same thing but with a different title. As you can see, it's identical to the creatures that started appearing in London back in 1860. Fortunately, they don't carry truncheons, which makes it a little easier for us."

"Who, besides the queen, lives here?"

"All the ministers of the government and their lackeys. The higher echelons of the Uppers. Also, I presume, our mysterious prime minister, whomever he might be."

They closed the bedroom door and continued on along the hallway. It ended at another junction. Burton whipped around the corner, facing to the right, gun raised. Trounce did the same, facing left.

"Head! Kill!" they chorused.

Ptooff! Ptooff!

Wells helped Burton to retrieve his victim while Swinburne assisted Trounce. They hoisted the equerries back to the junction and barged into what proved to be another sleeping chamber. A man, on the bed, sat up.

He was bald-headed, attired in bright-pink pyjamas, and so morbidly obese that he resembled a gigantic wobbling blancmange. In a bizarrely singsong voice, he warbled, "Hey there! What's this all about, then?"

Swinburne pointed his pistol. "Stun."

Outspreading ripples marked the point of impact. The man looked down at his stomach. "Ouch! That hurt! How dare you!"

His eyes rolled up into his head, and he plopped backward onto his pillows.

The chrononauts discovered that the mattress, straining beneath its occupant's weight, was too close to the floor to provide a hiding space, so instead shoved the two equerries into a wardrobe.

"For how long will Mr. Humpty Dumpty remain unconscious?" Wells enquired.

"Long enough," Swinburne replied. "I expect he'll be famished when he wakes up."

They returned to the junction. Halfway along the left-hand branch, they saw the head of the main stairwell and ran toward it, their feet padding on the soft, luxurious carpet.

They jerked to a stop at the top of the steps, weapons directed downward, but no one was ascending.

Faintly, from far below, an incoherent shout echoed, whether one of anger or merriment, pleasure or pain, they couldn't discern.

Treading carefully, they went down, passing polished suits of armour standing on display to either side of every tenth step, gauntlets clasped around the grips of broadswords, the blades' tips resting between pointed sollerets.

A Grecian-style statue dominated the landing of the next floor. It portrayed Jessica Cornish, naked but for flowing material around her hips and a laurel wreath on her head.

As they rounded to the next flight, two female voices floated up to them.

"Why, my dear Baroness, I feel thoroughly wearied to the bone."

"Of course you do, my lady. It is exceedingly late. I, too, must take to my bed. This whole business has quite exhausted me. I'm certain I'll lie awake fretting over it."

"Nonsense! You're being far too theatrical. It will blow over. It's merely a hiccup of some sort."

"Hiccup? How can a hiccup so thoroughly detach the government from its people? Do you not perceive the seriousness of our position? The palace is utterly cut off, dear thing. Utterly! Worse still, we've lost all control over the commoners. The implications are frightful."

"You suggest they might break the law, Baroness?"

"No. I suggest they might indulge in unfettered breeding."

"Heaven forbid! Now I shall have nightmares."

Burton said, "Good evening, ladies."

The two Uppers stopped in their tracks and looked at him. He saw them register, with mutual gasps of consternation, the pistol he was brandishing at them. Their eyes flickered as they took in Swinburne, Trounce and Wells, all standing at his back.

"If you attempt to call for help, I'll shoot you," he said.

Both women were exceedingly skinny—almost emaciated—and possessed of protruding joints and absurdly large breasts. Their faces were painted so heavily they resembled masks, and they had ridiculously tall and extravagant wigs balanced precariously on their heads. The pair wore gowns of a vaguely Elizabethan design.

"Who on earth are you?" the one on the left asked.

"My name is Burton. And you are?"

"I am the Baroness Hume of Goldaming, heiress to the sugar beet estates of Sir Jacquard Hume, the Marquis of Norwich and the Norfolk Broads. My companion is Lady Felicity Pye of the Brick Lane Pyes, wife of Earl John Pye, overseer of Bethnal Green Road and chairman of the Pye and Keating Corporation. Burton, you say? What more? Your title, if you please."

"I am Captain Sir Richard Francis Burton, Knight of the Order of St Michael and St George, Fellow of the Royal Geographical Society."

"Oh my dear thing!" Lady Felicity Pye cried out. "Why didn't you say so? Can we be of some assistance?"

"You could tell me how to find the House of Lords."

"You don't know? How marvellously extraordinary! Why, you must go down another three flights, turn right, go all the way to the end of the hallway, right again, and it's straight ahead. The entertainment is already under way, so you'd better hurry up."

"Forgive me for asking," Baroness Hume said, "but is that a gun? Why are you pointing it at us?"

"To assure you both of a thoroughly good night's sleep."

"Oh, how perfectly terrific!"

"Would you both sit down, please?"

"Sit down? On the stairs? Is it a game?"

"It is."

"Hooray!"

The women sat and clapped their hands eagerly.

Burton said, "Stun both."

Ptooff! Ptooff!

"Take one of them over your shoulder, William. Algy, Bertie, you carry the other. I'll find a room in which to deposit them."

While his companions took up the two limp ladies, Burton stepped down into a vestibule from which three corridors extended. In the one to his right, two equerries were walking, heading away. They turned a corner and vanished from sight, not having spotted him.

Turning back, he gestured for his friends to follow, moved to the left, and opened a door. On the other side of it, in a room filled with what looked to be shelves of bottled cleaning fluids, an equerry stood facing him, a heavy metal case—perhaps a toolbox—in its right hand.

"You are not—" it began.

The king's agent whipped up his pistol, saw the red dot on the creature's face, and pulled the trigger.

The creature's head snapped back, and its knees buckled. The case fell from its grip and hit the ground with an almighty crash. Tottering backward, the equerry fell into shelves and slid to the floor, taking bottles with it. They smashed and clattered noisily around it.

"Damnation," Burton hissed.

"That," Swinburne commented, "was an unholy racket."

Wells, who was holding Lady Felicity Pye's ankles, dropped them and announced, "We have company."

Burton turned. The two Spring Heeled Jacks he'd seen a moment ago were returning, bounding along the corridor. Wells and Trounce shot them down.

"There's more!" Trounce said. He lowered Baroness Hume to the floor and, kneeling, raised his pistol and started shooting.

"By Allah's beard!" Burton cursed, as he saw equerries appearing in all three corridors, rounding corners and stepping from rooms. "There's a lot of them! Back to the stairs, quickly."

Leaving the two Uppers where they were lying, the chrononauts raced to the landing.

"Intruders! Intruders! Intruders!" the equerries shouted.

"Head, kill," the men responded. "Head, kill. Head, kill."

Ptooff! Ptooff! Ptooff!

One after the other, the spring heeled creatures went down.

With his companions at his back, Burton sprinted down the stairs to the next floor, where, before he saw it, an equerry pounced on him and bore him to the carpet.

"Off him! Off him!" Swinburne shrieked. He kicked the side of the creature's head and, as its chin jerked around, pressed his pistol to where an ear should have been and pulled the trigger. Plastic, bone and pig brains splattered outward.

Burton heaved the corpse to one side and regained his feet in time to kill another of the stilt men before it managed to grab Wells.

"I have the distinct impression," Swinburne said, "that our presence is no longer a secret."

Their destination was one flight of stairs away, but the steps were fast crowding with equerries, all yelling, "Intruders! Intruders!"

"You may be right," Burton said breathlessly.

Now there was no time even for the order *Head! Kill!* They simply pointed their weapons, fired into the mass of white figures, and forced their way forward.

"No!" Trounce yelled.

It was too late. Swinburne's pistol gave a deep cough, and, with a deafening bang, equerries flew into pieces, those at the front being hurled forward onto the chrononauts.

Burton's ears jangled. Pinned down by a struggling figure, he jammed the barrel of his Penniforth Mark II under its chin, averted his face, and fired. Its head exploded. He shoved the twitching carcass to one side and raised his pistol to shoot another, which was looming over him, its cranium already half shorn off, blue fire playing about the horrible wound. Before he could pull the trigger, it knocked the pistol from his hand. The weapon went spinning away over the banister and clattered out of sight.

Burton drew up his knees and kicked out, his heels thumping into his opponent's stomach. The equerry keeled over, already dead from the damage to its skull.

Struggling to his feet, half deaf, the king's agent fell over prone bodies, pushed himself back up, and was suddenly gripped from behind, iron-hard arms closing around him, crushing his rib cage until he couldn't draw breath.

His right ear popped as a voice, right beside it, said, "Your presence is unauthorised."

Something cracked behind his head. The constricting arms fell away. He turned and saw an equerry dropping to the floor, a hole through its brain. Another was ploughing through the carnage towards him. It, too, went down.

"Splendid weapons, these!" Herbert Wells called.

For the briefest of moments, there came a lull in the fighting. The stairs around Burton were buried beneath limp stilt men, shattered pictures and fallen armour. The walls were scorch-marked, the bannisters broken.

"So much for stealth," the king's agent muttered.

From the hallway below, more equerries came hopping.

He reached down and pulled a broadsword from a collapsed suit, hefted it, and found it to be well balanced.

Swinburne, a couple of steps above him, grinned down. "Uh ho! Now they're in trouble."

"Stand well back," Burton said. "And for pity's sake, don't fire another explosive."

"Sorry. It was more powerful than I—"

The poet's words were drowned out by cries of "Intruders!" as the Spring Heeled Jacks came vaulting up the stairs. Burton swung the sword up and behind his right shoulder then, timing it perfectly, swiped it forward horizontally, decapitating three stilted figures with the single stroke. With Swinburne, Trounce and Wells following, each of them firing shot after shot, he descended the last remaining stairs to the next landing.

Burton's expertise with the blade astounded his fellows. Weaving a web of steel about himself, he sliced, blocked and stabbed with such speed the weapon became nothing but a blur. Like a scythe through wheat, it carved a path before him. He battled his way to the mouth of the right-hand hallway and—while those equerries that avoided him fell to his companions' bullets—moved into it. Severed limbs fell and twitched. Heads bounced to the floor. Blue flame, spurting out of lacerations and stumps, arced around him, following his blade, and to Swinburne, the Romantic poet, it looked like his friend had been enclosed within a shield of light, as if the ancient gods had bestowed upon him magical protection.

A crowd of equerries was coming from behind now, descending from above. Despite the excessive results of Swinburne's ill-considered grenade, Trounce now resorted to another, firing it above them so it landed at their backs. The ear-splitting detonation sent dismembered torsos, pieces of banister, segments of armour, and shredded carpet raining down. Burton was far enough into the hallway to be protected from the blast, but Trounce, Swinburne and Wells all went down beneath the falling bodies.

For a moment, Burton was fighting alone.

He slashed upward from his right hip, cleaving off an equerry's face; barged into the creature and, as it collapsed, cut horizontally back to the right, chopping off another's head; then brought the sword swinging up and downward into the skull of a third. Momentarily, the flow of his movement was interrupted as the weapon jammed in his victim's hard plastic cranium. A stilted figure slapped its hands to either side of Burton's face and started to twist, attempting to break his neck. "Unauthorised!" it yelled. A hole appeared in the middle of its blank face. The hands slipped free as the figure fell.

Suddenly, there was peace.

The king's agent wrenched his blade free and stood panting. He saw Wells, on his knees, lowering his pistol.

"Much obliged, Bertie."

"Pardon? I'm deaf as a stone."

Swinburne emerged from beneath a quivering cadaver. "What did you say? I can't hear you. My ears are full of bells."

"Exploding bullets," Trounce grumbled as he pushed himself up. "Remind me to tell Penniforth to tone them down a little."

"A tipple?" Swinburne responded. "I should think we've earned one!"

An equerry tumbled down from the shattered staircase above. It struggled to its feet. "Intruders!"

"At your service," Trounce said. "Head. Kill."

Climbing over the fallen, the three men joined Burton. The chrononauts were all bleeding from superficial wounds, all feeling the effects of their exertions, but also all intoxicated by the heat of battle.

Burton pointed along the corridor. Through ringing ears, the others heard him say, "To the end and turn right."

Two equerries came leaping around the indicated corner. Swinburne and Wells shot them down.

The clamour in the chrononauts' ears died away.

Swinburne, surveying the massacre, said, "I'm not sure we'll find sufficient beds under which to conceal this lot."

His friends gave barks of amusement.

They moved on, senses alert.

Twice, equerries appeared behind them and were instantly dispatched. After that, a silence fell upon the palace, bringing with it a threatening air of expectation.

The chrononauts moved forward, past closed doors and countless portraits and statuettes; Jessica Cornish repeated over and over.

Wells observed, "What a grand obsession. As a monument to a single woman, even the Taj Mahal can't rival it."

"The Taj Mahal speaks of a dedicated heart," Swinburne said. "This of a magnificently sick mind."

They reached the junction with the next hallway and turned right. Ahead, the passage dropped a level, and as they went down steps to the lower, they saw tall double doors ahead of them and heard muffled voices.

"The House of Lords," Burton said.

"The plan?" Wells asked.

The king's agent shrugged. "Barge in. Assess in an instant. Shoot if necessary. Rescue Tom Bendyshe. Identify the prime minister. Don't kill him. Find out where the Turing Fulcrum is."

"That," Swinburne said, "is the best plan I've heard all day. What could possibly go wrong? We'll be back on the jolly old *Orpheus* in time for breakfast."

With his hands low, Burton raised the sword blade until it rested against his shoulder. "I'll cut down anyone who jumps at us." With a jerk of his chin, he indicated that Swinburne and Wells should prepare to thrust open the doors.

"It sounds like there's a crowd in there," Trounce said, as his fellows took hold of the gold-plated handles.

"No one with any sense would be up at this time of night," Swinburne replied. "So they're undoubtedly politicians. Ready?"

With his left fingers wrapped around the base of his right hand, Trounce raised his pistol, holding it poised to one side of his face. "I am."

Burton said, "Go."

The two smaller men threw their weight against the portal. The doors hinged inward. Burton and Trounce ran forward with Swinburne and Wells at their heels. The entrance swung shut behind them.

Their senses were assaulted.

For a moment, Burton could make nothing of the bedlam that surrounded them.

Piece by piece, it came together.

The sharp tang of ozone.

A babble of voices protesting, "Bah!" and "Boo!" and "Bad form!"

For a moment he thought himself in the midst of angry sheep.

A storm overhead. A big blue dome of crackling lightning, its jagged streaks snapping a concave course from the perimeter to the apex before streaming down into the top of a silhouetted bulk suspended in the centre; a black mass of indeterminate form.

Below the tempest, beneath Burton's feet, a round stage-like expanse of tiled floor, unsteadily and dimly illuminated by the hissing and spitting energy. In the middle of it, an X-shaped frame to which Thomas

Bendyshe was tethered, and encircling the area, row upon row of benches occupied by a braying crowd, the seats rising until they vanished into deep shadows that appeared to be immune to the strange blue illumination.

"By God!" Wells cried out. "What kind of arena is this?"

"Father!" Swinburne and Trounce yelled. They ran to Bendyshe.

A loud knocking caused Burton to spin, and he saw, on an ornate wooden chair over the door, a willowy and rather bird-like individual who was banging a gavel while shouting, "Order! Order!"

Uncertainly, the king's agent moved to join his companions.

"Order! Order!"

The crowd quietened. A woman, three rows back, stood up. She was dressed in tight brocades, with fluffy epaulets extending from her shoulders and a conical hat upon her head.

The gavel-wielder bellowed, "Dame Pearl Marylebone, Minister for Amusements and Daily Gratifications."

Raising her voice over the incessant sizzling from above, the woman said, "My Lord Speaker, may I, on behalf of the House, express dismay at this unwarranted intrusion and demand to know the identities of these— these—horrible *ruffians!*"

"Hear! Hear!" the crowd cheered.

The woman sat, a satisfied smile on her face.

Lord Speaker banged his wooden hammer again and blinked his large black eyes at the chrononauts. He pointed at Burton. "You, sir. Announce yourself."

Burton stepped backward until he was beside Bendyshe. Without taking his eyes from the Lord Speaker, he said to the Cannibal, "Are you all right?"

After giving a nod and moistening his cracked lips with his tongue, the prisoner managed a slight smile. "Hello, Sir Richard. It's good to see you again after all this time, though I—" He gasped and winced. "Though I regret that you find me in such a dire position. Be careful. They are all insane."

"Sir!" the Lord Speaker insisted.

Burton raised his voice. "I am Sir Richard Francis Burton. My companions are Algernon Charles Swinburne, Detective Inspector William Trounce, and George Herbert Wells. I demand that you release this man."

The gavel—*Bang! Bang! Bang!*—and, "You are in no position to make demands. You have no authority to be here. Which of the families do you represent? What corporation?"

"None and none," Burton replied.

In a sarcastic tone, Lord Speaker said, "What are you then? *Lowlies?*"

The crowd laughed.

Swinburne took aim.

"Stun."

Lord Speaker slumped.

"I'm sorry, Richard," the poet said, "but he was being rather boorish and I thought it best we assert ourselves."

"I say! Bad show!" a parliamentarian shouted.

"Aye!" another agreed. "Thoroughly unconventional!"

"Poor sportsmanship, I should say!" a third opined.

Above, the hemisphere of lightning turned a deeper shade of iridescent cobalt.

A man in the front row got to his feet. He was costumed as if participating in a *commedia dell'arte*. "My Lord Speaker appears to be resting, thus I will announce myself. I am Harold John Heck, the Duke of Deptford and Minister for Fashion, Jewellery and Accessories. Sir Richard, I demand that you explain yourself. Why have you interrupted parliamentary proceedings in such an irregular—and, frankly, thoroughly impolite—manner? You may address the House."

Trounce and Swinburne set about untying the bonds that held their father by his wrists and ankles.

Burton put his sword point to the floor and rested both hands on the weapon's pommel. He peered into the gloom at the edges of the circular chamber and tried to assess the size of the crowd. At least two hundred, he thought.

"We are here," he called out, "to rescue this man and to locate a device known as the Turing Fulcrum."

He saw little point in concealing the truth.

A woman in the front row jumped up. Burton vaguely recognised her but couldn't think how. "Lady Dolores Paddington Station, the Minister of War, Death and Destruction. The man you refer to, and whom your companions are untethering with absolutely no leave to do so, is an enemy of the Empire. He has attacked us. We have been attempting to establish whether he represents the United Republics of Eurasia or the United States of America. Since you are obviously aligned with him—and are therefore an awfully rotten scoundrel—perhaps you'd care to answer the question. U.R.E. or U.S.A., sir?"

"We insist upon an answer," someone yelled.

"Spill the beans!" another added.

"If we represent anyone," Burton responded, "then it's the majority. We represent the people. We represent what should be, but isn't."

"Nonsensical! You're a bad liar, sir," someone mocked.

"Surely you don't refer to the inhabitants of the London Underground?" Lady Dolores exclaimed. "That would be absurd."

Bendyshe slumped down into Trounce's and Swinburne's supporting arms. Struggling to raise his head, he shouted in a hoarse voice, "Neither Eurasia nor America are in any condition to attack, madam, and you bloody well know it."

"Mind your language, sir. And you are quite wrong. Those empires despise us. They are jealous of our advanced civilisation. We have this information directly from the prime minister. Don't you think we're rather more likely to believe him than we are a—a—a *commoner!*" She spread her arms. "Parliamentarians! Plainly, we are in the presence of enemy agents. I call for the death sentence. We must do them in. Slice their necks."

"Bravo!" someone cheered. "Hanging! Firing squad! Acid bath!"

"Could we construct an electric chair?" another shouted.

"Poison injection!"

"More of the carnivorous nanomachines! They are simply delightful!"

The crowd yelled its approval. "Huzzah! Carnivorous nanomachines! Huzzah! Huzzah!" They clapped their hands and stamped their feet.

Another women—her body and face almost entirely concealed beneath feathery garments—jumped up and cried out, "I object! I object! Let us not be impetuous!"

The hubbub subsided.

She continued, "I am Gladys Tweedy, the Marquess of Hammersmith,

Minister of Language Revivification and Purification. Lady Dolores, whilst your indignation is justified, you appear to have overlooked the fact that this man claims a title. *Sir* Richard. If he is, indeed, a knight of the realm, then we must extend to him a modicum of courtesy. We must hear him out."

Despite a scornful bray of "Liberal!" a number of voices were raised in agreement.

"It's the done thing," someone observed. "Though I must confess, I've never heard of the fellow."

A man, wearing a velvet cape and tricorn hat, stood and said, "I am Lord Robert Forest Beresford of Waterford, Minister for Executions, Suppression and Random Punishments. I would hear a full and detailed statement."

The crowd hooted its support.

"A contrary bunch of nutters, aren't they?" Swinburne muttered.

Lord Robert said, "You and your fellows have the floor, Sir Richard. Tell us in full why you consider it desirable to release this man—" he indicated Bendyshe, "who has wreaked such terrible havoc in the Empire's capital. Tell us what this—what did you call it? A Turning Fool? Whatever it is, tell us about it, and why you require it, and why you think we possess it, and what you intend to do with it. Speak!"

"Make it eloquent and compelling, if you please," another parliamentarian drawled. "I'm weary and my attention is wandering."

A ripple of laughter.

Lord Robert waved Burton forward, indicating that he should address the audience.

The king's agent hesitated, irresolute, and turned to his colleagues. "What can I possibly say to these people? They're like children."

Herbert Wells said, "May I?"

"Be my guest. Keep them occupied, Bertie. I need time to think."

"Your representative?" Lord Robert demanded, as Wells stepped forward.

"Yes," Burton answered. "Mr. Herbert Wells."

"Then the stage is yours, Mr. Wells."

The Cannibal cleared his throat. In his thin reedy voice, raised above the fizzling from overhead, he said, "I ask you to consider a preliminary proposition before I answer the questions you have asked. Though you set yourselves apart, though you inhabit these high towers while the rest are teeming below, you are human, all of you. You are human. So it is, you are subject to the wants of our species. You seek to satisfy your hunger. You desire shelter and warmth and good health. You want your families to prosper. No doubt, you also seek the satisfaction of knowing that you have contributed something to the world; that your existence will not pass without notice or any effect."

Someone shouted, "Dreary! Get on with it!"

"Order! Order!" another countered.

Burton moved to Swinburne, Trounce and Bendyshe. "What's going on here, Tom?"

"They were about to approve the invasion of the rival empires when I was dragged in. My torture has delayed mobilisation." He managed a weak grin. "At least I know the pain was useful for something."

"Are you holding up?"

"It comes in waves. I'm all right for the moment, but the nanomechs will start on me again in a short while."

Wells was saying, "Surely, out of this commonality, it is possible for you to find in yourselves an affinity for your fellow man? I urge you, discover your mercy. Embrace compassion. Ask what there is to admire in a world where the majority are suppressed and monitored and designedly distracted by falsehoods; where a few maintain their privileged position by deceiving the rest, by sucking at them like leeches, by looking down upon them as little better than animals, by jealously guarding their own interests at the expense of the majority. Where is your honour?" He threw up his arms. "Great heavens! My contemporaries had such high hopes for the future! We envisioned a world in which all men and women were equal; where every person would reap the rewards of their efforts and willingly make contributions toward the betterment of all. Can you people not see that the only true measure of success is the ratio between what we might have done and what we might have been on the one hand, and the thing we have made and the things we have made of ourselves on the other? Can you not understand that, by such a measure, you have failed utterly and miserably? I beseech you; destroy these terrible divisions you've created!"

As a body, the audience burst into raucous laughter.

"Please!" Wells pleaded. "Listen to me!"

Burton stepped forward. "Bertie—"

A deafening roar interrupted him. A ball of ferocious white flame blazed from the black hulk suspended above them. Bullets ripped down and thudded into Wells, shredding his clothes and flesh, crushing him to the floor and smashing the tiles around him.

The fire guttered and vanished. The roar slowed to a rapid metallic clattering then stopped.

Shiny blood oozed outward from the Cannibal's tattered corpse.

The king's agent, numb with the shock of it, watched as the life faded from Wells's disbelieving eyes.

The ministers' laughter gave way to enthusiastic applause.

Burton looked up and saw two pinpricks of red light in the bulky silhouette. Slowly, the shape descended. He heard Swinburne, Trounce and Bendyshe yelling but he couldn't process their words.

He saw the gleam of polished brass.

He saw thick legs and an armoured torso.

He saw five arms extended, Christ-like, and a sixth, to which a Gatling gun was bolted, still directed at Wells.

He saw that the red pinpricks were eyes.

He saw, floating down to the floor, with lines of energy cascading from the apex of the domed ceiling into his head, the famous engineer Isambard Kingdom Brunel.

CHAPTER 20

SEVEN BIRTHS AND A DEATH

Just because the stairs are there does not mean you have the right to climb them.
—Baron Friedrich Bruno Armbrüster,
Minister for Social Order and Stratification

The House of Lords fell utterly silent as the brass man descended.

In familiar bell-like tones, he said, "The Anglo-Saxon Empire is mine. I will not have its Constitution challenged."

His feet clunked onto the floor. He took a pace forward and looked down at Burton. The king's agent felt his skin prickling, reacting to the ribbons of blue energy that were pouring from the ceiling into Brunel's exposed babbage.

"Sir Richard Francis Burton," the engineer said.

"Isambard?"

Ignoring the enquiry, Brunel cocked his head a little to one side. "So, despite my efforts to prevent it, you have followed me through time. That is unfortunate for you, for now the manner of your demise depends upon the answer to a single question."

Burton took a step back and hefted his sword, eyeing the huge man-shaped mechanism, observing the gaps between its brass plates, wondering whether there was a part of it so vulnerable that a sword thrust could render the entirety inoperable.

"I shall tell you how I came to be," Brunel intoned. "Then I shall ask and you will answer. If I am satisfied with your response, you will die quickly. If I am not, you will die very, very slowly."

Burton remained silent.

"Know this, then, Burton: I have been born seven times, and through each birth this world was formed."

"Bravo!" a minister shouted.

"My first birth came at nine o'clock on the fifteenth of February 1860. Three hundred and forty-two years ago." With a quiet whir of gears and hiss of miniature pistons, Brunel closed his arms about himself. He lowered his face and regarded the floor. "No thought. No sensory stimulation. No knowledge of myself. What had its inception on that day was comprised of one thing and one thing only. *fear*."

Burton heard Tom Bendyshe groan and from the corner of his eye saw him buckle and fall to his knees. Trounce and Swinburne crouched and held him by the shoulders.

"Brunel! Stop this!" Trounce yelled. "For pity's sake! He's in agony!"

The gathered politicians bleated their objection to the interruption.

Without turning his head, Brunel extended his Gatling gun toward the three Cannibals. He didn't fire it, but the threat was enough to quieten the former Scotland Yard man.

Holding the pose, he went on, "My second birth came at nine o'clock on the fifteenth of February, 1950. A glimmering of awareness. A vague sense of being. Perhaps a dream."

Burton lowered his sword. "Turing's Automatic Computing Engine. Your presence, as you moved forward through time, resonated with its silicon components. It expanded your capacity to think." He took two paces to the left to avoid the pool of blood that was spreading from Wells's corpse.

Brunel raised his face and looked directly at the king's agent. "And it gave me a means to influence events as they unfolded." Without moving his levelled gun, he unfolded his remaining arms and held their four hands and one stump before his eyes, examining them, moving his fingers, extending the tools from the top of his wrists, making drill bits and screwdrivers spin, clamps and pliers open and close. "But what was I?

My body—this body—was in one place, my mind in another. I was dis-jointed. Incomplete. Scattered. And there were memories, nightmarish memories. I felt myself strapped down, at the mercy of a dreadful man with a swollen cranium. I saw an orangutan with the top of its head replaced by glass through which its living brain was visible. I was aboard a flying ship that was plummeting to earth. There were gunshots. And—"

An arm suddenly jerked forward, and a forefinger jabbed toward Bur-ton's left eye, stopping less than an inch from it. Burton stumbled back.

"And there was you. Sir Richard Francis Burton. The killer. The murderer. The assassin."

"No. Those events occurred in a different history and involved a dif-ferent me."

For a moment, Brunel stood absolutely motionless.

"Ah, yes," he said. He drew in his limbs, turned his palms upward, and raised his face to the crackling storm. Ribbons of energy danced across his brow and reflected on the curved planes of his cheeks. "Time. So vast and complex and delicate. Do you feel it as I do, then? Stretching away in every direction? History upon history? Variation upon variation? So many causes. So many effects. Innumerable consequences blossoming from each and every action. Possibilities and probabilities. What a beau-tiful, awe-inspiring, and truly terrifying equation."

Another pause; a silence broken only by the relentless lightning, a cough from the audience, and an agonised moan from Bendyshe.

Again, Brunel regarded Burton.

"A pattern. A rhythm. A third birth, this at nine o'clock on the fif-teenth of February, 1986."

"The Turing Fulcrum."

"Awake. Fully awake." Brunel fisted a gauntlet-like hand. "In a world gone wrong." He emitted a clangourous chuckle. "But wrong how? I didn't know. I didn't know."

He reached out. Burton tried to dodge away, but the brass man was too fast. The king's agent felt metal fingers close around his cheeks and jaw. The grip was surprisingly gentle, almost a caress.

"I dreamed that I was in a museum," Brunel chimed. "And you—you!—stood before me. I thought I had escaped, but here you were, in pursuit, determined to terrorise and destroy me. Burton. The man from the past. My demon. My would-be nemesis."

The fingers opened and withdrew. Burton glanced at his companions. Swinburne and Trounce were holding Bendyshe and gazing at Brunel. Their father was white-faced, glaze-eyed and trembling.

"My fourth birthday was at nine o'clock on the fifteenth of February, 2162. By then, my presence had been in every Turing device for a hundred and seventy-six years, yet I had no individuality. No Self." Brunel touched his own face, running fingertips over the line of his jaw, across the immobile lips, around the deeply shadowed eye sockets. "Suddenly, it came. I was me, in this body, half submerged in the mud of a narrow subterranean stream—a tributary of the Fleet River—beneath the ruins of the British Museum. Buried alive! Buried alive! A birth into primordial horror! Inch by frightful inch I pulled myself through that narrow tunnel, feeling my battery draining, until at last I came to the Fleet, which had become a part of the sewer system, and from there climbed to the surface to claim my rightful place. It was not difficult to convince those in power that I was the Turing Fulcrum incarnate. They were weak, while I was integral to every item of technology, and had long employed it to prepare them for my advent."

From the gathered politicians, a voice shouted, "Three cheers for the prime minister!"

Brunel whipped around his Gatling gun and pointed it at the man. "Shut your damned mouth, you cretinous heap. All of you. Not another word."

After a moment, satisfied that he'd not be interrupted again, he lowered his gun. Though his mask was fixed and incapable of showing emotion, he appeared to withdraw into himself and was silent.

Burton waited. A breeze brushed his skin. He looked at the dome of blue fire and noticed that the tendrils of energy were streaming from a great many nodes, flashing upward from one to the next before descending from the apogee in a long, twisting funnel to Brunel's cranium. The hissing storm, he felt sure, was increasing in power, and the air in the chamber was starting to move, as if being dragged slowly around the centre.

Brunel resumed his narrative.

"My fifth birth occurred five years ago, at nine o'clock on the fifteenth of February, 2197, when, amid the boundless chatter of information that passes through me, I discovered my queen. My saviour. Is it not said that only love can conquer fear? I know I have loved her before, though how and when eludes me. Perhaps I shall love her again, and the terror that drives me will finally be dispelled."

"You do not feel that love now?" Burton asked.

"While you—the source of my dread—are alive? No, I have no love. Only the hope that it will come when you are gone."

Brunel's head jerked, as if he'd just realised something. He turned to the benches. "Beresford, where is the queen?"

Lord Robert Forest Beresford stood and nodded toward Thomas Bendyshe. "The entertainments upset her, My Lord Prime Minister. She left the chamber and went to tend her flowers in the palace greenhouse."

"Fetch her. Bring her here."

"Me, sir? Surely it would be more appropriate for one of the royal equerries to—"

"Go, damn you, or I'll shoot you where you stand."

Beresford gave a submissive bob, ran from his seat across the floor, and exited through the double door.

Brunel surveyed the benches, and Burton sensed that, if the metal face had been capable of it, it would have been sneering.

The polished visage turned and lowered to regard him again.

"My sixth birth came at nine o'clock this very night, the fifteenth of February, 2202, when, while I was instructing my Parliament to vote in favour of an attack against our rival empires, I suddenly perceived six events occurring simultaneously and knew there must come a seventh. Seven births, seven events. Such are the intricate synchronies of time, such its patterns and echoes." Brunel raised a fist and extended from it a metal thumb. "A red snow began to fall, and I knew it to be from a different history." He unfolded the forefinger. "An explosion crippled the city, and I knew the enemy long hidden within the populace had finally made a move." His middle finger. "I remembered that it was you whom I fear, who you are, and where you are from." The fourth finger. "I felt time fold, and I knew you had arrived." The fifth finger. "I recalled my many births, and I knew I was almost complete." He extended an adjustable spanner from his wrist to make the sixth digit. "And I became fully myself when, out of time, all around me, there arrived these—"

He threw back his head and opened his arms wide. The dome of energy started to slowly drop down, and, as it did so, lights flared in the ceiling above it, in the walls, and from the edge of the circular floor.

Burton squinted and shielded his eyes from the glare, blinked, dropped his hands, and stared dumbfounded as the true nature of the storm was revealed. He saw burned, torn and blistered time suits—hundreds and hundreds of garments and helmets and stilted boots—all identical, all floating just inches apart and forming a downturned hemisphere. Chronostatic energy blazed from their Nimtz generators, connecting them all and flowing down into Brunel's babbage. As they gradually dropped, they rotated around a vertical axis, increasing speed, and now the air was moving faster too, quickly turning from a breeze into a wind.

"Power over time itself!" Brunel clanged loudly. "Now I could rid myself of that which has haunted me. Of you! Now I could send my equerries back to the source, back to 1860, where lay my genesis and my potential nemesis, there to hunt you, there to kill you. They never returned. Did you destroy them, killer? Murderer? Assassin?"

"Some," Burton shouted above the increasing din of the lightning. "Most vanished of their own accord. They were confused. Disoriented."

"Ah. Unfortunate. Perhaps when they leave my circle of influence they become erratic. I suppose those you allowed to live are lost amid the interstices of time. They have fallen between the lines of the equation."

"How did you send them?" Burton demanded. "By what method? Surely you couldn't—since nine o'clock this evening—so quickly have adapted them to travel through history?"

"No adaptation necessary." The brass man pointed a hand at the benches. From his fingers, zig-zagging lines of chronostatic energy lashed out and hit the woman who'd announced herself as Lady Dolores Paddington Station, the Minister of War, Death and Destruction. She screamed as it first enshrouded her then expanded to form a bubble. It popped and she vanished, as did a section of the bench and the arm of the man beside her. He shrieked, stood up, and fainted.

"I sent her to 1860," Brunel said. "She should have returned instantaneously. She hasn't. It appears that, like my equerries, she didn't fare too well there." He looked back at Burton. "I'm right to fear you. You are indeed dangerous."

Now Burton understood why he'd half-recognised the woman. "You deposited her right in the middle of a thoroughfare. She was hit by a vehicle."

He felt it apposite to exclude the fact that he'd been driving it.

"It doesn't matter. She was disposable. The demonstration is done." Brunel turned a hand in front of Burton's face. Blue sparks crawled up and down the fingers. "The stuff of time. I command it."

"I see," Burton responded. "And now you also have the ability to defy gravity. Floating down from the ceiling? Impressive, if somewhat theatrical."

"Time and space are indivisible, Burton. The accretion of time suits has endowed me with dominion over both. Once I've properly learned how to employ the power—"

"Employ it? What do you intend to do with it?"

Brunel chimed a chuckle. "You said you came here to locate the Turing Fulcrum? The device you refer to is long obsolete. Its functions became spread across millions of devices, which grew in number and shrank in size. Now they number in trillions and are naked to the human eye."

"Nanomechs."

"Yes, and this—" The brass man gestured at the suits, which were now blurring around them. "This is in them all. And this is *me*." He thumped a fist into his chest. "What shall I do? I have come home. I have fashioned the world. I am *everything*, and now I shall expand into the other histories and shape them, too. Every variant of every person will know their place; they will know where they belong and how they must contribute. They will feel safe. They will be content. They will have purpose."

Burton leaned into the air as it rushed around him. Above its howling, he yelled, "They will be enslaved. They will be subject to your insane whims. What of freedom?"

"A myth!" Brunel answered. "None of us are free. We are forever chained to the consequences of our actions. Time rules all. But I—" He put his head back and loosed a peal of demented laughter. "I rule time."

A hand closed around Burton's arm. He looked down and saw Swinburne at his side. His friend's red hair was whipping about his head like an inferno.

"Hey!" the poet screeched at Brunel. "Hey! What of the seventh?"

Brunel lowered his face. "You are Swinburne, I believe?"

"How do you do. Pleased to meet you. Charmed, I'm sure. What of the seventh? You said seven births and seven events. You've only ranted about six."

"Ranted?"

"Like a nutcase of the first order."

"Obviously, you don't value your life, little man."

"And obviously you don't value rationality. But enough of this delightful flirting. Number seven? Spit it out, old thing. I'm on the edge of my seat."

The engineer swung up his Gatling gun and pointed it at the poet. "The final birth is yet to come, and with it the final event." He slid the weapon sideways until it was aimed at the king's agent. "You will initiate them, Burton."

Burton raised a questioning eyebrow.

"As I have stated, I shall ask you a question," Brunel said. "Through your answer, I will be completed, and the seventh event will be your death, quick and complete or slow and recurring, as you please."

"Answer a question then die?" the king's agent said. "That doesn't sound like a particularly attractive deal. Why should I cooperate?"

"If you do not, I'll torture your friends in front of you."

"I thought you might say something like that. Very well, let's get it over with. Ask."

Brunel stepped closer and leaned down until his blank face was almost touching Burton's. From the dark eye sockets, his red mechanical eyes burned.

"Tell me. What is my name? Who am I?"

"My hat!" Swinburne cried out. "You don't know?"

Burton looked down and saw that one of Brunel's hands was gripping the blade of his sword. He felt cold fingers slide around his throat, holding it gently but—he knew—able to close with such speed and force that he'd be decapitated in an instant.

He gazed into the glaring eyes.

"You were once a good man, a historian, philosopher, engineer, inventor, and genius. You wanted the human race to be the best it could be. The things you created were helping it to achieve a new kind of consciousness. In addition to such an incredible contribution to the welfare of all, you also had personal contentment. You were married to a woman named Jessica Cornish, and your first baby was just weeks away from birth. However, you became obsessed with a crime committed by a distant ancestor, an impulsive and irresponsible act that was forever recorded in history. That preoccupation was your route into madness and death and this dreadful rebirth."

"What is my name?" Brunel repeated, so quietly that his voice was barely audible above the din of the chronostatic storm.

"It is the same as your ancestor's. It is Edward Oxford."

The air screamed around them. Time suits hurtled past, spinning ever faster, energy tearing from one to the next, flooding down into the motionless brass man.

For a minute, he didn't speak, didn't react, then his fingers eased from Burton's neck, his hand fell away from the sword, and he softly clanged, "Edward Oxford?"

He stepped back.

"Edward Oxford?"

He raised his hands to his face.

"Edward Oxford?"

He threw his head back and shrieked, "Edward Oxford!"

Toppling backward, the massive figure hit the floor, arched its back, and started to thrash its limbs. In a voice like shearing metal, it screeched, "My neck! Don't! Twisting! Don't! Don't! Please, don't! I didn't mean to hurt the girls. I made a mistake. I don't care about myself anymore. I'm a discontinued man. But let me restore history. Restore! Restore! Back! Back in time for supper! Edward Oxford!"

Ribbons of lightning started to peel away from the suits, crackling out in random directions. Burton saw a bolt hit a woman in the front row of benches. In an instant, she shrank and rolled out of her clothes, a mewling infant.

The politicians erupted into panic. They stood and began to crowd the aisles, pushing and pulling at one another, babbling and gesticulating, stampeding down to the floor and across to the exit.

The king's agent snapped into action. He yelled across to Trounce. "William, get Bendyshe out of here. This might be our only opportunity."

Trounce hauled Bendyshe upright while gawping at the convulsing machine-man. "By Jove! What the blazes did you do to him?"

"Told him the truth. Go! Back the way we came. Once you're clear, try to contact Lorena Brabrooke. She—"

"Yes! Yes!" Trounce gestured at Bendyshe. "She might be able to disable the nanomechs."

"I'm all right," Bendyshe moaned. He plainly wasn't.

Trounce dragged him toward the door. Swinburne moved as if to follow, dithered, then stepped back, closer to Burton. He shouted, "Save him, William."

Trounce gave a determined nod.

"My neck! My neck!" Oxford yelled. "In cold blood!"

"What's got into him?" Swinburne asked, looking down at the flailing body.

"Oxford has," Burton answered.

Floor tiles shattered beneath Oxford's drumming fists, elbows and heels. He bucked and writhed; hollered incoherently. Burton stepped closer to him, raised his sword, and looked for a viable insertion point.

Swinburne waved him back. "Out of the way. A grenade will do a better job of it."

Burton jerked his head in confirmation, but before he could move, the sword was yanked from his hand and thrown aside. Overbalanced, the king's agent fell forward and six arms clamped tightly around him.

Oxford rose, lifting Burton with him.

Swinburne backed away, aiming his pistol, unable to shoot without killing his friend.

"I am Oxford! Edward Oxford! How does it feel to change history? I haven't changed history. History is the past." Oxford laughed—or sobbed—a discordant jangling of bells.

"Remember!" Burton cried out. "Remember who you used to be. Remember the world you came from, the original 2202." He struggled to free himself, but his efforts caused Oxford to tighten his grip. With his ribs creaking under the pressure, Burton gasped out, "Can't you see how you've distorted everything? You sent history careening off-course. You broke the mechanism of time, and now you've created a future that's nothing but a grotesque mockery of the past."

"Maybe, maybe," Oxford clanged. His arms relaxed slightly. Burton sucked in a breath. Quietly, in his ear, he heard his captor whisper, "The problem, Burton, is that although the future might not be what it used to be, I like it the way it is."

In front of them, Sir Robert Forest Beresford entered, pushing through the last of the fleeing politicians. He skidded to a halt, ducked down and gaped at the spinning time suits.

Oxford levelled his Gatling gun and demanded, "Where is the queen?"

"He threatened to kill me!" Beresford shouted. He squealed in fear as a ribbon of energy snapped into the floor beside him. "That man—Trounce, was it?—I met him in the corridor. There are dead equerries everywhere. He threatened to kill me unless I let him pass."

"Stop yammering, idiot. The queen?"

"Gone. They've taken her."

Oxford bellowed a deafening cry of rage. The barrels of his Gatling gun whirled and spat flame. Beresford was thrown back into the doors and out into the corridor, leaving a smear of blood on the tiles.

Burton looked down at himself and saw a red dot of light crawling over his torso, passing over Oxford's brass plating—Swinburne, circling, trying to find a target, knowing only an exploding bullet would have any effect, knowing it would kill Burton, too.

The crushing arms closed like a vice. Fingers dug into the flesh of Burton's limbs, turning him until he faced Brunel's dispassionate mask.

"I'll break you," Oxford said.

The king's agent screamed in agony as his right arm was forced back and his elbow snapped with an audible crunch.

"Where is she?" Oxford demanded. "What have you done with her?"

Blinded by the pain, Burton hissed, "She's—she's safe. Gone. You'll never see her again, you insane bastard."

Oxford emitted a clangour of rage. He dropped to one knee and forced his captive backward over his thigh, bending Burton's spine to its limit. The torment was beyond anything the king's agent had ever experienced. It obliterated every other sense.

White.

Excruciating white.

A transcendental anguish.

From far away, a voice: "You object to the history I've created? Let's see how you feel about *your* history. Let's see what it would have been had I changed nothing."

He slammed a hand into Burton's face and closed his fingers hard. Cheekbones fractured, the jaw dislocated, teeth broke. Blue fire erupted from Oxford's digits and drilled into Burton's skull.

White. White. White.

Fragmentation.

Pain.

Decisions unmade.

Pain.

Successes and failures dismantled.

Pain.

Characteristics disengaged.

Pain.

Cohesion lost.

Pain.

Something of Burton observed and wailed and grieved as it watched itself forcibly shredded into ever-smaller components.

Reconstitution.

Pain.

Boulogne seafront emerged from unendurable torment. Two young women came walking and giggling along it, arm in arm, moving toward him. He recognised the scene at once. This was the moment he'd first met Isabel Arundell and her sister, Blanche.

He tried to call out to them but had no control over himself. His body did what it had done that day back in the summer of 1851. It even thought the same thoughts. He was nothing but a passenger.

As they passed him, Isabel—tall and golden-haired—glanced over. Burton felt a thrill run through him. He gave a small smile. She blushed and looked away.

He walked to a wall, took a stub of chalk from his pocket, and wrote upon the brickwork, *May I speak to you?*

He waited for her to look back and, when she did, tapped his fingers on the message before strolling away along the promenade.

The whiteness returned.

My back is breaking. My back is breaking.

Suddenly it was the next day, and beneath his words, others had been added. *No. Mother will be angry.*

Time always finds a way.

Instances of overwhelming suffering separated disjointed scenes as Burton encountered Isabel again and again among Boulogne's socialites. Then she was suddenly left behind, and he was no longer Richard Francis Burton. He was Abdullah, a *darwaysh*, embarking on a gruelling *hajj* to Mecca. A whole year as another man, subsumed into a character so convincing that it fooled even the pilgrims who travelled at his side.

The master of disguise felt the hot *shamal* blowing on his face. The desert stretched from horizon to horizon. Space. Freedom. He looked down at the sand and saw a scarab beetle rolling a ball of dung.

The beetle. That is the answer to it all. Life creates reality and rotates it through cycle after cycle.

He turned his sun-baked face to the sky and was blinded by its white glare.

White.

What is happening to me? Why am I back in Arabia?

He blinked his watering eyes and saw the low hills of Berbera, on the coast of Africa, east of forbidden Harar.

The Royal Geographical Society had given him its backing. He'd organised an expedition, recruiting William Stroyan of the Indian Navy, Lieutenant George Herne of the 1st Bombay European Regiment of Fusiliers, and Lieutenant John Hanning Speke of the 46th Regiment of Bengal Native Infantry.

The mania for discovery was upon him.

All that is hidden, I shall expose.

They'd landed at Berbera and set up camp.

They were attacked.

Burton watched and waited for Speke to die.

"Arm to defend the camp!" he yelled, as tribesmen descended upon them.

Spears flew. Scimitars slashed. Men screamed.

He looked over his shoulder just as Speke, emerging from a tent, was hit in the knee by a thrown rock. The lieutenant flinched. Burton heard himself shout, "Don't step back! They'll think that we're retiring!"

This is the moment Speke propels himself in front of Stroyan and takes a spear to the heart. The moment he dies a hero's death.

It didn't happen

Confused, he realised that Stroyan was on the ground behind the tents, dead.

No! It was Speke! It was Speke! He died just before—

A javelin slid through one side of his face and out the other, splitting his pallet and knocking out three of his molars. Suffering enveloped him. He felt his back breaking, his skin burning, his skull cracking.

Pain.

He had no idea why, but he thought, *I'll not be stopped.*

The Crimean War. He was there, but it was over before he saw any action. Disappointed, he sailed for London and upon arrival mingled with men of influence: Sir Roderick Murchison, Francis Galton—*but Galton is a madman!*—Laurence Oliphant—*Murderer! Stroyan didn't die in Africa. You killed him, Oliphant! You!*

Nothing felt right.

He met Isabel again. Secretly, they got engaged. Almost immediately, he left her and, with John Speke, set sail for Africa.

No! I flew to Africa aboard the Orpheus. *Stroyan, Herne, Sadhvi and I discovered the source of the Nile. Speke is dead. Speke is dead.*

He felt terror. He didn't want to see this Burton's life. He could sense horror lurking at its end.

He was helpless, forced along an unfamiliar path, spending two exhausting, disease-ridden years with a man who, increasingly, came to resent him.

"Don't step back! They'll think that we're retiring!"

Those words, taken by Speke as a slight, as an accusation of cowardice, fuelled a seething hatred.

The two explorers located and mapped Lake Tanganyika. Burton was immobilised by fever. Speke left him and discovered another lake—one so large it might almost be considered an inland sea. Upon his return, he claimed it to be, for certain, the source of the Nile.

"Show me your evidence," Burton said.

Speke had none.

Their relationship broke down. During the return journey to Zanzibar, barely a word was exchanged between them. Speke departed immediately for London. En route, he was persuaded by Oliphant to claim full credit for the expedition's achievements. Burton, after recovering from malaria, followed, only to find himself sidelined.

He turned to Isabel for comfort.

Her parents forbid their marriage. Burton was neither Catholic nor respectable.

Everything was going wrong.

It is wrong! It didn't happen this way!

Bitterly disappointed, angry and depressed, he embarked on a drunken tour of America with his friend John Steinhaueser. He lost track of himself; hardly knew who he was anymore. Ever since the fevers of Africa, he'd felt himself divided, two Burtons, forever disagreeing.

Burton the observer and Burton the observed.

Burton the living and Burton the dying.

No! No! Allah! Allah! He's killing me! Oxford is breaking my back!

To hell with it.

Defiance.

He and Isabel eloped.

He prepared a devastating critique of John Speke's claims.

Torture. His nerves afire, his vertebrae cracking, and Oxford's clanging voice like the chimes of passing time, the tolling bell of implacable history, of relentless fate: *"Thou shalt be reduced by flame to nothing."*

Burton watched as Grindlays Warehouse, where he stored his every memento, his every page of research, his journals and his notes, was consumed by fire. He was forty years old, and every recorded moment of his life prior to his marriage was turned to ash.

Now he had nothing but Isabel.

They were separated. He was made consul of Fernando Po, a tiny island off the west coast of Africa, and couldn't take her with him. He spent the first year of his marriage alone.

I'm going to die.

It was a white man's graveyard. No European could survive its rancid atmosphere, its infested water, or its torpid humidity. No European but Burton.

A further setback. In accepting the post, he'd inadvertently resigned from the Army and lost his pension.

Loss, loss, nothing but loss.

Anger. Isolation. Despair.

During his forays into the hotly dripping jungles of the mainland, he lashed out at everything he perceived as rotten and despicable in the human race. He railed at the natives, but really it was his own people who disgusted and disappointed him.

He returned to London, to Isabel, and to a final showdown with Speke.

Speke killed himself the day before the confrontation. Victory denied. Justice denied. Absolution denied. Satisfaction denied.

Is this how I die? Being dismantled piece by piece? Save me! Oh God, save me!

He was given the consulship at Santos, Brazil. Isabel joined him there. He could find no more mysteries to solve or secrets to penetrate, so wandered aimlessly, prospecting for gold, as if searching for something to value.

Patiently, Isabel waited.

A new post. Damascus. Allah be praised! How they both loved Damascus!

However, misjudgements, plots, accusations and threats soon soured their taste for the city and blackened even further Burton's already bad reputation. He was recalled by the government and given, instead, the consulship of Trieste. It sidelined him, kept him out of the way, and in effect castrated him.

Bad health slowed him down. He threw himself into his writing, became ever more dependent on Isabel, and finally realised the depth of his love for her. They did everything together.

At last, she had him.

He found a new way to expose the hidden. He translated the forbidden: the *Ananga Ranga*; *The Kama Sutra of Vatsyayana*; *The Perfumed Garden of the Cheikh Nefzaoui*; and, his triumph, an unexpurgated edition of *The Book of the Thousand Nights and a Night*. The books shocked his contemporaries with their explicitness but brought him further fame, notoriety, and finally, a grudging respect.

He was awarded a knighthood.

I'm already knighted.

He was content.

He wrote and wrote, and with every word he inscribed, he felt himself age, as if the ink that flowed from his pen was vitality draining from his body. His legs weakened. His hips hurt. His skin grew grey and wrinkled. His teeth fell out. His eyesight began to fail. His hair whitened. His heart struggled. His back creaked as the bones of his spine crumbled.

He began work on *The Scented Garden*, a book he hoped would shake the constrained and stifling morals of the British Empire to its roots; a book that would offer incontrovertible evidence that all cultures were an artifice that overlaid and suppressed the true nature of humanity.

It was his *magnum opus*.

At the age of sixty-nine, the day after finishing the manuscript, his heart failed. He cried out to Isabel, "Chloroform—ether—or I am a dead man!" The tinkle of camel bells filled his ears. The white sky of the desert spread over him like a shroud.

No! No! I cannot die! I cannot die!

White. White.

"Bismillah!" he shrieked. "Please! It's all wrong! All wrong!"

Oxford's metal hands were unremitting, the pressure on Burton's spine tremendous, the pain far beyond the explorer's comprehension. Chronostatic energy burned through his skull.

Now he was outside himself, watching as the remnants of his presence faded from existence like a dying echo.

Fire.

Grindlays Warehouse all over again, except this time it was Isabel, burning his every paper, his every journal, *The Scented Garden*.

The only thing he'd been proud to leave behind; the only thing that, after his demise, would have declared in uncompromising terms, "This is who I was. This is the essence of Sir Richard Francis Burton. By means of this, I will live through history." That thing, Isabel turned to ash.

It was the ultimate betrayal.

No. No. No. Isabel! Why? Why?

He howled his anguish.

I cannot die! I cannot die!

Oxford's insane laughter echoed through the domed chamber.

Swinburne screeched his terror.

Burton's spine snapped.

Oxford stood, lifting the king's agent like a limp rag doll, holding him face to face.

Through a fog of unutterable torment, through tunnelled vision, Burton saw himself reflected in Isambard Kingdom Brunel's death mask. He saw that his hair was sparse and white, his fractured face was sagging and lined, his life force was spent. He had become a broken old man. Oxford had sucked the life history out of him.

With his five hands, Oxford turned him so that he hung before Swinburne. The brass man hugged Burton close to himself and stalked forward, his feet thumping on the tiled floor. With one hand, he pressed Burton's head close to his own.

"See us together, little poet," he chimed. "The one has made the other. Death has danced around us while we've duelled upon the battlefield of history. I am victorious. Death is Time's tool, but I rule Time. I have snatched the scythe from his grisly hands. Now I apply its blade to your friend. Look upon my unchanging face and see beside it the decrepit features of he who was Burton. One gains all. The other loses everything."

Swinburne moaned despairingly. With a shaking hand, he aimed his pistol. Tears flooded down his cheeks.

"Before I kill you," Oxford said to him, "look into this old man's eyes. Watch the life leave him. Know that what is lost can never return." He crushed Burton's broken cheek into his own, a grotesque mockery of affection. "But know, too, that I can revisit any moment of his short span and there torture him. The one life he has to live can be made ever more dreadful, in every history, until he shall scream without surcease from the moment of his birth to the moment of his demise."

From the chest down, Burton was paralysed. Blood oozed from his face and stained his clothes.

Isabel. You betrayed me.

Weakly, he held out an aged, gnarled hand and examined in wonder its raised veins and transparent, liver-spotted skin. The targeting light from Swinburne's pistol skittered across it.

Old. Dead. Forgotten.

He felt the cool of Oxford's face upon his right cheek, the pressure of the brass man's hand upon the left.

The world started to slip away.

With his last vestiges of life, Burton looked straight at Swinburne, dropped his hand to his chest, and placed his forefinger over his heart. He silently mouthed his final words. "The diamonds, Algy."

The horror in Swinburne's eyes gave way to puzzlement.

Oxford started to raise his Gatling gun.

The poet hesitated. He suddenly understood. A wail of anguish escaped him.

Burton winked.

Swinburne pointed the pistol at him and said, "Heart. Kill."

An impact.

Sir Richard Francis Burton died.

CHAPTER 21

BODIES

> The long unmeasured pulse of time moves everything. There is nothing hidden that it cannot bring to light, nothing once known that may not become unknown. Nothing is impossible.
> —Sophocles, *Ajax*

Burton stepped out of his tent, straightened, stretched, and surveyed the distant horizon. It rippled and shimmered behind a curtain of heat. For a brief moment, the sea, which was many miles distant, eased into the clear sky. The mirage pulsed, folded into itself, and vanished.

Adjusting his burnoose, Burton knelt, reached into the tent, and pulled out a cloth bag. It contained cured meats, dried dates, and a flask of water. He sat cross-legged and broke his fast.

Movement caught his eye, a scarab beetle at the base of the tent's canvas, pushing a ball of camel dung across the scorched sand.

The beetle as the motive force. The manipulator.

Time is not an independent equation. Time requires a mind to give it form.

There was work to be done.

Burton opened his eyes.

The House of Lords was wrecked, fire-blackened, smoking and empty except for Algernon Swinburne and Sadhvi Raghavendra. Standing some distance from him, they were both aiming their pistols straight at his head. The poet's face was as white as a sheet.

Raghavendra said, "Two grenades will certainly destroy you."

"I don't doubt it, Sadhvi," Burton replied. His voice sounded like tumbling bells.

He looked down at his hands, five of them and a stump. "But you have no need to shoot."

His friends lowered their weapons and walked cautiously toward him.

"Richard?" Swinburne asked in a quavering voice.

"Yes. Thank you, Algy. My life may not have been saved, but I am, thanks to you, at least preserved."

The poet stumbled, dropped his weapon, fell to his knees, put his face into his hands, and began to weep. Raghavendra stepped past him, gently patting his shoulder, and stopped in front of the king's agent. She looked up at him, frowning. "It's really you?"

Burton tried to offer an encouraging smile but found he had no muscles with which to do so. Ruefully, he reflected that such impulses had never in the past offered much comfort to anyone, anyway. People had always found his smiles rather too predatory.

"It is," he said. He raised a hand—feeling disconcerted by his arm's whirs and hisses—and tapped the side of his head. "It worked. My brain's terminal emanation overwrote the electromagnetic fields in Brunel's diamonds. Oxford was erased from them."

"You took quite a gamble."

"He was holding my head right next to his own. I had no other cards to play." He examined the room. "I appear to have been oblivious for some time. How long?"

"About twelve hours," she replied. "There was some sort of backlash from his—from your—babbage device. The chronostatic energy ignited the room. Everything in it—apart from you, of course—burned ferociously. The time suits are destroyed."

"Resonance, I suppose. It started all this, now it has ended it."

With visible reluctance, Raghavendra pointed to the floor on Burton's right. He looked and saw what appeared to be a large and twisted stick of charcoal. Horrified, he recognised it as his own corpse.

"Your and Herbert's bodies were cremated," Raghavendra said. "There's little chance of cloning, apparently."

Burton acknowledged the revelation with a grunt that came out as a clink. He extended a metal foot and dragged a line through the ash. "The diamond fragments from the Nimtz generators and helmets must be among the ashes. We'll have to collect them. Where are Trounce and Bendyshe?"

"William went some hours ago to find Mr. Grub, the vendor. Unless someone gives the Lowlies focus, riots are inevitable. We're hoping Grub will spread the news that the prime minister and his cronies have been overthrown. Mr. Bendyshe, meanwhile, has taken Jessica Cornish to the *Orpheus*. Captain Lawless flew it here and landed in Green Park. We've all been waiting to assess your status."

"My status?"

"We could see the Brunel body was still functioning by the glow of its eyes, but we didn't know whether it was you or Oxford inside it."

"Ah, I see. And Bendyshe is all right?"

"Lorena Brabrooke did something to the nanomechs in him. 'Deactivated' is the word, I believe. As for the rest of it, all the equerries and constables have stopped functioning and the palace's inhabitants are wandering around like lost children."

"Would you see if any of them knows where Brunel's battery pack is, Sadhvi? It must be somewhere in the palace, and I feel I might require it soon."

She nodded, glanced at Swinburne, and looked back at Burton. "I'll organise a search party, if necessary. There's a well-appointed lounge one hundred floors down, which we've chosen as our base of operations. I suggest you settle in there to recover from your ordeal."

She smiled at him and left the chamber.

Burton clanked over to Swinburne. He felt disoriented and clumsy.

Isabel betrayed me.

He dismissed the thought. Time for that later.

I have all the time in the world.

With a hiss and ratcheting of gears, he squatted beside his friend, reached out, and prodded the poet's arm. "Hallo there."

Swinburne raised his wet face from his hands and smiled weakly. "What ho."

"Quite a rum do, hey?"

"I suppose so. You sound awful. Ding dong, ding dong. I hardly know if it's you or Brunel or Oxford. We shall have to make it Gooch's top priority to fashion for you a more human-sounding vocal apparatus."

"Thank you, Algy."

"Don't thank me, thank Daniel, he's the one who'll create it."

"I mean for what you did."

Swinburne suddenly giggled. "My pleasure, Richard. Any time you need shooting dead, don't hesitate to ask."

Burton whirred upright and held out a hand. Swinburne grasped it and got to his feet. He looked over to his friend's still-smouldering corpse and emitted a groan. "By God, Oxford aged you thirty years in a matter of minutes. I saw you become an old man."

"And I witnessed my life as it would have been had Oxford never altered history."

"And?"

"Let us just say, it had a theme."

Swinburne gave an inquisitive twitch of his eyebrows.

Burton ignored it and turned toward the doors. "I want to get out of this chamber, never to see it again. Lead me to the lounge, will you?"

They left the domed room, walked to the nearest lift, and entered it, a massive man of brass and cogs and pistons, and a diminutive red-haired poet.

"What a strange insanity," Swinburne mused as they started down, "to create a future from a jumbled, misunderstood vision of the past."

"Isn't that what we all do?" Burton asked.

His companion had no answer to that, and for the rest of the descent they stood in thoughtful silence.

The lift stopped, and they passed from it into a vestibule, and from there the poet led his friend to the grand lounge, which was filled with couches, armchairs, bookcases, tables, cabinets, and statuettes of the erstwhile queen. The walls were hung with portraits, every one of them depicting Jessica Cornish.

Gladys Tweedy, the Marquess of Hammersmith, Minister of Language Revivification and Purification, was the room's sole occupant. She stood as they entered.

"Prime Minister?" she asked doubtfully.

"Dead," the king's agent chimed. "I'm Burton."

"Really? How thoroughly singular. You're joking, of course."

"No."

Swinburne scampered over to a drinks cabinet and eagerly examined its contents.

"But you look and sound just like the prime minister," Tweedy protested.

"I know. I'm not particularly thrilled about it. Marquess, what is the situation with regards to the mobilisation of our troops?"

"Our forces are awaiting orders from the Minister of War, Death and Destruction, who, might I remind you, recently experienced a violent demise. You will have to appoint a successor."

"I'll do no such thing. The war is cancelled."

"Hurrah!" Swinburne cheered. "Hooray and yahoo!" He held up a bottle. "Vintage brandy!"

Burton said to the marquess, "Will you convey a message to your fellow ministers?"

"If you wish," she answered. "Or to those that survived, anyway. Quite a few didn't get out in time."

"Tell them that Parliament is suspended and all ministers are relieved of their duties. The people will fashion a new form of government in due course."

She widened her eyes and put a hand to her mouth. "What people?"

"You call them Lowlies."

She laughed. "But they're little more than animals!"

"Do as I say."

Gladys Tweedy swallowed, stuck out her bottom lip, put her hands on her hips, and stamped out of the room, pushing past William Trounce as he entered.

"By Jove! She looks annoyed! Have you—" He saw Burton and quickly drew his pistol.

"Steady, Pouncer!" Swinburne shrilled. "It's Richard."

"Richard?" Uncertainly, Trounce lowered his gun. "You mean—it—he's in—it worked? By Jove!"

"Why don't you stop 'by Joving' and have a tipple?" the poet suggested. He poured three drinks, met his companions in the middle of the room, handed a glass to Trounce, and held another out to Burton. He blinked and said, "Oops! Oh crikey. You poor thing."

A wave of grief hit the king's agent.

I can't taste. There's no physical sensation. I'm dead.

He pushed the emotion aside: something else to be dealt with later.

"Oh well," Swinburne muttered. He looked down at the drinks. "One for each hand."

Burton noticed, at the other end of the chamber, French doors, and beyond them, a balcony. He strode over, followed by Swinburne and Trounce, and pulled them open. Their handles snapped off in his hands.

"Damn!" he exclaimed. "I have to familiarise myself with this body. It's fiendishly strong."

"By my Aunt Penelope's plentiful petticoats!" Swinburne cried out. "Close the doors. It's freezing."

"In a moment," Burton said. He stepped out onto the balcony, into twelve-inch-deep scarlet snow.

Swinburne gulped one of his brandies, ran to the side of the room, and tore a couple of tapestries down from the wall. He wrapped one around himself and handed the other to Trounce, who did likewise. They joined Burton. The air at this altitude was thin but breathable.

They looked out over London.

Under a clear afternoon sky, the city sprawled, blanketed in red.

"I was born here," Trounce said. "But it doesn't feel like home. I miss the hustle and bustle of the nineteenth century. I even miss the smells."

"It's all down there," Burton noted. "Under the ground, waiting to be liberated."

"Humph! It is, but that hustle and bustle isn't *my* hustle and bustle."

"I miss Verbena Lodge," Swinburne said. "Twenty-third-century bordellos are absolutely hopeless. They have no understanding of the lash."

Burton asked, "Will you both come back to 1860?"

The question was met by a prolonged silence.

The poet broke it. "I don't know whether I can. I feel I have an obligation to fulfill."

"Likewise," Trounce said. "There's much work to be done here,

Richard. I fear I may never be reunited with my bowler or with Scotland Yard." He paused. "You'll go?"

"I have to. My brother will expect from me a full account of what has occurred here."

"And after that, what? Will you masquerade as Brunel?"

"I hardly know one end of a spanner from another." Burton leaned on the balcony's parapet then suddenly remembered his great weight and stepped back, afraid that it might give way beneath him. "I require time to adapt to this body before I return. Once I'm there—well, I'll see what happens."

Swinburne bent and scooped up a handful of snow. He examined it. "The seeds are sending out roots. The jungle is obviously up to something. I wonder what?"

Burton's neck buzzed as he turned his head to look down at his friend. "It's you."

"But I never know what I'm going to do next, even in human form."

Burton snorted. It sounded like the clash of a cymbal. "I can't imagine how it feels to know you're a vegetable."

"Probably not much different to the awareness that you're an accumulation of cogwheels and springs. My hat, Richard! Animal, vegetable and mineral. What are we all becoming?"

Burton looked toward the tower-forested horizon.

"Time will tell, Algy. Time will tell."

MEANWHILE, IN THE VICTORIAN AGE AND BEYOND . . .

ISABEL ARUNDELL (1831–1896)

Isabel and Richard Francis Burton met in 1851 and, after a ten-year courtship, married in 1861. Marriage brought a change of fortune for Burton, seeing him more or less abandon exploration in favour of writing and the translating of forbidden literature of anthropological interest. Notoriously, upon his death in 1890, Isabel burned her husband's papers, journals and unfinished work. She also consigned to the flames his translation of *The Scented Garden*, which he considered his *magnum opus*, and which he'd finished just the day before his demise.

ERNEST AUGUSTUS I (1771–1851)

Ernest Augustus I was the son of George III. When his niece, Victoria, became queen of the United Kingdom in 1837, Ernest was made king of Hanover, which ended the union between Britain and Hanover that had begun in 1714. Had Victoria been assassinated, Ernest would have been a prime candidate to replace her as the United Kingdom's monarch. With rumours of murder and incest attached to Ernest's name, this would not have been a popular choice.

CHARLES BABBAGE (1791–1871)

Mathematician, inventor, philosopher and engineer, Charles Babbage is considered the father of modern computers. He created steam-powered devices that were the first to demonstrate that calculations could be mechanised. However, his most complex creations, the Difference Engine and the Analytical Engine, were not completed in his lifetime due to funding and personality problems. By 1860, he was becoming increasingly eccentric, obsessive and irascible, directing his ire in particular at street musicians, commoners, and children's hoops.

BATTERSEA POWER STATION

The station was neither designed nor built by Isambard Kingdom Brunel and did not exist during the Victorian Age. Actually comprised of two stations, it was first proposed in 1927 by the London Power Company. Sir Giles Gilbert Scott (who created the iconic red telephone box) designed the building's exterior. The first station was constructed between 1929 and 1933. The second station, a mirror image of the first, was built between 1953 and 1955. Considered a London landmark, both stations are still standing but are derelict.

JAMES BRUCE, EIGHTH EARL OF ELGIN (1811–1863)

Lord Elgin, orator, humanist, and administrator, was the British governor-general of Canada and later served diplomatic posts in China, Japan, and India. He did not say, "Talk, talk, talk, and while you are talking, the Chinese are exacting yet another tax, . . ."

ISAMBARD KINGDOM BRUNEL (1806–1859)

The British Empire's most celebrated civil and mechanical engineer, Brunel designed and built dockyards, railway systems, steamships, bridges and tunnels. A very heavy smoker, in 1859 he suffered a stroke and died, at just fifty-nine years old.

EDWARD JOSEPH BURTON (1824–1895)

Richard Francis Burton's younger brother shared his wild youth but later settled into army life. Extremely handsome and a talented violinist, he became an enthusiastic hunter, which proved his undoing—in 1856, his killing of elephants so enraged Singhalese villagers that they beat him senseless. The following year, still not properly recovered, he fought valiantly during the Indian Mutiny but was so severely affected by sunstroke that he suffered a psychotic reaction. He never spoke again. For much of the remaining thirty-seven years of his life, he was a patient in the Surrey County Lunatic Asylum.

THE CANNIBAL CLUB

In 1863, Burton and Dr. James Hunt established the Anthropological Society, through which to publish books concerning ethnological and anthropological matters. As an offshoot of the society, the Cannibal Club was a dining (and drinking) club for Burton and Hunt's closest cohorts: Richard Monckton Milnes, Algernon Swinburne, Henry Murray, Sir Edward Brabrooke, Thomas Bendyshe, and Charles Bradlaugh.

CAPTAIN SIR RICHARD FRANCIS BURTON (1821–1890)

1860 was one of the darkest periods of Burton's life. Having returned the previous year from his expedition to locate the source of the Nile, he was engaged in a war of words with Lieutenant John Hanning Speke, who'd accompanied him during the gruelling trek through Africa. Though the expedition was Burton's from the outset, and Speke was the junior officer, the lieutenant returned to London ahead of Burton and laid claim to having discovered the source independent of him. Feeling sidelined and badly betrayed by a man he'd considered a friend, Burton hoped to find some happiness through marriage to Isabel Arundell. Unfortunately, her parents forbid it. With everything going wrong, Burton escaped to America and embarked on an ill-recorded and extremely drunken tour.

MICK FARREN (1943–2013)

A singer-songwriter, music journalist and science fiction author, Farren fronted the proto-punk band the Deviants. During the late sixties, he was for a brief period at the helm of the underground newspaper *International Times* and also ran a magazine called *Nasty Tales*, which he successfully defended from an obscenity charge. His essay for the *New Musical Express*, entitled "The Titanic Sails at Dawn," is considered a seminal analysis of the state of the music industry during the mid-seventies and a clarion call for the birth of punk rock. Farren continued to write novels, poetry and songs, and to perform with the Deviants, right up until his death onstage at the Borderline Club in London on July 27, 2013.

GEORGE V (GEORGE FREDERICK ALEXANDER CHARLES ERNEST AUGUSTUS) (1819–1878)

George V, the son of Ernest Augustus I, was the last king of Hanover. His reign ended with the unification of Germany.

SIR DANIEL GOOCH (1816–1889)

Daniel Gooch was a railway engineer who worked with such luminaries as Robert Stephenson and Isambard Kingdom Brunel. He was the first chief mechanical engineer of the Great Western Railway and was later its chairman. Gooch was also involved in the laying of the first successful transatlantic telegraph cable and became the chairman of the Telegraph Construction Company. Later in life he was elected to office as a parliamentary minister. He was knighted in 1866.

THE GROSVENOR SQUARE RIOT OF 1968

On March 17, Grosvenor Square, London, was the scene of an anti–Vietnam War demonstration that quickly turned into a riot due to what many regarded as heavy-handed police tactics. It ended with eighty-six people injured and two hundred demonstrators arrested. Mick Farren was present.

RICHARD MONCKTON MILNES, 1ST BARON HOUGHTON (1809–1885)

Monckton Milnes was a poet, socialite, politician, patron of the arts, and collector of erotic and esoteric literature. He was also one of Sir Richard Francis Burton's closest friends and supporters.

JOHN HANNING SPEKE (1827–1864)

An officer in the British Indian Army, Speke accompanied Burton first on his ill-fated expedition to Somalia, which ended when their camp was attacked at Berbera. Speke was captured and pierced through the arms, side and thighs by a spear before somehow managing to escape and run away. This expedition also marked the beginning of his deep resentment of Burton, caused by his misunderstanding of a command, which he took to be a derisory comment concerning his courage. When Speke accompanied Burton on his search for the source of the Nile from 1857 to 1859, their relationship quickly broke down. Speke then returned to London ahead of his commanding officer and sought to claim sole credit for the discovery. The two men fought a bitter war of words until 1864, when Speke shot himself while out hunting.

HERBERT SPENCER (1820–1903)

One of the most influential, accomplished, and misunderstood philosophers in British history, Herbert Spencer melded Darwinism with sociology. He originated the phrase "survival of the fittest," which was then taken up by Darwin himself. It was also adopted, misinterpreted, and misused by a number of governments, who employed it to justify their eugenics programs, culminating in the Holocaust of the 1940s. Spencer, unfortunately, thus became associated with one of the darkest periods in modern history. Bizarrely, he is also credited with the invention of the paper clip.

SPRING HEELED JACK

Spring Heeled Jack is one of the great mysteries of the Victorian age (and beyond). This ghost or apparition, creature or trickster, was able to leap to an extraordinary height. Helmeted and cloaked, it breathed blue fire and frightened unsuspecting victims, mostly young women, over a period mainly from 1837 to 1888 but also extending into the twenty-first century.

ABRAHAM "BRAM" STOKER (1847–1912)

Born in Dublin, Ireland, thirteen-year-old Stoker was still at school in 1860. In adulthood, he became the personal assistant of actor Henry Irving and business manager of the Lyceum Theatre in London. On August 13, 1878, Stoker met Sir Richard Francis Burton for the first time and described him as follows: "The man riveted my attention. He was dark and forceful, and masterful, and ruthless. I have never seen so iron a countenance. As he spoke the upper lip rose and his canine tooth showed its full length like the gleam of a dagger." Stoker's novel *Dracula* was published in 1897.

ALGERNON CHARLES SWINBURNE (1837–1909)

A celebrated poet, playwright, novelist and critic, Swinburne was nominated for the Nobel Prize in Literature in every year from 1903 to 1907 and once more in 1909. In 1860, Swinburne returned to Balliol College, Oxford, having been rusticated the year before. He never received a degree and after leaving the college plunged into literary circles where he quickly gained a reputation as a great poet, an extreme eccentric, and a very heavy drinker. Swinburne is thought to have suffered a condition through which he sensed pain as pleasure, which might explain his masochistic tendencies. He and Burton were very close friends.

"And grief shall endure not for ever, I know . . ."
—From *The Triumph of Time*

"I hid my heart in a nest of roses . . ."
—From *A Ballad of Dreamland*, Poems & Ballads
(second and third series)

TERMINAL EMANATION

Though it's been theorised for many years, research was published during the writing of this novel that supports the proposition that the brain sends out a strong electromagnetic pulse at the moment of death. According to the *Washington Post*: "Scientists from the University of Michigan recorded electroencephalogram (EEG) signals in nine anesthetized rats after inducing cardiac arrest. Within the first 30 seconds after the heart had stopped, all the mammals displayed a surge of highly synchronized brain activity that had features associated with consciousness and visual activation. The burst of electrical patterns even exceeded levels seen during a normal, awake state." (Source: "Surge of Brain Activity May Explain Near-Death Experience, Study Says," Washingtonpost.com, August 12, 2013.)

HERBERT GEORGE WELLS (1866–1946)

A prolific writer, Wells is best remembered for his science fiction. He was also a proponent of the idea that the world would function best under the auspices of a single state.

"The only true measure of success is the ratio between what we might have done and what we might have been on the one hand, and the thing we have made and the things we have made of ourselves on the other."

"Adapt or perish, now as ever, is nature's inexorable imperative."

"The Anglo-Saxon genius for parliamentary government asserted itself; there was a great deal of talk and no decisive action."
—From The Invisible Man

"Socialism is the preparation for that higher Anarchism; painfully, laboriously we mean to destroy false ideas of property and self, eliminate unjust laws and poisonous and hateful suggestions and prejudices, create a system of social right-dealing and a tradition of right-feeling and action. Socialism is the schoolroom of true and noble Anarchism, wherein by training and restraint we shall make free men."
—From New Worlds for Old

AFTERWORD

Throughout the Burton & Swinburne series, I've used real people from history as the basis for many of my characters. Mostly Victorians, they are long dead and thus cannot be properly known, no matter how many biographies of them might be read. However, the truth of their many achievements can be explored, and to compensate for the liberties I've taken with their personalities, I've added to each novel an addendum to highlight aspects of their real lives, hoping that my readers are curious enough to research a little further.

With Mick Farren it's been different. With Mick, when I started this novel, I was introducing into the series a man who still lived.

For those of you unfamiliar with him, Mick was an important voice in the UK counterculture who rose to prominence during the late 1960s. He was the editor of the alternative newspaper *International Times*, a song-writer and lead singer in the rock group the Deviants, a music journalist (he accurately predicted and supported the advent of punk), and a science fiction novelist.

You can probably understand that I felt rather apprehensive when I approached him and asked if I could hijack him for a work of fiction. I sent him the first three Burton & Swinburne novels to read. I told him what I intended. I made it clear that the Mick I wanted to portray would be, at best, an approximation of the real thing.

He was delighted. Really. He laughed, he enthused, and he said he was thoroughly flattered. "Damn! I love it. I'd be delighted. Do your worst. Burton has always been a major hero of mine."

So I went ahead, got writing, and sent the early draft chapters to him. He gave me a thumbs-up. We communicated regularly over a period of about six months.

Then he died.

This man, who was one of my heroes, who was fast becoming my friend, got up on stage with the Deviants on Saturday, July 27, 2013, and, after two songs, suffered a heart attack, collapsed, and didn't regain consciousness.

He never got to read this novel.

I never got to say thank you or good-bye.

So I'll say it now. Thank you, Mick. You inspired me, impressed me, entertained me and intrigued me. Thank you for the Deviants. Thank you for the novels and many brilliant articles. Thank you for so enthusiastically embracing what I have done with you in *The Return of the Discontinued Man*.

And good-bye. I'll miss you. I hope everybody who reads this novel looks you up on *Wikipedia*, listens to your music, and buys your books. I'm glad you went out rockin'.

Mark Hodder
Valencia, Spain

ABOUT THE AUTHOR

Photo by Yolanda Lerma Palomares

Mark Hodder was born in Southampton, England, but has lived in Winchester, Maidstone, Norwich, Herne Bay, and for many years in London. He has worked as a roadie; a pizza cook; a litter collector; a glass packer; an illustrator; a radio commercial scriptwriter; an advertising copywriter; and a BBC web producer, journalist, and editor. In 2008, he moved to Valencia, Spain, where he settled with his Spanish partner, Yolanda. Initially, he earned a living by teaching English, but then he wrote his first novel, *The Strange Affair of Spring Heeled Jack*, which promptly won the Philip K. Dick Award 2010. Mark immediately and enthusiastically became a full-time novelist, thus fulfilling his wildest dreams, which he started having around the age of eleven after reading Michael Moorcock, Robert E. Howard, Edgar Rice Burroughs, Fritz Leiber, Jack Vance, Philip K. Dick, P. G. Wodehouse, and Sir Arthur Conan Doyle. He recently became the father of twins, Luca Max and Iris Angell.